THE STORY OF CANADA

A BESTSELLING FIVE-PART
SAGA OF ROMANCE AND ADVENTURE
SPANNING TEN TUMULTUOUS
GENERATIONS

"ADAIR AND ROSENSTOCK KNOW HOW TO TELL
A STORY . . .
Fans seeking historical fiction and romance will find
plenty to keep them turning the pages . . . with physical
violence and personal turmoil . . . action fast and furious
. . . battles, sex, and narrow escapes . . . keeping the story
moving quickly."
Toronto Quill and Quire

"EPIC . . . ENTERTAINING . . .
The action is compressed and carefully plotted."
Calgary Herald

"A CRACKLING GOOD ROMANCE"
Ottawa Citizen

"A BLOCKBUSTER SERIES . . .
Its considerable strengths are its meticulous historical fidel-
ity and its interesting, lively characters."
West Coast Review of Books

"EXCITING NARRATIVE"
Books in Canada

THUNDER-GATE

BOOK 3: THE STORY OF CANADA

DENNIS ADAIR AND JANET ROSENSTOCK

AVON
PUBLISHERS OF BARD, CAMELOT, DISCUS AND FLARE BOOKS

THUNDERGATE: Book III: THE STORY OF CANADA is an original publication of Avon Books. This work has never before appeared in book form.

AVON BOOKS
A division of
The Hearst Corporation
959 Eighth Avenue
New York, New York 10019

First Avon Printing, September, 1982

AVON TRADEMARK REG. U. S. PAT. OFF. AND IN
OTHER COUNTRIES, MARCA REGISTRADA, HECHO EN
U. S. A.

Printed in the U. S. A.

WFH 10 9 8 7 6 5 4 3 2 1

FOREWORD

Between 20,000 and 2000 B.C., there occurred a great glacier melt-off. It created the gorge of the Niagara River and the dipping, rolling topography of the St. Lawrence, Mohawk, and Hudson valleys. The area became a kind of northern Garden of Eden, rich with natural vegetation and animal life.

The same melt-off created the falls at Niagara, one of the natural wonders of the world. The Indians once made human sacrifices to placate the thundering falls as they tumulted into the rocky gorge of the Niagara. The Niagara River, above and below the falls, leads to a network of inland waterways that connect half the continent. But to reach those waterways, the eighteenth-century traveler was forced to use the portage trail that became the gateway to western expansion. Today we call the area Niagara Falls; yesterday the Indians called it Thundergate.

ACKNOWLEDGMENTS

The authors would gratefully like to acknowledge the contribution of Jay Myers, the historian and researcher who worked with us on *Thundergate*. Among the reference books used in preparation of this novel were: *The American Revolution 1775–1783*, by John Alden; *The Devil's Backbone: The Story of the Natchez Trace*, by Jonathan Daniels; *A History of the Old South: The Emergence of a Reluctant Nation*, by Clement Eaton; *Thundergate: The Forts of Niagara*, by Robert West Howard; *Canada and the American Revolution 1774–1783*, by Gustave Lanctot; *Quebec: The Revolutionary Age 1760–1791*, by Hilda Neatby; *Benedict Arnold: Traitor to His Country*, by Jeanette Covert Nolan; *Louisana: A Bicentennial History*, by Joe Gray Taylor; *The United Empire Loyalists: Men and Myths*, in *Issues in Canadian History*, by L. F. S. Upton (ed.); and *Revolutionary Ladies*, by Philip Young.

CHAPTER I

Montreal, April 1, 1779

The rain continued unabated, just as it had for the past three days and nights. Streams of water ran rapidly between the cracks in the cobbled streets, and passing carriages splashed the water of deeper puddles against the large old houses that lined the narrow street.

Like most of the houses in old Montreal, the house the Macleods lived in was built at the very edge of the cobbled street. It was a large stone edifice with two double chimneys that released curls of white smoke into the gray afternoon. April or not, the weather was inclement; it was unseasonably cold and damp. The snows of winter had melted by the first of March and by the middle of the month the days were warm and sunny. But the two last weeks of March had only been a cruel joke of nature. The warmth had greened the grass and caused premature buds to awaken to a false spring. Now those same buds shriveled in the cold rain; the long-awaited spring was in retreat.

Janet Cameron Macleod sat stiffly on the settee and stared at the empty teacup on the little table in front of her. Abstractedly, she pushed a strand of hair off her forehead. Janet's long russet tresses were streaked with gray and she no longer allowed them to fall loose to her shoulders. Rather, her hair was pulled back and up, offering a high rounded frame for her fine-featured face and accentuating her long white throat.

A few feet away, Helena Fraser, Janet's oldest daughter, held the pewter teapot by its dark wood handle. "More tea?" she queried.

Janet responded with an affirmative nod. "Where's your

1

father?'' There was a touch of annoyance in her voice and Helena knew why. Her mother's irritation was not with Mathew, but rather with Helena's younger sister, Jenna, and with the uncomfortable situation Jenna had created.

Within the hour, Stephan O'Connell was coming to call, and Stephan O'Connell was not well liked by Mathew Macleod. Moreover, Stephan was coming to ask permission to court Jenna.

The prospective courtship had met with various reactions, none of which was favorable. ''She's too young!'' had been Mathew's first objection, and that pronouncement was followed by a long list of other negatives. ''He drinks too much. He's not responsible. He's got a reputation as a womanizer.'' And finally, Mathew had gotten to the heart of his objections: ''He's a young, hot-tempered, rebellious Bostonian!'' But, of course, Mathew would not have objected to a Bostonian as such. Stephan O'Connell might have been born in Boston, but his parents were from Ulster and were Protestants who were militant anti-Catholics. Now that they had moved to Montreal, they were virulently anti-French Canadian, disliking intensely the role of the Church. In Ireland Catholics were forbidden to gather for Mass and were forbidden education. The O'Connells thought the same treatment was due the French Canadians, whom they regarded as a defeated people.

''And you don't approve of his family,'' Janet added. She understood only too well. Stephan's father was a wealthy merchant, a man with power and stature in the English-speaking community of Montreal. Mathew saw the O'Connells as agitators against British rule.

In the sixteen years since the end of the Seven Years' War, many English-speaking merchants from Boston and Philadelphia had immigrated to Montreal in order to take advantage of the business opportunities offered by the busy St. Lawrence port. After all, Boston, Philadelphia, Quebec City, Montreal . . . they were all part of one great empire, they were all British North America. But the newly arrived English-speaking merchants from the Thirteen Colonies brought with them their own ideas. Chief among them was the desire for a constituent assembly modeled on the assembly of the Massachusetts Bay Colony. And true to their prejudices, they wanted to exclude the French Canadians from government and eventually forbid them the right to worship publicly. They believed in forcing the English language on the continent and in having the northern part of British North America ruled in the same way as the Thirteen Colonies. They were therefore called Continentalists.

But the British, Mathew Macleod noted, had responded to the pressure from the Thirteen Colonies with uncharacteristic caution. They honored the Treaty of 1763, which protected the rights of the French Canadians. Further, the British Parliament passed the Quebec Act, which forbade the Continentalists a constituent assembly, but which instead guaranteed the French inhabitants freedom of religion and the right to speak French and educate their children in French. The Quebec Act deeply angered the Thirteen Colonies. They cried foul and the Quebec Act, together with the various tax acts affecting the Thirteen Colonies to the south, were labeled the Intolerable Acts.

As a result of the so-called Intolerable Acts, the Thirteen Colonies were in full rebellion, a rebellion that had begun with small acts of terrorism against the British and grown into a war. But as in all such situations, there were more than two sides.

There were United Empire Loyalists, who were loyal to the British Crown in the Thirteen Colonies, and there were in Quebec rebels supporting the Continental Congress. And between the United Empire Loyalists and the rebels, there were men like Mathew Macleod, men prepared to support the British as long as they were fair to the French Canadians, men who loved the land above all; men who mistrusted the methods and outcome of rebellion and who believed there was room in Canada for English and French alike if they respected one another.

But the O'Connells were anti-Catholic and therefore anti-French Canadian. They considered the Quebec Act intolerable only because it denied them the right to rule, as a minority, over the majority of French-speaking inhabitants of Quebec. Their sympathies were with the rebellious colonies and they made no secret of it.

"Papa is wrong," Helena said abruptly. "He's wrong to deny Stephan the right to court Jenna. It will only make her

3

angry and more set in her ways. If he courted her, Jenna would get to know him, she might outgrow her attraction to him." Helena hesitated for a moment, then continued, searching for the right words. "Mama, forbidden fruit always is more desirable. I know Jenna and I love her, but she always wants what she cannot have."

Janet smiled at her oldest daughter. There was more than a little wisdom in Helena's comment. On the other hand, Janet remembered her own liaison with Richard O'Flynn. It had taken her a long time and much bitter experience to see him for what he was. Her strongest impulse was to try to protect her younger daughter from the same kind of shattering experience.

"She is our youngest child. It's natural to be more protective of your youngest."

Helena set the pot down on the table, placing it on a heavy crocheted mat, then sat down in a chair facing her mother. "Jenna's ten years younger than I. But she's twice as stubborn. When she's told not to do something, she wants to do it more. Mama, you must not let Papa send Stephan away."

Janet's hands clenched the dark material of her skirt. In all the years of their marriage, she and Mathew never had disagreed about rearing the children. She had never set herself against her husband simply because they were always of one mind; they were two people still deeply in love; two people perfectly attuned to one another. They moved and acted as one. This was the first time any disagreement had loomed on their horizon. And it certainly was not total disagreement. Janet had no argument with Mathew's assessment of Stephan, but she did share Helena's misgivings. Mathew's reasons were correct, but his method of dealing with the problem might well be wrong.

"It's more than Stephan's politics," Janet said, trying to work through her own conflicting thoughts. "Jenna is—"

"Jenna is Papa's baby. Jenna looks exactly like you, and Papa is very protective of her."

"He loves you every bit as much," Janet quickly put in. Even as she said the words, she knew they begged the question.

Helena looked at her mother and arched an eyebrow. "I've been married to John Fraser for eight years now. Papa

4

likes John, and Papa regards me as a grown woman. I never gave Papa any grief, not like the grief Jenna's going to give him. And I tell you, Mama, the more grief she gives him, the more he's going to love her. She's spoiled. She's spoiled like Mat, Andrew, and I never were spoiled.''

Janet's eyes searched her elder daughter's face. Helena's tone held no bitterness. Helena loved her sister, but she understood what motivated her.

"It won't do any good to tell Jenna about Stephan and his tavern women, and you certainly can't appeal to her on political grounds. She has no interest in politics. Not until she finds out for herself what a rotter Stephan is, will she give you and Papa any credence at all."

The familiar clatter of carriage wheels caused both women to stop talking for a moment. "I think he's here," Janet said. She glanced at the empty teacup again and wished she had drunk something stronger. "Would you be so certain of what to do if it were your daughter, Abigail? Would you risk Abigail's future by giving a person like Stephan O'Connell permission to court her?"

Helena stood up and smoothed out her skirt. She met her mother's question with a frown. "Every situation is different," Helena allowed. "But children are loaned, not owned. If you deny Jenna, you might risk her future within the family, you could cause her to act emotionally." Helena thought of her many conversations with Jenna. Jenna had a full-blown infatuation with Stephan and would hear no criticism of him.

Janet stared at the floor as Helena picked up the cups and teapot to take them back to the kitchen. "Yes," was all Janet could manage to say in the face of Helena's insights. As Stephan O'Connell banged the great iron door knocker, Janet straightened herself up and pulled back her shoulders, "Call your father, will you?" she requested, trying to smile but wishing that the visit were already over and done with.

Helena left the room, and Janet moved toward the door, opening it to greet young Stephan O'Connell. It was not difficult to understand Jenna's attraction. Stephan was tall and slim. He had thick, dark hair and deep blue eyes and his mouth twisted slightly when he smiled to reveal straight, gleaming teeth. Stephan's complexion was fair and he was,

5

by any woman's standards, a fine-looking man. Perhaps, she mused, his roguish reputation made him even more desirable to young women, who no doubt saw him as a person with a wild nature that needed to be tamed. For some, and probably for Jenna, Stephan O'Connell was a challenge. It was all such a misconception! Men do not change, nor can they be changed. But a young woman, especially a beautiful young woman, always overestimated her own abilities. Janet herself had been guilty of that, and it was a lesson hard learned. ￫

Stephan stood for a moment and then stepped into the foyer, doffing his hat gallantly and bowing politely from the waist.

"Madame Macleod," he said, kissing Janet's extended hand.

"Mr. O'Connell," Janet acknowledged. "Please come in."

Stephan unfastened his cloak. "I'm afraid it's quite wet," he apologized as he handed it to her.

"One could hardly expect it to be otherwise." Janet forced a smile. "My husband will be joining us shortly. Please come into the parlor."

Stephan walked behind her. "Have you British soldiers still billeted here?" Even the biting way he pronounced *British* seemed to indicate his feelings.

"Yes, but they are gone during the day."

Stephan shook his head and sniffed. "It must be crowded," he intoned.

He was sizing up the house, noting immediately that it was not as large as his parents' house. "We manage," Janet replied. She could hear Mathew at the top of the stairs. He dragged his game leg along, suffering more pain than usual because of the terrible dampness that caused his leg to stiffen when he stayed in one position for too long.

"Good day," Mathew said coldly. Mathew was a handsome man; the years of the outdoor work had honed his muscles, and his hair, still thick, was turning steel gray. The only aspect of him that belied his strength was his leg. Because of two old wounds to it, he now was forced to use a cane in order to keep his balance on the uneven cobbled streets. Normally, Mathew bore a cheerful expression, but

6

as he greeted Stephan, his countenance was less than friendly.

Janet moved instinctively between her husband and Stephan. "Would you like something to drink?" she offered, motioning their guest to a nearby chair and wishing she had discussed this situation more thoroughly with Mathew beforehand.

"Brandy, thank you," Stephan requested.

Mathew sat down on one end of the settee and stretched his leg out before him. "Is your leg troubling you, sir?" Stephan asked.

"An old gunshot wound," Mathew explained without elaboration. He still retained his Scots reserve with outsiders. Family stories were confined to family. In any case, it was obvious he had no desire to prolong this visit with unnecessary conversation.

Janet poured the brandy and served Stephan and Mathew, taking a snifter for herself as well. Then, she sat down on the settee, positioning herself nervously on its edge. For Janet, the stiff formality of the scene was all too reminiscent of Robert's courtship of Marguerite Lupien. But, she thought, during the Seven Years' War things were simpler; all the parties involved had been on one side. Today Montreal was a city divided by what seemed a hundred allegiances. Then, Janet reflected, Robert had been serving with General Montcalm, and little Marguerite had fallen in love with him. They had been wrenched apart by war, by circumstances beyond anyone's control. But for Jenna and Stephan the situation was different. They were about to be separated by family animosities. Were Jenna and Stephan truly in love as Robert and Marguerite had been? Janet could not answer the question and she dared not consider the implications of the possible answers.

"Did you get your wound fighting with the French?" Stephan's voice had an edge to it; his anti-French sentiments were all too obvious.

Mathew straightened up abruptly and looked at the young man defiantly. "No," he answered tersely. "I got it from one of your Ulster countrymen while being held against my will."

Countrywomen, Janet mentally corrected, as a vision of

7

Megan, an Irish spy who had acted for the British, drifted across her memory. It all seemed so long ago, so many years back.

"But you were pro-French then?" Stephan questioned.

"I was pro-Canadian," Mathew snapped, "and I still am."

"Supporting the British now is pro-Canadian?" Stephan's clipped New England accent made his words sound more sarcastic than he intended them to be, Janet noted. Though his words were sharp enough.

"The rebellion—the possible success of the rebellion—is more dangerous to Canada than the influence of Britain." Mathew paused and narrowed his dark eyes. "Experience has taught me that evolution is better than revolution." Mathew did not wait for Stephan's reply. He cleared his throat. "The British have supported freedom of religion; they have refused to give a minority of people from the Thirteen Colonies in Quebec the right to run everything! As an Ulsterman who came to Canada by way of Boston, you ought to know the perils of oppression."

"I know the perils of the Pope," Stephan answered quickly, taking a gulp of his brandy. "France is aiding the rebels. How long do you think the French of Quebec, the farmers, the *habitants,* will remain neutral?" Stephan referred to the new alliance between the rebellious colonies and the French. Like so many others of his ilk, he believed the French-speaking population of Quebec would join France.

"And if your little rebellion succeeds, how long would you allow freedom of religion and language?" Mathew asked.

Mathew looked steadily at Stephan. The young man did not understand; he had not been in Canada long enough to understand. "The French-speaking people of Canada are not the same as the continental French. They have no real desire to return to the rule of France, or to the French feudal system. They fought the Virginia expansionists at Fort Necessity to defend their land. They know men like Washington, they know your blessed two-faced patriots. You can't have it both ways. You can't have French-speaking Canadians as allies while at the same time condemning their religion and language. They see your rebellion as a family fight between two kinds of Englishmen—one born here who still exhibits intolerance, the other born in England who governs with more understanding than might be expected. They'll remain neutral.''

"I had hoped you would see things more logically.'' Stephan's face had reddened and Janet could almost feel him struggling to contain his famous Irish temper. She could see the effort he was making to be conciliatory. "The colonies want freedom,'' he continued, "they want justice, they want liberty and the right to free trade. Mr. Macleod, they want assemblies of their own choosing to tax them, not some foreign power.''

"You play your words both ways,'' Mathew replied. "You want repressive laws in Quebec and freedom in Virginia and Massachusetts, where, I might remind you, Catholics are still forbidden to worship. What kind of freedom is that? High-flown words, you people have. Freedom for whom? If your rebellion succeeds and takes hold in Canada, we will become a colony of Massachusetts. If it fails, we will remain a colony of England. I prefer the enemy I know.''

Stephan remained silent for a moment. And Janet noted that, whatever else the young man was, he was not stupid.

"We live in a state of confusion,'' Stephan finally said.

"It's better than living in Virginia,'' Mathew answered, hardly bothering to try to conceal his own anger.

Stephan smiled his enigmatic half smile and his eyes twinkled. Janet could not help thinking that he seemed to enjoy arguing politics. He cleared his throat and took another gulp of brandy. "I apologize,'' he said after a long moment. "I know we stand far apart, I know my family views things differently from you and your family. But things will take their course, things will be settled. I did come here for personal reasons, not for political arguments. I came to ask permission to court your daughter, Jenna.''

Mathew stared into his own brandy snifter. "I don't see how you even can ask,'' he remarked coldly. "Your family comes from Ulster, you were settled on your land by Cromwell when he overthrew the rightful Stuart heir to the

9

throne of England. We come from Jacobite stock; we stand now as we have always stood. I do not bear the same grudge my grandfather did, nor even the same grudge I bore some thirty-three years ago when I stood knee deep in the blood of my clansmen at Culloden. But allow my daughter to marry a militant Protestant rebel! It's out of the question!''

Mathew's voice had been low, even, and steady. Janet saw that his chin was set and her heart ached. Jenna never would understand. Mathew had what seemed new allegiances, though she knew they were not so new. All Mathew wanted was to see Canada free. All he wanted was to be able to take his family and return to the Niagara. He wanted, above all, to live in a land without the hate that filled some Protestants and some Catholics. He wanted the Protestants and Catholics to live side by side, to build a nation together and leave the futile wars of Europe behind. No man wanted to forget Culloden more than Mathew Macleod. No man was less able to. For, in the end, if the bitterness was gone, the lesson still was there. Mathew did not object to Stephan O'Connell because he was a Protestant, but because he was a militant Protestant and a rebel; a young man capable of rekindling old flames and fanning them into new fires of destruction. Mathew wanted to build, Stephan wanted to tear down. Mathew had chosen a kind of middle ground between English and French, between Catholic and Protestant. He had chosen it because he loved the land under his feet. It was Canada; and Canada was where he intended to remain.

"This is not an easy time," Janet said, speaking for the first time. "You must understand, or try to."

Stephan hardly looked at Janet as he stood up abruptly and put his brandy snifter down with some force. "I love Jenna," he announced in a deeper voice, a voice that matched Mathew's for coldness. "And she loves me. You are making a mistake."

"Then it's my mistake," Mathew answered.

Mathew pulled himself up, but Stephan had already turned and was striding toward the front door. Janet watched as Mathew followed him. She felt rooted to the edge of her chair. The front door opened, then closed. Stephan was gone.

Mathew returned to face his wife. "You're upset," he ventured.

Janet lifted her eyes to meet Mathew's. "I'm not certain we did the right thing."

'He's simply not suitable—I have a hundred arguments, but it comes down to that."

"And who would be suitable?" Janet asked, then added more softly, "Can we prevent our children from making mistakes? Can we bear their hard times for them? Experience is something a parent can't pass on."

Mathew's eyes flickered. She was talking about herself, she was trying to tell him that no amount of advice could have stopped her when she was younger. "I don't want Jenna to be hurt." Mathew's voice sounded defensive.

"Stephan never would hurt me!" Mathew turned and Janet's mouth parted. Jenna was in the doorway, her eyes misty and her face pink with anger. "You sent him away! How could you?"

"It's for your own good," Mathew replied. "He's not the sort of person I want you to marry."

Jenna's hands were grasping the sides of her long skirt. "You want to ruin my life! Love and romance and happiness are all right for you and Mother! And adventure too! But you want me to rot in Montreal—closed in my bedroom, away from the whole world!" The tears had welled in her large green eyes and now they tumbled down her face as she trembled with anger and outrage. "You always told me I should marry for love! You always said you didn't believe in arranged marriages! Now you send the man I love away and tell him he can't court me!" Her words were barely intelligible.

"You don't understand!" Mathew shouted. "You're too young!"

"Mother was my age when she met you! She was almost my age when she was in Paris at court, when she—"

Jenna did not finish her sentence because Mathew had seized her wrist roughly. "Go to your room!" he ordered. "Before you say something you'll regret."

Jenna turned her head away and Mathew dropped her wrist. In a whirl of taffeta she was up the stairs, her hands over her face as she sobbed.

"She'll get over it," Mathew said as he turned around.

Janet shook her head, slowly. "Will you?" she asked. But Mathew didn't answer and Janet sunk back against the settee in silence, a hundred jumbled thoughts crowding her mind. None of this would have happened had they not left the Niagara, but of course they had to leave. Her mind strayed to their homestead, the place they had called Lochiel. Mathew was bitter when they had to give it up, but there was no choice. The final treaties of 1763 forbade settlement in the area, reserving the land, save that around the fort, for the Indians who had allied themselves with the British. They had moved onto the land that surrounded the fort and there they had remained for many years. Mathew had received a license to trade, and their trading post had proved profitable. He also was able to work as an engineer within the fort, and that too gave him pleasure. When the rebellion in the South had started, Mat and Andrew had both joined the British Army. Andrew remained at Niagara with Butler's Rangers. Mat went south to fight and now served in the same Scots unit with Helena's husband, John Fraser. But there wasn't one member of the family who didn't want to return to the Niagara. Mathew had come to Montreal to work with the British because he believed that after the rebellion the land in the Niagara would once again be opened to settlement. There already was talk of it, and the promise made their temporary exile in Montreal easier.

If they had remained in the Niagara, Janet thought, Jenna probably would have married a soldier, someone of whom Mathew approved. But here in Montreal, Jenna was thrown into the whirl of society. Rather than the hardworking frontiersman she might have met, she met young men of wealth and station, men who did not earn their fortunes but inherited them. And Mathew had all of his strong Scots morality. A man should work hard, he should earn his own way, he should build for the future. That was Mathew's way, and Mathew wanted a man with the same values for his daughter.

"You disapprove of my decision, don't you?" Mathew's question broke into her thoughts.

"Jenna's stubborn. She won't accept your decision."

Janet's voice became a mere whisper as she murmured, "Forbidden fruit."

"I won't allow it," Mathew railed. "I won't allow her to ruin her life."

Janet restrained herself. She would have to talk to him again about it, but it was too soon now. Stephan's jarring visit was too fresh, Mathew's anger was too close to the surface.

April was kinder to Philadelphia than to Montreal. The near thirty-five thousand inhabitants of Philadelphia had enjoyed the warm winds of spring for some weeks and in the four main squares, each supplemented with graceful fountains, trees and flowers were in full bloom.

Ideally located at the confluence of the Delaware and Schuylkill rivers, the city had access to both the rich farmland that lay inland and to the wood that supplied its blossoming industry. Prior to the outbreak of the rebellion, Philadelphia had been the third most important business center in the British Empire; it was a city of trade, and trade was nearly everyone's business. Foodstuffs and wood went to the West Indies, where they were exchanged for sugar, rum, and spices. These were taken to England and exchanged for British manufactured goods that were, in turn, shipped to Philadelphia. It also was a city of printers, more than twenty of whom plied their trade, concentrating, now more than ever, on political subjects. Meeting place of the First Continental Congress, it was widely assumed that Philadelphia would lead a new nation when the rebellion knew its final success.

But if trade and the need for free trade had spawned the rebellion, Philadelphia, like Montreal, was a city in turmoil. A surprising number of Philadelphia's traders, especially those residing on Society Hill, were loyalists who still nervously pledged themselves to the British Crown.

Such a family lived in a large three-story brownstone on Fourth Street. They were the Shippens. Like all the wealthy of Philadelphia, they enjoyed the richness of life and endless rounds of parties in spite of the fact that the British Army had fled and the city was now commanded by General Benedict Arnold of the Continental Army.

"There was never a social season as gay as that in 1777 and 1778," declared one of young Peggy Shippen's friends. "The Continental Army is not . . . not as well bred as the British."

Peggy Shippen, seventeen and full of life, could only partially agree. Blue-eyed, petite, with blond hair that fell in natural ringlets, one expert on such matters had proclaimed her the most beautiful woman in America. "I shan't soon forget General Howe's farewell party," Peggy said with a sigh. "I was there and I was not there." A bemused expression came over her heart-shaped face and she snuggled up against the huge satin-covered pillows that lay against the headboard of her mahogany four-poster bed with its deep blue canopy of brocade. Her close friend Anne Stearns stood poised before the mirror, trying on a succession of broad-brimmed hats.

Peggy closed her eyes and thought of Major André. He was so handsome! So considerate. When the British had controlled Philadelphia, Major André had planned all the better parties. He was tall and dark, suave and well educated. He wrote poetry, he collected fine art, he played several musical instruments. And he had been Peggy's friend and close confidant, though not her lover. This Peggy Shippen could not quite fathom. He was in great demand and he was pursued by every woman in Philadelphia. Still, without hesitation, he chose to spend all his time with her. He spent endless hours toying with her long blond hair and delighted in coiffing it for her into a myriad of styles. In preparation for General Howe's farewell, which in the end her father had not allowed her to attend, Major André even had designed a dress for her. Oh, and what a dress! It was pure white and as filmy as a cloud. It draped daringly off one bare shoulder and a wide swath of material drew in her tiny waist before the gown fell in graceful folds over her well-rounded little hips. "It's a Turkish gown," Major André had declared. Peggy thought it more Greek than Turkish, but Major André insisted it was Turkish. "And besides, my sweet," he whispered, "I should rather think of you as a harem girl than a disciple of Sappho." Still, Peggy reflected, their relationship was strange. Though they met daily and danced nightly, he never kissed her lips. His sole

14

interest was in dressing her like a precious doll and in fixing her hair. And she in return felt warmth and friendship for Major André, but little else. His long, graceful, well-manicured fingers did not excite her; his deep, dark eyes did not beckon her to the bedroom.

"The American officers are not nearly as much fun," Anne complained.

"Except for Ben," Peggy replied wistfully.

"Well, I should expect you to say so. You're going to marry him."

Peggy hugged her ankles as she sat on the bed leaning against the headboard. "I'm so excited. I think I shall swoon at my own wedding."

"Only if you want to," Anne replied knowingly.

Peggy closed her eyes and thought about her very masculine Benedict Arnold. He had proved himself the bravest and most competent general in the Continental Army. Moreover, he lived as lavishly as General Howe had. He was no boar like so many of the so-called patriots. General Benedict Arnold was an officer and a gentleman. And much to Peggy's delight, he had serious second thoughts about the rebellion and its outcome. These thoughts he had confessed to her and her alone, but Peggy held his confession close. She did not mention it to Anne, who, although a true loyalist, was known to chatter far too much.

"I shouldn't say it," Anne hesitated. "But I am your friend. Are you certain about Benedict? I mean, his leg does give him a great deal of trouble. He hardly can stand unaided. And he is much older than you . . ." She did a quick count on her fingers. "Nearly twenty-one years older."

Peggy laughed lightly. Beneath her pillow was a letter from her Ben. "Open your heavenly bosom to me . . . let it expand, accept me, for I am nothing without you at my side." Peggy shivered as she thought of the words and imagined Ben's hands on her. Much as she loved him in a sisterly way, Major André had never caused her such exciting thoughts. "Oh, I am quite certain," Peggy said. "Quite, quite certain."

Robert MacLean crouched behind the gnarled trunk of an old cyprus tree and stared down the sloping hill toward the wide, muddy river. Somewhere across the water, hidden by the low scrub bush on the far shore, there were British soliders keeping a silent vigil.

Robert let out his breath and strained his senses to listen. But he could hear nothing save the shrill cry of the katydids calling to one another from their nests among the reeds. The long, green insects infested the growth on both sides of the river; theirs was a night song.

Robert patted the ground and judged it dry enough to sit down. There was no need to be uncomfortable, as he could have a long wait. Indeed, he hoped he would have a long, futile wait. This was not a good night for subterfuge, it was far too bright and the British were far too close. He could not see them, but in spite of their stealth, Robert knew the British patrol was there, and their presence made his own position dangerous.

Robert kept his eyes fastened on the water. The Indian tribes who spoke the Algonkian tongue called the river "the Father of Waters," since in their language *misi* meant "big" and *sipi* meant "water." It was those same Indians who had led the French to the Mississippi, taking their birchbark canoes from Lake Michigan to the Fox River and then portaging them from the Fox to the Wisconsin and from that tributary onto the Mississippi. The French had called the wilderness the Louisiana Territory. In the fifth year of the Seven Years' War, a war in which Robert MacLean had fought on the side of the French in Quebec, Spain had entered the conflict and sided with France against the British. As a result of the Treaty of 1763, which ended the war, the Louisiana Territory was ceded to Spain.

Robert smiled to himself as he thought about the artificial boundaries drawn in the wilderness. The exact terms of the treaty called for France to give up Canada and surrender her claim to the land south of the Great Lakes and east of the Mississippi, except for New Orleans. Isle d'Orleans was set off by the Bayou Manchac, the Amite River, and lakes Maurepas, Borgue, and Pontchartrain. As a result of this twisted line on the map of conquest, New Orleans remained part of the Louisiana Territory, while the ceded portion east of the Mississippi became British West Florida.

Robert touched the earth with his finger and drew a circle

in the loose soil. Sitting, as he was, beneath the large cypress tree on the west bank, he was in Spanish territory. But across the river, the British patrolled the waterway. They maintained garrisons at Natchez, Baton Rouge, Mobile, and Pensacola. The object of the garrison at Natchez was to prevent Robert MacLean from sending gunpowder upriver. But as Robert knew full well, the British would not hesitate to cross the river in full pursuit if the gunpowder he was expecting were to be delivered while they were on their nightly patrol. The river was a road and by making it the dividing line in the treaty, a new bone of contention had been created between traditional enemies.

"You know what they write in them treaties?" old Fou Loup, a French-Mohawk half-breed and riverman, had asked Robert more than fifteen years earlier. "They write down all the things that cause the next war."

Well, Fou Loup should know, Robert thought. His old friend and companion had known war and fighting for the better part of seventy years and he had survived it, only to succumb to river fever in his seventy-fifth year.

Robert MacLean had thought that Fou Loup merely was being cynical. But as the comment came back to him, he recognized it as a statement of universal truth.

The Treaty of 1763 had resulted in a British army being placed in North America. It had resulted in taxation. Moreover, the merchants of the Thirteen Colonies were furious over the Intolerable Acts, which included trade restrictions. The resentment had boiled over until it finally grew into a full-fledged declaration of independence and rebellion against the British. Louisiana was a long way from Bunker Hill and Valley Forge, but here, on the western frontier, there was plenty of trouble.

The French had seen their opportunity to even the score with the British for the loss of Canada and the Louisiana Territory. They had declared war on England and now aided the rebellious colonies. Spain, one of England's traditional enemies, sat on the fence, attempting to judge which way to jump in order to land firmly on the winning side.

Ah, life is complicated, Robert thought. And war, especially this war, made strange bedfellows. The British forces in West Florida posed a distinct threat. But the rebellious colonies also were a threat. Virginia was expansionist; her boundaries extended to the Pacific Ocean. And the Spanish King did, after all, rule many colonies around the world. Rebellion was not to be encouraged.

"If we get involved at all," the tavern strategists in New Orleans maintained, "it must not be directly on the side of the rebels. We would only be joining the French—just to weaken the English, you understand." Such conversations were common; Robert had heard them, participated in them, and made his own choices.

The choice he made came as a result of another of Fou Loup's lessons. "You don't sell wood in a forest, or fish at the lakeside. You take advantage of scarcity." He and Fou Loup had done that during the latter part of the Seven Years' War, when they had traded scarce furs. Now Robert was at it again. The commodity was gunpowder. The Mississippi, Robert decided, was the dividing line between war and peace; it was a winding, muddy line between military adventure and pure commerce.

Natchez, just across the river, held British soldiers and a considerable number of settlers from the rebellious colonies. On the west bank, near the fledgling community of Vidalia, Robert MacLean operated a trading post. Owing to the secret support the Spanish governor extended to the rebellious colonies, the colony of Virginia in particular, trade in gunpowder provided Robert with considerable funds and a small mortgage on the treasury of Virginia.

The former governor, Don Luis de Unzaga, had been given specific orders to observe all events in North America that might come to affect Spain and her colonies. He also had begun the secret and quiet trade in which Robert MacLean had come to play a leading role.

It began when Captain Robert Gibson had come to New Orleans with a letter from General Charles Lee asking for help. Governor Unzaga was happy to oblige. He accepted a large bank draft on the government of Virginia endorsed by a wealthy New Orleans merchant and close friend of Robert MacLean's, Mr. Oliver Pollock. The funds were used to purchase ten thousand pounds of gunpowder that were forwarded up the Mississippi by Robert MacLean to Fort Pitt and Wheeling, West Virginia. George

Rogers Clark was grateful indeed for his new supplies.

In addition to running gunpowder, Robert also was charged with Indian relations. This effort consisted of distributing over seven thousand dollars' worth of goods to the Indians in order to ensure their cooperation and silence. The Spanish continued to smile sweetly at the British, but the Spanish clearly were preparing for a major British attack launched from Canada down the Mississippi.

Robert forced himself out of his reverie and looked heavenward. The progress of the rising moon indicated that several hours had elapsed since his arrival. He moved his body into a half-standing position and let forth with a low, birdlike whistle. His signal went unanswered.

The night sky was like a rich black velvet cloth studded with unusually bright diamonds. A fine night for lovemaking, or for reminiscences, but a bad night for work that ought to go unobserved.

Robert bit his lower lip and surveyed the scene. The moonlight shimmered off the water and illuminated the river's banks. He hoped the Indians would not come tonight.

A few moments passed and Robert heard the unmistakable sound of paddles in the water. He cupped his hands over his mouth and made a shrieking noise, a sound that emulated a night bird.

Immediately the east bank was alive with gunfire and the voices of shouting men. The shots crackled through the air, wild shots aimed more toward Robert than in the direction from which the Indian canoes were coming. Robert knew his warning would have halted the flotilla before it came into sight. The Indians would be gone, dispersed into the bush before the British could cross the river.

Suddenly a flare lit up the west bank, and Robert realized that his silhouette was clearly outlined against the darkness. There were voices and more gunfire. With horror, Robert realized that the gunfire was coming not only from across the river, but also from the low scrub brush below him. He turned quickly and headed for his horse, tied among the poplars above the cypress tree. A blast from an unseen musket ripped through the air, and pain became Robert's main reality. He fell to the ground, his fingers digging into the soft earth.

CHAPTER II

April 8, 1779

Jenna Macleod studied her image in the mirror that hung on the wall of her bedchamber. Her long russet hair was pulled back and tied with a green ribbon. Her green eyes were steady and clear. Everyone said she was the image of her mother, tall and well proportioned. The dress Jenna wore was made of a rough, dark material and trimmed with stiff white cloth. In spite of its modest cut, it failed to hide her voluptuous body, though it did give her a prim appearance, which was acceptable on the streets of Montreal. "It looks like a nun's habit," Jenna complained. "And I'm going to end up a nun too." Her bottom lip thrust forward. "It's not fair." Jenna stomped her foot for added emphasis.

Helena sat on the edge of the bed and watched her sister. "You're young," she commented.

"It's not that I'm young, it's that I'm the youngest! You're married. And who ever worries about Andrew and Mat? Nobody. I am the one who can't go where I please, or see whom I want. I'm a prisoner. It's unfair!"

Helena suppressed a smile. Jenna was full of outrage and indignation. Only one so young could feel injustice so hotly. "You can see anyone you want, but Papa will not tolerate your being courted by Stephan and you know why."

Jenna whirled around to face Helena. "I love Stephan!"

"You *think* you love him," Helena corrected.

"I *know* I love him, and Papa has no right to forbid him to come, just because he's a Protestant. I don't care about that. I don't care about the Church! I hadn't noticed we were all so religious that we spent all of our time in church! Mama and Papa have Protestant friends. This never was an issue before!"

"Being religious really has nothing to do with it. Not all Protestants are anti-Catholic. Stephan is militant and drinks too much; he isn't a moral person."

"He's wonderful to me," Jenna retorted. "And I don't believe any of the stories about him."

Helena forced herself not to reply. She realized she was sinking into a trap, doing what she had vowed not to. She was making Jenna more defensive, just as Mathew had done when he banned Stephan from the house. Jenna was reacting just as Helena had warned her mother she would. Willful to the core.

Jenna turned back to the mirror and with a single motion pulled the ribbon from her hair and picked up her hairbrush. She began to pull it through her hair vigorously, the anger still apparent on her face.

Helena got up and walked toward the dressing table. "I'm not going to give you any advice," she said softly. "But think about it before you do it."

"Do what?" Jenna said, pouting.

"Do whatever you're thinking about doing."

"I'm thinking about being a nun. Suitable for such a religious family!"

Helena laughed. "I hardly think they would have you. You're vain."

"I am not vain," Jenna protested.

Helena shook her head. Jenna was a beautiful child-woman. Her looks gave her an aura of maturity, but she was emotionally immature.

Jenna set down the brush and pulled her hair back again, tying it securely. She put on her bonnet and picked up her shawl. "I'm going out," she announced.

"If you really were a prisoner, as you keep saying you are, you couldn't go out," Helena reminded her.

"There are different kinds of prisoners," Jenna sniffed. "Papa has done something unforgivable. He doesn't own me!"

Several miles from the house Jenna was about to leave, Stephan O'Connell stood in a wooded area atop Mount

21

Royal and surveyed the scene below. This, legend had it, was the spot where Jacques Cartier had planted the first cross in Montreal, claiming Canada for the French. But the historic significance of the spot was of no interest to Stephan. Nor indeed was Montreal itself of interest.

Just as Jenna was alienated from her family, Stephan was alienated from his. His father urged him to return to Boston and fight with the patriots in the Continental Army led by General Washington. But Stephan rejected that request. The rebellion interested him only in that it opened up new opportunities in the West and, however fine the potential of Montreal, it did not hold nearly the possibilities for gaining wealth that the West did. In any case, the southern climate beckoned Stephan. His uncle had traveled through the Cumberland Gap and settled near Natchez. Across the river, Stephan knew, there was rich land aplenty and the opportunity he desired so much.

If he went south and then west, he reasoned, he would escape his parents' prodding. Moreover, the Spanish remained neutral and they offered fine land grants in the area. His mind was made up; there was but one thing left to settle.

He listened at the approaching sound of hoofbeats and looked anxiously through the dense trees. Jenna pulled in her horse's reins and looked about.

"Here!" Stephan called out. He ran to her and helped her dismount, gathering her in his arms and kissing her.

"I thought you wouldn't come. I was about to leave."

"I came," Jenna answered breathlessly. She pulled herself away from him. "But Papa would be furious. And I can't stay long."

Stephan allowed his eyes to feast on her. There was no question about it, Jenna Macleod was among the most desirable women in Montreal and, he thought, the most high-spirited.

Beneath the boldness of his gaze, Stephan could see Jenna blushing. He did not let go of her hands but pressed them harder and studied her expression. "Do you love me, Jenna?"

"My father has forbidden it," Jenna answered. She looked away.

"That's not the question I asked," Stephan persisted.

"Damn your father! Do you love me?" His voice had grown deep and demanding and it sent a chill down her spine.

"Yes, I love you. I think I love you. . . ." Jenna blinked at him.

"I'm going away," Stephan said slowly.

"Not back to Boston to fight?" Jenna's face paled and she threw herself against him. Thoughts of her adopted sister Madelaine flooded her mind. Madelaine's husband had been killed. Helena's husband was away too and Helena was lonely. Jenna's arms went around his neck, "No, no, Stephan. Don't go, I couldn't bear it!" Jenna felt the warm excitement she always felt when she was near Stephan. She snuggled against his chest and closed her eyes, filled with the anxiety that he would go away, leave her. Again Stephan pushed her back, but this time he bent and kissed her again, passionately moving her lovely lips with his and quickening to the fact that she responded fully, moving her mouth beneath his. After their long kiss, Stephan brushed a tear from her cheek. "I will go and fight," he said, "unless you run away with me." He paused and added, somewhat dramatically, "Without you, I might as well be dead."

The look on Jenna's stricken face was plain evidence of her feeling. But as Stephan well knew, beneath her present anger, Jenna's loyalty to her family was strong.

"Run away with you? How? To where?" Jenna's wide eyes were incredulous, questioning. Stephan's hands were on her shoulders, and his eyes seemed to be devouring her. "We'll go south," he answered. "We'll go where there's no war, where we can make our own fortune, have our own lives without interference."

The warmth of his hands seemed to burn through her dress. Jenna's first impulse was to throw herself again into his arms, to promise to follow him to the ends of the earth. "Oh, Stephan . . ." She could not finish her sentence.

"We'll go via the lakes, down the Mississippi,". he was saying.

"To New Orleans?" Jenna questioned. Stories darted through her mind, stories about the gay, free, uninhibited French port. "I have an uncle there," Jenna said, thinking of Robert MacLean, her mother's brother-in-law. Robert

23

wasn't really her uncle, he was the brother of Janet Macleod's first husband. But Robert MacLean had escaped from Scotland with Janet and together they had come to New France. There were family stories by the hundred about Uncle Robert. Jenna had heard them all.

"I'm a decent woodsman," Stephan was saying. "It won't be such a difficult journey. And we can be married in Fort St. Louis. It's Spanish Territory."

Jenna sucked in her lip and looked at him. "You'd have a priest marry us?"

Stephan nodded. "In Spanish Territory we won't find much else. Jenna, I will take care of you. I have some money and once we get to St. Louis there is no danger at all. Will you come? Will you be my wife?"

Jenna met his questioning eyes. "Papa was wrong to deny you the right to court me, and he's wrong about you too—all the things he said! I'll never forgive him."

"But do you love me enough to come with me?" He cleared his throat and looked away. "Or shall I go back to Boston and fight? I can't go west without you. But I will go home and fight with Washington, even if it means . . ."

Jenna let out her breath. Excitement and apprehension filled her all at once. In her mind's eye she imagined her first night under the stars with Stephan. She thought of them traveling into the unknown together, bound by their love and seeking their freedom. They would be like Adam and Eve, innocents in the wilderness.

"Oh, I'll do it!" Jenna suddenly promised. "I'll come with you!"

Stephan seized her and again kissed her. "We'll have to make plans." He seemed to be considering the various provisions they would require. "We'll be able to go soon, perhaps in a fortnight."

Jenna shook her head affirmatively.

"You'll have to dress like a boy," Stephan suggested, "if you can." The thought of her curvaceous figure made him smile. Jenna would be most difficult to disguise. "And we'll have to travel light. Bring no more than one dress."

"And the provisions?" Jenna asked.

He placed his large hands on her small waist and squeezed her to him. "I'll take care of everything, and when we get to

New Orleans, I'll dress you the way you ought to be dressed.''

Jenna smiled up at him lovingly. "You're shameful," she said, blushing again. The thought of Stephan dressing her filled Jenna with excitement. And the thought of making love! He was so handsome, so strong! She shivered in his arms. "Shameful," she repeated.

"And you love it," Stephan answered as he again kissed her.

Peggy Shippen's mother was a small woman, under five feet. Her snow-white hair was pulled back, but not in the severe fashion of so many matrons. A few waves were allowed to form behind her ears and around her little face. Mrs. Shippen had sparkling blue eyes, a ready smile, and her grooming was always just so. Her husband would have described her as a trifle nervous, and it was true that she tended to speak in rapid phrases.

Mr. Shippen was not small, nor was he at all nervous. He was in truth a portly giant of a fellow, a man who drank too much rum but who held it well because he knew the value of both money and silence. His wife called him an old dear, and by that she meant that he was extraordinarily wealthy but a bit rough around what she considered important edges.

Few who knew the Shippens could imagine them making love, but they must have done so because they had three children. Peggy Shippen was younger than her brother and sister by many years, causing the gossips to comment, "She must have been conceived when he was a bit drunk and she was a bit tithered." The response was, however, always the same. "Well, if she was conceived as a result of too many rum toddies, the outcome is hardly undesirable."

The wedding was not the lavish affair one might have expected from the Shippens, considering that Peggy was their youngest daughter and the toast of Philadelphia. "The constraints of war," Mr. Shippen explained. "It's really elegance that matters," Mrs. Shippen added.

"Does it distress you, my dear, to have your lovely daughter marry a rebel general?" one of Mrs. Shippen's friends inquired.

"Politics does not interest me," Mrs. Shippen said in defense of her new son-in-law, General Benedict Arnold. "Manners, breeding, and substance are the only real indicators. General Arnold is a true gentleman, an honorable man."

Mr. Shippen was hardly less delighted. The commander of Philadelphia who now stood at his daughter's side hardly seemed a rebellious colonial at all. Indeed, he was put upon by the financial restraints of the Colonial Army and unhappy with the course of the rebellion. "If things persist," Arnold had confided to Mr. Shippen, "we shall end up a collection of little kingdoms ruled by louts and liars. A confederation of selfish little states simply cannot succeed in the eighteenth century! The Articles of Confederation are doomed! They provide for no central leadership. Virginia goes its way, the Massachusetts Bay Colony goes another." With that statement, Arnold had sighed, puffed on his pipe, and looked heavenward for guidance. "I would not willingly trade the British Crown for an American King named Washington. He'll have to tax the people more than the King, if only to pay his expense accounts for one week!"

Mr. Shippen had smiled happily and, in spite of his advanced state of inebriation, checked his impulse to agree too heartily. There would, he had reminded himself, be more than enough time to talk politics with his new son-in-law. And poor General Arnold! He had enough trouble with the colonial government to turn him into a complete loyalist. First, he had been passed over repeatedly for advancement, though clearly he was the most competent general among the rebels. Now, there was all the difficulty with the charges against him made by the Executive Council of Pennsylvania. Well, one could hardly expect the commander of Philadelphia to live in poverty! One had to make investments, one had to maintain a certain position. Mr. Shippen shook his head as he thought about it. It was quite disgusting. Clearly in this so-called new society, favoritism and patronage would continue to be the bywords. One might as well remain a loyalist! It was a question of who the new favored were to be.

Mr. Shippen gazed at his beautiful blond daughter. She was utterly radiant in her snow-white gown. And beside her, leaning on the arm of Major Franks, General Arnold also looked handsome. The drawing room was filled with smiling faces, though Mrs. Shippen was crying just a bit. She always cried at weddings.

Arnold's sister Hannah was there, as well as Arnold's sons by his first wife, who had died four years ago. Arnold's other close friends, Eleazar Oswald and General Philip Schuyler, were not present. All the other guests were members of the extended Shippen family; cousins, aunts, and uncles abounded.

Mr. Shippen's eyes came to rest on Thomas Bolton, the foundling lad the Shippens had taken in so many years ago. Tom had been eight years old then. Apprenticed from the foundling home to the Shippen firm, Mr. Shippen had brought the lad home and seen to his education. Tom Bolton was now a widower of thirty-two. He still worked for Mr. Shippen, but that was not his sole source of money nor his only avocation. Tom had grown up into a good-looking, well groomed young man; a born loyalist with good sense. For a boy who knew so little about his origins—save that he had lived with a Quaker family named Stowe—Tom Bolton was well adjusted and well suited to meet the challenges he faced. His position with the Shippen firm offered him fine cover for his real work with Major André, chief of Intelligence Services for General Sir Henry Clinton, the commander of the British forces in North America. Mr. Shippen had a special pride in Tom. The young man to whom he had extended his helping hand was a potential hero, a man willing to perform great services for the Crown.

The wedding ceremony came to its conclusion and now people mingled, congratulating the groom, who sat on the settee, and kissing the bride, who stood by his side.

"He's such a fine man," Mrs. Shippen whispered to Tom as she nodded toward General Arnold. Tom could not but agree. At thirty-eight, Benedict Arnold was suave and distinguished-looking, broad of shoulder and straight of nose. He had an honest, open face and he was widely acknowledged as a fine woodsman. He had fought with Ethan Allen in the successful colonial attack on Fort Ticonderoga, and he had led seven hundred men through the wilderness of Maine to attack Quebec in the dead of winter. But Montgomery's reinforcements had come too late, and the attack

27

was a failure in spite of Arnold's personal success. Wounded himself, Arnold had saved most of his men and returned a true hero.

Then, Tom thought, came the politics and indignities of the rebellion. General Arnold was not given a decent fighting command because the colonies fussed over what general came from which colony. And in the end they decreed that there could only be one general from each, or that they be apportioned in equal number. Even the arrogant Washington was known to have mumbled, "The management of the Revolution has become a matter of geography rather than of military talent." But Tom Bolton suspected, as did Mr. Shippen, that Arnold was neither bitter nor unhappy. He seemed to have come to the conclusion that the colonies would fall apart as soon as they won against their common enemy. *If* they won. Tom moved to the settee as soon as Arnold's sister Hannah was engaged in conversation by Major Franks.

"I congratulate you, sir. Peggy is a wonderful girl." He extended his hand, and Arnold shook it vigorously. He had met Tom Bolton many times at the Shippen house.

"I fear I'm not worthy of so fine a young woman," General Arnold said, blushing slightly.

"You are most worthy," Tom assured him. "No woman could ask for more than a man of your stature and honor. Your house—I should call it a castle—is magnificent!" Tom smiled warmly. He was referring to Mount Pleasant, the estate General Arnold had so recently purchased, the home he and Peggy would move into this very evening. On the outskirts of the city, Mount Pleasant was a rambling mansion located on the banks of Schuylkill River. The main house was surrounded by lawns, gardens, and a multitude of smaller buildings that housed servants, horses, and carriages.

General Arnold smiled back at Tom, but Arnold's eyes followed his petite, blond bride. "I could provide no lesser setting for a woman as lovely as Peggy," he answered. Then, on a poetic note, "She is like a fantasy come to life. Her voice is music, her presence gives me every pleasure." Tom's eyes also followed Peggy Shippen. He would not have described her in quite the same terms, though he could well understand why General Arnold was so smitten with her. He had known Peggy since the day she was born and was, therefore, one of the few men immune to her charms. She was a trifle frivolous, but she also had talents. Chief among them was her acting ability. She could cry at will, faint whenever it seemed useful, and she always was coquettish. Whatever Peggy asked of a man became that man's command. And that, Tom thought, would be most useful for his purposes.

Peggy walked across the room and bent down, taking both of Benedict Arnold's hands in hers. "It's time we left," she whispered. "Tom, will you be a dear and help Ben to the carriage?"

Tom stood up. He was the tallest man in the room and he bent slightly, always conscious of his height. "Sir," he said, offering General Arnold his arm. "With your permission, I will drive your carriage to Mount Pleasant." General Arnold nodded and struggled to his feet, leaning on Tom Bolton's extended arm.

Two hours later, in their bed chamber, Benedict Arnold watched his blushing bride as she emerged from her boudoir to join him. Her long, blond curls fell to her bare white shoulders, and her silken nightdress revealed her small, perfectly shaped little breasts. Peggy smiled at him, her cornflower-blue eyes wide and glowing.

Arnold ran his finger around his own tight collar and then loosened it. It was a moment of self-consciousness and it occurred to him that wedding nights ought to be forbidden. Peggy was so young, so lovely, and so inexperienced. He looked at her full, rounded lips and felt a combination of acute embarrassment mixed with overpowering desire. He had been a widower for four long years and because they were years of war, he had remained totally faithful to the memory of his wife. Looking at Peggy, he could see the glint of apprehension in her young eyes, he could feel her unspoken questions.

With the aid of his cane, Arnold hobbled across the room to her side. His dark eyes devoured her. "Do not ask," he said softly. "Do not ask if you are more lovely than Margaret, do not ask if I love you more than I loved her."

Benedict was aware that he sounded pleading. He was terribly aware of how Peggy must feel. Surely she wanted to know if he loved her more.

"Peggy . . ." Her blue eyes looked away, down at the richly carpeted floor.

"I've never been married," she whispered. "I've never . . ."

"I know you haven't." Arnold heard his own voice and was aware of how formal he sounded. He swallowed hard and chastised himself for not having spoken to her earlier about his first wife. But his courtship with Peggy had been a proper Philadelphia courtship. They had seldom been alone, their togetherness had been a round of gay parties, concerts, theater, and receptions. They talked about books, about political tracts, about the rebellion.

"Margaret was a lovely woman, Peggy." It was a difficult beginning, and he took a deep breath. "She bore me three sons, and I cherish her memory. I don't think I love you either more, or less. I only know that our love will be different, that you are special, unique." He was struggling for words as he pulled her into his arms. She buried her face in his chest and they stood silently. Then he bent down and caressed her long white neck with his lips, finally seeking her full mouth. When he kissed her, she moved her lips beneath his and he felt suddenly relaxed.

"I would trade my soul to the devil to be able to sweep you up and carry you to our marriage bed. But you have made a bad bargain, you have marrried a man whose legs no longer carry him willingly."

"You are strong and brave, wounded in battle." Her arm went around his waist and she helped him across the room to the bed. Benedict sat down and touched the snow-white pillowcases with their embroidered silken flowers, flowers created by Peggy's own needle. He unfastened his shirt and took off his trousers, then, with difficulty, he lifted his lame leg and lay out on the bed. Head on the pillow, he could smell the woody aroma of the linens so recently released from Peggy's hope chest. He lifted his hand and caressed her cheek, her neck, the outline of her small, firm breasts. Peggy smiled, then slithered down the bed and pressed her lips to the scars on Ben's leg. She kissed them again and again, murmuring, "I do love you, I do."

He ran his fingers through her thick curls. "You are my golden princess, my true love."

Peggy moved up and leaned over him. "Oh, Ben, forgive me for being so selfish. I love you more for being faithful to Margaret's memory. I cherish your loyalty, your honor. It's what makes you special."

Benedict loosened the top of her gown and gently pulled it down. He touched her little breasts and delighted as her nipples grew hard and firm. "Be gentle," Peggy whispered. "Be gentle, love me, and be loyal."

He answered her plea with a more intimate caress and she pressed herself to him, her arms around his neck, her lips partly open, her eyes closed. "I pledge myself to you and you alone," he said.

"And I to you," came Peggy's reply.

His fingers toyed with her till she moaned and he moved his hands expertly from her mound of soft golden down to her nipples. "Sweet rosebuds," he whispered as he separated her legs and continued his caresses. When he felt her damp, he penetrated her as gently as he could. "My virgin princess," he said, "I adore you." Peggy again moaned and he could feel the heat of her body and see the flush of desire in her face. When at last they both knew full pleasure, he extinguished the lamp and lay beside her in the darkness.

"Are you asleep?" Peggy asked after some time.

"No, thinking," he answered. His mind had been wandering from his personal loyalties to his political loyalties. "Have I made a mistake?"

"In marrying me?"

He laughed gently and his hands ran through her hair. "Oh, no! I was thinking about the rebellion, the suffering it has caused. Have I made a mistake? Should I be involved at all?"

"In your heart, you are true to the King, aren't you?"

He nodded. " 'To thine own self be true,' " he replied, quoting his favorite play, *Hamlet*.

" 'And it must follow, as the night the day, Thou can'st not then be false to any man.' " Peggy finished the quote and turned in his arms. "You will do the right thing."

31

"The time will come when my honor will be questioned."

"I shall not question it," Peggy promised.

A memory image of Janet Macleod floated across Robert's mind. In his vision, Janet was ageless, frozen in his memory as a beautiful woman of thirty-eight. "I wanted to come back," his lips formed the words, but he made no sound. His dream continued. He was lying down; Janet was standing over him and the expression on her face was one of concern and understanding.

"I have so much to say to you, so much to tell you," he said in the dream. The years had fled like weeks, his time spent on the river had eclipsed. They had written to one another. Long letters, delivered through a precarious series of exchanges. Letters that traveled the waterways and across the Great Lakes, letters that went into buckskin pouches, carried near an unknown courier's heart. But now there were no letters. The rebellion had ended the always tenuous line of communication. Besides, a letter from Louisiana, from Spanish Territory, might cast suspicion on the Macleods. We are divided by war and by loyalties. But we are always together spiritually. In his mind, Robert remembered his escape from Scotland with Janet. He had only been seven and she had saved his life. She was the widow of his dead brother, but she had been both a sister and a mother to him.

"Angelique and I have three children," he wanted to tell her. "But of course they are not children anymore. The twins, Will and James, are sixteen, and Maria, our daughter, is fourteen."

In his dream, Janet smiled and her lips formed a reply. Then suddenly, he was seven and grasping for her skirts: "Don't go away, don't leave me. . . ." The image of her face faded and Robert felt a hot flash, followed by a cold chill. He was enveloped in darkness, lost among the trees, deep in some dense, lush forest. He heard Fou Loup's laugh and reached for his hand, then remembered that Fou Loup was dead. Robert inhaled and out of the blackness, he heard a voice.

"He's a strong man. No load of grapeshot in the hip's going to keep him down." The voice was deep and husky with a raspy quality, as if the vocal cords were covered with sand. He couldn't tell if it was a male voice or a female voice.

"Are you certain he'll be all right?" The second voice was small and frightened, but it was unmistakable. It was his wife, Angelique.

Robert forced his eyes open and the room wavered before him. It was small and stuffy; the only light came from a single lantern that sat atop a crude table in the center of the room. The smell of menthol permeated the air and, on the fire, a cauldron filled with leaves and water boiled up.

"Angelique?" Robert slurred her name. His eyelids were heavy and he felt unnaturally weary, as if he had been drugged.

"I'm right here." He felt her cool hand take his. "We're at the conjure lady's. She's given you medicine."

Robert shook his head in acknowledgment. The inside of his mouth felt dry and there was the lingering taste of something bitter. "What happened?" Robert asked, remembering the British attack.

"The Indians said the British shot you, that they had crossed the river, that they were waiting. But it was a small force and the Indians chased them back across the river. Then they brought you here."

"Were any Indians killed?" Even in his drugged state, Robert searched for information. If any Indians had been killed, it would mean more trouble. It would signal the start of something bigger.

"No, none," Angelique assured him. She sniffed and pressed his hand. "I told you not to get involved in this. You could have been killed. It's too dangerous! And for what? Don't you care about me? About the children?" The words poured out of her mouth. Anger followed her relief, chasing away her tone of concern. "Robert MacLean, you should have been home. This war is no concern of ours. None."

"I wouldn't doubt the Spanish will enter it anyday now," Robert argued.

"I don't care who enters it. I hate the Spanish!"

Robert struggled to focus his eyes. Even in the shadows, he could see the expression on Angelique's face. Though she was only in her midthirties, Angelique had grown brittle

33

and tight. She's still beautiful, he thought. But she's changed. Angelique was no longer a willow that bent in the wind; she was like a dry branch ready to snap in two.

It had begun five years earlier with her younger brother's death. And since Grande Mama and Fou Loup were gone, Angelique was too much alone. The children had become involved in their own interests. As she grew older, all her resentments had seemed to surface, resentments Robert had thought were gone or forgotten. But Angelique had not forgotten. She dreamed of Acadie, of her childhood, and of her family. Her hatred of the British increased daily; their cruelty to the Acadians, Angelique's people, burned inside her. But Angelique could not accept the Spanish either. They had violated her and murdered her father. Irrationally, she also blamed her brother's death on the Spanish, though he had died of a fever. "He caught it from the Spanish," she often said.

"Let go of your hatreds," Robert had begged her many times. But Angelique could not and would not let go. She refused to return to Canada and to live there because it was part of British North America. She hated staying in Louisiana Territory because it was governed by the Spanish. And where the rebellion was concerned, she was adamant. "They're all English," she maintained. "It's only a family quarrel."

Robert's eyes fastened on Angelique. She was a knot of frustration, of bitterness. He loved her still, he tried to help. But it seemed he could do nothing.

"We'll go home now," Robert suggested. He struggled to move but discovered that his legs were numb and refused to obey him.

"The conjure lady says you have to stay the night. I'll bring the wagon in the morning."

Robert squinted and looked past Angelique into the face of the conjure lady, who stood a few feet away. The old woman looked impassive. She was standing with her wizened hands folded across the front of her long black dress; her eyes studied him without moving. The skin on her face was like the shell of a walnut, tan in color and deeply grooved. The conjure lady had a place of honor in the small community. She cast spells and healed wounds; she didn't bless newborn babies, as the priest did, but she said incantations over them. The priest, who visited now and again, shunned her, but even he did not challenge her or her authority over the inhabitants. The conjure lady had vast knowledge of every local plant species and bit of wildlife, and often she was seen during a full moon collecting the specimens that made up her pharmacy. Robert could not see them in the half light, but he knew the shelves of her small cabin were lined with containers of every sort and that those containers held rancid fats, mysterious pastes, powders made from the crushed wings of insects, and great barrels full of leaves from assorted shrubs. The conjure lady was as mixed as her remedies, a combination of races who, it was said, blended together under the Haitian sun. That she came from Haiti was quite clear. She spoke the patois of the island: Spanish and French mixed with some unknown African tongue.

"What have you given me?" Robert demanded to know.

"Medicine," she answered vaguely. "A little something to ease the pain, and there's poltices on the wound."

Robert nodded and suppressed a smile. He remembered when Fou Loup was alive and used to come to the conjure lady to obtain medicines. But more than that, Fou Loup had come to her when he wanted a good fight. The old woman always was good for that. She and Fou Loup argued constantly about the best cure for this or that. They cursed one another but one could only conclude that their medicine was equal. Either that, or the gods ignored their spells, since their curses worked on neither of them. Moreover, Fou Loup refused to pay the conjure lady for any of her remedies. He believed she should supply them without payment, as a sort of professional courtesy—one medicine person to another.

"I would stay here with you," Angelique said, "but Will and James are gone again. God knows were they go, and I can't leave Maria alone all night."

Robert closed his eyes. Not now, he thought. Angelique sounded as if she were about to begin a familiar litany. She could not accept the fact that Will and James were sixteen, they had lives of their own. Every time that they went off, Angelique thought of it as a personal affront. Robert cautioned himself to be patient. "I don't mind staying till morning. I'll be asleep anyway."

Angelique leaned over and kissed him on the cheek. It was a quick, dutiful kiss, a wifely kiss. She stood up and smoothed her skirts and turned to press some coins into the conjure lady's extended hand. "And you'll have a fresh chicken every week for a month," Angelique promised. It was the standard payment.

"The Indians are waiting to see me home," Angelique told him. Robert nodded and his eyes followed her as she walked across the room and opened the door, letting in the night air. In a moment she was gone.

By the fire, the conjure lady lethargically began to stir the brew in her cauldron.

"You got trouble with your woman," she commented. It was a statement rather than a question.

"We love each other," Robert protested.

"Some love eats," the conjure lady replied as she stood up and walked toward him, pulling down a skin of liquid from the shelf. "Some love devours everything, eats till there ain't nothin' left. Some sicknesses do the same, they eat away and make a person different."

She opened the skin and lifted it to her mouth, gulping down whatever was inside. She passed it to Robert. "Not medicine, just rum."

Robert took it from her and gulped down a long drink. It burned his throat and warmed his chest; it combined with the conjure lady's medicines to make him tired and groggy.

"A good woman can smother," the conjure lady went on. She leaned over and looked into Robert's face. "You ain't the type who should be smothered. Some plants don't grow in pots, no matter how good they grow in the bush." With that, she took back the skin and took another swig, wiping her mouth with her hand.

"Conjurin's an art," she mumbled as she crossed the room and disappeared behind a curtain that divided the cabin in half. "So's marriage, but disease . . . disease eats."

Robert didn't hear the last of her words. His head ached and his eyes were heavy as he fell into a deep, drug-induced sleep.

CHAPTER III

April 20, 1779

Jenna Macleod pulled the loose-fitting jacket around her. It was Mat's jacket, one he had worn when he was younger. The buckskins were Mat's too. They were a bit tight in the hips, and too loose around the waist. Jenna's woodsman's boots were Andrew's; she had stuffed material into the toes so they would fit her better. Into her pack Jenna had stuffed one dress, her brush, and clean undergarments.

She looked in the mirror and shrugged. She looked terrible! Jenna leaned forward; the silver chain that held the Roman coin was just visible. "It's our family heirloom," her father had told her. "Without it I would not have found your mother." Jenna sniffed and blinked back tears at the thought. A wave of indecision and guilt swept over her and hot tears began to tumble down her cheeks. "I do love you, Papa," she said aloud. "But I have a right to my own life!" Jenna stood an instant longer and then she shouldered the pack and crept quietly out of the house into the dark night.

As her mare carried her to the meeting place she and Stephan had decided on, Jenna grasped the coin. "I had one," her father had told her. "And your mother had the other. She gave hers to Robert and when I found Robert, I knew I had found your mother as well." It was such a romantic story, Jenna thought. "You had your romance," she whispered into the night. "But you didn't want me to have mine."

Jenna reached the clump of woods by the river and drew in the mare. She climbed down and again shouldered the pack. She waited in the darkness, praying Stephan would not be late. She started when she heard footsteps, and she crouched down behind a tree and listened.

"Jenna?"

"Stephan?" Jenna stood up and saw him as he emerged into the small clearing.

"You did come!" He took her into his arms and kissed her.

"I almost didn't come. I hate to hurt Mama and Papa this way." Stephan squeezed her. "They'll be all right. After a time they'll accept it." He kissed her lightly again. "We don't have much time. Your father is bound to come hunting for you. We have to leave now."

Stephan was leading her along the shore of the river. It was cloudy and the black water lapped against the rocks. Presently Stephan stopped, then moved knowingly to a pile of branches near a felled tree. He cleared them quickly and uncovered the long birchbark canoe and the two packs he had stored. The clouds broke, and in the moonlight Jenna recognized the dark outlines of the canoe and the packs. "You take these," Stephan advised, pointing to the packs.

Jenna went to the packs and felt grateful that her father had taught her so much about canoeing and surviving in the wilderness. Having grown up in the Niagara would help on this romantic adventure. She swung the lightest pack over her other shoulder with a groan and dragged the other, exclaiming in a loud whisper, "Oh, they're heavy!"

"Heavy or not, you'll have to carry them for a bit."

Stephan bent down and lifted the canoe onto his shoulders, wobbling on his feet under the heavy load. They walked following the river till they came to a sandy area. Stephan waded into the water a few steps to unload the canoe as silently as possible. But it slipped in his hands, hitting the water with a noisy *whap*. "Dammit!"

"Are you all right? You're making so much noise," Jenna whispered as she let her packs slide off her shoulders and drop to the sand.

"The ground's uneven," Stephan said, only too aware that his skills were not as expert as he had led Jenna to believe. "Hand me the packs."

He loaded the canoe, trying to distribute the weight as

evenly as possible. "Get in the far end," he instructed Jenna, pointing to the stern of the canoe.

Jenna lifted the paddle and peered at the canoe. "But that's the stern. You're supposed to be there," she protested.

Stephan looked up. "Oh, of course," he mumbled. He turned the canoe around and steadied it as Jenna, placing her paddle across the gunnels, climbed in.

Stephan climbed in after her and, using his paddle, pushed off into deeper water. Jenna paddled in her best silent Indian style, but Stephan splashed his paddle repeatedly.

Jenna blinked. They were headed out into the middle of the river where they could easily be seen. Besides, it was only April. The water was freezing cold and it was safer to stay close to shore.

Jenna stopped paddling and turned toward Stephan. A splash from his paddle hit her square in the face, sending icy water running down the open neck of her shirt. "Good God! I thought you knew what you were doing! We're going in circles. Can't you paddle properly?"

"I haven't done this for a long time," Stephan protested.

"If at all," Jenna answered. "Do it this way and head closer to shore. If you dump us, we'll freeze!" Stephan's face went red, but Jenna could not see him in the darkness. Luckily, they were heading for shore and Stephan was beginning to paddle correctly. Soon they were gliding swiftly along in silent unison, hearing only the gentle slurp of their paddles and the distant call of a lone whippoorwill.

Jenna relaxed some, sorry that she had lost her temper, but somehow fully aware that Stephan was not the woodsman he claimed to be. She sighed. He simply would have to learn.

Helena sat at the table next to her three-year-old, Abigail. "Come on," she cajoled, looking at the golden-haired infant. "Just a few more spoonfuls. That's it." Helena smiled as little Abby opened her mouth and accepted, albeit reluctantly, another spoonful of gruel.

"Perhaps she'd eat more if you fed her some potatoes with fresh-churned butter."

Helena frowned at her father, who was sitting at the far end of the table, a copy of the *Quebec Gazette* in his hands. "Not for breakfast. It's not healthy. Hot gruel is healthy."

Mathew smiled. "Where's your sister?"

"Still asleep, I expect." She turned to face Abby's mischievous little face. "She can sleep because she doesn't have a baby with a timepiece in her stomach to wake her up."

Janet came into the kitchen. Pulling her kerchief off her head, she set down a large basket of food on the corner of the table. "I got a big chicken," she announced, then said with a sigh, "You have to be at the street market early to find good food these days."

"Grandmama!" Abby squealed. Janet turned and bent down lovingly to kiss her granddaughter. "How's my baby this morning?" Abby giggled, drooling gruel from her mouth as she did so.

"The trouble with being a grandfather is that everyone else gets kissed first," Mathew said.

Janet straightened up and raised one eyebrow. "Now, now," she smiled. "The best always comes last, always." She bent over and kissed him tenderly. Mathew touched her face with his hand. "You're beautiful," he whispered, "and much too young to be a grandmother."

"Aren't you going to eat any more?" Helena questioned after Abby shook her head vigorously in the negative when approached with the brimming, gruel-filled spoon.

"Isn't Jenna up yet?" Janet asked. "She's supposed to be at Madame Rouge's by ten."

"No, she isn't up yet. And she told me last night she wasn't going to her lesson."

"Well, she is going!" Mathew said with irritation as he put down his paper. His face filled with exasperation. In the past fortnight the tension between him and his younger daughter had seemed to grow daily.

"Let me have the spoon," Janet said to Helena. "I'll feed the little minx her gruel. You'll eat for Granny, won't you?" Abby shook her curls and smiled. "Go wake Jenna," Janet said, hoping Mathew would not see the look the two of them exchanged. It said: Bring Jenna down and tell her that

Mathew's upset. Helena understood; she and her mother had long practiced silent communication.

Helena left the room and, lifting her skirts, climbed the stairs to the second floor. She knocked on Jenna's door.

"Jenna!" Helena waited. "Jenna!" There was no answer and Helena turned the knob, opening the door.

Her eyes seemed to take in the whole room at once: the unslept-in bed, the open window, and, on the desk, a parchment weighted down with a prayerbook.

Helena sucked in her breath and bit her lip. As surely as she stood rooted to the spot, she knew her sister was gone and would not come back. "Oh, dear God," she murmured under her breath. Quickly, Helena closed the door and went to the desk. The writing on the parchment was large and full and open; the curlicue letters stared up at her.

Dear Mama and Papa,

I have gone away with Stephan. I know you won't understand, but I hope you will forgive me someday. You and Papa have your love, but you would not let me have mine. I am no longer a child. Stephan and I will be married. We are going far away and when I can I will write to you. I will be safe and I know I will be happy. Kiss Helena and Abby for me; when Mat and Andrew come home, tell them I love them too. May you have all the happiness I know I will have. And Papa, Stephan *is* a wonderful man. He loves only me, he is honest and intelligent, handsome and brave. Someday you will get to know him and you will change your mind.

Your loving daughter,
Jenna

Helena closed her eyes and let the parchment fall to the desk. All her instincts bade her to remain in Jenna's room with the door bolted, or to make some excuse and say Jenna had gone out early. But there was no sense in prolonging the explosion and the pain. "Oh, you stupid, stupid little girl!" Helena swore under her breath.

She inhaled deeply and exhaled. She picked up the parchment and walked across the room as if she were in a dream. She wished her mother had come upstairs instead of her, she wished she did not have to be the messenger delivering this news.

Helena paused for an instant in the doorway to the kitchen. Janet had urged Abby to eat most of the gruel, and Mathew had lit his pipe, curls of white smoke now enveloping him. Even from the back, Helena could sense his relaxation. It was Saturday morning, a half day of rest. Mathew's bad leg was held out stiffly in front of him, extended onto the seat of an adjacent chair. The irony of the scene flooded Helena. The warmth of the kitchen, Mathew's grandchild happy and loving, Janet peaceful and secure. That was it, of course. They had security now after a lifetime of struggle, but there was new trouble caused by their beloved younger daughter.

Janet looked up and saw Helena's face. It was ashen.

"What is it?" Janet quickly rose to go to her daughter's side. Helena wordlessly thrust the parchment forward. Helena passed her mother and swept Abby into her arms, fleeing the kitchen while her astonished father looked on.

Janet read the parchment, closed her eyes, and handed it to Mathew.

Mathew read it and slammed it down on the table. "I'll kill him!" he yelled.

But Janet's hand was on his sleeve. "You won't," she said evenly. "Mathew, come with me."

Mathew followed as Janet led him into the parlor. Her hand on his arm betrayed her tension. She closed the door, shutting them away from the rest of household.

"Sit down," Janet pleaded. "We have to talk."

"How can you sound so reasonable? Don't you realize she's run away with that miserable Irish bastard? There isn't time to talk about this—I should go after them and bring them back!"

Janet had fished her handkerchief out of her apron pocket. She twisted it in her hands, making it a small rope. "You can't bring her back," Janet said flatly. She looked up and searched her husband's eyes. "Oh, Mathew, she's so willful and so stubborn. Not unlike me, I suppose. Mat, she's gone. She's been gone in spirit since the day you forbade

Stephan to court her. We can't keep her soul in this house—don't you see, she's gone and bringing her back physically won't really bring her back at all."

Mathew pushed his chin forward defiantly. "I want to bring her back," he mumbled.

"Well, you can't. When she returns—*if* she returns—it will be of her own accord."

Janet stood looking at her husband and saw tears in the corners of his eyes, just as she knew there were tears in her eyes. Her shawl slipped away from her shoulders and dropped to the floor, and she put her arms around Mathew. "I love you," she said softly. Then, pressing her face to his chest, "Let it be enough for now. Mathew, let it be. She'll come back. I know she'll come back."

Mathew didn't answer, but Janet felt him slacken as he buried his face in her neck. "She's so young," he said haltingly. "Too young."

Janet agreed. "And foolish," she might have added. Janet continued to lean against her husband. Ten years ago, she thought, I would have let you go after her. But you're not well and I can't let you go. She felt torn between her willful daughter and her husband. She could do nothing but pray that Stephan was not as bad as Mathew thought he was, that he would take care of Jenna, and that they would return.

Janet and Mathew embraced silently for some time, each drawing strength from the other. Mathew seemed gradually to accept the reality of Jenna's feelings.

"You're a strong woman," Mathew admitted.

"And I reared a strong daughter," Janet added. "She will come home. Let it be on her terms, Mathew. Let it be right."

"I see him!" Jenna panted as she ran, stick in hand, to a clump of bushes near the small clearing by the lake.

"Make him come out into the clearing so I can get a direct shot," Stephan shouted from fifty feet away. He held his musket at the ready.

This was not the way her father had caught rabbits when they used to travel along the Mohawk Trail, Jenna thought. She flailed at the bush, causing a cloud of flies to erupt in a dark puff. She barely caught a glimpse of their furry prey as it hopped into the clearing, then turned and bounced off into the woods. "There he goes!" she called frantically.

"Where? Where?" bellowed Stephan, trying to get a bead on the flashing brown speck. Not seeing his quarry for more than a second, he ran for the woods, with his musket across his chest, cursing under his breath.

Jenna lost sight of him, but she heard a thud and a loud groan. She dashed toward the sound, only to find Stephan between two trees, doubled over his musket and moaning and cursing in pain.

"What happened to you?" Jenna asked, her voice filled with disdain.

"Missed the damn rabbit," Stephan grunted as he rolled over, still holding his gun.

"Looks as if you were defeated by two trees—you didn't fire a single shot."

Stephan glared at her and tried to regain his composure. He felt every bit the fool he was. "I'm better at shooting birds," he mumbled. "There are no damn trees and bushes to get in the way."

Jenna suppressed a smile and reminded herself that there weren't many men like her father. Her standards were high. "I heard some geese this morning down the shore from our camp. Maybe a few will pass by for an evening drink in the marsh."

"Let's go there now," Stephan responded. "Come on, before it's too late. We will have fresh food tonight, we will."

Together they plodded down the beach, heading for the tall reeds where the sand beach turned into a marsh. "Shh!" Jenna said, coming to a halt. "Listen." From the reeds came the sound of the geese. "You stand here," she instructed. "Be ready. I'll frighten them out and into flight."

Stephan frowned, but did as she said. Jenna ran to the edge of the reeds clapping her hands and yelling. In moments a flock of geese noisily took flight and Jenna heard Stephan's musket fire, followed by his cry of triumph.

Within the hour, the fire crackled as fat from the roasting goose dripped into the flames. Jenna sat huddled beneath a blanket while, on the opposite side of the fire, Stephan watched the light and shadow dance across her face. They had been five days on the St. Lawrence and now were on Lake Ontario. They had been backbreaking days with both of them paddling and carrying packs whenever a short portage was necessary.

Each night they had both dropped exhausted into their bedrolls, sleeping beneath the overturned canoe. There had been kisses but no lovemaking. Jenna was adamant that they wait till they reached St. Louis and were married. Stephan, who had no intention of waiting, was only temporarily compliant because of his exhaustion. But now the days did seem easier—partly because travel on the lake involved no portages and partly because his muscles, exercised by this uncommon physical activity, had ceased to ache—and he found himself feeling more romantic than he had since the journey began.

"It smells good!" Jenna exclaimed as she watched the goose. "You are better at shooting birds than rabbits." It would be their first fresh meat in seven days. They had brought biscuits and some jerky, and since it was spring, there was no shortage of berries. Jenna had only just eaten some of the wild fruit, and her full lips still were ruby red with their color.

"I would give anything for a bath," Jenna complained. "But Papa always said the insects were worse if you bathed." Jenna rubbed her arm at the thought. She had two large, red, angry-looking mosquito bites.

"Heat some water after dinner," Stephan suggested. "You can wash off a bit."

"It's cool," Jenna commented. "But perhaps I will wash a little."

Stephan turned the goose and immediately more fat hit the flames. "Soon we'll be far enough south to risk bathing in the river." An image of Jenna bathing immediately entered his thoughts, and he felt a strong surge of sexual desire.

"It'll have to be a lot warmer!" Jenna said and laughed. "I put my hand in the water today and it's freezing. You know, this is the most dangerous time of year: The ice up north is just beginning to melt off."

"I know that," Stephan answered.

"Well, you treat me as if I didn't know anything. I did grow up on the Niagara!" Jenna thrust her lower lip forward. "I'm as good a woodsman as you, if not better. Remember who was steering the canoe on our first night. And as a rabbit hunter—well, you leave something to be desired."

"Woodswoman," Stephan corrected. "And you might be a good one, but it's certainly not what you were meant for."

A mischievous look danced in her magnificent green eyes. "And what was I meant for?" Jenna questioned playfully.

"For ornate gowns, for jewels . . . you were meant to be my lady."

Jenna smiled. "It's hard to think of such things, we have such a long journey. Besides, I have never known luxury, though Mama has told me about Paris. Did you know Mama knew the King of France?"

Stephan nodded and thought about Jenna's mother. Though Janet Macleod certainly was in her late forties, she was a handsome woman and Jenna most certainly looked like her. He thought about Janet Macleod in the corrupt court of Louis XV and wondered just exactly how she had maintained herself. The thought appealed to him. "Was she one of the King's mistresses?" he asked boldly.

Jenna's musical laugh echoed through the deserted woods behind the sand beach where they camped. "Of course not! Madame de Pompadour was the King's mistress. She had just become his mistress when my mother came to France in . . . in . . ." Jenna counted on her fingers, "in 1746."

Stephan did not press her for more details, though he was reasonably certain that a woman who looked like Janet Macleod could not have been a vestal virgin in the court of the infamous Louis XV. Doubtless, Jenna's mother had a very spicy past.

"I think the goose is ready," Jenna announced.

"I'm certainly ready for the goose," Stephan answered with enthusiasm.

Stephan clumsily removed the goose from the spit and set it on their one tin plate. Then he cut off a piece with his knife and handed it to Jenna.

For a time they ate in silence, savoring the delights of the gamey meat.

"Oh, enough for me," Jenna finally said, burying the bones in the sand. "Perhaps I will heat a little water." With that, she took a small pot and walked down to the shoreline, where the water lapped up onto the sand. She scooped up some water and returned to the fire, where Stephan was wrapping up the remaining pieces of meat.

Jenna set out the pot on the fire while Stephan positioned the canoe on two rocks. Upside down and several feet off the ground, it made the ideal shelter. He laid out the bed-rolls.

Against the fire, Jenna's profile was clear. She had removed her hat, and her long hair hung down her back in a single braid. She lifted the water off the fire with a long stick and began to wash her face and arms with a small cloth. Then, slowly, she undid her shirt and sponged her torso. She was facing the placid lake, back to Stephan. Stephan watched her movements and imagined the soft water-soaked cloth as she moved it across her milk-white flesh. He imagined her pink nipples erect in the cool night air, and he thought about the long white thighs hidden beneath the baggy breeches she wore. Watching her in the moonlight, Stephan was transfixed. She certainly was more beautiful than Claudine, the Montreal prostitute he had visited frequently. He felt his own face flush with the memory of past sexual exploits even while he thought about the one to come. He grew aware of his own excited hardening. He closed his eyes for a moment and considered the situation. Jenna would most certainly object. She was totally committed to marrying first. But what could she do? They had come much too far for her to turn back alone. And he reasoned that she would enjoy it; it would be all right afterward.

Stephan crept toward her silently and when he was directly behind her, he seized her shoulders and kissed her neck. Jenna jumped.

"Stephan!" Her hands flew to her open shirt and pulled it closed over the delicious mounds of white flesh. But he forced her backward into his arms and with one hand dipped into the shirt to caress her bare skin.

"You mustn't!" Jenna cried with indignation. "You promised me!"

"I must, I can't wait," he heard himself reply as he panted breathlessly. She was struggling now as he pressed her down. Her strong legs were kicking him and she had let go of her shirt to wrestle. Stephan fell on her breasts, ignoring her cries, his mouth kissing and biting her nipples. "Oh, I must, I must. You will like it! I love you! I can't wait!" But Jenna pushed him with all her might and rolled out from beneath him, struggling to her feet. Stephan grasped the sand where she had been and pulled himself up on all fours ready to lunge at her. But Jenna had grabbed the canoe paddle and as he jumped toward her legs, she hit him. Stephan groaned and sprawled forward, face in the sand.

She dropped the paddle almost instantly and looked at him. "Stephan?" He didn't move and fear filled her. "Oh, dear God. I've killed him." Jenna felt her legs go weak and she knelt down and gently rolled him over. Tears had formed in her eyes and were rolling down her cheeks. "Stephan, oh, Stephan. Please don't be dead. Please." She cradled his head against her and rocked back and forth. Then she leaned down and listened! He still was breathing! He was alive!

Jenna lay his head down gently and ran to the water's edge. She dipped the cloth in cold water and came back to his side, carefully wiping his face and brow. His eyes flickered open. "I didn't mean it!" Jenna cried. "I want you too! Oh, my poor darling, I almost killed you." Stephan snuggled against her breast and allowed her to caress him. Silently, he lifted his hand and slipped it inside her shirt, this time gently touching her. Jenna closed her eyes and let his hands move over her. The multiple sensations swept through her and she began to feel flushed and warm all over in spite of the cool night air.

Stephan's head hurt, but seeing that his prize now was willing, he pressed his advantage, leading her toward the canoe and the bedrolls. Silently, he struggled with her clothing until finally she lay naked and white beneath the moon and the stars. His well-practiced hands caressed her gently and he began kissing her all over, holding her lovely white feet and moving his lips upward till once again he reached her breasts, which now heaved with anticipation and excitement. He explored the hidden area beneath her mound of red-gold hair and Jenna pressed herself to him, moaning with pleasure. "You have to want me," he breathed, moving his hand away for a moment. His tongue traced her nipple and she groaned again, struggling to return to the pleasure his hand brought. But he continued to tease her till she wrapped herself around him and finally admitted she did want him. Then Stephan entered her, moving slowly till she went stiff, then whimpered with pleasure in his arms. He reached his own pleasure almost at once and, cradling her, said softly, "I'm a much better lover than woodsman."

Jenna nodded against him. "Will you still marry me?"

He ran his hand through her hair. "Of course," he promised.

Tom Bolton shifted in the straight-backed chair. He was aware of perspiring and of the fact that his collar was entirely too stiff for comfort—he preferred open-necked garments. There was no need to be nervous, he reprimanded himself. General Benedict Arnold was practically a relation. Surely there could be no suspicion cast on a visit from "one of the family." Still, Tom thought, coming right to Arnold's headquarters was a bit unusual. But where else was there? There were too many ears at Mount Pleasant, and these things were not to be accomplished at family gatherings. The secret of survival in Tom's profession was secrecy and guts. To come marching into Arnold's headquarters, the headquarters of the Continental Army in Philadelphia, with this kind of proposal was outrageous. General Arnold will do one of three things, Tom told himself. He will ask me to pretend I never came and never made such proposals; he will accept my offer; or he will have me hanged. The latter was a most disconcerting thought, though Tom considered it the most unlikely of the alternatives. To hand a near member of the Shippen family over for treason would cast a pall on Arnold's loving relationship with Peggy. No, all in all, it was not likely. In any case, he would not have come had Peggy not led him to believe that Arnold was a loyalist at heart. And confessions, especially those made in the bedroom, nearly always were true.

Tom shifted again and silently cursed the straight-backed Duncan Phyfe chair to which he had been directed by the officious young lieutenant from Connecticut. The reception room was elegant and certainly befitted the commander of Philadelphia. It was richly carpeted and furnished with highly polished deep mahogany furniture. The four-paned windows extended from floor to ceiling and were draped in rich blue fabric. The sun's rays which poured through the long windows danced on the facets of each finely cut glass bobble of the crystal chandelier hanging overhead.

Tom thought of Major André, who had sent him on this mission. André had chosen well when he had selected intelligence work. The man was kind and sensitive, unsuited to the rigors of actual front-line warfare, but well equipped for winning people over with his considerable charm and wit and then extracting from them useful information. It was rumored that André confined his lovemaking to a young blond lieutenant from Bristol, and that the lieutenant adored André. But such rumors were common, and Tom neither listened to them nor cared about them. General Clinton was quite right in his attitude: As long as André performed his job and bothered no one, his personal tastes were not to be questioned. Major André had a sharp mind and always seemed to have his priorities straight. Thus, even if his bedroom choices made him the butt of cruel jokes, the man was admired for his more important qualities.

Tom patted the chair arm and thought: The trouble with American furniture is its rigidity. Unlike the velvet-cushioned chairs imported from Britain, the straight chairs made in Boston seemed designed to make one suffer. One was molded into a Puritan from the bottom up!

The two double doors opened suddenly and another officer came through them, clicking his shiny boots together. The long musket the officer carried looked ridiculous in this setting and certainly was unnecessary.

"The commander will see you now!" The man stood at attention as his announcement echoed through the large, high-ceilinged room. Then Tom stood up and followed the soldier.

The inner-office windows were draped in deep red fabric and furnished with plush chairs. Behind a huge dark desk, General Benedict Arnold sat with a pile of papers in front of him. When Tom entered, he stood up and smiled broadly, extending his hand. "Tom Bolton," he said cheerfully. "To what do I owe the pleasure of this visit?"

"Business," Tom answered, glancing around toward the wide-open doors. "Personal business."

Arnold motioned to the officer. "Leave us," he commanded. The great doors swung closed tightly and Arnold sat back down. "Mind if I smoke?" He already was stuffing his pipe.

"Certainly not," Tom replied, studying the man and wondering what the next few moments would bring.

"And what business do we have?" Arnold asked politely. His arched eyebrow betrayed real curiosity and interest.

"It's a delicate matter," Tom replied. "A very delicate matter and I'm not certain how to broach it."

Arnold frowned. "We do not know each other well, Tom. But rest assured, you have my favor."

"I must ask you to keep all that passes between us confidential . . . unless of course you choose to have me hanged."

Arnold raised his eyebrow once again. "Hang you?" His mouth twisted in a curious smile. "Oh, my wife wouldn't like that."

Tom relaxed against the cushion of the chair and withdrew his own pipe. Casually he stuffed it with sweet Virginia tobacco and took Arnold's tinder box off the desk. As he lit the pipe with a burst of flame, he said, "Sir, you are the Continental commander in Philadelphia, but neither the Executive Council of Pennsylvania nor General Washington seem to appreciate you."

"I have requested a formal court-martial to deal with the absurd charges of the Executive Council," Arnold said, his mouth forming a hard line. "But it's true that Washington has not yet replied."

"Sir, you performed heroically. You are reputed to be the most competent general in the army . . . your march through Maine was a triumph. You're certainly more competent than Washington."

"That's not the greatest compliment!" Arnold roared with laughter. "In any case, I admit to being more honest. My expense accounts for a year do not equal his for a

51

month! And I never lost to the Canadians, nor did I starve my men at Valley Forge.'' Arnold paused and grunted. ''If this rebellion succeeds it will be by accident.''

Tom shook his head in silent agreement, then added, ''You must know my sympathies,'' he hedged. ''Is it safe to talk here?''

Arnold nodded. ''The bumpkins don't listen at the door; besides, it's as thick as Washington's head.''

''Sir, I have more than sympathies. I work for Major André.''

Tom's words hung in the silence for a moment, but Arnold did not pale. Indeed, his expression hardly changed.

''My British predecessor in Philadelphia,'' Arnold finally said. He tipped back in his chair, balancing it on its two back legs. ''He used to escort Peggy about.''

Tom nodded.

''I was jealous, you know,'' Arnold confessed. ''I thought they had been lovers. But when I asked, Peggy broke into such reams of delightful laughter I knew there was no basis for suspicion. She showed me a delicious poem André had written—not to her, but to one of his young men. You do know about his young men?''

Again Tom nodded. ''His tastes are strange. But he does his job well.''

Arnold made a waving gesture with his left hand and smiled. ''That's the important thing,'' he acquiesced. ''So your Major André is more of an Athenian than a Spartan. No matter.''

''He's the head of British Intelligence.'' Tom leaned forward instinctively.

''British Intelligence!'' Arnold exclaimed. ''Well, that explains everything, including his tastes. And what may I, the commander of the Continental Army in Philadelphia, do for Major André?''

''Sir, I am a loyalist. I hope to bring you around, to persuade you to join us.''

''So that I might do what?''

''So that you might serve King and country, sir.''

Arnold allowed his chair to fall back upon four legs as he leaned forward. His hand went to his brow and for a moment he closed his eyes against the earnest young man who sat before him. "To serve King and country," he repeated in a low voice.

Then he stood up and turned to look out the window. In the square below, the trees were in full bloom and the grass was alive; a carpet of green velvet. A small huddle of children played together under the watchful eye of a severely dressed young matron. Arnold followed the scene with his own eyes; his thoughts drifted. Then he slowly turned around. "I have been part of this rebellion," he said, looking down. "I am a traitor, and being a traitor has troubled me. I never dreamed, never thought it possible that a traitor might be welcomed back into the service of our King, might once again be allowed to know peace with honor."

"You could be of great value, sir. You are a loyalist." Tom smiled kindly. Arnold was clearly a man of honor, a man great enough to recognize his mistake, a man prepared to make amends for it.

"I am," Arnold admitted, "and I'm sick to death with this rebellion, tired of the senseless terrorism, the wanton destruction. . . ."

"Then you will help us?"

"I will do anything."

Tom stood up and anxiously circled his chair. "At the moment we want you to do nothing, save request another command."

"A more vital command," Arnold guessed.

"West Point," Tom suggested. "We want you to ask for West Point."

Arnold let out his breath, but he did not look shocked or distressed. "A command worth surrendering."

"Yes," Tom said with finality.

"This will be dangerous. I have to think of Peggy."

"I give you my word, Peggy will be safe. You will be completely reinstated, sir, and you will be well paid. An escape plan will be made."

"I shall be sent to England?"

"Or to Canada."

Arnold nodded. "So be it." He extended his hand and Tom grasped it. "We shall see one another again soon," Tom promised.

"Godspeed," Arnold replied. "I'll write Washington today. I'll request West Point."

Tom turned and let himself out the great white doors. On the far side of the room, Arnold's secretary, the young officer who had admitted him, sat behind a small desk, attempting to look busy. At the far set of doors, the young lieutenant stood guard, his ungainly musket in a relaxed pose. As Tom approached, the lieutenant snapped to attention and opened the doors. Tom stepped through and a whiff of spring air hit his nostrils. Suddenly he felt full of hope. Perhaps it wasn't too late. Perhaps British North American could be salvaged.

CHAPTER IV

May 1779

Janet's eyes followed Mathew as he sank into the love seat in the parlor. His face was pale and his leg seemed to be troubling him more than usual. He persisted in going to his office each day and he persisted in bending over plans and working in dull light well into the night. He absolutely refused to slow down or to rest. Since Jenna ran away, Mathew seemed to be running from time.

"You don't look well," Janet said softly. "You're working much too hard. It's not necessary."

"I'm fine. I just miss the outdoors." He shrugged, then winced a little. "I guess the indoor life is not for me."

"Are you in pain?" Janet prodded.

"Just my arm, it aches a little. I think it's just the dampness."

Janet shook her head but said nothing more. She might count her blessings that Mathew was not participating in the spring Highland games like so many of their friends. At least he seemed to realize he was not well enough to be carrying logs about. There was a loud knock on the front door, and Janet started. "Now, who can that be?" she complained. "This is no time to come calling."

She stood up and walked to the door. On the stoop, two British officers stood stiffly. In unison they doffed their hats and bowed from the waist. "Madame Macleod and Mr. Macleod?"

Puzzled, Janet led the two into the parlor. "My husband, Mr. Macleod." She assumed they had come to see Mathew on business.

Mathew struggled to his feet, leaning on his cane. "May

we be of service?'' Then he added, ''I shall be consulting with the general later in the day.''

''We come on personal business,'' the lieutenant replied. ''It is a matter quite apart from your position as an adviser to the British Commander.''

Janet watched them curiously and suddenly was aware of their guarded formality. They looked ill at ease.

''Is there something the matter?''

They both shifted from one foot to the other, avoiding eye contact as they looked off to some neutral point. ''You have a son, Mat Macleod?''

Both Janet and Mathew nodded and Janet's heart began to pound as a slow fear filled her.

''We have deep regret to have to bring you this news. It's . . .''

Janet's hands had flown to her face and the color had drained away. ''Mat!'' Her green eyes flooded with tears, her shoulders began to shake. ''Something's happened to Mat!''

Their eyes told the rest of their message. They looked at the rug on the floor, studying its designs. ''He's dead, killed as a result of wounds received at Vincennes.''

Janet let out a long gasp, and a shudder ran through her. When she looked at Mathew, she could see that his face was a deep red and that his breathing was exceptionally hard. He was rubbing his arm. He looked pain-filled and stricken. ''Mathew!'' His name had not escaped her mouth when Mathew Macleod fell to his knees, gasping and clutching his chest, sucking desperately for air.

''Oh, my God!'' Janet screamed as she turned to the two horrified soldiers. ''Fetch a doctor! Immediately!''

Her eyes blurred with tears over their loss and the terrible fright she now felt for Mathew, Janet bent over and undid his shirt. ''Oh, dear God! Please, please.'' Janet clasped his hand. ''Oh, God!'' she moaned again. It seemed as if they were totally alone. She mentally counted his breaths, listening to each one as he struggled for life. ''Not yet, not yet,'' she prayed aloud. The distance was filled with running feet, and the faces of one of the soldiers and her older daughter, Helena, wavered before her. ''You can't die, you can't!'' Janet whispered urgently. And it seemed as if they were breathing together during some period of endless time.

Janet felt strong hands around her waist, pulling her to her feet, and she saw some men lifting Mathew and carrying him away upstairs. "No! No!" she screamed while strong hands restrained her. Then, exhausted from her struggling, agony, and fright, Janet fell into merciful unconsciousness.

Robert's hip wound proved to be only a superficial injury and it healed quickly, allowing him to return to his role in the transshipment of gunpowder to George Rogers Clark. It was a waiting game, a game he now knew to be more dangerous than he had originally thought. But this night had been another spent waiting in vain and, tired and tense, Robert returned home.

He drew in his mare and slipped from the saddle. His boots sunk into the mud that always surrounded the hitching post in front of the cabin. Grass never grew there: too much water slopped over the side of the nearby trough, and the earth was churned constantly by the shifting of the horses' hooves as they stood tethered and waiting for a rider. Robert tied the mare's reins and patted her neck. "Tomorrow night we'll go for another ride, old girl," he promised. The horse twitched her ears at the familiar buzz of a hungry mosquito and flicked her tail.

Robert walked up the narrow path to the house and scraped the mud from his boots on the edge of the wood step that led to the front door.

"Robert?" Angelique's voice called out.

"It's me!" he called back to reassure her. The boys weren't home. Their horses were missing at the hitching post.

Robert opened the door and walked inside. All the familiar odors greeted him: the fish stew that had been prepared for the afternoon meal, the wild flowers that sat in containers along the windowsill, and the dried herbs that hung above the door.

The inside of the sprawling cabin was too warm. The cooking fire still smoldered in the hearth and the welcome night breeze off the river had not yet begun to drift through the windows to cool off the center room.

Angelique frowned with concern. Her dark hair was

pulled back behind her head, but a few damp wisps clung to her forehead. Abstractedly, she wiped her hands on her crisp white apron. "I was worried about you," she said in a somewhat exasperated tone. "You were wounded less than three weeks ago. Look at you! You're at it again."

Robert shrugged off her concern. "It hurt like hell, but it wasn't a deep wound. If you must know, the conjure lady's medicines left me with a headache more serious than the wound."

"I still worry about you. I always worry about you."

"There was nothing to worry about: They didn't come tonight, and besides, the British are elsewhere. It's a big river. They have more than me to worry about."

Angelique glanced away. Robert's cavalier attitude toward life and death angered her. And the fact that the expected shipment hadn't come tonight made it worse, not better. At least if it had come it would be over for a few weeks.

"There's always tomorrow," she said bitterly.

Robert moved toward her and pulled her into his arms. "And I'll come home tomorrow night as well." Angelique was stiff to his touch; she let out an audible sigh and then pulled away.

"Trust me to know how to stay alive," Robert said assuringly. "I've done more dangerous things."

"You're not immortal and you did those things before you were my husband, before you had a family. You have responsibilities now. But there you are, off playing at war and subterfuge!"

Robert looked at her steadily. Her dark eyes were luminous, her skin as smooth and ivory-colored as the day they had wed. But there was no denying the change in her: She no longer had the *joie de vivre* she once did. Her sense of adventure had fled and in its place there was a coldness he could not explain, a veil of prudery he could not abide.

"Where are the boys?" he questioned, seeking to change the subject.

"Visiting," Angelique answered. "I expect they'll be home soon. Maria's asleep."

Robert nodded. If the boys said they were visiting, Angelique never questioned it. In one sense, it was wise of them to offer such excuses. The offering of excuses was a luxury he did not have. Angelique knew full well where he was and what he was doing. Even if he had tried to lie, she would not have believed him. But her constant worrying was annoying to him, however natural it was.

Still, what could he expect? Angelique had endured a great deal and survived. Their life on the western frontier had been difficult and Angelique had done more than her share of the work. What they had achieved—the comfortable house, the lucrative trading post, the financial security —they had built together. He supposed that now she simply wanted to enjoy what she had earned while he, on the other hand, was bored by inactivity and could not accept a less active role in life than he had always played. Angelique, however, did seem to worry more about him than she did about the children. And that Robert found puzzling.

If the twins said they were "visiting," it was equivalent to saying they were "going out to play." But Robert knew full well that Will and James were children no longer. They were men. At sixteen, no frontier boy was a child. The boys might well have their own dangerous involvements—involvements that might cause their mother grave concern if she had been aware of them. And there was Maria. Maria shunned relationships with other girls her age, and her dark, brooding eyes troubled Robert more than he cared to admit.

"Hungry?" Angelique asked. "There's soup left."

"I'm more ready for a drink," Robert said truthfully. As he said it, he opened the sideboard with a smile and withdrew a skin of rum from the lower cabinet. The amber liquid came with the gunrunning, a shipment of good Caribbean rum with every cargo of powder.

Angelique handed him a mug and Robert poured a few ounces from the skin. "Want some?" he asked, even though he knew she would say no.

Angelique shook her head and wiped her brow. "It only makes me warmer. I'm far too warm already." She walked to the window and looked out into the night. "I wish the breeze would come up," she said after a long silence broken only by the sound of Robert sipping.

He swigged down more rum and savored the taste. It brought a wave of nostalgia for New Orleans and for carefree days and nights spent drinking and talking with old friends.

"It's Will," Angelique said, turning. "He rides like you. I can recognize him in the dark."

Robert laughed. "I didn't realize that men rode distinctively."

"They walk distinctively and they ride distinctively. You and Will sit straight when you ride, James hunches over." Angelique smiled. "And that old free Negra man, La Jeunesse, he moves his head up and down and keeps time with the horse as it moves along."

Robert grinned back. Angelique had lost much of her true Acadian accent and in its place developed a pronunciation that hit somewhere between French and Spanish. She never said "*neegro*," like the people from Massachusetts and New York. She always said Negra, which was a cross between the Spanish *negro* and the French *nègre*. The way Angelique said it sounded proper and refined. Unlike others in the area, she avoided the term "darkies" and the disdainful pronunciation of the Virginians, which always came out "nigger." But Angelique's feelings for the La Jeunesse family and for the other Negroes in the area was reflected in her friendliness toward them. She thought of them as dark-skinned Acadians. Just another people brutally rounded up and scattered over the face of the wilderness. "We have something in common," Angelique often said. "We're both strangers in this land, refugees."

"He's running!" Angelique cried, leaning toward the window. Will had tied his horse and was running toward the front door. Robert could hear his son's quick steps. Angelique had hardly finished her announcement when Will burst through the door.

"Spain is going to join the war!" Will blurted out. "The news just came up from New Orleans! They're going to honor the Bourbon family compact! They're coming in on the side of France!"

Angelique gripped the windowsill and stared at her son. Robert nodded knowingly. It was hardly a surprise. He had expected it for months. Nor, he reasoned, would it change his situation much. The small garrison of British soldiers across the river at Natchez wasn't much of a threat. They could, as he had so recently learned, be a dangerous harassment. When and if the Spanish moved militarily, it would be against the larger British forces at Baton Rouge, Mobile, Pensacola, and in the Caribbean. The garrison at Natchez would be forced to surrender because it would be surrounded by hostile forces. Indeed, the garrison's sole threat was to Robert himself.

"I'm going to join Governor Gálvez!" Will announced without hesitation.

Angelique gasped. "You'll do no such thing! This isn't our war! You're only a boy!"

"I am not a boy!" Will shot back. "Father was my age when he fought against the British in Quebec!"

Angelique turned to face Robert accusingly. "This is your fault! Filling his head with stories! He's full of romantic notions about war! If you weren't involved, he wouldn't be. Tell him he can't go! Tell him he's too young! Say something!"

Robert looked from his wife to his son. Angelique's face was pink with anger, and Will's was filled with excitement. It was true that Will was only sixteen, but he was over six feet tall, broad of shoulder, and strong like his Highland ancestors. He had been reared on the frontier and he was skilled as well as knowledgeable. He's like me, Robert thought with pride. He's filled with adventure and he has courage. Nevertheless, Robert sought to make peace, to temper his son's decision.

"This is no mere adventure," Robert warned. "War is life and death."

"I want to go!" Will interrupted. "I've been in touch with Gálvez. I've been training with some Acadians and free Negras."

"Is that where you've been?" Robert asked pointedly as he mentally tallied all the nights and weekends Will had been gone. In his own heart, he had suspected. Everyone believed Spain would enter the war soon. The young boys had been preparing.

Will shook his head in the affirmative. He glanced sheepishly at his mother. "Sorry," he mumbled. "I didn't want you to worry."

"Worry!" Angelique's eyes were filling with tears.

"And where is your brother? Is he training too?" Her voice had become high-pitched. Robert could see her struggling for control.

"No, he's over at old La Jeunesse's place. Helping him do something or other, said he'd stay the night and be back in the morning."

"It's nice that one of my sons tells me the truth," Angelique uttered with undisguised sarcasm.

"You're not being fair to the boy," Robert interjected. He felt torn between his admiration and pride in his son and Angelique's possessive fear. "He's old enough to know his own mind." Robert's voice fell to a lower pitch, and he was aware of feeling defeated. He had said too little too late.

"He's not old enough to go warring."

Will took a step toward his mother, but Angelique turned to face the dying embers of the fire. Her eyes fastened on the charcoal remnants of a log. It glowed red along its jagged edge. She remembered the Battle of Louisbourg and the expulsion of her people from their beloved Acadie. She thought about the terror-filled journey to Louisiana, the death of her mother, the murder of her father at the hands of Spanish sailors. She remembered with bitterness her own rape by those same sailors, and she thought about the horror-filled nights she and her little brother had spent marooned in the bayou. Her brother died of malaria before he was ten. If she had a single blood relative besides her own children, she didn't know where. For a while, when she was young, her pain seemed to have disappeared. But as she grew older her memories returned and Angelique felt a strong hatred of the Spanish, a loathing that seemed to grow and fester like a wart. She could not rid herself of it.

"I want to go," she heard Will saying.

"I won't stop you," she heard Robert answer after a moment. "Let me talk with your mother alone."

Angelique did not turn around, but she heard Will leave the room. She turned and faced Robert. "You have given my son permission to fight for the Spanish. I cannot forgive you, I cannot!"

"Angelique . . ." Robert started to say.

"I won't discuss it," she interrupted coldly. With that she

turned, clenching her skirt with her hand. "Not ever," she added as she retreated to their room.

For the first week after Mathew's attack, Janet had sat beside the bed night and day. Sometimes she fell asleep, but it was a restless, uneasy sleep. She seemed always to be listening for his breathing, terrified that it would stop. During the day, when Mathew was awake and protesting his illness, they talked. Helena brought tea and supper, realizing that her mother would not leave her father's side.

A full month had passed and the late-June weather was warm. It was a year without spring. The weather had gone from winter to summer and now the sun shone through the louvered windows of the upstairs bed chamber. Janet, awake and tense, embroidered a sampler to pass the time. The tiny cross stitches of gold and orange thread were patterned to make a garden of brilliant flowers with a border of minute cross stitches representing green grass. Wearily, Janet let the embroidery hoop fall into her lap. She stared at the sampler, which had, in the past few days, taken on both form and color. Janet looked up and sighed. Mathew was propped up against a pile of white down-filled pillows. His face still seemed pale, but his breathing was easy and he seemed a little stronger.

Mathew's eyes opened. "Oh, you are awake," Janet said after a moment. "I thought you were asleep."

Mathew nodded and pulled himself up in bed. "Have I been napping long?"

"Less than an hour," Janet answered. "How do you feel?"

"Fine, like getting up, like sitting in the garden."

Janet frowned. "I don't know if you're strong enough. You're so pale."

"Of course I'm pale. I've been inside for the better part of a month!" He smiled slightly. "You know, the longer I stay in this bed, the stiffer my leg is going to get."

"The physician said you needed lots of rest."

"I've had a lot—too much." Mathew reached out and took her hand. "I know you're worried, but I can't spend my life in bed. I'll want to go back to work soon. I have to get some exercise."

63

"Oh, Mathew, not too soon. The physician said—"

"Damn the physician. He's not inside my body. I have no intention of becoming an invalid waited on hand and foot by my daughter and wife."

"I almost lost you." Janet squeezed his hand, then lifted it to her soft lips and caressed it with a kiss. "I couldn't bear it. Please don't do too much too soon. I need you, I need you more than ever now." Janet blinked back her own tears as the rush of emotion she had closed out for so long flooded her. Her son was dead. Mat was dead and never was coming home.

Mathew nodded. Mat was dead and Jenna was gone. "I won't leave you," he promised.

Janet inhaled, then let out her breath. She wondered if time would ease their pain. "It's a terrible thing to have your children die before you," she said in a soft voice.

Between them there was understanding. Mathew rolled back the sheet that covered him and, with effort, swung his legs over the side of the bed.

"Can you help me into the garden?" He pulled himself up and Janet handed him his cane. She circled his waist with her slim arm, and Mathew leaned against her. Then he bent and kissed her neck lovingly.

"You've been strong for both of us," he whispered. "It's time we went back to being strong together."

Janet looked up into his soft eyes. "I shall always love you, Mathew Macleod, but perhaps never as much as I do now." He kissed her again and slowly they moved across the room together.

In the garden, Janet arranged cushions on the bench and Mathew sat down in the sun. "You'll have to be careful not to get a sunburn," Janet cautioned. "You've been inside for a long while."

"And you, my dear, have freckles."

"And don't you like freckles?"

"I love yours," he answered.

"Mama!" Helena's voice rang out from the kitchen and into the garden. "Mama, someone's here to see you."

Janet shrugged, wondering who would have the audacity to come calling without notice. Especially since the black wreath of mourning still hung on the door.

"Who is it?" Janet asked when she reached her daughter.

"It's Madame O'Connell, Stephan's mother," Helena whispered. "I didn't want Father to hear, it might upset him."

Janet nodded and smoothed her hair with her hand. "Quite right. Go talk to your father, try to keep his mind off . . ." She couldn't say Mat's name. "Off everything," she finished.

Mrs. O'Connell sat primly on the settee, her gloved hands clasped in her lap.

"Good afternoon," Janet greeted her, trying to sound pleasant.

Ivy O'Connell was a small, dark-haired woman with bright blue eyes. She was older than Janet Macleod by some ten years. Stephan, Janet knew, was the youngest of her five sons and two daughters. Like her husband, Ivy O'Connell had been born in Ulster and she spoke with an accent that betrayed the place of her birth even though she had lived in Massachusetts Bay Colony since she was thirteen years old. Both she and her husband were fiercely Protestant. The O'Connells were typical of the non-French in Quebec, more so than Janet and Mathew who, if only nominally, clung to the religion of their forefathers. "It is not so much Catholicism—after all, High Anglicans fought with us—" Mathew was fond of saying, "but the blood that flowed for the *right* to be Catholic."

Janet paused. "Would you like some tea?"

Ivy O'Connell looked at her coldly. "I think not," Ivy replied. "I think one should take tea only with one's friends, not with one's enemies."

Janet straightened up. "Enemies usually don't come to call," she replied testily. "If you do not come in friendship, why do you come?"

"To see what kind of mother can rear such a tart of a daughter." Ivy did not disguise her animosity. Her blue eyes were narrow, like hard little stones set in a wrinkled, disgruntled face.

"Tart! How dare you call my daughter a tart!" Janet's hands grasped her skirt in anger. "How dare you come to my house and insult my daughter, who has been stolen away by your bastard son!"

Ivy stood up and glared at Janet. "She's a tart! A thieving little Catholic bitch! First she seduced my Stephan, then she encouraged him to steal! He stole for her!"

Janet was shaking with rage. Her green eyes blazing, she took a step toward the older woman. "Jenna has never stolen in her life, and if any seductions have been done, I daresay it was Stephan and not Jenna. She's only a child! He is, or should be, a responsible adult."

"She's a tart and she made our Stephan steal the gold!"

"What gold?" Janet snapped.

"All the gold in my husband's strongbox. All we had saved in this world. It's gone, the lot of it's gone! Now, you don't tell me that a good boy—and Stephan is a good boy—would steal from his own father and mother unless he was put up to it by a Catholic whore!"

Janet had drawn back her arm automatically and in her blind rage she brought it forward with some force, slapping Ivy O'Connell across the face and sending her backward onto the settee like a crumpled piece of taffeta and old lace. "How dare you come into my house and make such accusations! My husband is ill and my son is dead. And your son has virtually kidnapped my daughter!" Janet's eyes narrowed. "If you ever come near me, my children, or my husband . . . if I ever see your son . . . Get out! Get out!" Janet was well aware that her voice had reached a hysterical pitch. She hoped Mathew had not heard.

Ivy O'Connell's mouth was agape and Janet leaned over and grasped the woman's hand roughly, pulling her to her feet. A good head taller than Ivy, Janet propelled the woman around toward the front door. "Out!" she repeated, slapping Ivy across the bottom. "And don't you dare come back. Go home and ask yourself about your son. He didn't steal for Jenna, he stole for himself. Go and ask the tavern girls, go ask how much money he spent there!"

Ivy looked at Janet Macleod with hatred. "It's people like you who tolerate the French and support the putrid Pope! When we Americans win this revolution, we'll outlaw Catholicism, and girls like your little slut—indecent girls—will be put where they belong."

"In this country," Janet shouted back, "everyone will worship according to choice . . . even you. You Americans have imported your petty little prejudices from Europe and you won't take Canada, I promise you that!'' Janet's blood boiled with indignation. "My son has just died defending this land,'' she said more evenly. "And one day it will be free and independent. We reject your kind of freedom. We'll earn ours. And when that day comes, there won't be room for the likes of you with your hatreds.'' Janet had regained control of herself and she added, "If your son has wronged you, look to yourself. What kind of man could be seduced by a slip of a girl whose only fault is misguided romanticism and the fact that she made a bad choice? Jenna is stubborn and willful, I admit that. But she's good too and I suspect I couldn't say that of your son.'' Her hand was on the door handle. She flung it open and pushed Ivy O'Connell out before the spiteful woman could answer. Then, with some force, Janet slammed it hard.

For a long moment, Janet stood with her eyes closed. Stephan *was* as bad as Mathew had thought. What kind of person would steal from his own parents? "Oh, be safe, Jenna. Be safe,'' she said aloud. "Stephan is not the man you think he is.''

The early-morning sun streamed through the floor-to-ceiling windows at Mount Pleasant. Peggy Shippen Arnold was languorously spread out on the bed. Her lovely white legs were bare and her nightdress was thigh high with one shoulder askew, revealing a perfect white breast. Her blue eyes still were closed and a halo of blond hair was spread out on the white pillowcase.

Since before dawn, General Arnold had been at the tiny writing desk on one side of their bedroom. There he had prepared a message to General Clinton and Major André, a message in which he outlined his acceptance of Tom Bolton's proposition and described in some detail his own needs. Enclosed also, to bind the bargain, Arnold included some information on troop movements.

He finished and folded the letter and placed it carefully in a pouch. He would give it to Tom today. The deed would be done.

He turned around and looked at Peggy. His tired eyes feasted on her sleeping form. Almost in a trance, he walked to the bed and leaned over her. Asleep, Peggy looked like a little girl; her face was untroubled, her expression one of pure innocence. But she was no child, she was a desirable woman, a woman who could awaken a man and make him feel like a boy again.

She blinked open her eyes and, lifting one hand, rubbed them. "Oh, you're all dressed," she murmured, taking his hand and placing it on her breast. His fingers moved and her nipple hardened instantly, something that always fascinated him. He leaned over and kissed it, caressing it with his tongue. She moaned and wriggled slightly. "Oh, why are you dressed? It's naughty of you," she cooed, running her delicate hand up his thigh and across his organ.

"I had some letters to write," he admitted.

She applied some pressure with her hand and moved her hips provocatively, pulling up her nightdress farther. "To Major André, no doubt."

In spite of his feeling of sexual excitement, he paled. "You know?" he mumbled, confused by the rush of sensations both physical and mental.

She moved her hand and began to unfasten the strings that wove his breeches together. "Of course I know. I know everything. I know you will be loyal to the King and to me. I intend to help you. I'm your partner."

She had slipped her hand inside his breeches, and her fingers were gentle, prodding. No matter how great his distraction at her words, he responded instantly to her touch.

"It's much too dangerous for you to be involved," he stammered, wishing to God this conversation were taking place under other circumstances.

"There's no need to worry about me. Women are never in much danger," she smiled. She blinked her wide blue eyes. "General Washington would never hurt a hair on my head."

Looking at her, it was difficult not to believe her statement was completely true. At the same time a surge of jealousy ran through him. "What's between you and Washington?"

She smiled coquettishly. "Nothing, you silly old dear." She tugged to free him from his breeches. "But there is something between us."

He smiled at her and started to remove his pants.

"No, no . . . keep your clothes on, take mine off," she giggled. "I always wanted to do it that way. I think about it sometimes." He felt his face redden, but he made no further move to take off his clothes. Instead, he slipped her filmy nightdress away and withdrew his organ. "Oh, feel me all over," Peggy asked. "Touch me as you did before, kiss me." Her eyes closed and she moved beneath his hands, groaning now and again and guiding his hand where she wanted it to be. At last, driven by the sight of her undulating hips, he threw himself on her and she moaned beneath him till at last she let out a cry of relief and joy.

"Oh, see how nice it is," she said as he rolled off. "The image of your jacket buttons are on my skin." And so they were, a little line of red on her snow-white skin. She let out a deep sigh. "Oh, I love it that way! It makes me feel taken! Ravished!"

"You would not like to be ravished in reality," he teased.

"Oh, of course not. It's just a daydream."

He rocked her in his arms. "I still don't want you to be involved," he reiterated. "It's really much too dangerous."

Peggy thrust out her little chin. "I will be. And we will go to the King of England together. You will be an important general. . . ." She bit her lip and her eyes were aglow. "Ask for some land in Canada," she suggested. "And don't dare accept less than twenty thousand pounds!"

CHAPTER V

July 1779

"Do you realize this is the route followed by the early *voyageurs?*" Jenna remarked enthusiastically. "It's the same route my uncle, Robert MacLean, followed, and my father was this way once too! When I lived at Fort Niagara I heard so many stories that I feel I have been on this river before!"

She looked across at Stephan. Under the persistent sun, his face had tanned and his dark hair had taken on a reddish-brown hue. "We're a mess!" Jenna said cheerfully. Her own hair needed washing and her face and arms were pinkish and freckled.

"I'll be glad to get to Fort St. Louis," Stephan replied. "I've had enough of your *outdoors* for a while."

"We should be there within the hour," Jenna remarked. "And we have a long, long journey after that."

"All on down current," Stephan said with relief in his voice. "No more portages, no more paddling."

The bluffs on either side of the river had grown higher and now and again one saw a cabin or a fisherman down by the river's edge. Jenna would wave and the fishermen would wave back.

"It is not as I imagined it at all," Jenna exclaimed when they finally reached St. Louis. "It's hardly a town at all!" She had not known what to expect, but it was impossible to stifle her disappointment. It had rained the night before their arrival and the streets, such as they were, had been reduced to muddy paths. Moreover, it was unbearably hot and humid as the water on the ground and in the river rose to meet the merciless sun.

There was, Jenna noted, a church. But apart from the

church and a few stone houses, the majority of the dwellings were shacks. It was, nonetheless, a bustling place, a major trading center, and one of the most westerly outposts of civilization.

"Stay dressed as you are," Stephan warned. "There are few women in this town and most of the men haven't seen a European woman in years."

Jenna looked at him teasingly. "It was the same at Fort Niagara. They're just fur traders."

Stephan grumbled and wiped his brow with his hand. "I want to sleep in a bed tonight," he intoned.

"And I want a bath," Jenna said, laughing.

"In good time," Stephan said suspiciously. "It might be better to look around first, get the lay of the land. This is Spanish territory."

"I hear the Spanish are very tolerant. There are lots of French and Acadians in the territory, lots of people from the Thirteen Colonies too."

"Confederation," he corrected her. "And if the people in Quebec had any sense, they'd petition to be the fourteenth state."

Jenna ignored his political comments. They walked the miserable streets for some time and finally returned to a tavern down near the river, one that offered rooms. "This place will do," Stephan muttered. "I doubt there is better. And do keep your mouth shut."

The downstairs of the tavern was given over to an airless drinking room where the accumulated smell of raw rum, whiskey, and brandy was almost overpowering. There were long tables and crude benches and a variety of men who looked as if they had not moved from their seats in days. For the most part they were bearded; a dirty, disheveled lot. Not one of them looks even remotely trustworthy, Jenna thought. She heard some of the men speaking French, but the majority spoke English and appeared to be from the colonies.

Jenna glanced around uneasily and followed Stephan up to a gross, fat creature who sat, unconcerned, behind a table, studying what appeared to be an ill-kept ledger.

"Have you rooms?" Stephan asked.

The man wiped his mouth with his hand; his small, dark

71

eyes studied the young couple suspiciously. "Might have," he answered in what Stephan recognized as a Boston accent.

Stephan smiled. "You're from Boston," he observed. "So am I." The man responded with a half grin. "Are you now?" he said noncommittedly.

Stephan did not pursue the matter. "Do you have a room?"

"Depends on what you're paying with," came the quick answer accompanied by a wink.

Stephan withdrew some greenbacks from his pocket.

The man immediately scowled. "No way I'm accepting that play money," he snapped back.

Stephan hesitated and then opened his shirt. From his money belt he withdrew some gold coins. "Gold, then," he offered confidently.

"Oh, gold, is it? Well, I think we might just have a room for you and your, uh, friend." His eyes fell on Jenna and he shook his head. "Come along." He stood up, and in spite of the bulk of the upper half of his body, which gave him the appearance of a large man, he was quite short. Several inches shorter than Jenna.

He motioned Stephan and Jenna to follow as he led them away from the tavern's main room and up a flight of rickety stairs to the second floor. There, at the end of a long, dark corridor, he opened the door to a small room. Its one window looked down on the muddy street below and it was furnished only with a bed, a small table, and a tin mirror that hung from the wall.

"Chamber pot's there." He pointed to a cracked earthenware vessel under the bed. "Have to empty your own, outside." Vaguely, he pointed off toward what must have been the back of the building.

"It'll do," Stephan said.

The man raised a bushy eyebrow. "Will that be French gold?" Stephan nodded his head in the affirmative. "One sovereign," the man announced.

"That's a lot!" Jenna exclaimed. It was an absolute outrage to charge so much. Her sense of Scot's thriftiness overcame her.

But Stephan only shrugged. "For that I expect a tub filled with hot water to be brought up."

Again the man's eyes fell on Jenna. "For the lady?" he asked, winking. Stephan flushed slightly. Unexpectedly the man reached up and pinched her cheek. "Either a lady or a very pretty lad . . . none of my concern either way."

Jenna's face flushed with embarrassment. The man laughed. "Glad I haven't forgotten what they looked like. Don't see much around here except for squaws." He thrust out his lower lip and shook his head up and down with approval. "I'd keep her covered up and out of the way if I were you."

"I intend to," Stephan answered. "Thanks for the advice."

The man held out his pudgy hand. "John O'Hara," he introduced himself.

"Stephan O'Connell," Stephan replied. "And this is my wife."

Jenna smarted at Stephan's bold-faced lie. Still, there was a church and she hoped to be married to Stephan as soon as possible.

"How long will you be staying?" O'Hara asked.

"A few days, headed for New Orleans."

"Isn't everyone," O'Hara answered blandly.

"I'm setting up a business there," Stephan announced proudly. He began to feel at ease with his fellow Irishman. "With all your gold?" O'Hara asked with another wink.

Stephan nodded. "I have plenty. Enough to buy land, enough to establish myself."

Jenna's eyes had widened and she was aware her mouth was open. Gold? What gold? Stephan had mentioned nothing!

O'Hara thrust his hands into his pockets, depositing the sovereign as he did so. "I'll send up the tub and some women to fill it. You can take meals downstairs. It's not Boston, not the old Union Oyster House, but we have fine catfish! A good meal with good rum right from New Orleans."

"Thank you for your kindness," Stephan said, closing the door behind Mr. O'Hara.

Jenna looked around. It was a depressing room without color and with only a minimum of comfort. But the window did have some cloth netting and she relished a night without the constant buzzing of mosquitoes. She turned back to Stephan and realized she felt more than a trifle annoyed. "You should have bargained for this room, Stephan. My father would have bargained. We could have gotten it much cheaper!"

Stephan scowled at her. "I am not your father. And besides, we have plenty of money."

"You didn't tell me you were rich!" Jenna said sarcastically.

"It's not necessary for you to know everything," Stephan replied.

Jenna bit her lip. "When you have money, you shouldn't waste it. And if we are to be married, you have to share secrets with me. Stephan, where did you get so much money?"

Stephan's eyes narrowed. "I stole it," he answered, unabashed. "For us."

Jenna's face paled. She drew in her breath and stared at him. "Stole it!" she exclaimed. "From whom?"

A half-smile twisted Stephan's face. "From my parents."

"How could you?" Jenna gasped.

"I do what I want, when I want. But then, you should know that."

Jenna shook her head and looked away from Stephan. Perhaps there was truth in his claim that she had tempted him beyond endurance; but then too, she had given in rather easily. But he was a thief! Jenna could not believe it. Stephan appeared completely without morals.

There was a dull knock on the door. "Come in," Stephan called out, glad to have this conversation come to an end. The door swung open and an old black man entered with a large wooden tub. Behind him, four Indian women carried pails of steaming hot water.

Silently, the black man unburdened himself and stood back to supervise the pouring of the water into the tub. One woman set a pile of cloths down on the bed, "For drying," she announced. The old man shook his head. "Mighty hot day for a hot bath. Bathing's unhealthy," he mumbled.

Jenna watched them fill the tub with water. Hot or not, it looked delicious. The woman fished an oddly shaped cake of lye soap out of her pocket. Like the mold in which it had been set, it was bent. "Here." She put it down and looked at Jenna curiously. Then, almost reverently, she stroked the top of Jenna's head, marveling at its red color. "Funny hair," she observed.

When the last bucket was emptied, the little troop went away, closing the door behind them.

"Well, you wanted a bath," Stephan said, pointing to the water.

"Stephan," she said seriously, "are you still going to marry me?"

"Of course."

"I can't marry you unless you promise me that you will tell me everything in the future. You also have to promise that we'll send back the money."

"Are you insane? We need it to get started!"

Jenna shook her head resolutely. "We'll send back most of it and pay back what we spend. I can't marry you unless you agree."

Stephan shook his head. "All right, if it makes you happy."

Jenna's face broke into a smile and she put her arms around him, planting a kiss on his lips. "It makes me happy, but you must promise never to steal again."

Stephan nodded through his growing excitement as she pressed herself to him. He had not the slightest intention of ever sending back any of the money. But Jenna didn't have to know that.

"Let me give you a bath," he suggested, touching her neck and running his finger around her ear. Jenna blushed again, though this time not in anger. All their encounters had been by moonlight and though he had felt every part of her, she experienced a strange sensation at the thought of undressing before him in the light.

"Let me help you," he suggested as he undid the ungainly shirt she wore and pulled down the breeches that disguised her full, rounded hips.

She shivered once as her last piece of clothing slipped to the floor and then she stepped into the hot water, lowering herself into the tub. "Oh, it feels wonderful!"

Stephan smiled and Jenna could plainly see that he was

75

aroused. "What feels wonderful?" he said, massaging her shoulders gently. She closed her eyes, giving in to the pure sensation of his fingers. "You do," she answered in a low, sensual voice. "Oh, Stephan . . . do that again. . . ."

Downstairs in the tavern's main room, O'Hara had taken a large jug of rum over to a corner table. There he joined three compatriots: Samuel Hughes, Willie McNair, and Robbie Ryan.

Hughes was a large, gruff man who was bearded, unkempt, and unclean. Willie McNair was shorter and, like O'Hara himself, was broad of shoulder and short of leg. A man in his midthirties, McNair had been a street fighter, a rowdy whose services always were for hire. Robbie Ryan was the youngest, a pallid blond who, unlike the others, lacked facial hair. His light blue eyes were red from lack of sleep and too much drink, his cheeks were hollow, and he seemed underweight. The others teased him about being sickly because of his frequent coughing fits, but each of them knew that in spite of his appearance, Robbie was the most dangerous among them. He wielded a knife like no other man, and they knew not to test his temper. Calm, Robbie appeared harmless enough; angry, he moved his wiry body quickly and his knife artfully. He had killed more men than the others, and each of them knew that as well. At night, when it might be necessary to dispatch a guard, Robbie moved with lightning speed and utter silence. He could make himself one of the shadows, and when he used his knife, there was no need for a noisier weapon and no need for a second stab. The price on his head was evidence enough of his ferocity. He was wanted by the British for his part in the Boston Tea Party, he was wanted by the government of the Massachusetts Bay Colony for murder.

"I have paying quests," O'Hara confided, revealing his dark, tobacco-stained teeth.

Hughes nodded and O'Hara motioned them to keep their voices low. "Right jolly paying quests. A young man loaded with gold and his companion, a right fair piece of mutton!"

Hughes raised an interested eyebrow. "Gold?" How much gold?"

"Enough, and he'd be an easy one to crimp too. Probably stole it himself . . . too young to have earned it."

"Do unto others . . ." Willie put in with a wink.

O'Hara's eyes roamed over his motley crew. The three of them still wore the tattered uniforms of the Continental Army, from which they had recently deserted. Even as dirty and disheveled as they were, the uniforms were vaguely recognizable.

"They'll be staying a few days, then they're heading downriver. That'll be the time."

Willie wiped his lips with his sleeve, which still bore the residue of his last meal. "I ain't mowed me a piece of mutton in a hell of a long time! That'll be a real bonus!" The three of them laughed. "And Robbie here, he ain't never mowed one."

Robbie's mouth tightened and grew red with anger. "I have so, you heavy arse!"

O'Hara threw a look that silenced them. "A bonus is a bonus, but it's the gold that counts. What you do with the girl I don't care. But I do care about getting caught by the Spanish authorities. I suggest we wear disguises—I'm not swinging for any of you."

Willie slapped Hughes on the back. "Let's dress up like red-skinned savages!"

Hughes laughed and cursed under his breath. "The way we did in good old Boston town when we dumped all that Tory tea in the big drink?"

"What works once, works twice." Willie slapped his hand on the table.

O'Hara looked menacingly at them. He knew his deserter friends all too well. "And you'll do it right and we'll split the goods. Then you'll keep going and take the girl. I won't risk getting into it with the soldiers at the fort."

Robbie plunked his mug down on the table. "More," he slurred.

O'Hara stood up, stretched, and walked away. He shouted back, "Good to have the lot of you gone. You're drinking me out of a tavern!"

Robert felt himself divided as never before. Part of him wanted to take Angelique in his arms and hold her, to make

77

her understand her son, and to accept his decision to fight with Gálvez. But his rational nature urged caution. In the past few days, Angelique had been withdrawn and silent. She was deeply hurt, angry, and afraid all at the same time. Some women, Robert reflected, would have shrieked till their husbands retreated with a pounding head. Others would have spewed forth sarcasm, causing bitter and lasting pain.

Robert watched Angelique. She had turned her back on him and was preparing some meat. She cut it with a fury that illustrated her frustrations. She uses her silence more effectively than other women use their tongues, Robert thought. The tension between them was unnerving. In all their years of marriage no such veil of unspoken words had fallen between them and nothing had so divided them. But now Will was gone. James seemed to spend all his time away, and Maria was growing more sullen by the day. My own daughter is a stranger to me, Robert admitted to himself. She erects one kind of barrier while her mother builds another.

"What are you preparing?" Robert finally asked.

"Sweetbread," Angelique answered, though her voice was barely audible. She didn't bother to turn around, and Robert did not need to see the expression on her face. He knew it was tight; her lips would be pressed together and she would give the impression she wanted to suck her whole body inside itself.

He waited a moment and then said calmly, "It's past time we talked about this." An image of her at night flashed across his mind. For months, long before Will announced he was going off to fight, she had curled herself into an untouchable ball. When he reached for her, she shook him away, coldly sending her unmistakable message of rejection. It *is* more than Will, he thought. Will is only the twig that snapped; the tree already was dying.

"I don't want to talk," she said distantly without turning around.

"Well, I do!" Robert heard himself shout. "I want to talk now!"

Angelique whirled to face him and lifted her dark eyes defiantly. "I didn't nurture my son to have him fighting for the Spanish! I didn't rear him to lie to me and I didn't expect you to side with him. You let him go, Robert MacLean. You let him go and I never will forgive you.'' Having spilled forth her bitterness, she sucked silently on her lip and turned back to the sweetbread. ''At least I have one good son,'' she exclaimed.

Robert clenched his fists and fought to hold back the words that flooded through his mind. Her gentleness was gone; she was like a different person, a stranger.

''Will is a man and he has made his own decision. He lied to protect you, not to hurt you or make you angry. You're unreasonable and stubborn, Ange.'' He knew his voice sounded cold, the inevitable result of struggling for control.

But she continued her work at a furious pace. Robert shoved his chair back and its legs scraped against the floor. ''I'm going downriver. James will look after you and Maria. I'm certain you'll enjoy a vacation from me. At least you won't have to sleep on the edge of the bed!''

Robert strode into the bedroom, a silent curse on his lips. He slammed the door behind him with some force and stood for a moment looking around. Along one wall was the sideboard he had made himself; against another wall there was a small table. Behind the table was an ornate mirror he had carted upriver from New Orleans, a special present for Angelique on their tenth wedding anniversary in 1773. Spread out on that table was Angelique's precious handwoven cloth, her only keepsake from her childhood in the pine forests of Acadia. On the cloth there was a silver brush and a set of tortoiseshell combs. Like the mirror, they too were gifts. And across the room was their bed, the bed they had shared for over sixteen years, the bed where Will and James were birthed and where Maria had been conceived. It stood there now with its rumpled coverings and seemed to laugh at him. The distance from one side of that bed to the other had once been less than a breath; now it was long, empty miles.

Robert yanked open the sideboard and took out some of his city clothes. ''Horse dung and feathers!'' he mumbled as he began jamming his clothes into his satchel.

Angelique equated all Spaniards with those who killed her father and violated her. But there could be drunken sailors of any nationality. The Spanish rule in the territory had been good and Governor Gálvez was a fine man. But the Spanish were only part of her problem. She had denied him his rights as her husband. She guarded her side of the bed as if it were a fort under siege and her body as if it were loot about to be plundered.

Robert flung open the door and stormed through the center room, hoping that Angelique would stop him. But she was not going to confess that her anger was misplaced and even as he whisked past her she stood with her eyes fastened to the cooking in front of her.

Robert walked out into the night and as he passed the muddy area by the horse trough, he thought, This is one night I don't have to worry about tracking the damn Mississippi red mud into the house! He strode on downhill to the jetty by the trading post. Will had proven himself a man, which was more than Robert could say for his other son, James. But Angelique favored James, and Robert supposed that he himself had favored Will, although he always had intended to treat them equally. But he and Will shared mutual interests while James, like Maria, was off brooding. Robert had a fleeting memory of his own brother, for whom James was named. His brother had been moody too. He had married Janet Cameron, but he did not love her. Shouldn't have named him James, Robert thought. He paused at the end of the jetty before he undid the river raft. "There's bad blood in my family," he said aloud. "And trouble follows us."

Louisiana Territory was an area of strange and diverse population; it had been settled by a hotchpotch of peoples. At the end of the Seven Years' War, settlers began to take advantage of the generous land grants offered by the Spanish custodians of the territory. Over five thousand Acadians had found their way to Louisiana and settled in the Attakapas region, while still others settled near Bayou Lafourche and on up the Mississippi. Two large areas south of Baton Rouge became known as the Acadian coasts. The Acadians, or Cajuns as they were called, spoke their own dialect of French, danced to their own music, and enjoyed their own distinctive cooking.

A large number of settlers also had drifted in from the

Thirteen Colonies to the east. The Spanish allowed Protestants, but only Catholics could worship publicly. Few Spanish colonists came to the territory in spite of its being ruled by Spain. The exceptions were a group from the Canary Islands who had settled north of Lake Marepas and a group of people from Málaga who established New Iberia.

The French-speaking added to their population in the territory with additions from the Caribbean. There were Scots, Irish, and Germans too, but like Robert MacLean, they were often adventurers who came via third countries. Indeed, the former governor was one Alejandro O'Reilly, an Irishman who had gone to Spain to escape religious persecution.

The black population of the territory increased as fast as the white. Slaves were imported by the Spanish, many from Santo Domingo and some from Haiti.

Unlike the Thirteen Colonies, emancipation of slaves in Louisiana Territory was reasonably simple under both French and Spanish law. Thus, some of the Africans who came were free when they arrived; in fact, a few were slave owners themselves.

The family La Jeunesse were one such family. They were free blacks who now cleared and farmed a plot of land some ten miles from Robert's trading post.

Mama La Jeunesse was round from the tip of her toes to the top of her close-cropped head. Even her smile was round. She was as black as pitch, with white gleaming teeth and a short pug nose. Her laugh was hearty and regularly punctuated with snorts.

Papa La Jeunesse was only half African. He claimed that the Ashanti had captured his grandfather, an Ewe warrior, and sold him to the Portuguese, who in turn took him in chains to Haiti, where he was sold to the French. There, his granddaddy married an Ashanti slave. Their daughter was bedded by a French sailor, and Papa La Jeunesse was the result of the short but satisfying conjunction.

Papa La Jeunesse himself had sired twelve children and buried seven. Among his surviving brood was one daughter, fifteen-year-old Belle. Belle was the color of rich chocolate with full, sensuous lips and a ripe body that belied her age.

James MacLean had watched Belle working in the fields, had spied on her when she bathed naked in the small stream behind her father's house, and had walked behind her as she swung home from market with her purchases in a basket atop her head. Belle's hips moved to a mysterious rhythm when she walked and every part of her curvaceous body was visible beneath her long, thin cotton dress. James had lusted after Belle for over a year and on more than one night he had possessed her in his dreams, awakening to find himself spent.

Unable to wait longer and feeling himself a man, James approached Papa La Jeunesse, whose need for money was a legend in the parish. It was true that Papa La Jeunesse had two slaves and it also was true that his land was productive. But he drank. He drank his profits and he could not always afford enough seed to plant his indigo.

James had taken some money from the MacLean family hiding place and brought it to the La Jeunesse farm. There he arranged with Papa La Jeunesse to enter into a relationship of *placage* with Belle. The custom was accepted but uncommon. The agreement enabled a young white man to take a free black woman as mistress till he married. He could, if he wished, keep her thereafter. The full agreement included payment to the woman's father and a written promise to provide food and shelter for the woman.

James had considered it long and hard. He had no desire to keep Belle permanently and a contractual agreement he alone could break was ideal. For a time, he had considered forcing himself on her—as he often did in his dreams. But such an act would have had consequences. Quite simply, Belle would have told and his father would have killed him. James MacLean knew his father well. Women were to be treated with respect and he and his brother had been taught never to force themselves on any woman. "Women are to be made love to, but only if they desire it," Robert always told his sons. No references were made to Angelique's experiences, though both boys knew her story. But James had been told the story of Culloden and of how the British soldiers had raped Janet Cameron. James therefore had rejected the idea of raping Belle. His father's wrath would be far too great.

Placage offered the best solution. Proud or not, willing or otherwise, Belle would be commanded to his bed by her father because she had been paid for. Papa La Jeunesse was happy with his gold, Mama La Jeunesse was silent, and Belle could say nothing for fear of her father's anger.

Of course, there was more than the payment. James was obligated to build a cabin for Belle and, toward that end, he had worked during all his spare time to construct the small cabin on the far edge of the La Jeunesse land. There he intended to maintain his reluctant mistress without his father's knowledge.

On the night that Robert left home and headed for New Orleans, James went to his long-awaited rendezvous. The cabin was at last a reality and Belle was waiting.

It was late when James set out. The moon had risen full over the rows of indigo, and the crickets were singing their night song while the plentiful frogs in the nearby marsh croaked away. As James approached the La Jeunesse land, he could see the lonely, isolated cabin outline etched against the star-filled sky.

Inside, Belle sat crouched on the edge of the bed pad. She held herself and rocked back and forth. She had ceased crying, although at this moment her world seemed as black as the interior of the cabin.

Her mother had talked and talked and tried to explain what would happen. Belle moaned at the thought. She had seen the pigs and she had watched her mother birthing. The thought of the pigs and the horrid sight of a child being born filled her with a feeling of nausea.

"We are free Negroes!" her father had proclaimed.

"Free Negroes!" Belle muttered under her breath. "Speak for yourself, Papa! You may be free, but you've sold me!" Belle could feel the hot tears behind her eyelids, but she vowed not to cry again. She held them in and thrust out her lower lip in defiance. James MacLean was a bastard! She had felt his eyes on her and she had been aware of his hungry looks. That's what bedding was all about. She'd slept in the same bed with her parents for fifteen years and she'd seen her papa full of rum and hungry for her mama. When Papa got hungry for Mama, food didn't satisfy him.

"He's going to touch you, girl," her mama had warned.

"He's going to take off your clothes and touch you all over. He's going to touch your teats and touch your bare ass, honey."

"No!" Belle had shrieked at her mama.

"You'll get to like it after a while," her mama said. "It's not unpleasant."

How could it not be unpleasant if even the thought was unpleasant? Belle felt ill, empty, and sick in the pit of her stomach. Her mama's reassurances gave her no comfort.

"You gotta do it sometime, every woman gotta do it sometime." That's what her mother had told her. And her papa? He had just sat in the corner and relished his money. "It'll make life easier," was all he would say. Then he looked up at her and grinned. "You're past age. You should have been married when you were thirteen like the other girls. You're ready, like a ripe melon you're ready."

The door of the cabin creaked open and Belle looked up to see James MacLean silhouetted against the moonlit sky. He was big and strong-looking, with dark, deep-set eyes and thick, dark hair. Belle could not have said just what it was she disliked about him. He wasn't unattractive. It was, she had decided, his mouth. His lips were thin and there was something about his face that Belle could not abide. Maybe it was the way he smiled, when he smiled. There was a harshness about him, a sort of cruelty, or what she suspected was cruelty. But what she disliked most was the way he came to her. He hadn't asked her, nobody asked her. He simply had paid, as if she were a pack of seed. It struck Belle as strange that two twins could look and act so differently. Will MacLean would never do such a thing as James had done. Then Belle's mind turned to their sister, Maria. She was a strange one, even stranger than James.

James walked across the dark room. Behind him the leather-hinged door of the crude cabin swung gently in the night breeze. It was a bright night and the light from the moon and stars came through the window and the open door, casting long shadows on the sparsely furnished interior.

James could clearly see Belle on the edge of the bed pad. She was crouched like a waiting cat; the hunch in her shoulders told him she was fearful and tense, and that knowledge added to his excitement. On the far side of the room there was a fireplace, and in the room's center, a hand-fashioned table and two stools.

James undid his shirt and laid it casually across the table. Then, sitting on one of the stools, he pulled off his boots and kicked them under the table.

"I brought you a little washbasin," he commented. "It's outside in my saddlebag. I forgot to bring it in."

"I don't want it." Belle's voice was barely audible. "I don't want anything from you."

"Then I'll use it when I'm here." He glanced at the door and decided not to close it. Total darkness didn't please him on this occasion and he didn't want to go to the trouble of getting a fire started. James dropped his breeches and walked over to where the silent object of his lust waited apprehensively. He sat down beside her.

"This is your house now," he said matter-of-factly. "I'll fix it up some more; when it's finished you'll like it."

"I won't ever like it!" Belle spit out the words and her obvious bitterness surprised him.

James turned and his large, strong hands seized her shoulders, pressing her backward and down onto the bed pad. His face was directly above hers, their noses only inches apart. In the light from the window, Belle could see James' face. She cringed at his twisted smile, that smile she hated.

"You could have ended up with some dirt-poor buck, or maybe your papa might just have kicked you out. You're a lucky girl, and I don't give a horse's shit what you like. This is my house, you're my mistress, and I'll keep you till I'm tired of you. You're only a black woman, you know. Just what rights do you think you have?"

His voice was filled with his meanness, but he paused and cleared his throat. "It doesn't have to be like this. I tried to be nice to you."

Belle closed her eyes so she wouldn't have to look into his face, but an image of it remained planted in her mind.

"I've wanted you for a long time," she heard him saying. "Near a year now, ever since I saw you naked in the river. I've wanted to touch you, feel you. . . ." His words trailed off and one hand moved from her shoulder to her throat. It was not a gentle motion; she could feel the pressure his hand exerted as it moved across her flesh. Belle froze completely as she felt his hand dip into her dress and grasp her breast roughly. He prodded and molded it in his hand and she heard him emit a deep, guttural sound.

James fumbled with the top of her dress and then pulled it away. He fell on her bare torso, touching one nipple with his mouth even as he grasped her other breast.

"Oh, sweet Jesus!" Belle let out a cry as she began to struggle beneath his hands. She could feel his left leg forcing her to separate her own legs, and his white hands seemed everywhere on her dark skin. His body completely covered her as he plunged into her without hesitation. Belle screamed, but James did not seem to hear her.

As he pumped away, Belle remembered the stallion. She had seen the huge horse coupling with the placid mare. She'd seen dogs too. Somehow, in spite of her mama and papa and their frequent animal-like encounters, she had hoped it was different with people. Her fists doubled and she was only half aware of flailing James' body in her rage.

"I hate you!" Belle screamed into the uncaring night. There was no response. The cabin was far from human ears and her parents would not have come in any case. James MacLean's sweaty body held her in place and his love filled her. Belle shrieked once again in sheer pain and James arched his broad back and shook violently against her. Then he collapsed and lay on top of her, panting and mumbling.

"I hate you," Belle repeated. This time her tone was less hysterical, though it was filled with the venom of her resentment.

James had ceased panting and he positioned himself over her ominously. "You're paid for, and I will exercise my rights!" His dark eyes narrowed and the twisted smile returned to his lips.

Belle stared back at him and tried to muster the defiance that had given her strength earlier. But her position beneath him seemed to make defiance useless: she was an easy victim.

Again, James' hands were everywhere and, after a time, he began again. It was slower than before and even as Belle lay beneath him, she felt her mind drifting above the bed pad, free from his assault. Even though he penetrated her with his mysterious bonelike appendage, Belle felt only a physical oppression. As she listened to him, she came to the sudden realization that during this act, James MacLean was nothing more than a crazed animal, while she retained total rationality. The man-animal above her desired her to respond. He wanted her to touch him, to kiss him, to move beneath him. Instead, Belle imagined herself as a receptacle —a cold, inanimate jar. In spite of her repulsion and her youth, Belle began to understand. The power might belong to James MacLean, but the glory of ignoring him belonged to her. He could only possess her body; he could not subjugate her thoughts.

Again, the dog above Belle completed his act and again he hovered over her triumphantly.

"Are you through?" Belle asked calmly.

"I will take you when I want," James threatened.

Belle opened her eyes wide and stared back at him. "You'll have to," she hissed, "because I'm never going to give you anything!"

The distance between Philadelphia and New York was not great, but with the rebellion going on, it was a difficult journey. One always had to have a pass from the proper authorities. One passed through many checkpoints, and at each the traveler was expected to produce the correct scrap of paper. Both the British and the Continental armies issued such traveling passes to well-known merchants. It was stupid to allow the war to interfere with commerce! Woe unto either side if they tried to keep the inhabitants from making money.

On occasion, Tom Bolton personally trekked to visit Major André, but this time he entrusted General Arnold's letters to Joseph Stansbury, an old family friend of the Shippens and one of Philadelphia's most talented merchants. Stansbury owned a glass and china shop and he was a loyalist from the tip of his shiny boots to the top of his round, balding head. He was a man whose business interests took him from Philadelphia to New York often, a man so openly loyalist that no one suspected him of being a spy. That he was not suspected illustrated the atmosphere of the rebellion. All spies, it was assumed, would pose as patriots. But a man who flew the red, white, and blue of the British flag was far too obvious to be suspected.

"Did you have a good trip?" Major André inquired when he met Stansbury in New York.

"Nothing out of the ordinary," Stansbury replied blandly.

André chuckled. It was no doubt true. In all likelihood Stansbury had been stopped twenty times and each time he had only to show so many documents as to give the guards a headache. None of them could read, of course; they didn't know a British pass from a pass issued by the Continental Army. But if there was sufficient paper they were impressed. Such was the way of war in the colonies.

André took the letters out of the pouch and read them. "I do love dealing with a man of intelligence and charm. A classicist lends life to this dreary business. Look at that: He has signed all the letters *Monk*."

For all his loyalty to King and country, and in spite of his ability to select and sell the very best chinaware, Stansbury was a dull, slow-witted man. "Monk?" he questioned. "Is he turning Catholic and going to a monastery?"

"No, no, no," André said and smiled. "He signs himself Monk after General George Monk, a famous general who changed sides in the midst of a war and was richly rewarded for his loyalty. Well, our General Monk will be rewarded too. By King George! The man does have style! It takes an exceptional person, Stansbury, a very exceptional person to admit he's made an error in allegiance and committed an act of treachery against the King of England. But our man has honor and a sense of real loyalty."

Stansbury cleared his throat. "Don't you think the price is a trifle high?"

André laughed. "For this man's services I would gladly pay more. Now, let me see . . . we will want to know the numbers and location of the rebel troops, the size and location of the ammunition stores, and the movements of Washington's regiments." André again laughed. "Of course, with some luck Washington may starve his own army to death. God knows where he would be without Lafayette!"

Stansbury frowned. "The Frenchman—the general? The one who is defending Virginia?"

Major André nodded.

"Oh, I've heard he's a reformer. And a very dangerous man. I wouldn't want to be leading the regiment that met him in battle."

"Oh, I'd love to fight him," André said with a smile. "But not on a battlefield, he's so—well, he has style too!" André waved his hand flamboyantly and sent a paperweight tumbling from the table. Stansbury flushed. There was something about the head of British Intelligence that made him uneasy. But then, the man did send Mrs. Stansbury nice gifts . . . dresses that simply could not be purchased in Philadelphia now that the rebels had taken over.

"Shall I return next month with his answers?" Stansbury asked. "Or do you prefer another messenger?"

"Are you under suspicion?" André questioned.

"I think not," Stansbury replied.

"Well then, I shall see you next month." He held out his well-manicured hand and shook Stansbury's. "Oh, I will be glad when this inconvenient rebellion is squelched. It's so tiresome not being able to get French wines! And decent food! It's been an age since I had a decent piece of meat. It's all tiresome! Come to think of it, America is tiresome. The people are so—so concerned with themselves. If I hear the words 'freedom' and 'justice' one more time, I think I shall vomit. It's all so crass. No wonder every man I meet swoons over an ample female breast . . . this country is being weaned too young!"

Stansbury laughed. If he didn't understand Major André in other ways, he had to admit the man had wit. Although sometimes he didn't understand his wit either.

Jenna watched as Stephen undid the rope that held the raft to the jetty. He had sold the canoe and purchased the river raft in a less-than-profitable bargaining session. He simply couldn't be forceful enough and money obviously meant very little to him. "You have to work for it, or it doesn't mean a thing!" her father would have said. "Look at the children of the rich in Quebec and Montreal. Spendthrifts and laggards all! Well, I'll not have my children that way. You'll earn your own.''

Jenna hated to think about it, but her father was not entirely incorrect. Stephan was handsome, but he was spoiled. He certainly was not flawless. But who is? Jenna asked herself. I'll change him and everything will be all right. Stephan only needs guidance.

She closed her eyes and thought about their wedding. It was a simple Mass performed by the local priest. He did not ask about Stephan's religion but simply made the assumption that he too was Catholic. Well, I am married, Jenna thought. I'm Jenna O'Connell for better or for worse.

She opened her eyes and watched Stephan, who was stripped to the waist, shove the flatboat away from the jetty. He seemed to know more about this than about canoes. And he is handsome! she thought. His strong arms glistened with beads of sweat in the morning sun, his well-toned muscles rippled as he exerted pressure against the long pole. His skin was darkly tanned now, and he looked refreshed after their stay in St. Louis.

Their newly purchased supplies were neatly piled in the center of the flatboat. Jenna sat by them, her legs folded beneath her. The raft floated easily on the current.

The sun was a blazing ball now and by noon, she contemplated, it would be burning hot on the river. Over low-lying spots on either shore a humid haze hung heavy and, on the distant horizon, several large blackbirds swooped, gliding on the wind drafts.

They journeyed downriver for nearly two hours, staying close to the shore of the west bank, as Mr. O'Hara had instructed them to do.

"It's certainly easy," Stephan commented. "The current just carries you along. But I hear it takes six strong men to come upstream."

Jenna pulled her cap down. Warm as it was, the day *was* beautiful. Huge butterflies flitted among the wild flowers on shore, and the trees were reflected in the calm waters of isolated pools cut off from the main body of the river by long, barren sandbars. "It's very wide here," Jenna observed. "Is it this wide all the way to New Orleans?"

"It narrows in some places, at least on the map. We're not far from St. Genevieve."

"Is that another fort?"

"It's a village settlement with a few troops, the first French settlement west of the Mississippi."

"Did Mr. O'Hara tell you that?"

Stephan nodded, and Jenna closed her eyes as the sun and the motion of the flatboat combined to make her sleepy. She thought that she could probably sleep all the way to New Orleans if the weather remained so hot and the river so placid. She was on the very edge of sleep when an ungodly cry ripped through the silence. Jenna's eyes snapped open.

Ahead in the water on another flatboat were four Indians, guns drawn. Stephan was standing like a statue, stiff and pale, pole in hand. There was no time, not even time for Jenna to scream. A shot crackled through the air and Stephan staggered, then fell into the river, blood gushing from his chest.

It was then that Jenna screamed, covering her face with her hands. She couldn't move from where she sat. Time seemed to stand absolutely still. She was aware of crying out again, of calling Stephan's name. She heard male voices, the clamoring of feet. They had somehow pulled the two boats together and boarded. Yet through her fog of shock, Jenna noticed their language was not Indian! They were speaking English, in the same accent as Stephan.

A rough arm pulled Jenna's hand away from her face.

"C'mon, wench, on your feet!" Jenna opened her eyes and stared at them. They definitely were not Indians. They were all white men with stained bodies and loincloths and painted faces. And one of them was Mr. O'Hara!

Jenna's mouth was open and her green eyes were wide with fright. They were searching the packs. "It's gotta be here somewhere!"

One of them fished out the money belt—Stephan had taken it off when he removed his shirt. They ripped it open. "Heavy!" Hughes said, grinning.

Jenna's eyes fastened on Stephan's body as it bobbed up and down close to the edge of the raft. "You've killed him!" she shrieked as if the reality had just come to her.

O'Hara's eyes surveyed the shore. One could never tell

when a patrol might come along. "Shut that piece up," he muttered with irritation. "Hurry up. I have to get out of here."

Hughes was counting out the gold pieces and the greenbacks. "That's the lot." He shoved a pile toward O'Hara. "Take it and get off with you, if you're so anxious to leave."

O'Hara stuffed the gold into a small pouch and, without pausing, leaped from one of the flatboats to the other. He unsheathed his knife and cut the rope that held the two boats together, and Willie McNair took the long pole and shoved the other way, out into the river.

O'Hara was on his way, but the other three remained with Jenna. She shook violently, her mouth was dry, and she thought she might vomit. "Oh, Stephan!" she cried again. As McNair had separated the two flatboats, Stephan's body had floated away. It was almost as if it were following them into open water.

Hughes looked at Jenna. "Shut up!" he commanded angrily. Jenna looked into Hughes' bearded face. He loomed over her and she could smell the foul odor of rum on his breath. Her fingers dug into the side of her pack and, unable to hold back the tears, she began to shake.

"Better tie her up!" McNair advised. "Cover her up, too. You can't tell who might come along."

Jenna looked at their evil faces. "What are you doing? Where are you taking me?" She was gasping and her sobs were violent. Hughes grabbed her shoulders and shook her violently. "Wherever we want, to do what we want! His hand moved to her throat and tightened. His finger rubbed her windpipe and Jenna gasped, fighting for air. "Don't worry, you won't die fast," he said, his eyes glowing. He ran his tongue around his mouth. "Not till you're well used." Jenna shuddered and Hughes allowed his hand to run over her breast. "Such a curious little piece," he sneered. He squeezed her breast. "But you have your purpose."

"No!" Jenna wailed, but he pressed her throat harder and she coughed. She felt things going black; their faces, their threats had reduced her to a shaking mass of terror, but still she fought for breath. Then he dropped his hand and yanked her to her feet.

Robbie tossed him a bit of rope and Hughes whirled Jenna around and tied her wrists tightly.

"I think we can take this mess off now," McNair was saying. "Nobody's around and nobody saw us."

Robbie already was wiping the stain from his skin and putting on his clothes. Jenna's horror-filled eyes followed his movements. Hughes pushed her downward. "She's a good girl, not struggling."

Jenna's legs had nearly buckled as he exerted pressure on her shoulders. She felt like a stone and she had gone totally limp with fear and shock. "Ah, are we going to have fun with you," he said menacingly. "But later." Jenna shuddered. Hughes rolled her under the flatboat's shelter. A veil of darkness dropped over her world and he covered her with a blanket.

Hours passed under the blanket in the hot, unbearably stuffy darkness. Jenna cried till there were no more tears, and she gagged once when the vision of Stephan's floating body returned to her. In her mind, she saw it bloated and floating behind the flatboat, following them downriver and being eaten by fish till it was nothing but a skeleton with empty eye sockets.

Stephan is dead, Stephan is dead, she kept saying to herself. And these men, whoever they were, were taking her downriver. She was vaguely aware that the sun must have gone down, because it began to get cooler. They're going to kill me, she thought. And she began to shake again. Stephan was dead and she was torn between wanting to die herself and wanting to stay alive. The thought of Hughes' fingers on her throat returned. It was horrible!

Suddenly Jenna's senses became alert. The flatboat had ceased moving. She tried desperately to organize her thoughts, but all she could think of were Hughes' threats.

Someone pulled the blanket off her and Jenna breathed deeply of the cool, fresh night air. Another man pulled her up and lifted her into his arms, carrying her ashore.

The young one had started a fire and the man who carried her set her down like a sack of potatoes on the ground.

The light from the fire cast shadows on their faces and Jenna was consumed by helplessness and fright. She looked from one to the other apprehensively, her eyes darting about like a trapped animal. They were all criminals, all murderers.

"Let's see what our little bundle looks like," McNair suggested. He and Hughes both laughed, but Robbie sat sullenly against a tree, neither joining in the laughter nor bothering to stand.

Jenna cringed as McNair walked over to her and pushed her onto her back. He undid her shirt and tore away the camisole she wore underneath. As he did so, Hughes pulled off her breeches, yanked her legs apart, and tied her down.

McNair covered her breasts with his hands. "A nice piece of mutton," he said, repeating his favorite phrase. Jenna squirmed, but there was no escaping them. The other had his hands between her legs and she let out a shriek as he touched her intimately. "Nice," Hughes muttered, pinching her nipple. Jenna moved again, a compulsive jerk. "I'd hate it if you were still," he said, exploring her body as McNair did.

"Which one of us will go first?" McNair asked.

"Does it matter? She's not a virgin." They both laughed and Hughes ran his hand the length of her long leg. "Untie her legs. I like a good struggle." McNair laughed and quickly obliged.

Hughes fell on her and Jenna closed her eyes. McNair left his hands on her breasts, rubbing them roughly. The weight of his hands held her down, but Jenna, her legs now free, struggled against Hughes' weight. She let out a scream as he was about to plunge into her, but a shot rang out, followed by another and another. The man on top of her fell downward and the other, whose hands were on her breasts, fell face forward, covering her completely. Jenna wiggled out from under them. She struggled to her knees and looked up. Silhouetted against the fire, the youngest of the three stood with a smoking pistol. His light blond hair fell across his face and his pale blue eyes were totally emotionless. Jenna stared at him in disbelief and again began to shake violently. Robbie took a step toward her, the pistol still in his hands. Jenna felt nausea, and a cold darkness seemed to overcome her. She gave way to it completely.

CHAPTER VI

Late July 1779

"You look wonderful!" Janet exclaimed as she smiled into Madelaine's lively eyes. "The country air agrees with you." Impulsively, Janet hugged Madelaine Deschamps again. It was good to have her back. She had been in Trois Rivières for nearly three months, visiting her brother Pierre and his brood.

Janet had written to Madelaine about everything, but writing was not the same as having her home. At thirty-two, Madelaine was petite, lively, and as beautiful as her mother had been. But Madelaine was not her mother, even though she had inherited her olive skin and dark eyes. With her sharp intelligence, wit, and charm, she was more like her grandmother.

Janet had only to look at Madelaine, her adopted daughter, to know the resilience of the human spirit. The death of Madelaine's parents and grandmother had cast a pall over her childhood. But Madelaine had survived and grown into womanhood on the frontier, marrying a handsome young Frenchman named Marcel Gérard. When Marcel had been killed, leaving Madelaine a childless widow, Janet had wept with her and, in time, the pain healed. The experience had caused Madelaine to grow into soft maturity, rather than hardening her into cynicism, as might have happened. And although Madelaine was slow to fall in love again, she often allowed men to call on her. She, like her brothers, was a fine example of the will to survive. They had all passed through the most terrible of ordeals and still managed to rebuild their lives.

Madelaine chose to remain with Janet and Mathew;

Pierre had returned to rebuild his father's estate near Trois Rivières; and René, the most adventurous of them all, had gone west, out to Rupert's Land, as the English called it. But he had gone with the North West Company, a Scots firm that favored French employees. There, in a place called Pembina, René worked with C. J. B. Chaboillez, setting up a North West Company trading post.

Madelaine drew back from Janet's embrace. "How is Mathew?" Madelaine asked. "How is he, really?"

Janet nodded and motioned Madelaine to a chair. She sat down herself. "He had his heart stop," Janet answered. She still had trouble thinking of it, or talking about Mathew being ill or weak. For days and weeks she had walked around saying it to herself: Mathew's heart is weak. She repeated it to make it real, as if forming the words over and over would take away her fear and remove the threat that it might happen again. "The doctor says he is recovering well, but . . ." Her voice trailed off.

"But you are afraid he will have another attack and you can't get him to rest enough because he won't give up working." Madelaine's hand covered Janet's warmly.

Madelaine's bright black eyes could be penetrating as well as lively. "You were strong for me once," she said softly. "You gave me the love that Papa didn't give me, and you and Mathew protected us, all of us." Madelaine paused and Janet felt the pressure of Madelaine's loving squeeze on her hand. "You haven't wept for Mat's death, you haven't allowed Mathew to weep either. You can't keep it inside you, you can't bury your mourning in your fears for Mathew. He is ill, but for him to change his whole way of living would be another kind of death for a man like Mathew Macleod. You must take the days as they come, you must mourn together and be together." Madelaine unconsciously felt the gold cross around her neck with her fingers. "One day we'll all go home to the Niagara," Madelaine said with conviction. "We'll all go. Mathew is strong, you are strong. Don't try to protect him from himself, you can't make him an invalid."

Tears were forming in the corners of Janet's eyes. Madelaine was right. "He blames himself for Jenna's running away, he blames himself for Mat's death."

"He blames himself for not being the one to die instead of his son. Fighting behind a desk is not good enough for him. Go to him, talk to him. Stop hiding from it, let him mourn."

"I can face anything except Mathew's dying," Janet admitted. Her confession came in the smallest of whispers.

"When it happens you will face it as you always have faced everything. What you have built cannot be destroyed."

Janet wiped a tear from her face. She stood up and smoothed out her skirt in a nervous gesture. "I'm so glad you're back. You give me courage."

Madelaine smiled. "You have courage and I did not give it to you."

Silently, Janet turned and looked at the staircase. Mathew was upstairs. She left Madelaine and climbed the stairs to the bedroom.

Mathew was not asleep, as Janet thought he might be. He was sitting on the edge of the bed, his face toward the window.

"Is it as warm as it looks outside?"

Lately they had begun every conversation with her asking how he felt. He was waiting for her to answer his question and ask hers.

"It's quite warm," Janet replied. But she did not finish the rest of their routine. She walked to the bed and sat down beside him.

Mathew turned and looked into her face. "Have you been crying?"

It was a sudden rush of emotion too long restrained. Tears flooded down her face, and she fell into Mathew's arms. Her sobs seemed to come from deep inside her; there was no controlling them. "It seems like only yesterday and Mat was a little boy . . . and we . . . we gave him his first hunting knife, and he built the canoe with you . . . and . . . and . . ." Her voice seemed to dissolve and she trembled against him. "Why is my little boy gone? I want him back. . . . I want you back. . . . I want us to be together. . . ."

"I want him back too," Mathew said after a time. "That's two sons I've lost."

"It's not fair," Janet said and sobbed.

"We're not the only ones to lose a son." Mathew pressed

her to him and stroked her hair. "You protected the children and nurtured them, you gave them all you had to give. You couldn't protect them forever, Janet. Nor could I stop Mat from going to fight. . . . I think I wanted to," he confessed. "But dammit! I was proud too! Proud that he was brave and believed in something."

"That's how you taught him to be." Janet breathed into his chest.

"It's how *we* taught him to be," Mathew corrected.

They sat for a long time holding each other, Mathew rocking Janet in his arms, realizing that for the first time they were sharing both their sorrow and their fears.

Mathew gently lowered her to the bed and kissed her face and neck tenderly. "I won't leave you," he promised. "I'm going to get better, Janet. I'll grow strong again. Stop being afraid for me too."

Her eyes, like deep green pools, searched his face. "Just hold me for a while," she asked. "Hold me and don't let me go for anything."

They lay in one another's arms for the better part of an hour, both drifting into a light sleep, both knowing the comfort of their mutual love.

"Are you asleep?" Mathew asked when he opened his eyes. The sun had dropped on the far horizon. The room was shrouded in shadows, the pink and gold shadows of twilight.

Janet moved in his arms and answered only with a soft moan.

Mathew leaned over her, watching her sleeping form take life, smiling as she opened her eyes. "I want to make love to you," he whispered as he bent his head to kiss her ear.

"You never have to ask," she answered softly. "I am yours always. . . ." He began to undress her slowly and lovingly. His own passion grew as he explored her and he thought: She is always new to me, always a joy. "We move as one," he told her as he lay against her smooth skin, his hands caressing her with mounting desire.

Janet opened herself to him and he moved within her with agonizing slowness till their mutual pleasure obliterated all other senses and she cried out, clinging to him. So attuned to one another that they seemed to breathe together, their passion peaked at the same moment, carrying them away and setting them down softly.

Janet marveled at his touch; it had been so long. They had begun by comforting one another and it had dissolved into tender, wordless lovemaking. It was as if they had gone on a perilous journey and returned together, stronger than ever, united as before.

Janet lifted Mathew's hands to her lips and kissed them.

"Our strength is together," she told him. "I forgot that for a little while."

Maria MacLean dipped her finger into the brown water of the little stream, withdrew it, and shook it off. Almost everyone said she was a pretty girl. But having said that, they paused to think about the comment, and almost without exception there was no elaboration.

She was fourteen, near fifteen, and had light brown hair streaked golden in some places by the strong southern sun. Her eyes were brown too and her dark pupils were ringed with gold. "I wish you would wear your bonnet," her mother often implored. "A lady has to keep her skin snow white; tanned skin is vulgar."

But Maria would not wear her bonnet and, as a result, her skin was dark. If Maria's looks had any flaw beside the color of her skin, it was the shape of her mouth. It was thin and narrow like her brother James'. "Those two young ones are like peas in a pod!" everyone said of James and Maria. "She ought to be his twin instead of Will."

Idly, Maria clamped her hand over a grasshopper that poised on the edge of a flat brown rock. "You didn't think I saw you, did you? That's why you sat so still. Still, just like a little stone." Her dark eyes glistened for just a moment, then she lifted her hand a tiny bit and watched the struggling insect. "You're not a large hopper," she murmured. With her other hand, Maria pulled off one of the hopper's flapping half wings. She smiled as the wounded insect writhed, then she flattened it against the rock. "Can't stand watching something struggle for life," she said. "Miserable thing!"

Maria lifted her hand, which now bore the stains of the insect's body. Tobacco stains. All hoppers seemed to spit tobacco.

Maria lifted her eyes to the small cabin, and a smile crossed her face. She had been waiting over an hour and for most of that hour, her imagination had been going at full tilt. It was fed by the periodic noises from the cabin, James moaning while Belle cursed. In her mind, Maria conjured up a checkerboard pattern of white on black. James and Belle. James was doing unspeakable things, though Maria would very much have liked to speak about them.

"I'll just mind my time." Just then the door of the cabin swung open. Maria quickly crouched down behind the rock and hid. It was James, all right. He came out into the sunlight and was walking to where his horse was tethered. He was doing up his shirt.

Maria smiled and then tore away the top of her own calico dress. She rolled over in the high grass and let out a piercing scream.

James halted and whipped around to face in the direction from which the scream came. It was beyond the cabin, back in the tall grass down by the stream. The first shriek was followed by another and James did not notice the door of the cabin fly open, nor did he see the wide-eyed Belle as she stood in the doorway.

James bounded into the high grass shouting, "Who's there?" He nearly stumbled over the prone body of his own sister. She was lying face down in the dirt and mud. Her long, dark hair fanned out on her back and she looked ominously still.

James knelt over her. "Maria!" He grasped her shoulders and lifted her as he turned her over. He saw her torn dress. "Maria!" He shook her and her eyes blinked open. She flung her arms around his neck and buried her small face in his shoulder.

"Thank God it's you!" Maria sobbed as she leaned against him. Shaking, she began to cry. "I thought you were that boy come back for me. I thought he was going to hurt me again!"

Maria felt James' body stiffen with all the rage she knew him to be capable of.

"What happened?" Belle's voice cut through the summer

100

afternoon. She stood above them looking down, her skin still glistening with dampness, her huge eyes wide with fright.

"He hurt me!" Maria wailed.

James pulled her back and looked into her tear-stained face. "Who hurt you?" he asked. "What did he do?"

Maria sniffed. "Pulled my dress and, and . . . and hurt me. He pulled it clear up and tore the top and . . . and felt me. . . ." She dissolved into tears again and her words grew muddled: "He touched me all over!"

"Who?" James demanded. "Who did this to you?" He muttered a curse under his breath.

Maria lifted her face once again and her fingers dug deep into her brother's arm. She turned her eyes slowly to meet Belle's. "Her brother, that's who! Her brother, the big one!"

Belle's hand automatically flew to her mouth. "He wouldn't!" Belle screamed back at Maria.

"He did! He did!" Maria shouted defiantly. "He's wearing that old red kerchief round his neck, I know him. I can see his face in my mind right now. . . . I can see his . . . his thing! He tried to—" Again she buried her face and sobbed, thinking it was a good thing that she had met Belle's brother on his way to the fields only a few hours ago. She congratulated herself on remembering the kerchief.

"He wouldn't," Belle whispered as she took a step backward. Her face was a study in agony. No one was going to believe a Negro boy over the word of a little white girl, no one.

James struggled to his feet and scooped Maria into his arms. His eyes met Belle's for a single instant. "I'm taking this child home," he announced. "But I'll be back for your brother."

"No!" Belle screamed as she whirled and took off across the rough ground, running to warn her brother.

"She'll tell him," Maria said.

"I'll find him," James vowed. "I'll find him and skin him alive."

Maria said nothing as James carried her toward his horse. She buried her face in his chest and suppressed the joy she felt inside.

James put Maria gently in the saddle and climbed on behind her. They rode for a few minutes, Maria staring straight ahead, James feeling his sister's hair in his face as it blew backward in the wind.

"What are you going to tell Mama?" Maria asked.

"I'm going to tell her you were attacked."

"Are you going to tell her how you came to find me? Are you going to tell her you found me behind Belle's cabin and that you come to Belle all the time, that you keep her?"

James hands tightened on the reins. Until this moment he had forgotten his own secret. He drew the horse in. "That's a secret," he answered. "I don't want you to tell Mama about it. She wouldn't like it."

"Why not?" Maria asked.

James suddenly felt defensive. "Because Mama believes in love and marriage. Mama doesn't believe in fraternizing with the Negras, says mixed blood is unhealthy."

Maria almost lost control and laughed. Fraternize? James must have thought her a baby. "What if I tell her?" Maria said, her voice full of sweetness.

James shook her shoulders. "You won't," he said in a semithreatening voice.

Maria twisted in the saddle and looked at him. Her face was set and filled with meanness. James had seen her look mean, but never as sly as she looked now. "You can lie to Mama and you can keep things from Papa. You even can steal Will's money and keep your old Belle. But don't you threaten me, James MacLean. I know you—we're cut from the same cloth, you and I."

James' mouth was dry as he took in the look of pure evil on his sister's face. "Nothing happened to you back there, did it?" His realization was swift. No Negro had attacked her.

"It doesn't matter," Maria replied. "You're going to kill him anyway."

James looked at her in amazement. "I'm not," he protested.

"Yes, you are," Maria said confidently. "Because I'm going to tell about Belle if you don't." Maria smiled at James. "I like secrets," she said.

James felt a sudden sense of defeat and it mingled with

the knowledge that his sister was not mentally right; she was something more than a devious little witch. At the same time, he had to admit she knew how to manipulate both people and situations. Those were valuable assets he felt he could put to good use in the future.

James burst into sudden laughter. "What if I kill you?" he asked.

"You won't," Maria answered. "I'm the only one who understands you."

She tossed back her hair. "Do we have a solemn pact?"

Wearily, James nodded his head. "We have a pact," he promised.

Governor Bernardo de Gálvez was in his thirties, a tall, good-looking Spaniard with a mixed reputation. He was well educated, he wrote poetry and enjoyed good music. But Bernardo Gálvez was an adventurer too, a man who might have been more comfortable in the days of buccaneer glory, the days of the Spanish Main. A soldier and an accomplished seaman, he anchored his proud little flagship, the *Gálvez town*, at New Orleans.

Since he had become governor of Louisiana Territory, Gálvez had set himself the task of reinforcing the defenses of New Orleans. His greatest fear was the possibility of a British attack sent out of Canada and down the Mississippi.

He had spent the years of peace gathering information on all the British activities in West Florida. He had obtained plans of the two largest British forts—Mobile and Pensacola—and had begun training small groups of men throughout the territory for positions of leadership. "We will be few in number compared to the British," he told them. "But we know the land, and planning can triumph over numbers. The British are spread out, and we can outnumber them in specific locations if they can be kept apart, unable to unify their total forces."

When word came that Spain had, at last, entered the war on the side of her ally France, Gálvez was specifically named by Charles III to lead the campaign. The three reasons given were: Gálvez' friendly relations with the Choctaw nation, relations carefully built by Robert MacLean and the merchant Oliver Pollock; his knowledge of the various groups that populated the territory; and his good relations with the struggling Continental Congress.

Will MacLean, Jacinto Panis, and Gálvez stood in the governor's study in his once-lovely mansion in New Orleans. The recent hurricane had been as devastating to the mansion and its courtyards as it had been to the rest of New Orleans.

"The best-laid plans . . ." Gálvez intoned, shaking his head to Panis, his second-in-command. All the maps were water-soaked; indeed, everything was water-soaked. Gálvez turned to Will. Gálvez had personally selected Will MacLean because of the young man's facility with languages, his intimate knowledge of the Choctaw Indians, and his intelligence and calm. Like Will's father, Robert MacLean, who was well known and well respected by the Spanish governor, Will was eager and ambitious. Heaven knew, a young man of his caliber was hard to come by on the frontier. But he was forced to admit that, even if he had a hundred Will MacLeans, they could not change the results of the storm. The unexpected had happened. Somehow it always did.

August was not the traditional month for hurricanes, but nevertheless there had been one. It had happened two days earlier, on August 18, and it had been the most violent storm within living memory.

Gálvez' carefully assembled little fleet had sustained severe damage. Many of his ships had been sunk, and what did not sink had been ripped to shreds by the same merciless winds that had ripped the roofs from houses, sent tiles flying through the air, and reduced the river market to a sunken, muddy shambles.

"¡Madre de Cristo!" Gálvez exclaimed. "Our plans to take Baton Rouge have been completely foiled, not by the British, but by the ill wind!"

Will frowned. "We still have able-bodied men. Over six hundred."

Gálvez sucked in his lower lip and his eyes searched the water-soaked map. "And there's another six hundred waiting on the German coast, mostly good Cajun fighting men, men who have a strong grudge against the British."

"Sir, I think we should leave without our ships. We could

go overland, we wouldn't lose as much time. The longer we hold off the attack, the greater the British threat over the river becomes. Sir, the British forces are strung out now; it would be a disaster if they were allowed the time to amalgamate."

"Some of the men are sick," Gálvez argued. He always played the devil's advocate; it was how he tested the resolve of his officers and men. "Sick men weaken our strike force."

Will smiled. "Some of the British are sick too, sir. Reports indicate that a good part of the garrison at Baton Rouge is down with river fever. Those of us who don't have it are resistant to it."

Gálvez nodded and smiled. Will was enthusiastic. "Do you think we can take them?" he questioned.

"I think we have no choice," Will answered quickly.

Gálvez' dark eyes moved to his second-in-command. Panis was chewing tobacco and had a faraway look. "You think we ought to defend New Orleans, don't you?"

Panis shrugged. "Defense usually is less dangerous than offense."

"Sir, we *will* be defending this city. The only real defense of New Orleans is to wipe out the British garrison at Baton Rouge. We must control the Mississippi and we must control it completely."

"Without harassment," Gálvez added. He rounded his desk and came over to Will. He slapped him on the back and smiled. "We'll go overland!" he announced. "And by God, we'll leave for Baton Rouge only four days off our original schedule. Damn hurricanes! Damn the weather!"

"Damn the British!" Will said, smiling.

Gálvez nodded. "Mind you, we'll need new information. I'm going to send you ahead of the main strike force. I'll want you to spend a few days in Baton Rouge and, if possible, a few days at the fort. Then you'll return to us. I won't attack till I know what we're up against."

"Shall I go alone?" Will asked.

Gálvez shook his head. "No, take Tolly Tuckerman with you. He's a good man, he'll help with your cover. You'll both be using assumed names, you'll both be volunteering to help the British."

Will shook his head and smiled. He couldn't have asked for a better partner. Tolly Tuckerman was a man of many talents.

"You'd better leave right away," Gálvez advised. "I want you there well ahead of the main force."

Jenna could look back on the last two weeks and recall, without difficulty, every single nightmarish second.

She had opened her eyes and found the fire still flickering. The young blond man with his pale, sickly eyes was sitting against the trunk of a giant old poplar tree, staring at the embers with a distant, dazed expression.

Jenna shook her head to clear it and realized that her hands as well as her feet were untied. She glanced around her, and to her relief, the bodies of the others were gone. Abstractedly, she rubbed her wrists, which were sore from having been tied for so many hours. Then her eyes returned to her lone captor, who seemed to be paying her no attention at all.

It then occurred to her that her clothes had been replaced, more or less. The torn camisole still was on the ground, but her shirt was wrapped around her, though not entirely closed. The breeches that she had been wearing were pulled up awkwardly.

"Don't run away," the young man said, not looking at her.

Jenna looked around. Where would she run? It was pitch black beyond the light of the fire; the woods beyond the river were thickly forested. These were not woods she knew; her chances of survival on her own would be severely limited. Who knew what kind of animals there might be, how friendly or unfriendly Indians might prove, even what berries were edible? She shivered and pulled the shirt around her, buttoning it quickly.

"Gets cold at night," the young man said. "You'll need this." He tossed her a blanket and Jenna quickly pulled it around her, crawling closer to the warmth of the fire.

The young man watched her, his expression curious.

"What are you staring at?" he demanded. "Stop looking at me!"

"I'm sorry," Jenna mumbled. And she thought to herself: I'm going to cry at any moment. She tried to put Stephan out of her mind, she tried to hold back her tears.

The young man was holding a long, slim knife in his hand. The blade glistened slightly as the light from the fire glanced off it.

"Why did you kill them?" Jenna finally gained the courage to ask.

The man coughed violently, then spit on the ground. "Didn't want to watch them with you." His voice was bland, emotionless. More silence passed between them, and Jenna tried to understand. Did this mean he did not intend to molest her? Or, did he want her for himself? There was certainly one thing she couldn't deny, he was a killer. He had killed Stephan as well as the men who had been his friends.

"I should be grateful to you," she said with some hesitation.

His expression didn't change and he didn't look at her.

"What's your name?" Jenna asked.

"Robbie Ryan," he answered, looking only at his knife.

"Robbie," Jenna repeated. She had been looking at the ground and she hardly realized he had leaped to her side; he moved so silently. She jumped when she saw his shadow. He grasped her long hair and wound it around his hand, jerking her head backward and forcing her face upward.

"Don't say my name! Don't you ever say my name, you filthy little cunt!" His sickly blue eyes were aflame. "I know your kind! I know what you make men do!" He was holding the knife at her throat, teasing her with it. "I should kill you too!" He was shaking and Jenna cringed in terror.

Uncontrollable tears began to flow down her face and she shrieked back at him, "Then kill me! I'm not a . . . a whatever you said. I'm not! Go ahead, kill me . . . it doesn't matter! I only want to go home to my papa and now I can't! And you killed my husband and . . . and . . ." As her voice dissolved into violent sobs, Robbie let go of her hair and stepped backward. He kicked a loose stone with his foot.

"Oh, shit!" he said loudly into the night. "Shut up and go to sleep!"

Jenna literally tumbled backward onto the grass. She buried her face in her arm and pulled the blanket up over her, crying softly. Robbie Ryan gave every indication of being completely mad. His eyes terrified her and his hatred toward her was an enigma.

I shall force myself to sleep, Jenna thought. She longed to have the sun come up, hoping that things would seem less horrible in the daylight, praying that someone would rescue her from the lunatic who held her captive. Desperately, in order to force the horrific experiences of the day out of her head, she tried to picture the warm, comfortable parlor of her parents' home in Montreal.

She thought about her mother's tales of Scotland and about her mother's ordeal escaping from Sergeant Stanley. "Where there's life, there's hope," her mother often had told her. "How could you have stood it?" Helena asked. And Jenna had added, "How did you survive?" Janet's answer always had been the same: "You have to want to survive, you have to want to live."

Jenna felt her hands clasp together tightly beneath the blanket. Stephan was dead. Did she want to live? I do, Jenna answered herself. I do, I must. With that thought, she curled herself into a ball. I am alive, she kept saying over and over. Someone helped my mother and someone will help me. Jenna listened to the night sounds and to the river. She let her mind wander back to the time before she and her parents had moved back to Montreal. She could picture the fort at Niagara and her father's trading post. She remembered a time when she had crossed the meadow full of buttercups and stood looking across at the thundering falls of Niagara. The Indians called the falls Thundergate because they thundered and because the portage trail was the gateway west, the gateway to the great river systems. "I want to go home," Jenna murmured to herself. "Home to Thundergate."

In spite of her fears, Jenna fell into a deep sleep and woke only when the night noises had ceased and the birds began their wild song just before dawn. At first she did not remember where she was, or how she had gotten there. Then, in a flood, the events of the previous day swept over her and she jumped bolt upright, alert and fully awake.

The fire had gone out and Robbie was gone! Jenna looked around quickly and saw that everything was gone save the blanket she had been wrapped in. She whirled about and ran through the thicket to the river's edge. To her relief, Robbie was just loading the flatboat.

"You were going to leave me!"

He turned around and stared at her for a moment as if she were a ghost. "You can't leave me," Jenna protested. For, however much she feared him, she feared being left alone more. If he were going to let her go, then at least let it be on the edge of civilization and not at the mercy of the wilderness.

He shrugged, unconcerned. Jenna didn't wait; she scrambled aboard the flatboat without invitation. She crawled across it as it swayed in the water and positioned herself near the packs, crouching down beside them.

Robbie finished loading the supplies as if she didn't exist. He untied the rope that held the flatboat, climbed aboard, and pushed off onto the river without a word. After a time, he sat down, content to let the river carry the boat along. He took out his long knife and sharpening stone. Idly he scraped the knife along the stone, his pale eyes concentrating on the task.

Jenna watched him like a cat, looking away whenever he looked up at her.

"I've killed twelve men," he said after a time. The maddening sound of the knife on the stone continued. "And more women . . . whores mostly . . . wicked women." He looked up to assess her reaction. "Aren't you afraid I'll kill you?"

Her experience with him the night before made Jenna hesitate to answer. He was mad, but it was worse than mere lunacy. There was something else wrong with him. One could be quite mad and still have normal sexual desires. Robbie didn't seem to have them, and though that made her grateful in one sense, it made him more terrifying in another. She was unsure of what it all meant and she cursed her own inexperience. Her instincts all told her that it was good to keep him talking. "Why did you kill the women?" she asked.

He ran his tongue around his mouth as if he were savoring the memory of his past murders. "Women are evil. They make men do things."

Jenna forced herself to look at him fearlessly. Her green

eyes fastened on his blue eyes. "You could kill me," she said. "I'm not certain I care. I've made a horrible mess of my life, I'm not even seventeen and it's a mess!"

He looked a little surprised and Jenna thought: Like everyone else, he assumed I was older.

"Was that man really your husband?"

"Yes," Jenna replied. "Do you have a family?" she asked only to keep the conversation going.

But Robbie just shook his head and again silence passed between them. It was a silence broken only by the unnerving sound of Robbie's knife against the stone.

Jenna reached back and started to undo her own pack.

"What the hell are you doing?" Robbie's voice was belligerent and mean.

"Getting some biscuits," Jenna answered as she looked up uncertainly.

"You ain't got no food. Everything on this flatboat is mine!"

Jenna blinked at him. Heaven knew what might set him off. She remembered Stephan's gold. Robbie now must have all of it: she was sure he had killed the others. But knowing that didn't make any difference to her. She was hungry and thirsty.

"I want something to eat," Jenna said. "May I please have something?"

He looked quizzically at her and took a gulp of rum from the skin that he had laid near him. "Take off your blouse," he demanded in a low, threatening voice. "Take it off and let me look at you."

Jenna's face went bright red. Perhaps his tastes were not unnatural and she was in just as much danger of being assaulted as she had been with the others. "Take it off!" He made a movement toward her and held out his knife. It was a deadly, sharp, well-honed blade. Shaking, Jenna undid the shirt, revealing her breasts. She turned her eyes to the muddy brown water, but the hot blood of shame flooded her face as she felt his eyes on her bare, milk-white skin. Her breasts were full and well shaped, with tight pink rosy nipples pointing upward.

Ryan crawled over to her and she closed her eyes as she felt the dull edge of the knife against her breast. He pressed it flat against her flesh but did not cut her. "Bitch!" he spit. "Do it back up, cover yourself up!" Quickly, Jenna redid the buttons on the shirt. Why would he want to look at her and then call her names? From across the flatboat, Robbie tossed her some biscuits. "There's water in that skin," he said, pointing off to a full container of water near one of the packs.

Jenna bit into a biscuit and made herself eat slowly so it would last longer. She opened the skin and drank some water. It was warm but it didn't matter. Her lips and throat were parched. Across the flatboat, Robbie was at his knife again, his tongue licking his lips now and again.

By noon the sun was unbearably hot on the river, and Jenna had moved slightly under the half shelter in the middle of the boat. It wasn't very high, but it offered some respite from the sun.

Robbie stood up and stretched. He still held the knife in his hand as he walked across the boat toward her, his eyes glazed with too much rum, his fingers caressing the razor-sharp blade. Jenna tensed. He's going to kill me, she thought. He's going to slit my throat.

He knelt down and looked at her. "Tell me how it feels." he asked. "Describe it to me."

"What?" Jenna was perplexed.

"When a man has you, tell me how it feels!" His voice had grown menacing and Jenna cringed back from him.

"You slept with him, tell me."

Jenna tried to be vague, but she was quick to realize that the more she talked, the slacker Robbie's hand on his knife was. As she talked, his pale face turned pink with excitement and his breath came quicker. Then, after a time, he left her in peace.

For two weeks, Robbie had fed Jenna and made camp with her, but every day, day in and day out, he threatened her. More than once he held the knife at her throat, but every time he was calmed if she spoke to him about lovemaking. The more vivid her descriptions, the more intimate her details, the more satisfied he seemed. But that, as Jenna was soon to learn, was only the beginning.

111

CHAPTER VII

Late August 1779

Mathew put down the *Quebec Gazette*. "Fighting has all but come to a halt in the southern colonies." A smile crossed his face. "Because it's too hot! Not the problem we usually have here."

"Our winter is turning out to be our protection," Janet commented. "But in the colonies . . . they're going to win their independence, aren't they?"

"Looks that way," Mathew admitted. "In spite of Washington. You know, even some of the members of the Continental Congress have called him incompetent. I'm surprised he's still around after Valley Forge. Do you realize he did the same thing there he did at Fort Necessity?"

Janet smiled. The story of Washington at Fort Necessity was one of Mathew's favorites.

"Canada is changing," Janet observed. "First we had an influx of businessmen from the colonies, now all kinds of loyalists are coming." The French tended to call them *English* because English was their common language, but in reality a large number were German, Dutch, Scots, and Irish. They had moved into Nova Scotia when the colonies began to deport those loyal to the Crown. Others had fled to Montreal, Fort Frontenac, and into the Niagara. Behind them they had left their homes, their belongings, and their fortunes. Many were members of families divided by the rebellion. The British Parliament was sending what money it could, but there were new homes to be built, new businesses to be established, roots to be put down in a new land.

Mathew nodded his head. "A lot are arriving in the Niagara. It's a great worry to the governor. And the Mohawk are coming with them. There won't be time to plant and harvest enough supplies before winter. It's going to be bad; there even may be a famine."

Mathew had only to mention Niagara and she felt homesick. "It'll be changed when we go back," she said wistfully.

"Well, we won't be alone. They're certain to reopen it for settlement, there won't be any choice."

"Can we get our land back?" Janet asked.

Mathew nodded his head in the affirmative. "When grants are given, we'll get it back. The very same land in the very same spot. I've had assurances on that."

"And we can rebuild the house . . . it'll be like it was?"

"Better. We'll have neighbors."

Janet thought: The children will be home, we'll be together. She didn't say it, though. She didn't want Mathew to start talking about Jenna again.

"What are you thinking about?" he asked. Janet looked beyond him, out into the garden. "I was thinking that August is almost over." She sighed. "The summers are so short."

Robert pushed his hands into his pockets and picked his way through the muddy streets. The smells of New Orleans filled his nostrils, and a wave of nostalgia washed over him. It seemed a century since he had first smelled those smells. In reality it had only been a few years.

Robert turned the corner and headed up Bourbon Street. He saw the decaying house that once had been the brothel where he had met Juliet, a beautiful Creole prostitute who had taught him how to make love, but who had rejected him.

He wondered how his life would have been different if she had not sent him away. He discarded the idea quickly. I love Angelique, he reminded himself. *Loved*, in any case. But then he realized that he was unwilling to part with the memories of their love and of their years together. He felt the need to question himself hard. What had changed Angelique into the woman she had become? When had it happened? Was he in fact the cause of it? No, Robert thought. It happened so gradually I didn't notice. He searched his mind for the first signs of change in her. It was, he thought, right after Fou Loup and Grande Mama died. They had passed on within a year of each other. Perhaps it was being alone so much . . . perhaps Angelique simply had fallen out of love with him. It had begun gradually enough, with Angelique denying him every so often; then it increased, and now they hardly made love at all. But the other thing had happened too. Over the years Angelique had grown more and more bitter toward the Spanish. Irrationally bitter.

Robert paused momentarily in front of a tavern, then pushed the door open and entered the smelly din. It was so dim that Robert guessed a number of lanterns had broken during the recent storm. But it smelled like taverns all over New Orleans. Fish and rum and sweat. The heat and humidity were oppressive. Robert wiped his brow and sank onto one of the wooden benches that flanked a long common table.

At the far end of the table, four Spaniards sat drinking with a silent, sullen dedication. Their unkempt beards were gray and their faces were swarthy and dark. One of them spit on the straw-strewn floor; two of his front teeth were missing and the rest were stained dark from tobacco.

A fat black barmaid waddled over to him and plunked down a tankard of rum drink. Robert paid her and lifted the tin to his mouth, gulping down the mixture of liquor and fruit.

Robert drank in solitude for a time. Gradually the heat seemed to become bearable and the room took on a warm, rosy glow. Then, feeling thoroughly maudlin, Robert staggered forth and headed down the street toward the brothel that was currently in vogue, La Casa Roja. Everyone said it now was the city's finest establishment. Robert swore under his breath. Damned if he was going to sleep on the far side of the bed tonight! He weaved up the steps and tripped. He pulled himself upright and leaned against the door. "Open the door!" his voice pealed out. "Are you in business or not?"

The well-dressed madam opened the door. Robert looked at her with blurry eyes, but nonetheless noted the flicker of recognition in hers. He stood stock still and tried to focus

114

more clearly. It occurred to him that he ought not to have drunk so much.

She was older, much older. But then, so was he. She had been seven years older than he when they first met. She must now be forty-seven, Robert calculated.

The madam didn't say a word, she just grasped a hurricane lamp in one hand and motioned him into the parlor. Robert followed. There was no mistake: Juliet still was tall and straight, her dark hair was handsomely streaked with gray, her skin still was coffee-colored, and her eyes still were golden like a cat's.

"You've had a lot to drink," she observed. Robert searched her face. Her skin was remarkably taut, her mouth had not lost its divine pout.

"Do you remember me?" Robert asked, painfully aware of slurring his words.

"Of course." Juliet caressed him with her cat eyes. Then she said, a trifle defensively in case he misunderstood, "I do not sleep with customers anymore. I own this house. I'm strictly a businesswoman."

"I don't want to sleep with you!" Robert snapped. His suppressed anger toward Angelique suddenly surfaced and vented itself on Juliet.

But Juliet responded only with a shrug that revealed no emotion.

"I'm sorry," Robert apologized.

"For what? For having drunk far too much? I seldom see sober men. For being angry? For trying to use me? It happens all the time." Her cat eyes danced playfully. "All in a night's work," she said with sarcasm. "Follow me." She motioned him toward the winding staircase.

Robert suppressed a belch and followed her up and then along the corridor. Her long golden gown trailed in front of him, and Robert felt he was going to cry. On first seeing her he had felt only nostalgia; now he felt a powerful wave of loneliness sweep over him. Fou Loup was dead, Janet was far away in Canada separated from him by yet another stupid war, Will had gone off with Gálvez, James was off doing something he wasn't even sure he cared to know about, Maria was sullen and unreachable, and now not even Juliet

115

wanted him. Robert felt every one of his forty years and very sorry for himself.

"Here," Juliet said as she opened the door. Robert entered the room. To make matters worse, it was a room much like the one he had shared with Juliet so many years ago. He slumped onto the bed and inhaled. The odor of musk filled his nostrils. He closed his eyes and flung himself face down on the goose-feather mattress.

"You've had a lot to drink and you're much too sorry for yourself to be whoring tonight," Juliet observed. "If you like, I'll send someone in the morning."

Robert lifted his eyes and looked at her. "You seem to know a lot about how I feel."

"A whore is like wet sand," Juliet answered. "A man lies on her and leaves the impression of his body and the shadow of his thoughts." She arched a magnificent eyebrow. "We know you all well."

"I do want you," he slurred. "For old times' sake . . ."

Juliet shook her head. But a coquettish smile crossed her full lips. "Perhaps tomorrow," she replied.

They had made camp nearly an hour ago and the fire was a roaring blaze fed by the rabbit's fat as it turned on the spit. As she always did, Jenna sat quietly, afraid of sending Robbie into one of his mindless rages. But he was at the knife again, grinding it maddeningly against the stone.

He got up and walked over to her. "Tell me again," he said, "the way you did last night."

Wearily, Jenna started to talk, wondering why he never tired of this conversation. The words had lost all meaning for her and she only repeated them nightly to keep him from killing her. As usual, his face grew red while she talked, and his breath became quicker and more uneven. "Take off your clothes," he said hoarsely. Jenna blinked at him. It was the first time since they had been on the barge that he had asked for that.

"All of them?" she questioned.

The knife flicked at her throat. "All of them."

Jenna fumbled with her shirt buttons and took a second too long getting the garment off. The blade was back at her throat. She closed her eyes and slipped out of the breeches. She shivered in the night air. "Sit nice," he hissed. "And sit still."

He lifted his free hand and ran it over her flesh, stroking her slowly as if she were some sort of holy object. "Talk some more," he ordered her. Jenna began speaking again. He was running his hand over her, touching her skin with the flat blade of the knife. Then he removed his hand and opened his own breeches. Jenna tried to look away, but she felt the knife again. "Look at me," he commanded. Jenna's wide eyes looked down. He laid the knife down and continued to stroke her with one hand and himself with the other. "Go on talking," he urged. Rapidly, he brought himself to satisfaction and then ordered her to dress.

Over the next four days, Robbie seemed to relax somewhat and sometimes he even spoke to her decently. For Jenna it was all part of an evil game that she played only to stay alive as she prayed for someone to rescue her. Each night it was carried a step farther, with him having her strike various poses, or fondle him while speaking. She feared that he finally might possess her in some abnormal way, then being finished with her, kill her.

"You got a dress?" he asked on the fifth morning.

"One," Jenna answered.

"We're getting close to Baton Rouge," Robbie announced. "We need supplies."

Jenna glanced at the empty rum skins and thought that what he meant was he needed more liquor. But she held her tongue. She had nurtured the hope that she might be able to get away from him in a town, especially a town that was part of British West Florida.

Robbie turned around. "You better not try anything." His voice was low and his hand fingered the knife sheath. "I'm fast with it," he bragged. "I can have it out of the sheath and into you without a soul seeing, before you even have a chance to scream."

Jenna lifted her green eyes. "Why do you want to keep me?"

Robbie smiled a twisted smile. "You talk nice," he replied.

Jenna turned away and nursed her hope silently. Surely the moment would come. This nightmare could not go on forever.

"Put on the dress now," he ordered. "Can't leave you on the boat and I can't take you into town like that."

Jenna's hand went to her face. She wondered what she looked like. Her skin was pink from the sun and her nose was peeling. She had tried to stay covered up, but it was impossible. Her only bathing had been in pools near the river when they camped.

She opened the pack and searched through it. The dress was on the very bottom and, according to Stephan's instructions, it was a plain and practical dress, one that would not make her conspicuous in frontier communities.

Jenna crawled into the flatboat's shelter and struggled out of her men's clothing and into the dress. When she came out, she unbraided her long red hair and brushed it out, pulling it back and tying it with a single ribbon.

Robbie looked at her and grunted. "Don't forget to be a good girl," he warned. "I don't want to kill you . . . yet."

Tolly Tuckerman looked like a prancing show horse as he lifted his feet gingerly to avoid the muck and dung-strewn streets of Baton Rouge. He moved along ahead of Will as if he were blazing a trail through the heavy bush rather than walking down a village street. The sun had gone down and although it was not yet dark, the persistent insects already were buzzing about.

"Smells worse than Liverpool," he commented as they paused before a tavern. "Might as well have some drink. We can't march ourselves into the garrison at this hour."

"Why not?" Will asked.

" 'Tain't right, mate. Morning's the time; sentries get nervous after dark. We might be all right, but I don't fancy taking chances and ending up fodder for British bullets. Anyway, I fancy a card game."

Will looked around uneasily. "I suppose you're right," he allowed. "Anyway, we ought to discover what popular opinion is, which way the town dwellers feel, and which way they might jump when the fort's attacked."

Tolly shrugged. It was like Will MacLean to be finding

work to do in a place meant for having fun. "I doubt they'll jump at all," Tolly remarked. "Too hot for jumping. Do you think anyone in Baton Rouge cares? Long as no one burns the crops or stops the trade on the river, they won't give a tinker. This isn't Philadelphia, where the friggin' loyalists are so thick you could trip over them on a cloudy day. Everyone who's come out to this godforsaken swamp is too busy fighting insects to be fighting for or against the British." Tolly laughed. "Not much difference. They're all a bunch of bloodsuckers."

Will ignored Tolly's vituperative comments about the British. Will didn't care much for them, but he really didn't care that much either. He simply had chosen to fight with Gálvez and, quite simply, he had a job to do.

"Suppose they have rooms here?" Will surveyed the upper floor of the tavern.

"I suppose they have them somewhere. People coming and going all the time. I also suppose that where there are British soldiers there is rum, and where there is rum there is a card game."

"You're a single-minded bastard, aren't you?" Will said with humor.

"Pleasure before danger," Tolly said and laughed. "I intend to die, if at all, a happy man."

"I'd rather not die just now," Will said as he pushed open the door. He took a quick look around and saw that there were British soldiers. "Caution," Will whispered to Tolly. "And remember to use our cover names. My father is too well known to make a slipup."

Tolly nodded. It was quite true. The name MacLean *was* well known. And the British knew it best, Robert MacLean being the most active gunrunner on the river.

Tolly anxiously stepped into the tavern. "Over there," he said, motioning. Will followed as Tolly positioned himself at a table not far from the British soldiers. "Drink!" he bellowed out. "And a toast to the loyalists!" The British soldiers turned and acknowledged the friendly greeting with a wave of their hands.

Tolly didn't wait a second longer. He rummaged in his pack and withdrew a deck of cards. The tavern keeper brought a tankard of rum and set it down. "Well, pay for it," Tolly said to Will. "I do need my funds, meager as they are." Will shook his head and reached into his pocket, withdrawing the coins.

"A game of chance, my friends!" Tolly gestured toward the British. Two of them came over eagerly. Tolly spread out the deck. "Examine them," he offered. Then he took out a small pile of gold coins and set them in front of himself. "Go forth and multiply," he said, looking at them reverently.

Will leaned back, deciding not to participate. One thing was undeniable: Tolly Tuckerman had a certain flair.

The cards were dealt and the first hand saw the winnings go to one of the British regulars. Tolly remained cheerful and undaunted. Will caressed the coins in his money belt, fully believing that by the end of the evening it would be all they had.

Three more hands were dealt and again the winnings went to the British soldiers. Tolly didn't crack, though he once kicked Will under the table for no understandable reason.

Another hand had just been dealt when two more people entered the tavern. Will looked up and noted with amazement that one was a beautiful young girl—in fact, the most beautiful young woman he had ever laid eyes on. In spite of her dismal dress and her sunburned skin, she was a stunning beauty—and stunning beauties were rare on the frontier. She walked slightly behind but close to her companion. Her eyes seemed to be searching the floor and, for some reason, Will thought she looked distressed, though he could not have explained why. Perhaps it was only wishful thinking, he concluded.

Her companion was blond with sickly skin; red, blotchy, pimply skin. He had pale blue eyes, and Will's first thought was that he looked like nothing so much as a rabbit. But his expression did not have the softness of a rabbit's; it was cruel and Will's sixth sense put him on guard.

It was doubtless Will's concentrated expression that caused the others to turn around and survey the newcomers. Tolly looked up too and for a single instant, Will thought he looked surprised. "I'll be goddamned," he heard Tolly mumble.

Will assumed his friend was remarking on the girl, whose

eyes were still fastened to the floor, seemingly too embarrassed by the blatant stares of the assembled men to look up.

"Join us!" Tolly invited loudly, then added, "Or are you afraid of losing money?"

Robbie met Tolly's challenge with a hard look, but he came to the table and sat down. Then, glancing at Jenna, he pointed to a nearby table and said, "Go sit down over there."

Jenna sat down and folded her hands in front of her. There were British soldiers! But she was uncertain what to do. Should she stand up and denounce Robbie now? What would happen if they laughed at her, ignored her pleas? She shivered. Men in groups terrified her. They might not help. Robbie would simply offer her—they would all make use of her! Jenna fought back her tears. It could be her only chance, or it could be a horrible mistake. All the men were drinking heavily, all of them were young. No, Jenna thought. It was taking too great a chance because they all might turn on her. She decided to sit quietly, to see what kind of men they were, to make some sort of plan. Even if they were friendly, she couldn't put it out of her mind that Robbie might kill her or them.

More drink was brought and five more hands were played, one of which Robbie won while the rest went to Tolly, whose concentration seemed to grow with each deal of the cards. Will found himself stealing glances at Jenna. What was such a woman doing with someone as callous as the strange young man now engaged in the card game with Tolly and the soldiers? She looked like a forlorn doll, soft and fragile. She looked the total opposite of her companion. Yet he had ordered her to sit and she had, without a word of protest, without so much as a glance. Perhaps she was afraid of him. She did look weary, and Will decided she looked frightened too. She looked as if she might need help and did not know how, or was afraid, to ask. On the other hand, he cautioned himself, they might be married and he simply might be imagining everything. With my luck, Will thought, that's exactly the way it is.

"I've had enough!" one of the soldiers announced, standing up. "One more hand and I'll be cleaned out."

Another laughed and stood as well. "Better all pull out,"

he remarked. "We've a big day tomorrow, up at the crack of dawn for inspection."

Tolly's expression registered no change. He had won his money back and a bit more. "Too bad, lads," he said cheerfully. "You'll not cash in too, will you?" His eyes settled on Robbie, who met them unblinkingly, a trickle of rum running from the corner of his mouth.

Jenna looked up. A sense of panic swept through her when one of the soldiers touched her shoulder and squeezed it. "Nice," he slurred drunkenly. Jenna froze. They were so drunk they could hardly stand. What possible use could they be? Almost desperately, she glanced at Will. He looked nice enough. But who could tell by looks? Jenna felt a wave of helplessness sweep over her. Her opportunities were slipping away.

Tolly began dealing again and Robbie sent Jenna's eyes back to the floor with one evil look.

"Ever been in Boston town?" Tolly asked Robbie. The question sounded casual enough.

Will turned away from Jenna momentarily to listen. He had not missed the warning look given to Jenna. It was a quick glimmer in the eyes, a glimmer that made Robbie look almost animal-like.

"No," came Robbie's quick reply.

Tolly laid down his cards. "I think I have you," he said, giving his words some added weight.

"I don't like two-man games," Robbie mumbled. He lifted his drink to his lips and took a long gulp.

"Come and join us," Tolly said, motioning Will over.

Will looked away from Jenna, annoyed that Tolly was pulling him into a game when he knew full well he didn't like to play cards.

"C'mon, Will. I order you to play. The man doesn't like two-player games."

Order? Will thought. Was Tolly trying to tell him something? It was he, not Tolly, who was in charge. Will cursed under his breath and hoped that Tolly had some reason, other than the pure sport of it, for pulling him into this absurd game.

"Come and play with me and my new friend," Tolly slurred drunkenly.

Will looked at Tolly hard. He knew full well that Tolly had not had enough liquor to make him drunk, just as he knew that Tolly never used the word "friend" casually.

Will sat down and watched as Tolly dealt again. Robbie sat poised on the edge of the bench, leaning forward, obviously tense. He picked up the cards one by one.

Will picked his up too. There were two nines, a king, a three, and a seven. Will sighed. He kept the nines and the king and threw the rest away. Tolly dealt him two more cards and Will picked them up. One was a king and the other a nine of diamonds. He stared at the nine of diamonds. Since childhood he had heard that card spoken of as the Scottish Curse. He mumbled under his breath.

The other two men had discarded and received their cards. "I'll raise you two gold pieces," Tolly said confidently. Robbie looked at his cards and ran his tongue around his lips. He put down the three gold pieces.

Will felt like kicking Tolly for making the stakes so high. He seldom played poker, and this was the first time he'd ever had a decent hand, curse or no curse.

Will reached into his own money belt. I'm too good a Scots, he thought. Good hand or no, I really don't want to do this. But he did. Will put down four gold coins and tried to look suitably confident.

Robbie sucked in his lips. "That's it. I don't have any more money!"

Tolly didn't believe him for a moment. "What about the cunt?" he said, gesturing toward Jenna, who looked up, her mouth open and her green eyes wide at the suggestion.

Will stiffened. He had never heard Tolly use such language and he started to say something, but Tolly looked at him harshly. "I don't know you well, but you ought to enjoy her."

Will was all but stupefied into silence. Tolly was one of his oldest friends. Something *was* going on.

"All right, the girl," Robbie said. It wasn't true that he didn't have more gold, it was more that he didn't believe the others had any and he felt he had a winning hand. There was a nice pile of money on the table and he intended to have it all, no matter what outcome the cards dictated. Even though they were two, he calculated the odds and decided he had the advantage. One was stone drunk, the other looked like a country bumpkin. No match for his swift, skillful knife.

Jenna's heart pounded and her mouth still was open. She was too terrified of Robbie to say a word. But what kind of man would play a card game for her? What kind of man would speak of her in such disgusting terms? Her mind darted back to the scene in the woods when Robbie had so casually killed his friends. She sat glued to the chair, knowing that he would kill these two as well.

"Do you accept the girl as a call?" Tolly said, almost sprawling across the table.

Will nodded his head in the affirmative, still wondering what was happening and why. He spread out his cards; he had three nines and a pair of kings. "A full house!" Tolly exclaimed with delight. "I'm bust!"

Robbie's face twisted, but he lay down his cards and stood up.

What happened in the next few seconds happened so quickly that Jenna hardly even saw it. She only saw that Robbie's knife was unsheathed and that he made a move toward Will, who jerked to one side when Tolly tipped the entire table, throwing Robbie slightly off balance.

Tolliver Tuckerman was across the table in one adroit leap. "Watch the knife!" he warned. The razor-sharp edge just caught the sleeve of Will's doublet, but it did not touch his skin. Tolly's own knife was unsheathed and in his hand. He didn't hesitate for one split second. He expertly plunged the long blade into Robbie, sliding it up and under.

Jenna let out a shriek and Robbie's pale blue eyes bulged in their pink sockets as his hand went to the handle of the knife that had pierced him. For a split second he seemed to caress the handle as he had so often caressed his own knife. An evil smile crossed his face and he fell forward, his limbs askew and his mouth open with his last cursing gurgle.

"You killed him," Will said in amazement. He had known Tolly for a long time, and Tolly was not a killer. He would fight when attacked, but he never initiated an attack.

Jenna was totally paralyzed. Her hands covered her mouth and her green eyes seemed fastened on the nauseating sight of Robbie sprawled out across the table.

Somewhere behind them, Jenna was aware of the tavern's owner. He held a musket and looked confused.

"I killed him before he killed us," Tolly said by way of explanation. "And because I knew him."

"Don't move," the tavern owner mumbled. He was used to fights and violence. He had seen what had happened, but he could not see the knife in Robbie's clenched fist.

Tolly smoothed out his rumpled clothing and ran his hand casually through his mop of unruly hair. "He's a killer," Tolly informed Will and the tavern owner. "I knew him in Boston. He knows no side. He kills for money and for pleasure. He's a ripper." The tavern owner dropped his musket some but still looked wary. Tolly grinned. "He's got a price on his head. The British will pay you for his body—so would the Virginians. Feel free to collect it, my friend. I have other business."

All color had drained from Jenna's face. "You're not drunk at all!" she exclaimed.

Tolly grinned at her and, bowing from the waist, kissed her limp hand. "I seldom am." He winked at her. "Of course, I did win you."

"It was I who won her," Will corrected.

"Oh, yes. Quite right. Of course, I wasn't sure you'd want something won with the Scottish Curse. She might prove more trouble than she's worth." Tolly knew his Scottish folklore; the nine of diamonds stretched across the centuries, yet another symbol of the long animosity between clan Macdonald and the Campbells.

Jenna looked from one of them to the other. Their voices were mocking and cheerful. She stomped her foot. "I'm not won or lost in a card game!" Her green eyes flashed and Will burst out laughing.

Jenna's hand clenched the edge of the table and, as Will laughed, she burst into tears. "I'm not to be won! Don't you understand? He was holding me prisoner!" Her words poured out of her mouth amid quick, hysterical sobs and her entire body began to shake.

Will stopped laughing immediately and felt both stupid and foolish. "I'm sorry," he stumbled. But Jenna did not hear him. She was completely hysterical. "And I have no money and I don't even know where I am! And I can't get home! And . . ." Will looked helplessly at Tolly.

Tolly shrugged. "The Scottish Curse," he mumbled. Tolly bent over and quickly searched Robbie's body. He took off the money belt and shook it. "Ill-gotten gains, I'll wager." He handed it to Will. Then he grasped Robbie's shoulders, and the tavern owner, who had laid down his musket, took Robbie's feet.

"Let's put him in the back," the tavern owner suggested. "I'll turn in the body and collect the reward in the morning."

Will's eyes followed them out of the tavern. Jenna still was leaning against the table. She seemed unable to stop crying, but at least she had ceased screaming. He reached out to her. She cringed.

Tolly came back. "There's two rooms at the top of the stairs. It's all arranged. You can do what you want with your winnings. I'm going to bed!"

"Come along," Will said, gently tugging at the sleeve of her dress.

"I'm not going to bed with you!" she screamed. "I'm not a prize to be won! He didn't own me, I was kidnapped!" Her words were almost unintelligible through her sobs.

Will's face went red. How could she actually think he was going to take advantage of her? "Come on," he urged. "Just come on." He pulled on her again, but her fists doubled and she lunged at him, beating his chest and screaming. Exasperated and thoroughly embarrassed, he seized her by her slender waist and tossed her over his shoulder. She kicked, shrieked, and pounded his back with her fists. Tolly had long disappeared. Tolly always disappeared at the wrong time.

Will carried Jenna upstairs and opened the first door he came to. Like all frontier inns, it was furnished only with a bed and a small table. There was a lantern on the table, its candle half gone.

Will dumped Jenna on the bed face down and she immediately turned over, jumped off, and bolted for the door. But Will slammed it and stood in front of it.

"Let me out of here! You let me out of here!" Her face was streaked with tears, and she soon lapsed into unintelligible babble again. But she still was fighting him. She was a hellion, beautiful, high-spirited.

"I can't understand what you're saying!" Will finally shouted back. "You're hysterical!"

"Let me out of here!" She began pounding his chest again and Will, who never had hit a woman, seized her shoulders and began shaking her.

"Stop it!" he ordered in a deep voice. "Stop screaming. I'm not going to hurt you."

Jenna did not stop instantly. Her flailing slowed, then ceased. It was as if she were a tightly wound clock that just had to run down. She sagged in his arms like a rag doll and again began to sob. "You laughed at me. You don't know what I've been through!" She was pressing against him and Will automatically enfolded her in his arms, patting her gently.

"It's all right," he kept saying, "everything will be all right."

Gradually, Jenna relaxed in his arms. Then, after a time, she drew back and looked up at him. He had a warm face, a kind face. "You really won't hurt me?" she questioned, almost childishly.

"Of course not," Will replied instantly. But she was lovely. Lovely in spite of her swollen eyes and peeling nose.

He led her back to the edge of her bed. "Sit down," he requested. "Here, I'll sit over here." He moved away and sat on the floor. "Now, slowly, tell me your name and your story." He paused, then added, "Maybe I can help you."

Jenna sucked in her lower lip and took a deep breath. "My name is Jenna, Jennifer, really. Jenna O'Connell. She began her story in St. Louis and told him about Stephan's murder and how she was kidnapped by Robbie. "He was a lunatic!" she said between soft sobs. She told Will a little about how he threatened her with the knife and, blushing and sobbing and searching for words, a little about what he made her do.

Will listened carefully and tried to piece her story together. He felt deeply ashamed for having teased her earlier and for having laughed at her. But how could he have known about her ordeal? She was certainly not the kind of woman one would expect a person like Robbie to have been with.

127

She was an innocent, a victim of a dreadful sequence of events, events that she seemed to blame on herself.

"It is my fault," Jenna sobbed. "I ran away from home, I went against my father."

Briefly, Will thought about his mother. He had gone against her and he wondered if it would bring him similar luck.

Will handed Jenna Robbie's money belt. "The gold in there is yours," he said. "And I'll have Tolly take you to New Orleans."

Jenna looked stricken. "Can't you come too?"

Will shook his head. "I have important business here. But Tolly is very trustworthy. He wouldn't hurt you either, that I promise you." Will leaned over closer. "You must go to New Orleans," he said intensely. "There's a war on, you know."

Jenna's lips parted. "Spain has joined the war?"

Will nodded. "That's why you have to leave Baton Rouge. I'll find you in New Orleans. I'll get you home somehow."

Jenna reached out and took his hands. "I don't even know your name."

"Will," he answered pausing. No, he thought. I can't tell her my real name. If she was stopped, it might be dangerous for her to know a spy working for Gálvez. He could not take any chance on involving this girl, who already had been through so much. "Will Knowlton," he lied. "You had better get some rest. In the morning we'll make plans for you."

Will stood up and Jenna stretched out on the bed. He covered her with the insect netting and opened the window to let in the cool night air. Beneath the white netting she looked like an angel. Her red hair was fanned out on the pillow and already she had curled up like a child and closed her eyes.

He moved toward the door, and Jenna's eyes opened. "Where are you going?" she asked in a voice that betrayed some panic.

"Just next door," Will replied.

Jenna shivered again. "I'm afraid," she confessed.

Will smiled. "I'll get my bedroll and sleep on the floor beside you, then."

Jenna looked up at him gratefully. "Please," she an-

128

swered, laying her head back down on the pillow. Will retrieved his bedroll from the room where Tolly slept peacefully. Will arranged it on the floor and blew out the candle in the hurricane lamp. Before he closed his eyes, he could hear Jenna's even breathing as she fell into a deep, exhausted sleep.

CHAPTER VIII

September 1, 1779

The room in which Tolliver had slept was identical to Will and Jenna's. It was small, narrow, and airless. Tolly already was up, dressed in clean clothes and washed. His open pack was on the bed, and a small basin of lukewarm water, now gray from having been used, was sitting on the rickety table under the tin mirror.

Tolly looked at Will with some disgust. "I doubt the British will take you in; you look entirely disreputable, my friend." Tolly's penchant for cleanliness even under the most miserable of conditions was well known. He was, even at this moment, combing through his beard. "We haven't all day, you know," he said turning to Will with a wink. "Sleep well?"

"Not the way you mean," Will answered quickly. "I slept on the floor."

Tolly burst into laughter. "I go to all the trouble of finding you a bedwarmer and you sleep on the floor? Gad! You *are* honorable! She must have been a tiny bit grateful!"

"She's not what you think," Will protested. "She's been kidnapped. She's had some terrible experiences."

Tolly raised an eyebrow. Either the girl was a fast talker and Will was taken in, or her story might be true. Certainly Robbie was capable of anything.

"We hardly have time for her terrible experiences," Tolly reminded Will. "We have work to do."

They had made their plan on the way to Baton Rouge. It involved simply going to the British garrison to volunteer bogus information regarding Spanish troop movements. Posing as good loyalists, they would volunteer to stay and

130

fight. Real loyalists certainly would do just as they intended doing, but when Will and Tolly left the garrison, they intended to take with them plans of the fort and knowledge of the location of its defenses and the exact number of troops defending it. "You are a good team," Gálvez had praised them. "And you will fall under less suspicion because Tolly is British by birth and you speak English well."

Will stared at the back of Tolly's neck. He was leaning forward, toward the tin mirror. "We can't leave her here alone and we can't risk coming back for her. She has to leave Baton Rouge now, and one of us has to take her downriver."

Tolly whipped around. "I suppose you told her who you were? You know, she could be a spy herself. I didn't like the company she was with last night."

"I didn't tell her my real name and she hasn't got the slightest idea why we're here. Good God, she didn't even know Spain had entered the war. Listen, Tolly, I believe her."

"Well, believe her or not, we both have other things to do."

Will stood up. "We both don't have to go. I can go alone and you can take her downriver."

Tolly scowled. "And why don't *you* take her downriver?"

"Because I'm in command. Remember?" Will scowled back at Tolly.

"You'll get your head blown off without me—I never thought you of all people would pull rank!"

"I want to get that girl safely to New Orleans!" Will felt a wave of guilt pass over him. Jenna's safety had become as important to him as his assignment, and Tolly certainly could read that in his face and hear it in his tone.

"And even if I do agree to take her, what will I do with her when I get there? New Orleans is not exactly a sanctuary for *nice* young ladies who are unmarried and alone."

"She has the money—find her a place to stay," Will answered with irritation.

"It's not a matter of money," Tolly replied in an annoyed tone. "Escorting some helpless female is not my assignment."

"Well, I am reassigning you!" Will said with finality. Tolly mumbled a curse. "And is that an order?"

"It's an order."

Jenna stared into the muddy brown river. She felt she had spent half her life on rivers. I'm being carried with the current, she thought apprehensively. Then the flatboat made a turn around one of a hundred bends, and the jetty no longer was visible and neither was Will, who had watched till the flatboat was out of sight.

Jenna turned to Tolliver Tuckerman. He was a strange-looking and -acting man. He was tall and skeletal with a carefully combed beard. His chest and hips appeared to be exactly the same size; he was what some might call a bean-pole.

Jenna thought about the one called Will. He was quite the opposite. He was tall too, but broad-chested like her own father, and his arms were muscular and strong.

Tolliver Tuckerman did, however, have twinkling blue eyes that always seemed to be laughing in spite of the haughty tone his voice often had. He seemed to be a highly intelligent man, Jenna thought, and even his sarcastic disdain for the world around him did not make him unpleasant.

"You're angry, aren't you?" Jenna asked.

Tolly arched a dark eyebrow at her. "Oh, why would I be angry? Simply because I have been ordered to alter my life in order to look after a slip of a girl who's gotten herself into trouble? Come, come now."

"Ordered?" Jenna said in surprise.

"Ordered," Tolly repeated. There was no need to keep it from her now. Baton Rouge was behind them, New Orleans ahead. "It is a strange and unjust set of circumstances that caused me to volunteer to fight in the first place," he sighed, "and an even stranger set that placed a younger man above me in the chain of command."

Jenna's eyes widened. "Fight?" she asked incredulously. "Fight whom?"

"My dear, I am with the expeditionary force of General Bernardo Gálvez, and so is dear Will. We were on an important mission before encountering you. Now Will is alone on an important, and I might add, dangerous mission, and I have become a nursemaid. A cruel twist of fate.''

Jenna's mouth opened in surprise. "Fight the British?" Her face clouded over. "But what will happen to me? You are taking me to New Orleans, and I am from Canada. I'm a loyalist!"

Tolly broke into laughter. "And a woman," he said disdainfully. "You're not, nor will you become, a prisoner of war. Dear me, no. There are dozens—God knows maybe hundreds—of loyalist refugees in New Orleans. You have no idea how lenient the Spanish are!"

It must be like Quebec, Jenna thought to herself. Loyalists and supporters of the rebellion living side by side and the British not doing much about it. She sighed. Her uncle was living under Spanish rule, and the Spanish were at war with the British. Perhaps he too supported the Spanish.

Tolly was looking at her in amusement. "Besides, a beautiful woman has nothing to fear. They make the best spies. Are you a spy?"

"Of course not!" Jenna replied instantly and with some indignation. "I don't even understand this rebellion or war or revolution or whatever it is!"

"It's a rebellion," Tolly answered. "It won't be a revolution till it succeeds. And I can believe you know nothing about it."

"Is Will in any danger?" Jenna asked as a frown clouded her face.

"As much danger as any man spying. If he's caught, the British will hang him; if he succeeds, he could be killed in battle. Gálvez doesn't have that many men, and we don't know the British strength."

Jenna folded her arms around her. "I hate war," she murmured.

"It does rather interfere with one's social life, doesn't it?" Tolly answered scornfully.

"That's not what I meant," Jenna snapped. "I'm not the silly child you seem to think I am. I just meant that I've never really known peace. We had to leave our home in the Niagara because of the Indian wars and because the British gave the land to the Indians. And before that there was a war and now this—this rebellion."

133

Tolly shrugged. "You don't exactly sound committed to either side."

"I'm not," Jenna answered. "I just want to go home!"

"You should have thought of that before you left."

Jenna forced herself not to reply. Her mind was filled with confusion. Her eyes traveled the shore, which seemed to be peaceful enough. Was war really going to come to this wilderness? Jenna suddenly felt defeated, alone, and miserable again. She had just met Will and now she probably would never see him again.

"I hope Will is safe," Jenna said finally in a voice that was hardly audible.

Tolly looked at her, bemused. "I suppose there's some hope for you. Perhaps, under my careful tutelage, you might grow up."

Jenna scowled at him. "I am grown up!"

At that Tolly laughed. "You have the looks of a butterfly, the consistency of a firefly, and the good sense of a moth. Given a bright enough light, you'd fly right into it. I am afraid you are far from grown up!"

Robert had only just awakened when the door of the bed chamber opened and Juliet came in carrying a tray.

"You do look better than last night," she said, putting it down.

Robert propped himself up in the bed and rubbed his eyes. He was aware of being thirsty and of a dull ache at the back of his head.

"I've brought you some tea and bread," Juliet said with a smile.

Robert's eyes caressed her, but he made no move to get out of bed. She looked even lovelier than she had last night. She's incredibly well preserved, he thought with admiration.

"You look wonderful," he commented. Her long, dark hair was pulled back and tied behind her head. Even streaked with gray, it was rich and full. Her golden cat eyes looked at him and danced with a hundred secrets. Her skin was as golden as ever.

"I thought you didn't look after your customers yourself," he commented.

Juliet shrugged. "You're an old friend too, the only one of my customers ever to propose marriage. I suppose I have a soft spot for you."

Robert stretched and stood up. He walked over to the little table and sat down. The tea looked inviting. "Will you join me?"

"I brought two cups," she said, smiling. Juliet sat down and Robert could smell her perfume from across the table. Like the room itself, she smelled of musk and, he had to admit, the years had made her no less erotic and no less desirable.

"What brings you to New Orleans?" she asked. "I've heard you were doing well upriver."

"Do you know everything?"

"One who entertains the Spanish and the traders knows almost everything," she admitted. "I have an important, if not elite clientele."

"I wanted to see my son before he . . ."

"Went to join Gálvez," she finished his sentence. Then she added, "He's already gone. Is that what drove you to excessive drinking?"

Robert shook his head. "No," he answered without elaboration.

Juliet lifted the teacup to her lips. "Tell me about it," she requested.

Robert had already drained his cup and refilled it from the pot. His head ached less now and the tea calmed his churning stomach. He shook his head, searching for words. "My life is in disarray," he finally managed. "One of my sons is sullen and, I think, selfish. My daughter is a stranger to me and my wife . . . I loved my wife . . . she's grown cold and distant." He shook his head again. "I don't understand, because life was good for so long."

"It's the river," Juliet said mysteriously. Her golden eyes glowed as she looked into Robert's face.

"I don't understand."

"Winter winds cleanse, so you can begin again in spring," Juliet said with a faraway look in her eyes. "But it's always the same on the river. There's disease. They say it eats at the brain slowly until the weak succumb to it."

Robert knew that Juliet was speaking both in symbols and

in realistic terms. The death toll from river fever was indeed horrendous, and it was true that it could affect the mind. Juliet also was talking about a kind of rot of the soul, something the river symbolized to her. A wave of guilt passed over him. Perhaps Angelique was not well, perhaps the change in her did have something to do with a physical illness. Perhaps Maria had it too. But James was strong and healthy and he was strong and healthy, and so was Will.

"Good spirits can leave you," Juliet said with meaning. "They can desert you." He watched her eyes and again he understood. Juliet was a Creole and she clung to the beliefs of her people, beliefs that like the inhabitants of the Delta were mixed. A little voodoo from Haiti, Catholicism from the French and Spanish, incantations and a deep belief in the spirit world saved from Africa.

"Has my good spirit left?" Robert asked. "Is my protective spirit elsewhere?"

Juliet shook her head. "It hasn't left you," she replied. "Your aura still is strength. But you need a new challenge." Then, suddenly, she smiled. "I think your spirit is only bored."

Robert stood up and walked behind her chair. He placed his hands on her bare shoulders and ran his fingers up and down her swanlike neck. "Are you determined not to sleep with your customers?" he asked, toying with her delicate ear.

"Yes," she replied. "But I might sleep with a friend."

Robert bent over and kissed her neck. Her flesh was cool to his lips and as delicious as he remembered. He lifted her into his arms and carried her to the bed, laying her down gently.

"Do you still remember to do it slowly?" Juliet asked, touching him as he slipped away her gown and admired her fine body.

Robert rested his face on the smooth flesh of her flat belly. "I shall make you cry for me," he said, speaking the words that he knew she wanted to hear.

His hands moved over her, at times hardly seeming to touch her, at times applying a pressure that made her groan with pleasure and twist in his arms, seeking more of him.

"You are as fine a lover as I have ever known," she admitted in a low, throaty voice. Robert gently rolled her over and stroked her rounded buttocks, leaning over to plant kisses on them. He lifted her upward and, massaging her with one hand, entered her from behind while she moaned in pleasure and swayed before his eyes in rhythm to some unheard song. He was transfixed by her experienced movements and the hue of her skin; he felt carried to some unknown place. Then together they climbed toward that upward sweep of passion, those long moments of holding back till neither could hold back longer. Then together they reached the summit, the height of pure sensation.

In the hours that followed, Robert held Juliet in his arms and began to understand. With Juliet he had found the physical pleasure he had so long missed, but he did love Angelique. There was no erasing their years together, no running away from the memories they shared. Love, Robert reflected, was not what he had always thought it to be. It was something beyond the physical joy and exhilaration he felt with Juliet. It was something that had crept over him and possessed him. And even as he held Juliet, he longed to be with Angelique; he longed to make his peace with her.

Janet twisted her handkerchief into tiny, precise coils even as she stared out into the garden. Everything had been brought in and stored for the winter months. Her mind was on Niagara. This little plot of land in the courtyard behind the house in Montreal was laughable when compared to the rich fields they once had harvested near the fort. "I can't imagine it," she said to Mathew. "I can't imagine those fields not having sufficient food!"

Mathew put the dispatches down. "Even with the farm annexes near the fort, how can so many people be fed?"

"They can't," Janet answered. The area around Fort Niagara was bulging with loyalist refugees and with loyal Onondagas, Cayugas, and Senecas who had fled there.

"You're not really thinking about the food, are you?" Mathew asked.

Janet shook her head. "Of course not. I'm thinking about Andrew." She shivered. Andrew was at Fort Niagara, he was with Butler's Rangers, and she knew he already had seen battle; horrible battle, that special warfare used by the

Indians and encouraged by leaders on all sides, men Janet considered beneath contempt, regardless of belief or loyalties.

"I couldn't stand it if anything happened to Andrew," Janet said in a small, faraway voice. It was unthinkable; but they both had thought it and now, more than ever, he was in jeopardy. The dispatches that Mathew held combined intelligence reports with the latest correspondence from the mysterious Monk. New offenses were being prepared by the Continentals against Niagara.

It was known that the French were preparing a fleet of frigates off Newport in the colony of Rhode Island. And for a time proclamations had appeared on every church door in Quebec—THROW OFF THE TYRANT'S YOKE! they urged. But the French Canadians did not respond. They trusted the Continental Army less than the British and were uneasy at the thought that the Continentalists might have made a deal with the French to return Quebec to France. They had no desire to return to French feudalism.

Continental troops already had invaded Oswego, and a fleet of *bateaux*—special barges for river transport—were being prepared under Colonel Goose Van Schaick, among others. Van Schaick was known to be a terrible creature, notorious for his wanton massacres of helpless Indian women and children. And Van Schaick did not lead the only Continental militia on the move. Sullivan's men were coming up the Susquehanna River, General Brodhead was coming from Fort Pitt, and George Rogers Clark was headed toward Fort Detroit.

"Niagara has quite a reputation," Mathew joked. "They must think it quite well protected to attack with so many forces from so many different directions. They seem to be trying to catch the British between the pincers."

"And our only son is there! Mathew, it frightens me!"

"Fear's not unhealthy; it's an emotion bred into us by experience. But remember, Andrew knows every inch of the Niagara. He has friends among the Indians."

Janet knelt beside Mathew and buried her head in his lap. "I want it to end, I want to go home to a Niagara that is peaceful. I want to feel the spray of Thundergate on my face

138

and hear the rush of the river from my own house. I want my grandchildren around me. Oh, Mathew, I'm tired. I want an end to war." He stroked her hair but didn't offer any comforting words. The situation was far too serious.

Major André had moved his headquarters from New York to the British warship the *Vulture.* It maneuvered the Hudson River, often dropping anchor off Teller's Point. This mobile headquarters made it easier to move about—to drop anchor in dense fogs, to dispatch messengers and spies ashore. Moreover, the *Vulture* was an admirably outfitted vessel. It had reasonably large rooms, tasteful silver fittings, and even crystal chandeliers.

"A deceptive home away from home," Major André said as he paced the long room, staring at the fine carpet.

"It suits you," Tom Bolton replied. He had made his rendezvous with the *Vulture* some hours ago, but André had insisted on serving him dinner before they settled down to exchange information. "I have the latest dispatches from Monk." Tom withdrew a leather case from inside his waistcoat. It was a flat buckskin case, ideal for carrying papers but flexible enough to rest snugly against the body.

André spread the documents out on the desk and studied them, shaking his head. They contained more information on the pincers launched against Niagara.

Tom Bolton watched André carefully. André obviously was pleased to have yet more details, but he was agitated as well.

"Are you troubled, sir?"

"Not by this," André said, setting down the document he held in his hand. "The news is hardly pleasing, of course. But actually, I'm upset about you."

Tom looked up and André stopped pacing in front of him. "Have I done something wrong, sir?"

André sighed. "Not at all. You have performed every task to perfection. Indeed, that's the problem."

"I don't understand, sir."

André's face was knit in a deep frown. "I have reason to believe that the rebels are suspicious of your activities. I'm sorely afraid that your usefulness may be at an end." He paused before saying, ''More than that, I have reason to believe that if I don't send you away, you may jeopardize the safety of both Peggy and Monk.''

André's conclusions were not a total surprise to Tom. He had been a courier for months and one could only last so long before suspicion was cast and accusations made.

''Is Peggy in any danger now, or, uh, Monk?'' They both played the game of always referring to General Arnold by his self-given code name. But Tom thought it rather silly to use the code, especially when both he and André were safely aboard the *Vulture* and among his trusted allies.

André shook his head. ''No problems there,'' he said confidently. ''The court-martial has ironically diverted any possible suspicion from Monk.''

It was true, Tom thought. The stupid charges, which all had to do with money, had enveloped General Arnold. The good patriots of Philadelphia were more concerned with fraud than with treason. And, of course, Arnold would be cleared. If Washington rebuked him at all for becoming involved in private investments, it would be mild in the extreme. Washington's reputation being what it was, he couldn't afford too much public self-righteousness about money.

''And I doubt,'' André added, ''that Peggy ever will be in any danger. Washington and Hamilton melt in front of her. The one stumbles over the other just to kiss her hand.''

Tom smiled. ''You would stumble to kiss Peggy's hand too, if you were married to Martha Washington.''

André laughed. ''Very definitely a woman without class. Yes,'' André observed, ''I'd say the charges aganst Monk have acted as a fine front for his other activities. You know how people think: If a man is distracted and needs money, he obviously has nothing more important to think about.''

''Trumped-up charges in any case,'' Tom muttered. ''Only brought because he married a loyalist.''

André shook his head. ''God help us if they succeed in this miserable rebellion. God help the people who survive! They put a man in charge of running an entire city and they condemn him for living a decent life and marrying the most important woman in town. It's those wretched New Englanders and their ethics of poverty. They think it's a sin to make money and a sin to spend it. Good Lord, they've all been infected by Franklin's little morality books—except, of course, Franklin's rich enough. Probably the richest man in the colonies. Wish to God they could see how their penny-saved-is-a-penny-earned man lives in Paris! High on the proverbial French hog, I can tell you."

Tom smiled. André was honest. He was a man who liked fine clothes, fine food, good literature, and good theater. He was a man who relished the elegant life of upper-class Philadelphia, a man who perished aboard the *Vulture* and was no more comfortable in the British outposts of New York. If André hated the rebels for any one reason, it was for ruining his entertainments. André was infuriated with the hypocrisy of the writing produced by the rebellion.

"Why do they all keep talking about the common man and equality?" he railed. "Every one of them comes right out of a homegrown aristocracy! Well, no matter. Your time on this run is over and we have to get you away from Philadelphia and out of colonial territory, lest you end up on the end of a Continental rebel rope."

"What do you have in mind?" Tom asked.

"I have in mind sending you to Montreal. I want you to coordinate intelligence reports with our forces in Canada. You'll like it; it's a hotbed of activity, not unlike Philadelphia, but firmly in British hands." André tapped his fingers on the desk. "There are a lot of supporters of the rebellion, merchants mostly. The time has come to root them out, I'm afraid."

"And the French?" Tom asked.

"Neutral for the most part. They consider this something of a family struggle, none of their business."

"When do I leave, sir?"

"Tonight," André answered. "It's all been arranged. You'll be going with about fifty men, all regulars. When you get up to Montreal you are to report to Lieutenant Fitzgibbon. You'll be carrying some special documents on fortifications currently held by the rebels. Fitzgibbon has a consultant working with him—talented chap, an engineer. He's been at Niagara, and being an engineer, he visited many of the forts in British North America. He's a Scots.

141

Name eludes me, but Fitzgibbon will put you on to him."

"Thank you, sir."

André extended his hand to Tom. "Thank you," he replied. "I'll keep you informed about Monk and, of course, about Peggy."

Tom stood up.

"Let's have a brandy to toast your new assignment," André suggested, heading for the liquor cabinet behind his desk. "I wouldn't want to send a man off to face the Canadian winter without a drink."

André was pouring the drinks from a silver flask. "Oh, I remember his name." He interrupted his activity. "Macleod, that's it. Mathew Macleod."

Tom took the glass that Major André handed him. "Macleod," he repeated. "I'll remember that."

Maria MacLean stood in the waist-high grass and looked up at the twisted limbs of the ancient cypress tree. From its strongest branch, some eight feet off the ground, a piece of rope still dangled, its fibers hanging loose and blowing in the gentle southern breeze. Only a few weeks ago the rope had been strong and new. It had hung in a noose till it was tightened around the neck of Belle's brother. The crowd had cheered. Black men who bothered little girls were punished. Severely punished.

In her mind, Maria could still see Belle's brother swinging from the limb; she could still hear his cries, screams, and protestations that he was innocent.

She remembered seeing Mama and Papa La Jeunesse too. Their expressions had been hate-filled and it was clear that they believed their son. Nonetheless, they had no say and after the hanging, the crowd of angry settlers had driven them off their land. Their bundles of household goods had been piled on an old cart and tugged off by a half-dead horse. They had gone away fearing more reprisals.

"Freemen," Maria mumbled under her breath. "None of them ought to be free." Maria smiled. The Virginians were sure to win this rebellion and when they did, all the Negroes would be slaves. She sat down on the ground and idly picked a long piece of grass and put it in her mouth. It was sweet down near the stem where it was pulled out of the shoot. But her eyes remained fixed on the tree.

Mama was wrong to give the Negroes things. Maria's mind wandered back in time. She couldn't remember how old she was when Mama had given her clothes to a Negro family. "These are old clothes," Angelique had explained. "They don't fit you anymore." Maria had protested, she had been especially upset about the white dress Mama had given away. Papa should not have freed those slaves because after he did there was too much work to do. Papa said no man should be a slave, and Mama said the Bible said it was wrong.

"Well, it's not wrong!" Maria said aloud. "And someday the free slaves all will be slaves again!"

Maria's eyes wandered over toward Belle's cabin. Mama and Papa La Jeunesse had not taken Belle; they had left her for James. They left her because they blamed her for what had happened to her brother and because James had threatened them. "I'll get rid of you too," Maria promised as she thought of Belle.

"Maria!"

Maria stood up. "I knew you'd be here," James said.

"Been with old Belle?" Maria said meanly.

"That's none of your business. C'mon, we have to go home. It's not fair to leave Mama all the work."

Sullenly, Maria mounted her mare. "Mama wouldn't have all the work if we had slaves and if Papa hadn't left her to go down to New Orleans."

"He'll be back," James said flatly.

Maria turned her mare and they rode off. She tried to puzzle things out. For some weeks she had been preoccupied with James and Belle and Belle's brother. It had been her single-minded desire to get rid of the La Jeunesses.

Poor Mama, she had been so upset when Maria had told her about being attacked. She cried and cried, fretted and talked about her "little girl." She had mumbled then about Papa being away at times of crisis and she had praised James for handling the situation manfully. Mama still didn't hate blacks, though. But she was glad when they caught Belle's brother, saying, "Now you'll be safe."

Maria pensively biting her lower lip turned to James. "You could lay claim to the La Jeunesse land. You could lay claim to it for me, say it's compensation for what he did to me."

"Nothing happened," James answered. He was almost afraid to look into his sister's face. She had lied and he knew it, but she had stunned him by sticking to it, by telling the story over and over to all the neighbors. Now it was as if it had really happened, it was as if Maria believed it were true.

"It's rich land," Maria said. "It's near the river and it's rich land. You know, when Papa dies and Mama dies, our land is going to be divided. Will is sure to get half. But if we had the La Jeunesse land, we'd have more." Her voice had grown thoughtful and James knew she had a plan.

"More land's more work," James said irritably.

"Not if you have slaves," Maria answered quickly. A smile crossed her dark little face. "I'd like a proper house like the houses in New Orleans. I'd like over a hundred slaves."

"Papa doesn't approve of slavery," James reminded her.

"Papa's fighting for the Virginians and they believe in slavery. Anyway, Papa's not going to live forever!"

"Don't talk like that!" James rebuked his sister.

"Why not? If Papa finds out about you and Belle, you won't even get half the land. Will will get it all! You know Will is Papa's favorite." Maria paused. "But you're Mama's favorite."

James couldn't even look at her. Her words burned through him and he didn't bother to deny her accusations. Will was Papa's favorite; it was Will Papa took fishing and hunting; it was Will who always got the praise. Even Mama said they were alike.

"Papa's left Mama and who knows when he'll come back." You apply for the La Jeunesse land, James. You do it."

They were approaching the sprawling cabin now and from the knoll they could see the river winding its way southward. "The governor will cede it to you," Maria pressed. "It has to be you, James, 'cause women can't own anything."

James didn't answer her, though he knew he would do it.

He would do it because she would plague him if he didn't. Just turned fifteen, he thought. Maria frightened him.

"You children! You children come down here!"

James squinted his eyes and saw that the voice calling them came from the front door of the cabin. But it was not their mother who called them. It was the conjure lady.

"Where have you been?" she scolded. "I've sent everyone hereabouts looking for you two!"

Maria looked at the conjure lady in disgust. Her clothes were a sight. She was dressed head to foot in a tattered and torn collection of rags. But James wore an expression of concern. It was not usual for the conjure lady to leave her own lair unless she was fetched, and she wasn't fetched unless someone was sick.

"Why are you here? Where's Mama?"

"Your mama's inside. She's got a bad fever, she's real sick."

James brushed the old woman aside and went into the cabin. In her bedroom he found his mother, lying on the bed, covered only with a light sheet.

James took his mother's hand and held it; it was unnaturally warm and her skin glowed. Against the pillow, Angelique's dark hair was damp and stringy and when she opened her eyes, they rolled slightly backward as if she could not control them.

"Mama!"

Angelique's mouth formed his name, even as her fingers curled around his hand and dug into his flesh with a sense of urgency. "Mama, can you hear me?"

Angelique nodded her head. "Go for Papa," she gasped. There were tears forming in her eyes and she could hardly speak. "You're my good boy, go for Papa in New Orleans and bring him home to me." Angelique's dark eyes seemed to search his face. "Please," she begged. "Go now, go as soon as you can."

James nodded. "I'll go," he promised. He got up quickly and returned to the front room where Maria and the conjure lady waited.

"How did this happen?" James questioned. "She seemed all right this morning."

"She came and got some medicine from me near a week

145

ago, been taking medicine for a couple of years now." The conjure lady shook her head. "She collapsed this morning after you left. Old Jake found her. She's got some eating disease, something that eats at her from the inside out. She's got big bumps under her skin, they're hot like they're alive. I give her what I can."

"I have to go for Papa," James announced. The conjure lady shook her head. "I don't think you have much time."

A chill ran through James' entire body. The conjure lady's words had a finality about them. Again he found himself afraid to look at his sister, who had only just been discussing the death of a parent. Somehow he knew her expression would be hard set. She was unnatural, uncaring.

"You take care of Mama," James advised the conjure lady.

The old woman nodded her head in agreement. "I'll stay, but you make that trip as fast as you can."

CHAPTER IX

September 18, 1779

Will stopped alongside the babbling stream and sat down momentarily to catch his breath. He lay down on his stomach and splashed water on his face. He was perspiring heavily, having maintained a brisk pace since sunup. The back of his shirt was soaked with sweat and his hair hung damp and limp over his sunburned forehead. The cool water momentarily refreshed his senses, but he thought, I really can smell myself. I need about an hour in the water, right up to my neck.

It was, Will reckoned, five or six miles to his rendezvous with Gálvez. He had not been followed; indeed, it was all much simpler than either he or Tolly had imagined.

The British garrison was in a state of mass confusion. Gálvez had defeated the smaller garrison at Manchac and when Will had arrived, a steady stream of refugees, both civilian loyalists and British troops from scattered outposts, were straggling into Baton Rouge.

For some six weeks the British had been hastily erecting fortifications, but they were badly built fortifications that would not withstand a good storm, let alone cannon. Behind the walls of the garrison the British had no more than 400 regulars, a mere 150 Loyalist settlers, and a few terrified and armed blacks who had been promised their freedom. Will smiled to himself. Now there were only 149 settlers since he had been counted among them, and he had fled before dawn.

There was no question about it. Gálvez had more cannon and by this time must have gathered 1200 men. Moreover, the British were isolated. They could not bring up forces from Mobile because the Spanish now controlled the river, and the overland march around the lakes and the Gulf Coast would have taken too much time and too great a toll on the troops, who were unused to the country and fell ill easily. This battle, Will thought, would end any and all British threat to the river. The Spanish would control the Mississippi completely and without fear.

Refreshed, Will stood up and dried his face on his sleeve. He plodded on, anxious to tell Gálvez that victory almost seemed assured. Baton Rouge would be his!

Within two hours, Will met the main force. They reached the garrison at Baton Rouge on the morning of September 21 without detection and by midmorning had begun to attack with cannon.

The garrison was totally surrounded and the acrid cannon smoke mingled with the dense humidity. It was as if the swamps and shallow lakes were smoldering too. The fortifications were made of dry softwood and they burned easily. The British, distracted by putting out fires, were unable to return cannon fire blast for blast. By midafternoon the white flag of surrender fluttered over the British fort and a happy cheer went up from Gálvez' mixed army.

The British commander ushered Gálvez, Panis, and Will into his quarters. "You have won this round," he admitted, and it was obvious that he was glad it was over.

He ushered them to chairs and slumped down himself behind a table. "Let's drink to your victory," he offered. "And to my being out of this hellish rebellion." Wearily, the man leaned over and pulled a tray toward them. Panis' dark eyes sparkled; the Spaniard was fond of his rum.

The British commander poured. "To tell you the truth, I've never thought this part of the continent was worth defending," he admitted. "Too much fever."

Gálvez smiled and accepted his drink. "And this surrender also will include the garrison at Natchez," Gálvez pressed.

"There's no choice," the man confessed. "Give me the documents and I'll sign them." He smiled weakly. "The

148

garrison at Natchez has less than fifty men; they're cut off from supplies as well as from command.''

Will smiled. That would make his father happy. The removal of the garrison cleared the river completely for the gunrunners who would transship more powder to George Rogers Clark and his men. That left only the occasional sniping of the Chickasaw, who were mainly concerned with the Choctaw and some of the odd Tories who inhabited the area. But the British regulars would be gone and with them the threat to Vidalia. The river is ours! Will thought.

Gálvez slapped Will across the back when the negotiations for surrender were completed and they were out of British quarters. ''Pollock has a case of Caribbean rum waiting,'' he whispered. ''Much better than English rum.''

''This was nothing like we anticipated,'' Will observed.

''Not as difficult as our next objective.''

''Mobile,'' Will guessed.

Gálvez scratched his glistening black beard. ''Mobile indeed!'' He paused. ''But we'll have to go back to New Orleans first. I have need of fresh troops and for Mobile we'll need ships. Perhaps from Havana.''

Jenna and Tolly would be in New Orleans, Will thought. He could hardly wait to see her. He had found himself thinking about her constantly on his trek back to Gálvez from Baton Rouge.

Gálvez leaned over toward Will. ''You've done a fine job,'' he praised. ''I don't want you to go back to New Orleans. I want you to go to Havana with Estevan Miró and be my personal ambassador to Don Diego José Navarro, the captain general there.''

''Not go to New Orleans?'' Will repeated dumbly. Gálvez fingered his beard abstractedly. ''There's no time. The British will try to reinforce Mobile as soon as they possibly can. We must back one easy victory with a victory we deserve to win. I need you in Havana now.''

Will shook his head in reluctant agreement. Jenna would have to wait.

''Well, come along!'' Tolly looked back at Jenna with irritation.

"Where are we going?" she questioned.

"My dear little girl, have you ever been in New Orleans before?"

"No, but . . ."

" 'But' nothing; if you have not been here, my telling you where we are going is a total waste of time. You will take note only of where you have been. Where you are going is my problem."

"We have been walking for a long time," Jenna complained as she lifted her skirt to cross the muddy street.

"It's not much farther." As Tolly led her down a winding street Jenna gaped at everything.

"Have you been in the wilderness so long that you have forgotten what civilization looks like?"

"I suppose I have," Jenna conceded. New Orleans did not look as she expected it would, though, in all honesty, she had not known quite what to expect. The streets were filled with people whose skin was dark and who dressed colorfully, combining bright reds with orange and green with blue. The women wore kerchiefs on their heads, but not the way women in Quebec did. They did not tie them under their chins, but wrapped their hair into them and tied them over their foreheads, turban-style. And they did not carry their produce in baskets, but rather wrapped them in cloth and balanced them on their heads.

"Why are you so wide-eyed?" Tolly asked.

Jenna leaned over and whispered in his ear. "I've never seen black people before," she confided. "I didn't realize that people came in so many colors."

It was such a naïve statement that Tolly laughed. But he also wondered how it would be to see New Orleans through Jenna's eyes. Certainly she would have seen Indians before, but he could see why the racial variety in the streets of New Orleans must be baffling to her.

Jenna smiled as they passed another group of street musicians: young boys beating out a strange and haunting rhythm with reed sticks. And the smell of fish was overpowering!

On the street they had turned down, the houses were flush with the road, as they were so often in Montreal. But the houses were not flagstone. Rather, they were white and yel-

150

lowish brown sandstone and sometimes even pinkish in hue. Each had a tiny balcony that seemed to join the balcony of the adjoining house. Indeed, all the houses were connected in the French style.

On some of the balconies, women sat on low benches and looked down on the street below. The women all appeared to be overdressed for a warm afternoon and their faces were made up and some even wore powdered wigs and artificial beauty marks. Jenna was puzzled.

Tolly stopped in front of a door. "We have arrived," he announced flatly. "You need not look so puzzled. This is the finest whorehouse in New Orleans."

"Whorehouse!" Jenna exclaimed. "Why have you brought me to such a place?"

"Because, my dear, I am not in such high society that I can introduce you to the upper class of New Orleans —people who might offer you shelter. And I trust you realize that this is not Boston or Philadelphia, or even Montreal, for that matter. There are no suitable inns in New Orleans, no hostelries where a young woman might remain on her own. What exists is filled with raucous, deprived soldiers who would really give you a most difficult time."

Jenna's mouth opened. "But I cannot stay here!"

"You can and will. Please be quiet now and try to act as if you had a modicum of breeding. I should not like you insulting the fine lady who owns this establishment."

Tolly knocked on the door, which was soon opened by a statuesque woman of indeterminate age. Her skin was a warm coffee hue, her eyes a remarkable gold color.

"Ah, Tolliver Tuckerman." Her voice had a husky, sensuous quality.

Tolly bent gallantly and took her hand, kissing it. "My dear Juliet!"

Juliet eyed Jenna with her cat eyes, allowing them to travel slowly from the top of Jenna's head to the bottom of her toes. "What have you brought me?"

Tolly pulled Jenna inside and Juliet closed the door. "First," he said with some enthusiasm, "I think we could do with some tea."

Juliet laughed enchantingly. "But of course." She summoned a small black girl in a patois Jenna could not understand and, Jenna assumed, ordered the tea.

"Do sit down," Juliet invited, leading them into the parlor. "Ah, Tolly. It is wonderful to see you. I thought you had gone off with our gallant General Gálvez like most of the other interesting men in New Orleans."

The little girl, whose hair was patterned into a hundred braids, returned with an ornate tray and set it down before Juliet, who poured it into delicate china cups and passed one to Jenna and one to Tolly.

"I should be with Gálvez," Tolly replied, "but one of my young friends had an adventure that brings me here instead."

Juliet sighed. "You may be able to rejoin them soon. I understand they are all on the way back."

"What's the news?" Tolly pressed. Juliet was the finest source of information in all New Orleans. She received messages from upriver almost before they were given to the Spanish authorities.

"The news is that Baton Rouge was easily taken. You see, you were not missed at all."

Tolly smiled. "I must ask you a favor, but naturally, you will be paid."

Juliet glanced at Jenna. She was quite a pretty girl and redheads were always at a premium.

"I want you to take this girl in. She is quite alone and cannot travel home now; she must have a place to stay."

"I'd say she needed some cleaning up too. A new dress . . . definitely a new dress. She's really quite grubby."

Jenna jumped to her feet. "Don't talk about me as if I weren't here! I'm not a whore and I'm not staying in a—a brothel!"

Juliet's eyes narrowed. "Pity," she said sarcastically. "You could do a fine business and bring in some new customers, assuming, of course, that you are capable of learning some manners and controlling your fine young temper."

Jenna gripped the edge of her soiled dress. "Take me away from here!" She stared at Tolly and could feel herself once again on the verge of tears. This was too much!

"Sit down instantly!" Tolly commanded. "And do close your mouth. If I turn you out on the streets you'll

152

be in someone's bed by nightfall and, I'll wager, unwillingly.''

"So instead you are going to sell me into prostitution!"

Tolly raised his eyebrow. "Sell you? I'm going to have to pay for you to stay here." He turned to Juliet. "Ignore her," he advised. "She hasn't the patience to listen carefully. I didn't bring her here with the idea that she should work for you. However charming she looks, she is really quite bad-tempered and obviously a very bad judge of character. She wouldn't do your business any good at all. For all I know she bites."

Juliet laughed. "Oh, I have customers who would like that."

Tolly laughed too. "I've heard there are such men. But I merely wanted you to board her for a time. I have money for that. I realize it's a great favor, especially considering her obvious lack of gratitude." His eyes fell on Jenna. "Sit down!" he commanded.

Jenna sank onto the settee. She could feel her heart pounding and she knew her face still was red with anger. They both were treating her like a child and a silly child at that. And, she acknowledged, what made her mad was that she herself felt like a child. Tolly's intentions really had been honorable, but she had assumed otherwise too quickly. She bit her lip and stared at the floor.

"I suppose I shall be able to do something with her," Juliet replied. Again, she glanced at Jenna. Then, shaking her head, she repeated, "Pity. Redheads are so scarce."

Jenna looked up at Tolly. "You will tell Will where I am?" And she thought: *He* wouldn't let me stay in a brothel, not for one moment.

"I daresay I shall have to," Tolly answered. "I'm certainly not taking any responsibility for you. He's your knight in shining armor, not I. In the meantime, I suggest you get cleaned up, eat, and get some rest."

Tolly withdrew some money from his inner pocket. "For her expenses," he said coldly. "She does have some funds of her own as well. And do see if you can teach her some manners. Obviously I have failed."

Tolly stood up and looked at Jenna. "I bid you good day."

Juliet saw him to the door and Jenna sat stonily on the settee, the teacup still in her hand. "Oh, what's going to become of me?" she wondered aloud.

"I suppose you shall learn how to survive, my dear." Juliet was standing in the doorway. "Come along."

Jenna stood and followed Juliet up the winding staircase.

"First you will bathe and wash your hair," Juliet was saying as she opened the door to one of the bedchambers. "Then you will rest and when you awaken you will get properly dressed." She opened a large cabinet and displayed an array of gowns "Any one of them ought to fit you. They come from Paris, you know. Very nice gowns and there are camisoles in the drawer."

Jenna stared at the dresses and at the room. The bed looked comfortable and inviting and the gowns Juliet offered were the nicest she had ever seen. It also was quite true that she longed for a bath and for some peace. "Your customers won't bother me?" she questioned suspiciously.

"Not if you don't want them to," Juliet confirmed. "But you could make a good living, a very good living indeed."

Jenna looked at Juliet and replied with stubbornness in her voice, "Well, I'll not sell myself! I won't!"

Juliet shrugged. "I'll never understand girls like you. Giving away what you could make money on."

Jenna sank to the edge of the bed. "Well, I can't explain either!" she replied with dejection. This was a whole new world to her and she felt alone, totally alone!

James MacLean looked around the river market and wondered where to begin. This, he thought, was an ill-conceived adventure. He had left quickly and had not the slightest idea of where to look for his father. He thrust his hands in his pockets and began to walk. I'll have to start with the taverns, he thought.

The first one he tried was filled with soldiers, and while a few of them knew his brother, none of them knew or had heard of his father. Dejected, James moved on. The second tavern was filled to overflowing with loyalist refugees from Natchez who seemed, at this point, dedicated only to drinking and sulking. They were, they claimed, prisoners of war, held by a benign government that had no concern for their needs, their hopes, or their desires. They huddled in small, dismal groups and told stories of their escape to one another, or talked about the "good old days of British rule." They spoke disparagingly of the rowdy Continentals and of the Spanish and the French. Some of them even talked of heading upriver and of escaping into Canada.

James made his way about, stopping now and again to converse with one group or another. But it was no use whatsoever. No one had seen his father, though a few knew him as an ally of their enemies, so they cursed when his name was mentioned.

The third tavern was peopled by a strange mixture of humanity. But among the crowd James found several traders who knew his father.

"Is he in New Orleans?" one proclaimed with surprise. "The old rascal, he hasn't been here to see his old friends." James' heart sank. But the man thought for a moment. "Why don't you try Pollock's house? He and your father are good friends."

"Where is it?" James inquired.

The man gave him hurried directions and James left immediately in search of Oliver Pollock, the well-known and wealthy New Orleans merchant. James cursed under his breath; he should have tried Pollock's house first. He knew full well Pollock and his father did business together.

As James made his way to Oliver Pollock's house, he got lost twice. He had only been to New Orleans once before; it always was Will who came with their father. And that thought brought back James' last conversation with Maria. She was right, of course. Will was their father's favorite.

It was Will who had gotten the better rifle. "He hunts more," Robert had explained. "And as soon as possible, I will try to get you one like it." James remembered sulking about the rifle and he remembered his anger and hurt about other things as well. It was true that Will did do more hunting, but James could not admit that to himself. He only remembered that when things were divided, Will always seemed to get what *he* desired. And he thought: Maria's right about another thing. When the land's divided, Will might get the better share. It's the way it always has been. He would apply for the La Jeunesse land, he decided. In the morning, no matter what, he'd go to the Spanish authorities and file the documents.

James approached the Pollock house and saw that it was shrouded in darkness. He climbed the front steps and pounded on the door and waited. There was no sound from within and, in a fit of temper, James kicked at the door. No one was home. He turned dejectedly and headed back toward the river market. I'll have to find a place to stay the night, he thought. And tomorrow, even before I begin looking for Papa, I'll go to the authorities. He ambled off in bad humor, angry with himself and doubly angry with his father.

Robert MacLean walked toward Juliet's with some difficulty due to his drunken state. He had been with the Spanish adjutant and a more pleasant evening he could not imagine.

First he had learned the good news: The attack against Baton Rouge had been entirely successful, and Gálvez and his men were on their way back to New Orleans and Will, he thought gratefully, was safe. Moreover, the harassment on the river was over; that should make Angelique happy.

When they had finished talking, Señor Alvarez, the adjutant, had served a fine dinner of tasty, spicy Spanish rice and shrimp accompanied by more than one bottle of wine and followed by a bottle of fine French brandy.

"I'm quite drunk," Robert admitted to himself. But this time it was not a maudlin drunkenness. It was only the result of a good meal and good companionship. Now his only thoughts were for the white bed sheets and the feather-filled mattress of his room. And tomorrow, Robert thought, tomorrow he would return upriver to Angelique. He would make his peace with her somehow, he would try to understand her and make her understand him.

Robert walked unsteadily up to the door of La Casa Roja. He turned the handle and let himself into the dimly lighted hallway.

"Ah, you do return," Juliet cooed from the parlor as she peeked around the corner to see him.

Robert nodded sleepily. "Tonight, only to rest," he answered.

156

"You've been drinking," she chided with good humor. "You could have stayed here and done that."

"And other things as well," Robert answered. "But tonight I was not drinking alone. I was with a friend."

"Well, I suggest you go upstairs and lie down before you fall."

"I agree," he smiled, doffing his hat. With a wave of his hand, by way of good night, Robert climbed the stairs. At the very top he stopped and stared down the long, semidark hallway. He blinked and grasped the rail for an instant.

At the far end of the corridor was a vision in blue. Her long red hair fell nearly to her small waist and the snug fit of her gown revealed the lines of her figure. She was a tall girl and she paused and looked down the hall at him before she opened a door and disappeared.

"Janet," Robert exclaimed under his breath. But there was no sign that anyone had been in the hallway just a moment ago. "I'm seeing things," he mumbled incoherently as he reminded himself that Janet Cameron Macleod was far away in Canada and that, in any case, she was now nearly fifty and not a slip of a girl seventeen or eighteen.

Still, the image of the woman remained in his mind. From a distance she looked just like Janet in her youth. Robert staggered into his own room and closed the door behind him. A wave of loneliness swept over him, a wave of unhappiness for something lost. He fell across the feather mattress and closed his eyes. Wine and brandy combined, and Robert slipped immediately into a deep, dreamless sleep.

The utter gloom of the MacLean cabin was equaled only by the apprehension clearly visible on the conjure lady's face. Angelique lay in bed—a pale, small version of her former self. Her dark hair had fallen out by the handful and what was left emphasized the yellowish glow of her skin. The tumors that riddled her body gave her much pain; she was being consumed by an unknown disease.

The conjure lady bent over her and wiped her lips with a damp cloth. "She's got the jaundice," the woman reported.

Maria looked at her mother steadily, neither with concern nor with sorrow.

Mama is not a strong person, she thought. Mama is frail,

but she used that frailty. "You be a good little girl, Maria, or you'll make Mama sick." It was a phrase Maria had heard often, it was a phrase she had learned to ignore. Well, Mama always said she was sick and now she seemed to be.

"You're a good girl not to cry," the conjure lady praised. She patted Maria's hand. "You'll have to be a strong girl," she advised. "We might lose your mama—I don't like the jaundice, or the fever. It's not broken one bit, not one bit."

Maria stared into space.

The conjure lady stood up and shook off her ragged skirt. "I've got to get more medicine," she announced. "More root and more bark. You're going to have to stay with her alone. Can you do that? Can you watch her?"

Maria nodded. The conjure lady was wrapping her shawl around her shoulders. "I'll be back as soon as I can."

"I'll be all right," Maria answered vaguely.

"You gotta keep wiping her lips with a damp cloth, her mouth is bound to be awful dry."

"I'll be all right," Maria repeated, trying to hide her annoyance with the doddering old woman.

Maria positioned herself on the stool by the bed. She heard the front door close and she knew the conjure lady had disappeared into the night.

Angelique tossed uneasily and let out a small groan. Her eyes flickered open and her mouth began to move slowly. "Where's Papa?" she whispered.

Maria's emotionless expression didn't change. "He's gone to New Orleans, Mama. Remember? You made him go away."

Angelique shook her head. "No," she murmured. "No, I want him."

Maria folded her thin arms across her chest. "Well, he's not coming," she replied. "He doesn't care about you and he's not coming."

Angelique blinked back tears and tossed her head back and forth. Spittle ran down her chin. "Robert," she called out. "Oh, Robert."

"Why did you give away my clothes to those black people, Mama? Why did you do that?" Maria's eyes glowed with a strange intensity. She felt a sudden power, the same power she'd felt when she looked at the piece of rope on the

158

old tree; the power she'd felt when she saw Belle's brother's body hanging from the limb.

"So long ago . . ." Angelique said as she looked at her daughter. Maria's face seemed to be weaving in front of her; puzzlement filled her eyes.

"Will, tell Will to come," Angelique asked. "Tell him I forgive him and ask him to come."

Maria's features twisted evilly. "He's gone too," she announced with a flash of dark eyes. "Why Mama, don't you remember? Will's been killed in battle, Mama. Don't you remember anything?"

Angelique gasped as she drew in a breath. Her chest rattled slightly and her face seemed to grow even paler. "D-dead?" she struggled with the word. "Where? When?"

Maria shrugged. "You don't remember? I told you only yesterday."

Angelique closed her eyes against Maria's face and shook her head against the white pillow. "No, no, no," she kept repeating.

"Well, it's true," Maria said with conviction.

Angelique gurgled and then, as if fighting for breath, she managed to pull herself up, gasping. She let out a cry and retched. Blood and slime poured forth from her mouth and covered the sheet and her long nightdress. She gasped again and vomited. Her fingers clasped the side of the bed, and her eyes seemed to roll back in her head as, for the third time, her mouth filled with the sour, bloody mucus.

Maria jerked back from the bed. Her mother was sitting up and gasping for life itself. Her dark eyes were huge with fear and pain. Then she collapsed back against the pillows once again, breathing a little more normally.

Maria twitched her nose. The smell of the vomit was sickening. Her mother looked less than human. "Look what a mess you've made!" Maria yelled, narrowing her eyes. And at that moment all her irrational hatred for her mother surfaced. "You made a mess!" she screamed. Her own head was pounding, as it so often did. It was a dull, miserable ache at the base of her neck and when it came, Maria heard voices—whispering voices that told her what to do.

She lifted one of the white pillows and looked into her mother's terrified face. Then Maria put the pillow over

Angelique's face and held it there with all her strength. "You're going to die anyway!" she shrieked. "I can't stand looking at you! Or listening to you! I can't stand to see something struggling for life!"

Angelique struggled for only a moment and then her movements ceased and she lay quietly. But Maria did not lift the pillow. She continued to hold it down and she continued to scream. "You're making me do this!" She gradually grew aware of her own shaking and of the terrible fright she felt. Long moments passed and finally Maria released the pillow. "Are you dead, Mama?" Her whispered question seemed to fill the room with sound. Maria reached out and touched the edge of the pillow. As if it were something alive, she pulled it away and looked into her mother's face. Maria jumped backward at the sight of Angelique's wide-open eyes staring at her. "Are you dead, Mama?" Maria screamed the words.

Maria backed away, holding her fingers in her mouth. She moved to the far corner of the room and huddled there, unable to take her eyes off her mother's dead, horror-stricken face.

She might move, Maria thought. She's not really dead. She's going to get up and walk right across the room. She's going to touch me with her icy-cold hands. Maria shuddered. Mama's ghost was going to kill her. She struggled with herself, but she couldn't move. It was as if her legs had turned to jelly and her eyes were permanently stuck on Angelique's face. There was a loud, creaking sound and Maria's heart throbbed even as she jumped and let out a bloodcurdling scream.

The conjure lady threw open the door of the bed chamber and stood stock still for an instant. She saw Angelique's face and she knew her patient was dead. The conjure lady believed in magic, but she also believed in Christianity. She crossed herself rapidly three times.

Maria had dropped to her knees and was still shrieking.

"Hush!" the conjure lady commanded. "Hush, your mama's died."

Maria screamed again and the conjure lady lifted her hand and slapped her hard. "Hush!"

"Her ghost's coming for me," Maria wailed.

The conjure lady yanked Maria into the other room and shook her like a rag doll. "You're hysterical! Hush!"

"She's coming, she's coming. . . ."

"She's doing no such thing. She's just died, let her rest in peace. You were being such a good child. Now you're just acting like some wild thing!"

"You don't understand," Maria whimpered.

But the conjure lady paid no attention at all. She rummaged through her satchel and brought forth a vial of liquid. She yanked Maria to her and forced the contents of the vial down her throat. Maria coughed once, but the conjure lady rubbed her throat and Maria involuntarily swallowed.

The first sensation she felt was heat and the second extreme cold. She shivered again and her body went numb. Then Maria passed out.

"I trust this will not be too much of a comedown for you," the young British officer declared. "Montreal is not Philadelphia, though we do try."

"Better to have your head attached to your shoulders in Montreal than to be hanged in Philadelphia," Tom quipped. "I'm certain I'll adjust. I am, after all, a refugee."

He had crossed the St. Lawrence early that morning, but there had been little time to explore the city. Nonetheless, Tom Bolton was impressed. Montreal seemed far different from Philadelphia, Boston, or Arlington. It was more European, or what he imagined Europe to be like. And certainly the French influence still was strong. I like it, Tom thought. I'm certain I'm going to like it. On his way to Montreal, Tom had imagined that the French might be hostile. One could certainly expect hostility from people who had suffered as they had. But that did not appear to be the case at all. Thus far he had encountered only friendliness, though he was careful to speak French to those who were French Canadians. Mentally, he thanked the Shippens for seeing to it that he had a better-than-average education and that he had learned both French and German.

"I have to find a Mathew Macleod," Tom announced. "Major André wanted me to contact him as soon as possible."

"Ah, Mr. Macleod," the young officer said knowingly.

"He's not been too well, been working at home lately."

"Might I call on him at his house?" Tom suggested. "Would that be considered rude?"

"Not at all. But why not after the midday meal? It would be rude to appear at suppertime."

"Of course," Tom agreed.

"Why don't we have some lunch in the *auberge* across the square," the officer suggested. "You have yet to sample Quebec cookery. They have fine bread, wine, and cheese."

"Sounds agreeable," Tom said, smiling.

The young officer stood up. As the officer had been sitting, Tom had not realized he wore a kilt. Though, Tom thought, I should have known from the band on his hat. The red coat trimmed with gold was much like that of any officer in the British Army, but below the waistcoat the young man wore the green and blue kilt of the Royal Highland Regiment, better known as the Black Watch. He had red and white argyle stockings to the knee and black shoes with gold buckles.

"You're a Highlander," Tom commented.

The officer held out his hand. "Mactavish," he said, introducing himself.

The two men crossed the square. "It's going to be an early fall," Mactavish observed. "No Indian summer this year."

"Aren't kilts a bit cool in the Canadian winters?"

Mactavish laughed. "No, because in the winter we put on a wee bit underneath, don't you see?"

They entered the crowded *auberge*. "They have fine food here," Mactavish confided, "far better than the officer's mess." He winked at Tom. "You know, we Scots may fight for the British now, but we always did have a taste for French food and wine, especially a good claret."

Again Tom smiled. There was always something enviable about the Scots. Perhaps it was that they remained Scots no matter where they were or how long they had been there. He remembered the evacuation of Philadelphia by the British. It had been a dignified withdrawal and the army had been piped out by the Royal Highlanders. "Oh, I don't like bagpipes!" Peggy had cried. "They sound like old women wailing!" Tom remembered saying that he rather liked them, that he felt stirred by their music for some inexplicable reason.

Mactavish marched to a long wooden table at which a number of men sat family style. "Mackenzie!" he exclaimed with glee. "Don't tell me you've decided to part with some of your hard-earned cash in order to eat out?"

Mackenzie looked up almost guiltily. "It's only a little cash," he whispered. "And don't you look all spit and polish."

Mactavish grasped Tom's elbow. "I'd like you to meet a young countryman of mine—the woods are full of them. This is Alexander Mackenzie; Mackenzie, be introduced to Tom Bolton."

Tom leaned over and shook the large hand extended to him.

"Mackenzie here works for Finlay & Gregory; keeps account books, he does." Mactavish lowered his voice. "A good loyalist lad, his father and brother are in the army. He's only fifteen, but he's finished his schooling and he's a strapping fine boy already making money. And Finlay & Gregory are loyalist too. That's something—a lot of the merchants lean toward the Continentalists. Get three people together in Montreal these days and you have five political opinions."

Mackenzie laughed and passed Tom a great hunk of black bread and a glass of wine. "Bolton," he repeated. "You're not Scots?" Tom shook his head. "British Intelligence, from Philadelphia."

Mackenzie roared with laughter. "British Intelligence! That'll be the day. It's a contradiction in terms."

Tom looked at him quizzically. "I thought you were a loyalist."

"Oh, I support them, but admitting they're intelligent is quite another matter. Why, man, this country needs the Scots to take charge of it and pull it together. If the British hold onto anything in North America they'll be lucky!" Mackenzie looked into Tom's eyes with humor. "Are you certain you're not Scots? You're built like a Highlander and you have the coloring too."

"Now, there's a compliment," Mactavish put in.

Tom felt his face redden. "As a matter of fact," he stumbled, "I was adopted. I have no idea where I come from."

Mackenzie roared again and slapped him on the back. "Then tell people you're a Scotsman. It puts you right between the British devil, the Continentals' deep blue sea, and the French *joie de vivre*."

"Watch out," Mactavish cautioned. "He's softening you up to pay the bill."

"I'll pay it for good company," Tom agreed as he bit into a large piece of pale cheese.

The total meal consisted of fresh greens, a thick, rich soup, and more bread accompanied by more wine. When the bill came, Mackenzie handed it to Tom unabashedly. "You volunteered," he reminded him.

Tom paid the bill and waited while Mactavish wrote down the directions to the Macleod house. "You'll like them," he advised. "They're Scots too, very hospitable people."

CHAPTER X

October 1779

Tom followed the winding maze of streets according to the directions Mactavish had given him. The smells of fall were in the air and most of the leaves already had turned.

Tom had left Philadelphia in late August and met with Major André aboard the *Vulture* in early September. Now it was the third of October. His trip had been difficult because now there was so much activity in upper New York. The forces of the Continental Army were moving toward Niagara, and although they seemed disorganized, they managed to make travel difficult as well as dangerous.

Tom paused momentarily to look at the Sulpician Seminary and the Church of Notre Dame. Then he walked on and after some time turned onto Rue Bonsecours. The finest house on the street belonged to a Huguenot merchant, one Pierre du Calvet, who had been charged with treason and now was in jail. Mactavish had told Tom to mark the house of Calvet, which the British had confiscated and now used to board officers, and count five houses more. "The fifth after Calvet's is the Macleods'."

Tom paused before the house and saw that the name Macleod appeared on the front door. He climbed the three steps to the door and used the large black wrought-iron knocker.

Janet was halfway between the parlor and the kitchen of the rambling stone house when she heard the knock. She hastily wiped her hands on her apron and pushed a stray hair back off her forehead. Glancing around, she saw that the dishes were cleared from the table and, all things considered, the house was not in bad order.

"Just a moment," Janet called out. She swung open the large oak door and stood totally paralyzed as she looked into Tom Bolton's puzzled face.

The young man who stood before her was just over six feet tall. He had those same soft brown eyes she had looked into for thirty years and the same shock of sandy hair falling casually over his brow. His shoulders were likewise broad and strong; his mouth even had the same slight twist. The person at the door was the near-perfect image of Mathew Macleod thirty years ago!

She only vaguely saw the red coat and the white breeches tucked into the black boots. So startling was the person before her that she felt dizzy, as if she were losing her mind and seeing some apparition.

"Who are you?" she blurted out.

"Mrs. Macleod?" Tom asked with more than a little apprehension. The woman looked stricken and he felt stupid and silly. "Are you all right?"

Janet grasped the side of the door for support, but she could feel her knees weakening. She held out her hand to him just as she began to crumple. A startled and bewildered Tom Bolton caught her in his arms and heard her murmur, "Mathew!"

"Janet?" Madelaine hurried down the stairs when she heard Tom's anxious cry. She stopped short and stared at him, torn between the startling sight of a young Mathew Macleod and Janet crumpled in his arms.

"She—she opened the door and just fainted," Tom tried to explain in a husky voice. His own expression was one of total confusion. Were all the women in this house mad? One had looked at him as if he were a ghost and passed out; now another simply stood and stared at him as if he had dropped off the moon.

Madelaine's lips parted, but she found herself unable to speak. Instead she pointed dumbly toward the parlor and a chair. Tom easily lifted Janet into his arms and carried her to the chair, sitting her down gently. He jostled her slightly and turned to Madelaine, who still stood in the doorway, her mouth slightly open and her lovely large dark eyes wide with disbelief.

"Have you no smelling salts?" Tom asked. God knew,

he should be used to women fainting. Peggy fainted all the time—indeed, whenever she pleased.

"In the other room," Madelaine mumbled.

"Well, could you get them?" Tom asked, trying to be patient. What was wrong with these people? Mactavish had said they were hospitable, not insane.

Madelaine shook her head and fairly fled the room. She returned in a few minutes holding the vial of crystals soaked in ammonia. Tom took it from her, opened it, and waved it beneath Janet's nose. Janet coughed and blinked open her eyes. "Mrs. Macleod? You are Mrs. Macleod?" Janet only blinked up at him and nodded her head.

"What is it? Can you tell me what's the matter?" Tom asked. But she still looked as if she had seen a ghost. He turned to Madelaine. "What is the matter with you two?"

Nervously, Madelaine rubbed her hands on her skirt. "Who are you?" she asked, finding her lost voice at last.

Tom's arm still was under Janet's head. Carefully he eased it away and tucked a loose cushion behind her. "I'm Thomas Bolton, recently arrived from Philadelphia, and I have business with a Mr. Mathew Macleod who, I am told, resides in this house."

Madelaine leaned against the side of the doorway and let out a long-held breath. Janet's hands grasped the tapestry with which her chair was covered. "From Philadelphia?" she asked.

Tom straightened up and looked from one to the other of them. "I'm sorry if I've come at a bad time. I . . . I seem to have upset the two of you for some reason I don't understand." He was stumbling over his words and felt distinctly ill at ease. These women, beautiful as they were, appeared strange in the extreme.

Janet shook her head as if to clear it. "I'm sorry," she apologized. "You say your name is Bolton?"

Tom again shook his head. "Yes, from Philadelphia by way of Major André."

Janet tried to smile. The young man could not possibly understand what she herself was only beginning to hope: her heart was still beating wildly and she could not put the possibility out of her mind that this young man, who so coincidentally had appeared at her door, was indeed Mathew's son

Tom. The resemblance was uncanny. This young man looked more like Mathew than either Mat or Andrew. He looked more like Mathew than either Jenna or Helena. Even his mannerisms were similar.

"I'm terribly sorry," Janet reiterated. She straightened up and held out her hand. "You certainly have not come at a bad time. I don't even quite know how to explain my behavior to you. Please do sit down."

Tom smiled but still felt bewildered. Nonetheless, he sat down on the settee opposite Janet. Silently, Madelaine also sat down, though she did not—indeed, could not—take her eyes off the young stranger whose looks were so utterly familiar to her.

Janet sucked her lip. "Philadelphia," she said again. "Bolton." Her face was knit in a frown. "You will think this very rude of me, Mr. Bolton, but I ask you to indulge me. Mr. Bolton, tell me about your family—are you any relation to General Bolton? Tell me why you have come to Montreal?"

"I'm no relation to General Bolton," Tom answered. "I'm with British Intelligence. I've come at Major André's request to consult with Mr. Mathew Macleod."

Janet took the words in. It was all some ghastly mistake, a coincidence. This young man was not in search of his father after all. He was here for quite a different reason. "About your family?" Janet pressed. "I must know about your family."

Tom stared back at her. Her intensity was unsettling. Though he had no idea why she asked the question, he decided it did not matter. "My father's a merchant in Philadelphia. My sister is married to a general in the Continental Army—though we are loyalists," he quickly added.

Janet's heart sank. "Your father? Your father is Mr. Bolton?" Janet questioned. Perhaps the resemblance was just that, an unrelated resemblance. They say everyone has a double, Janet thought. Still, Philadelphia is where little Tom had been taken and, then too, there was the name, Tom.

Again Tom frowned. "Well, if you must know," he replied, "my father's name is not Bolton. It's Shippen. I was adopted and renamed. Well, I mean, it wasn't a real adoption. I was a foundling and the Shippens took me in.

They named me after a friend who had died. They educated me." He had no idea why he was babbling on, telling her so much. "But of what possible interest can this be to you?" he asked.

Janet's lips parted and a chill ran down her spine. Tom could not help but notice the sudden color in her face and the sparkle in her eyes. She looked quite a different woman from the one who had just fainted in his arms. She and the quiet, lovely young woman who sat opposite now looked alive with curiosity. Tom cleared his throat. "You asked me to indulge you," he said politely. "Now please indulge me and tell me what this is all about."

"What do you know of your real family?" Janet pressed. "Does the name Stowe mean anything to you? Have you heard it?"

Tom blinked at her. It was his turn to be totally shocked. His mouth had gone dry. He could only manage to nod in the affirmative.

"Oh, my God!" Janet said, trembling. Tears had begun to run down her face. She felt moved by such an emotional thrill she could hardly speak. Her hand had flown to her lips, and her green eyes were wide.

"You know my parents?" Tom finally managed.

Again Janet shuddered. "The Stowes are not your real parents," she informed him, struggling over every word. "You were left in their care in 1747. They took you to Philadelphia. They were killed."

Tom looked into Janet's eyes with amazement. Her face was deeply flushed. She held out her hands to him. Tears ran freely down her face. "We tried to find you, my God, how we tried . . ."

Tom too was shaking. "You're my mother . . . ?"

Janet quickly shook her head. "You are the son of Ann Macdonald and Mathew Macleod. Your mother died in childbirth. Your father is upstairs."

Tom felt a sudden moisture in his own eyes.

"You are exactly as your father was at your age. When I opened the door, I thought I was seeing an apparition. I was transported back thirty years." Tears were running down her face. "We tried, Mathew tried, I tried . . . we wanted to find you."

Tom wiped his own ruddy cheek and thought it was undignified for a grown man to cry. For years he had searched for remnants of his own family, believing them to be the Stowes. At absurd moments—wonderful moments —absurd thoughts enter one's mind, Tom thought. He recalled his lunch with Alexander Mackenzie and Mackenzie's comment that he looked like a Scots. I am a Scots, he thought.

Tom pulled himself to his feet and walked over to Janet. He reached out and took her extended hands, pulling her to her feet. He folded his arms around her and hugged her tightly. His search for his family was at an end, over when he least expected it to be.

After a few moments, Janet drew away from him and looked into his face. "Your father, your real father, recently has had a heart attack. If you don't mind, I will have to tell him, prepare him. You have no idea how long he searched for you, how much he longed to find you."

"And I him," Tom responded. Then, in a lower voice, "I have a family. My God, I have a real family!"

He looked beyond Janet to Madelaine. "Are you my sister?"

She shook her head and smiled. "I too am adopted," she informed him. "We are no blood relation."

"Good," Tom beamed. "I should not like to think the most attractive woman I have seen in Montreal was my sister."

Madelaine blushed.

"You have a half brother and two half sisters," Janet explained. "And Madelaine has two brothers whom we also adopted, but they are on their own now." Janet lowered her eyes and, almost choking, added, "You did have another half brother, but he was killed recently." It still was hard for her to think of Mat as dead. "It was his death that caused your father's attack." Janet patted the sleeve of his uniform. "Let me go and tell him his lifelong dream has come true."

"Let me get used to it too," Tom replied, sinking back into the chair.

Janet turned quickly and, lifting her skirts, began to climb the staircase. She could hardly suppress her joy. She wanted to cry out, "Tom is here!" But she did not. I will have to tell him calmly, she thought. But he will be overjoyed! And the news will make him well again. I wanted to find him as much as you, she thought. Oh, Mathew, I wanted to find him because you wanted to, because he is your son and a part of us.

The Spanish officer in charge of land grants was a model of officiousness. He rattled through piles of hand-copied documents and pondered maps on which large tracts of land were marked off.

He carefully wrote down everything James told him, pausing only to twirl his long, dark, waxed moustache or arch an impeccably plucked eyebrow. "I shall, quite naturally, have to check the details of your story with local officials. If indeed the land you refer to has been deserted, and if indeed you claim it as compensation for a wrong against your family, I see no reason why it cannot be transferred into your name." He completed the forms slowly, concentrating on each word and, seemingly, on the ornate flourishes with which he wrote them.

"How long will it take?" James questioned, trying not to sound irritable, though the office was unbearably stuffy.

"Well, there is a war going on," the official mumbled. Again, he tweaked his moustache. "So quite naturally we are short of staff. But it will be seen to as soon as possible. Certainly within the year."

James frowned. It was October. "Three months?" he confirmed. "Surely it can be done more quickly than that."

The official moved from one side of his chair to the other. "These things take time," he hedged.

James reached into his waistcoat and withdrew a small leather pouch. From it he took two gold sovereigns. He placed them on the desk. "Five more if it can be done within two weeks," James offered. "A man such as yourself, a man with such obvious good taste, surely can use some extra gold."

The officer smiled, revealing his uneven, tobacco-stained teeth. He tapped his fingers nervously and picked up another parchment. He narrowed his eyes and studied it for a few moments. "My schedule does indicate some free time toward the end of next week. I think I might manage to see to your request at that time."

"I'm grateful," James said, rising from the chair. The sooner the better, he thought. He could move immediately onto the land and begin to improve it. It was his chance to get away from his father and to make his own fortune. In the back of his mind, James considered Maria's suggestion. Amalgamated, the La Jeunesse and MacLean land would make a large and profitable estate. And I will purchase slaves, James thought. Father has not properly developed his land because he is opposed to slavery, but I will have slaves.

James bid the officer good day and again found himself under the hot New Orleans sun. He went to several more taverns before returning to the house of Pollock the merchant. James even asked for his father, at the seedy inn and at the river market, but no one had seen Robert MacLean, no one knew of his whereabouts.

James looked up Bourbon Street and thought: The only places I have not looked are the brothels. Well, I will have to go to them as well. He spit on the ground in anger at the idea that he might find his father in a brothel. You always preached to me about respecting women, he thought bitterly. And in all likelihood I will find you in a whorehouse. You would be furious if you found out about Belle, but a brothel is no different. But of course you would say that Belle was forced to do something against her will and you would insist that the women in brothels enjoy their work and do it voluntarily.

James hastened his step and thought about his mother. If Papa was in a brothel he would never forgive him! But on reflection, the rift between his parents pleased him. His mother was deeply angry with Will, but she had praised him for remaining home and for ignoring the war. "I would never fight for the Spanish!" he had told her, and Angelique had cried, "You are my good son, you never have lied to me!"

Robert awoke late after a troubled night of strange dreams. He had awakened at least three times during the night, twice with a terrible thirst caused by drinking too much and once with the sudden memory of the vision he had seen at the end of the semidarkened corridor. After that, he had drifted off into dreams about Janet, Mathew, and their children. But he had not slept deeply; his sleep was composed half of conscious thought and half of dreams. He had thought about the cool forests of Quebec and the clear-bottom lakes and rivers of Canada. He had dreamed of Angelique too, and in his dreams she was as she had been and there was nothing between them save love and understanding.

As Robert came fully awake, he rolled over on his back, stared up at the ceiling, folded his hands across his stomach, and thought about his children. No man, he thought, can dislike his own children. But Robert had to admit that he felt cut off from James and Maria. It was as if they had begun as ripe, firm pieces of fruit and had disintegrated in the southern sun, growing soft. James and Maria had picked up the beliefs and prejudices of their neighbors, and both had unreasonable expectations of great wealth. Robert recalled an argument he'd had with James about slavery. "Straight and simple," he had told his son, "owning another human being is wrong." James had retorted, "Slavery is the means by which we will achieve wealth and power; you are old-fashioned not to accept it; it will rule this land whether you like it or not."

Maria had agreed, of course. She always agreed with James. But Maria did not argue. She only nodded and her face grew cold and hard; it was an expression Robert could not stand. The girl is too much alone, he told himself. She's too possessive of her belongings, she always refuses to share.

Will was different. He was open and honest, and he worked hard. I've treated him with favor, Robert admitted. But which came first—the favoritism, or Will's ready acceptance of the values Robert held dear? He only knew that his son James took after his namesake, Robert's brother.

The sunlight was pouring through the windows, and the heat of the day already was oppressive. He drew his long legs over the side of the bed and stood up and stretched. I'm going home to Angelique, he decided. I'm going this very morning.

He dressed quickly and walked down the corridor to the winding staircase. From the kitchen below came the enticing aroma of breakfast being prepared.

At the long wooden table, Juliet would be presiding over the steaming teapot and there would be a large platter with dark bread, roast pork meat, and greens. The "girls" who inhabited the house would be gone. Each morning, they left early in a group to go to the river market. Imported clothes from Spain and France were sold there as well as household items. Sometimes the girls went to shop, sometimes only to walk about. Morning in the river market was, after all, as much a social occasion as it was an adventure in commerce.

Robert walked into the kitchen and stopped short. Juliet was at the table with her tea, but she was not alone. The girl who sat with her was his vision from the night before. Her long red hair cascaded over her bared white shoulders and she turned to greet his startled expression with clear, emerald-green eyes.

He stared at the girl. Up close, she did not look that much like Janet, he thought. It was only her build and coloring; certainly the nose was different. Robert smiled at his own silly fantasy.

"Sit down," Juliet invited. "This is Jenna," Juliet said by way of introduction. Then, misunderstanding Robert's bold stare, "She is not one of my girls, only a temporary guest."

"Forgive me," Robert apologized. "It's only that you remind me a little of someone I know."

Jenna frowned at him and again lifted her green eyes. He was a well-spoken man and she could hear a trace of his Scots accent, the same accent her mother had.

Robert's eyes had fastened on Jenna's throat, or more specifically on the pendant that hung around her neck, dangling from a long silver chain. In the light blue gown that Juliet had given her, the gown that fell off her shoulders and bared her long white throat, the pendant was quite visible.

Almost in a trance, Robert reached across the distance between them and, much to Jenna's surprise, seized the pendant in his fingers, turning it over. The ancient Roman coin imprisoned in the silver setting still bore the clear imprint of the profile of the Roman emperor Severus. Could there be a third such pendant? Robert had one. It was in fact around his neck now; he never took it off. It was the pendant Mathew had given Janet, and Janet had given him. It was one of two. The two coins had a long and strange history in the Macleod clan. It was said that they were taken from a Roman soldier in one of the many attacks launched against the Roman invaders of Scotland in the second century. It was after the attack that the Romans had restored Hadrian's Wall, marking off their conquered territory from Scotland, where fierce tribes had prevented further conquest. The coins, so the story went, marked the beginnings of clan Macleod and they had remained in the family and were worn into battle as a symbol of good luck.

It was the pendant that had enabled Mathew Macleod to recognize Robert so many years ago when Fou Loup had brought him as a lost and bewildered child to Fort Frédéric.

Jenna jerked backward and Robert released the pendant that fell back against her neck.

"Where did you get that?" he demanded.

"It belongs to my father!" Jenna replied with irritation. "And don't you touch it." Her hands had flown protectively to her neck, and her emerald eyes flashed.

Robert smiled. He had seen those eyes flash before. "And who is your father?" he asked, softening his voice.

"Mathew Macleod," Jenna said instantly. "I'm from Canada."

"I'm Robert MacLean." He held out his hand toward her. His head was full of questions.

Jenna's mouth fell open. "Robert MacLean! Are you really Robert MacLean?" Tears filled her eyes and she began to shiver. "I thought I would never find you!"

A sense of confusion and relief flooded Jenna. This man was her uncle! He was not her real uncle, of course, but that did not matter. He would help her get home, and that meant her nightmare was at an end. Robert was the brother of her mother's first husband, and Robert and her mother had escaped Scotland together many years ago. He was not a blood relative, but he was bound to the Macleod family by ties of love and emotion. He would protect her, he would help her.

175

Robert smiled and it was a wild, good-humored smile. An almost infectious smile. He held out his hands to her. "How did you get here?" he asked with amazement. Janet and Mathew had been on his mind a great deal lately; seeing their daughter seemed like a dream.

"I have a long story," Jenna said slowly. "An unhappy story." Tears were running freely down her face.

"Begin at the beginning," Robert suggested. "Tell me everything."

James paused at the door of La Casa Roja. He had been to four brothels and felt discouraged as well as tired and hot. Perhaps his father was not in New Orleans at all, perhaps he had already left and was making his way upriver. It was late afternoon and an orange sun was burning in the western sky. James felt resentment and anger. A trip to New Orleans ought to be enjoyable, but this one had not been. There was no time to pleasure himself, or to sample the night life of the city. Instead, he was spending every moment searching for his father.

He knocked on the door and waited. In a few moments the door was answered. "It's a bit early in the day," Juliet purred as she examined the tall, dark, good-looking young man before her.

James let his eyes roam her well-shaped body. She was probably older than his father, but the Creole woman was stunning. He cleared his throat. "I'm looking for one Robert MacLean," he announced, staring into her hypnotic, almond-shaped eyes. If this were the madam, he could but wonder what the women of the house looked like.

"Robert," Juliet called out in a voice that was deep and sensual, "you have a visitor!"

"We're in the parlor," Robert's voice shouted. James stiffened at the word "we."

Juliet motioned him in and James followed. She walked like a willow reed, moving gently from side to side; each step seemed to be an invitation.

Robert was seated in the parlor and with him was the most stunning young woman James had ever seen. Her long red hair tumbled loose over snow-white shoulders and she turned wide green eyes to him.

176

"James!" Robert stood up, clearly startled. James' eyes moved from the beautiful creature on the settee to his father and back again. She could not have been more than seventeen!

James' eyes narrowed. "I've come for you," he said quickly. "Mama is terribly ill! You must come home at once!" He emphasized the word "Mama" and looked hard at Jenna. Her facial expression hardly changed at all, nor did she blush with any sort of shame. James turned to his father. "I see you have not been too lonely, but couldn't you have picked a whore who was older than your daughter?" James' voice was heavy with anger and bitterness.

"This is Jenna," Robert stuttered.

James' eyes bore through her. Her skin was truly lovely, white like magnolia blossoms, and her full lips seemed to offer a secret promise. Certainly, he thought, it was a promise her curvaceous body easily could fulfill. Angry as he was, he had to admit that his father showed excellent taste.

Robert's face was red with embarrassment. "This is not what you think," he stumbled. "This is no whore."

"Really." James' voice was filled with hatred and disbelief.

"She is no whore," Robert repeated with as even a voice as he could master. "This is Jenna Macleod, daughter of Janet and Mathew Macleod. She will be going home with us."

James blinked at the stunning redhead. She walked to him with her hands extended. "You are like a long-lost brother to me," she said softly. "You must believe your father; circumstances are not always what they seem."

"How ill is your mother?" Robert questioned. Angelique had been ill before, but she had always gotten well. In fact, in the past few years she had taken to her bed a number of times.

"She is deathly ill," James said slowly. "The conjure lady sent me after you."

Robert's face contorted. The conjure lady would not have sent James unless Angelique were truly sick. A wave of guilt passed through him. "Oh, God," he murmured. "We must hurry."

James still looked at Jenna and his mind was full of questions. He knew about the Macleods, he knew all the family stories.

"We'll tell you everything when we are on our way," Robert said, turning to his son. "Come along, Jenna, you must get your things together. It's a long journey upriver."

Jenna looked at the silent Juliet. "When Tolly comes back, you'll tell him where I've gone, won't you?"

Juliet nodded. "Of course," she agreed. Her eyes fastened for a long moment on Robert's anxious face. Then, smiling, she said, "Go home, Robert MacLean. Go home and be happy."

The conjure lady had fallen asleep on the bed pad which she had pulled into the center room of the cabin. She was curled up like a cat and covered with a light sheet. Even in her sleep she clutched the material, grasping it and holding it close to her. Her tangle of wild hair, knotted and uncombed, partially covered her face. Her eyes were closed, but her mouth was open and a trickle of spittle ran out and down onto the arm that cradled her head.

Maria crouched on the bed pad across the room. She watched the conjure lady with wide-open eyes. The room was in partial darkness; Maria had not allowed the conjure lady to extinguish all the lamps. On the table in the far corner, one flickered, its candle half gone. The flame cast strange shadows that seemed to form wavering shapes as the breeze came through the open window.

Maria shuddered. The conjure lady finally had fallen asleep in total exhaustion. She had given Maria some more medicine, but Maria's eyes still had not closed. She huddled, listening and waiting. Her eyes watched every flap of the curtains over the window; every shadow seemed threatening. She held the corner of her own bed covering in her hands and she twisted it over and over, finally putting it in her mouth and sucking on it.

All cats are friends of the devil, the conjure lady once had told her. But dogs, except for the white dog with yellow eyes, are the devil's enemy.

It was a long time ago that the conjure lady, the teller of tales, had told Maria the bloodcurdling stories. Maria blinked; the white curtains were flapping again and the conjure lady's tales were blending into her reality.

"Tell me about the great white dog with the yellow eyes?" Maria had asked long ago.

"Oh, the white dog is the devil incarnate—pure white, pure, pure white, and you can see right through him. He haunts the evil ones, he come to fetch them and take them to hell. And his eyes, his eyes glow yellow in the darkness and where the white dog walks he leaves a trail of white pawprints on the ground. That's how the evil ones know he's tracking them."

Maria shivered and stared into the flickering lamplight. She imagined she saw the bright yellow eyes of the dog and out of the darkness the fingers of her mother's hand clawing at her.

There was a scratching at the door and Maria went rigid. It was the dog! He had come for her! In a trance of terror, she crawled off the bed pad and over to the door. With a shaking hand, she opened the door and saw, in the moonlight, a large white dog ambling off toward the barn. On the steps, the telltale white prints looked up at her. She let out a piercing scream that filled the whole cabin and jolted the conjure lady into consciousness.

"The white dog's come! He's come for me!" Tears were running down her ceeks and she was gnawing at the sheet she had carried with her to the door.

The conjure lady rubbed her eyes and stared at the pawmarks on the porch. She too shivered. "The white dog!" she repeated it in a voice nearly as shaky as Maria's. "He came," she whispered. "I never thought I'd live to see him!"

Maria buried her face in the old woman's skirts and screamed again. "Do something! Don't let him have me! You do something!"

The conjure lady braced herself and looked out into the night. She searched her memory. The tale of the dog had been told to her by her grandmother in Haiti and there was a conjure to ward off the white dog. She bent down and examined the pawprints reverently. There was no doubt about it. The dog had come.

"Did you see him?" she whispered, her large dark eyes wide with fright. "Did you actually see him?"

Maria shook against her. "He scratched at the door," she murmured. "He's come to get me."

"Why you? You're just an innocent. Maybe he came to get me." The conjure lady's eyes moved about, searching the area in front of the house.

"No! No!" Maria shrieked.

The conjure lady turned to look Maria in the face. The child's eyes were wide with terror.

"He won't come again tonight," the conjure lady said with confidence. "We'll do a spell tomorrow, we'll do it at midnight when the moon is full."

"Will he go away then?" Maria asked.

"We'll sacrifice the blood of a chicken," the woman said seriously. "To ward off the devil seeker, to send him away."

The conjure lady pulled Maria back into the house and closed the door. Her own heart was beating as fast as Maria's.

She had heard the tale all her life and repeated it often. But not till tonight had she dreamed it could come true. None of her other horrific tales ever had come to pass and, in truth, she considered them to be warnings, means of keeping people good. But there was no denying the prints on the steps. The white dog had come. His spirit must live here too, she thought, and not just in Haiti, where her grandmother had told her the tale.

"Lie down and close your eyes," she told Maria, leading her back to the bed pad. "He won't come twice in one night."

Maria lay down and forced her eyelids closed. The medicine she had been given earlier seemed to be taking effect and she felt her whole body going numb. But she was afraid to sleep. Afraid because when she did she had dreams of her mother rising from the grave to kill her.

"There's evil here," she heard the conjure lady mumble. "Some sort of evil."

CHAPTER XI

November 1779

"Are you warm enough?" Tom inquired. Madelaine Deschamps was weaving her magic thread from one side of the taut cloth to the other. Sitting on the very edge of her chair, she leaned forward over her needlepoint frame. Each push of the needle brought yarn through the material and added to the design she was fashioning. Her long, amber dress fell down to her petite ankles, and her hair hung loose, giving her a comely, girlish look. Tom was perched on the long stone hearth, fanning the embryonic fire with the bellows while, outside, a bitter November wind, the harbinger of an early winter lashed across the St. Lawrence River.

Madelaine lifted her dark eyes and smiled. "Quite warm, thank you."

Tom nodded. He wondered how he could advance his relationship with Madelaine. She was always kind and friendly toward him, yet she kept a discreet distance between them. She was the quiet type, he acknowledged, and she was both intelligent and beautiful. But Madelaine was treating him like a relative rather than a single man to whom she was unrelated.

He had been with the Macleods now for nearly a month. And each passing day, he felt more a part of the clan. The first days had been difficult. Mathew Macleod obviously harbored great guilt over the way Tom had spent his childhood. But as Mathew came to understand that Tom had been well looked after, his guilt seemed to lessen. And the two of them had spent long hours talking alone. Day by day, the feeling between father and son had forged itself into a strong bond. Mathew had related all the family history and even told him a great deal about his mother, Ann Macdonald.

"She was a gentle creature," Mathew told him. "A good woman who was responsible for making me seek a life in a new world. You are Macdonald on one side—the name means world ruler—and Macleod on the other. Your great aunt, Flora Macdonald, who was instrumental in the escape of Bonnie Prince Charlie, lives in North Carolina and, like us, has become a loyalist. But you also have a young cousin, a fifteen-year-old called Jacques Étienne Joseph Macdonald, from a part of the family that settled in France.

"We are two of the proudest clans in the Highlands. We have a long history that cannot be forgotten. It's a history I pass on to you, and you must pass it on to your children." Tom remembered smiling at his father and reminding him that he was a widower without children. "You will have them eventually," Mathew proclaimed confidently.

There followed an oral history of both clans that went back as far as Kenneth MacAlpin, King of the Scots in the ninth century. Mathew also told his son the long and complicated history of the Jacobite rebellions and of the division of the Highlanders. Those who fought for the Stuart cause were Catholics and High Church Anglicans. Those who fought for the British were Protestant. There was bitterness in the tale and Mathew emphasized the point that most of the Scots now coming to Canada were Protestant. "But we all wear the kilt," Mathew said, smiling. "It unites us here, and in this land we are more united than we have ever been." Mathew then showed Tom a kilt made of the Macleod dress tartan and, while he was at it, he explained the history of the tartan.

For his part, Tom developed a feeling of belonging. He was no longer a mere Englishman, a member of some great amorphous group. He was a Scots; a Macleod.

And Mathew was not the only member of the family who made him feel welcome. Janet was both loving and understanding. She treated him as if he were her own son and confided in him. He also found himself an instant uncle to Helena's children. Helena, like her parents, accepted him completely.

Tom roused himself from his reverie and turned to look at

Madelaine. She was deeply engrossed in her sewing and he took advantage of her distraction to steal a long glance at her. She was the one person in the household he had failed to get close to; the distance she kept from him made it difficult for him even to begin a conversation. She was, Tom knew, his own age. He also knew she was a widow, just as he was a widower. Perhaps, the thought, it is because she and I are no blood relation. Then he thought, hopefully, it was because she was attracted to him as he was to her. It is not only friendship that I want, he admitted to himself.

Madelaine suddenly looked up as if she had felt his eyes on her. She tried to smile, but the color rose in her cheeks.

"I'm sorry," Tom apologized. "I didn't mean to stare at you."

Madelaine's dark eyes glowed warmly and she murmured, "It's all right."

"It's just that you are so beautiful," Tom blurted out, blushing himself for being so bold. He was painfully aware that this was one of the few times they had been alone together and he suddenly felt brave enough to take advantage of the situation.

Madelaine's blush deepened at the compliment. But she did not answer him. He noted, however, that she did not look displeased either.

Tom stared at his own clasped hands for an instant. "I feel foolish," he admitted. "You know I am a widower." He shook his head. "A man who has been married, who has courted before, should not be acting so much the novice." He lifted his eyes to look into her delicate, heart-shaped face and found her expression somewhere between benign amusement and embarrassment. "I should give off the aura of experience and of maturity," he stumbled on. "I simply should ask if you would accompany me to official functions—and if you would allow me to court you."

Madelaine stuck the long needle into the cloth and dropped her hands into her lap. She lifted her dark eyelashes and met Tom's steady gaze. "Nor should I, a matron, be playing an ingenue," she sighed. "Sometimes, Tom, I feel like this cloth stretched on a frame." Madelaine paused. "My husband has been dead for some time," she explained, "but we were very much in love."

"Does that mean you cannot love again, or at least know another man in marriage?"

"I have tried to love," Madelaine confessed.

Tom knew she was telling the truth. Madelaine was the toast of Montreal; Helena had told him about her many suitors. "She can be gay and flirtatious," Helena assured him. "But I think she stays distant and cherishes the memory of her husband too much. It prevents her from becoming serious about any one man. And you must remember," Helena warned him, "though Madelaine had been reared in a Scots home, she is French Canadian. She has conflicts, and because of her unique background, those conflicts are both emotional and political. She was born into Quebec's upper class. Her brother Pierre had reclaimed and rebuilt the family *seigneurie;* her other brother, René, has chosen to ally himself with the Scots merchants of Montreal. Pierre is a traditionalist, René an entrepreneur. Madelaine is in the middle. She does not care about the Church because of what happened to her mother; she is morally against many of Quebec's institutions. But she also is suspicious of the British. She is bilingual and has divided loyalties. She is torn between two worlds and two cultures; like so many in Quebec she finds it difficult to walk on one side or the other. For a French Canadian, language is culture. We Scots had our language ripped from us, but we managed to survive culturally. With the French Canadians, it would be different. Their language is so tied to the definition of culture that they all fear losing it. It is that which divides us."

Tom had considered Helena's words well, but he was not to be put off. He felt some strength now. He had begun the adventure and he intended to see it through. He stood up and walked over to Madelaine. He reached for her hand and took it in his. "You have not tried with me," he replied. "Let me take you to the governor's reception next week. Let me court you properly."

Again Madelaine flushed. "You have a great advantage, you have that advantage of constant proximity. We do live in the same house."

Tom caressed her small hand and thought how delicate she was. He lifted her hand to his lips and kissed it. "If that is an advantage, then I shall press it," he said in a low voice.

Madelaine's eyes had fallen on the golden hairs of his hand. He towered above her and she knew that if she stood, she would hardly be as tall as his elbow. Like Mathew Macleod himself, his son Tom was tall and strong and his muscular shoulders strained the material of his shirt. He had a protective quality about him; he seemed to be a man a woman could count on, a strong man who was gentle. "You have another advantage," she said softly.

"What is that?"

"You are the image of my childhood protector." Madelaine felt a chill of apprehension. She could not deny that she herself had a longing to be loved and to be possessed.

"I am Scots," Tom said, remembering Helena's words. "But I was reared in an English home," he reminded Madelaine. "You are French Canadian, and I am trying to understand all of what that means to you and ought to mean to me. You know, this land has a future; it is a future that can be built only if the English and the French settle their differences, when they become united in one goal."

Madelaine smiled and answered him in French: "Two people cannot unite a country."

Tom smiled and lifted her gently to her feet. He bent over and kissed her on the forehead. "It's a beginning," he said, light of heart. "We shall explore our future together."

Madelaine lifted her eyes to his handsome face. "Let us take our time," she suggested. "Only the very young and foolish must hurry."

Unlike the trip downriver, which was fast and quick, the trip upriver was slow and agonizing. It was partially accomplished on land, partly on water. Robert, James, and Jenna went by water from one settlement to another, exchanging raft for horses when bends in the river could be avoided by overland travel. The small settlements along the river, Jenna learned, operated almost a relay system for travelers going upriver. Some nights were spent outdoors, others were spent in the cabins of settlers, still others were on the river itself.

"It doesn't matter how well you know the route," Robert told Jenna, "it still takes time and it is impossible when the rains close in and turn the banks of the river into seas of silt and mud.''

Jenna's first impression of James was far from favorable. She had thought him quick-tempered and rude, and certainly there was true antagonism between father and son.

But soon Jenna concluded that James was deeply concerned about his mother and deeply angry that his father had run off to a brothel in New Orleans. The rift between father and son caused Jenna to think a great deal about her relationship with her own father. James is like I am, she thought. He is headstrong and rebellious, he does not realize what he is doing.

She learned that James had a sister called Maria and a twin brother named Will. She started at the name Will, remembering her encounter with the young man in Baton Rouge whose first name also was Will but whose last name was Knowlton.

Jenna soon felt drawn to both Robert and James. She liked them in different ways and for different reasons. It is not my place to pry or to probe or to make judgments, she decided. It is my place to do my share of the work and to help as much as possible.

After James heard all of her story, he appeared sympathetic and understanding toward her. For her part, as the days passed, Jenna felt taken with his dark good looks and with his gallantry toward her. He carried her ashore through muddy waters and helped her to make her bedroll at night. He covered her with netting so she would not be eaten alive by the ever-present insects. Together, Robert and James looked after her completely. They caught or purchased food along the way and Robert spoke often of Canada and told her everything about his long journey into the Louisiana Territory and his life on the river.

One early-November night, Robert had gone to lay trap lines, and Jenna and James remained behind, sitting by the flickering fire on a knoll above the winding river.

"We're only a few days from home now," James said absently as he stoked the fire.

"It'll be nice to be in a house again," Jenna admitted. "I like being outdoors, but sometimes I want material comforts

186

too." She did not say anything about yearning to be with other women, though it was on her mind. For eight months now, she had been primarily with men, and that represented a great change for Jenna, who was used to having Helena, Madelaine, and her mother about all the time.

"It's not a grand house, not like the houses in New Orleans. It's a small farming community, indigo mostly." James paused. "But one day it'll be a rich community. It's on the Natchez Trace."

"Natchez Trace?" Jenna questioned.

"The trail west. There'll be settlers going west and goods going north and south. And it's good, rich land too. Ideal land for cotton, if we can get enough slaves to pick and plant it."

Jenna looked at James curiously. Stephan had spoken of slaves too, and of the advantages of owning slaves. "Slaves?" Jenna repeated.

James laughed. "Don't you have them in Canada?"

Jenna thought for a moment. There were some families from the colonies who had come to Montreal with slaves, but they were few in number. And, as she recalled, there were some Indian slaves up North. They were ill treated and always seemed to get sick and die young. "There are a few, I think," Jenna admitted.

"But you don't own any?" James asked curiously.

Jenna shook her head. Her parents, she suspected, would not approve of slavery. They didn't even have servants. She herself had never really thought about it. But she had been aware of feeling vaguely uncomfortable around black people in New Orleans. It is because I have never been around them, she thought. And I can't understand their patois either.

"I guess that Africans couldn't survive in Canada," James allowed. "They come from a hot climate. I guess they would die in the winters up there."

Jenna laughed at the idea. "If we don't, why should they?"

"Because they're used to the heat," James insisted.

"That's foolish," Jenna retorted. "It's hot, very hot in Canada in the summer, but still we live through the

187

winters.'' Jenna paused for a moment. ''You've been brought up in a hot climate. If you went to Canada, don't you think you'd survive the winter?''

James looked slightly annoyed. ''I'm white. We're stronger, better able to adjust than the Africans.''

Jenna cocked an eyebrow. ''If you're so much stronger, why do you need slaves to do your work in the first place?''

James only mumbled an answer, but he pondered her comment. It was clear that Jenna, like his father, did not believe in slavery. But, he told himself, it is silly to be arguing with a woman anyway. What do women know about economics? ''You would like having someone to do all your chores,'' James retorted confidently ''You'd like someone to comb your hair and dress you. You'd get used to it.''

Jenna only smiled at him.

''One day,'' he boasted, ''I'm going to have myself a real house. A house with a great wide green lawn and stables filled with fine Spanish horses. I'm going to have hundreds of slaves and I'm going to be the wealthiest man on the river.''

''Do you think the land on the trace will be that valuable?''

''I know it will be,'' James confirmed. ''The trace is the trail westward, the path to the whole southwestern part of this continent.''

''It's like Thundergate,'' Jenna mused. ''That's the route to the Northwest, the gateway to all the waterways.''

''Why do they call it Thundergate?'' James asked.

''Because of the falls—they're huge falls, magnificent.''

''Then you must realize,'' James pressed, ''how valuable such land is. People are going to move westward, Jenna. The center of commercial activity will be at the crossroads between what they leave and what they are going to.''

''My parents will move back to Niagara when the fighting is over. Not just because it might become commercially valuable, but because the land is rich and it's beautiful.''

''And you'll have to work it yourselves,'' James replied. ''That's not for me. I want my land worked for me. I want slaves and lots of them.''

''My father says the only reward comes from doing the

188

work yourself. He says you have to start something and finish it. He says we all have to build for ourselves and earn our own way."

"Your father sounds like my father," James said with a touch of disgust.

Jenna folded her arms around her knees and looked across the fire, studying James' face. He was doodling in the dirt with a twig and he looked preoccupied. Slaves are the custom here, she reminded herself. And as she looked at James she decided he would at least be kind to his slaves. He certainly was kind to her. There was something about James that reminded her of Stephan. They both had dark good looks, she thought. Perhaps it was that, perhaps it was something in their mutual attitude. It is strange, Jenna thought. I know more about James now than I did about Stephan when I ran away with him. She thought briefly of Will, the young man she had met in Baton Rouge. But he was gone and, like James' brother Will MacLean, off fighting with General Gálvez. No, Jenna thought, I probably shall never see Will Knowlton again.

James looked up from across the fire. "I never really apologized to you," he said carefully.

Jenna tilted her head. "For what?"

"For calling you a whore when we first met."

Jenna laughed, thinking that it was good that she now could laugh about such misunderstandings. "Well, it was a brothel. You could not have known at that moment. You only thought the natural thing."

James smiled. "You are beautiful, you know. Far more lovely than any woman in New Orleans. I thought my father had shown excellent taste."

Jenna looked down at the ground. It had been ages since any man had told her she was beautiful. As kind as he had been, the young man in Baton Rouge had not told her she was beautiful. He had treated her as one might treat a small child. As quickly as she thought of it, she wondered why it bothered her. How, after all, had she wanted him to treat her? She had been alone and frightened, and he had only been kind. Still, Jenna now could safely admit to her own vanity. It did please her to have men look at her and it certainly pleased her that James thought she was beautiful.

"You are trying to flatter me," Jenna answered coquettishly.

James stood up and stretched. He met her flirtatious smile with a look of undisguised lechery. "Of course I am," he answered. But James did not make a move toward her. He dared not. His father would be coming back at any moment and he had to be on good behavior with Jenna Macleod. Her father is like my father's brother, he reminded himself. Jenna had to be treated with honor and respect.

Still, he thought, there is time. Lots of time. Jenna will be coming home with us and Jenna will have to remain there until it is safe to travel. Waiting, he admitted to himself, would not be easy. Twice on this journey he had awakened in the night thinking about her, longing to touch her, but only daring to watch her sleep peacefully under her veil of netting.

Her skin was as white as Belle's was black. Her breasts were full, well formed, and desirable. He imagined that she had rose-pink nipples and he could see she had a fine, round, firm bottom. But what fascinated James most was her hair. He had never before known a redhead and he thought about the mound of hair which was hidden from view, wondering if it was the same golden red as the hair on her head. James turned away from Jenna as she sat by the fire and walked a few paces into the brush. He could imagine her naked in his mind's eye, and he could almost feel his hands on her undulating buttocks. She would enjoy it as Belle did not, he told himself. He could feel himself stiffen at the images of Jenna that ran through his mind. He knew that he would not wait too long to make his fantasy a reality.

"What are you doing?" Jenna called out.

James closed his eyes and willed himself not to think about her sweet flesh. "I think I'll walk by the river," he called back to her. "I won't go far, don't worry."

Jenna watched him as he headed for the small stream that ran parallel to the larger river. James knelt down at its edge and splashed water on his face and arms. "She's a gift and I will have her," he promised himself in a whisper.

* * *

General George Washington had wintered at Morristown in New Jersey and had finally consented to allow the court-martial General Benedict Arnold had requested.

"It is the only way to clear myself of these absurd charges," Ben fumed to Peggy. He turned to her pleadingly. "I know it seems strange, considering where my loyalties lie, but I actually care, I care that my name is taken in vain, that my reputation has been sullied."

Peggy lifted her curly blond head and touched his cheek with her hand. "You have done nothing to be ashamed of, Ben."

"Do I look all right?" He had been fussing all morning and though he was dressed in his finest uniform, he still felt ill at ease.

"You look very handsome," Peggy answered, smiling. "And I shall be right there. I'll be by your side."

Ben's face knit in concern. "Are you certain you're up to it?" His eyes fell on her rounded stomach. Peggy, his darling Peggy, was six months with child. But she looked only a sweet, innocent child herself.

Peggy closed her eyes, took Ben's hand in hers, and placed it on her stomach. "Shh! Feel, see, it's moving." Benedict felt the strong roll and kick of the baby. "It's a miracle I can't fathom. Life—life is such a miracle."

Peggy nodded. "It's time we went," she said softly.

The trial was to be held in Norris' Tavern near the camp. It was quite true that Benedict Arnold did not intend to remain a Continentalist, but it was equally true that he had fought bravely, been badly wounded, and served well. He was accused of issuing a pass to a loyalist vessel and utilizing army wagons to transport its cargo. It was a cargo that Arnold himself owned half of. But it was such an unimportant thing! All the generals in the Continental Army had business interests—how else could they possibly survive? And without question every one of them at one time or another had used his influence to protect his investments. It was not the transport of the cargo of the *Charming Nancy*, and the pass he had issued the vessel that caused this trial. Nor was it the fact that he had been forced to close some Philadephia stores or imposed menial tasks on enlisted men, as he was accused of doing. It was more, much more. It was the prevailing attitude of bitterness in Philadelphia. It was the mean sniping and small-mindedness.

The problem was, the good people of Philadelphia were, in part, Quaker. They were opposed to and outraged at the way the British lived and most especially the way General Howe had lived. In Arnold's view, they were a provincial, Stoic lot who believed with all their hearts the propaganda of the rebellion. My God! They actually believed in equality! Don't give enlisted men menial chores, indeed! How else could one run an army? Did the pious people of Philadelphia, Quaker and non-Quaker, really believe that after the rebellion they would never again have to do menial work? Did they believe that everyone would live alike? If they did, they didn't know their leaders as well as Benedict Arnold did. Every general had an above-average education, every one of them had money, every one of them had privilege, and every one of them expected to keep it! But, of course, there would be the occasional sacrifice to egalitarianism. Arnold saw himself as the current sacrifice. Well, he thought, I shall win this battle and when I do I shall retrieve my honor and break faith with this band of highway robbers who call themselves patriots. How, how, he asked himself, had these rabble-rousers gained such a following? His only conclusion was that they pandered to the masses. Hadn't they, after all, taken a poor little seamstress, Betsy Ross, and elevated her to national stature because she sewed together a flag for them to fight under? Good heavens! She wasn't even the best seamstress! But never mind that, the Continental Congress adopted her little effort as the flag two years ago and now, thanks to Washington's efforts to make her famous, she had opened a shop and had a good, fat contract to design uniforms for the army.

Arnold leaned on Peggy's arm as they entered Norris' Tavern. His leg pained him and he leaned heavily on his cane. Peggy smiled at the chairman of the proceedings and took her seat. But as soon as the charges were read, her smile faded and she began to weep into her lace handkerchief.

The pass had been illegal and improper, the charges maintained. The use of the wagons also was not proper.

Arnold stood when requested, having decided to defend himself. He limped on his cane; the pain from his leg was obvious in his face.

"I was the first to appear on the field of combat," he said. "And never have I abandoned my true duty. I have won honors of war and from each of you, and from General Washington, I have letters praising my skill in battle and the military achievements made by the men I led."

He withdrew some of the letters from his case and read them aloud. There were murmurs through the courtroom, a wave of hushed whispers.

Peggy bit her lip as she watched her handsome, brave husband. He was angry and proud; he had given his all and now he was being sacrificed because Washington needed to placate the merchants of Philadelphia. She stared at the military judges without blinking, allowing her tears to flow freely down her cheeks. Benedict was reading a letter of warm praise from Washington. It was sad, it was ironic.

"How could I win such honors and then sink into a code of conduct unworthy of a soldier?" Benedict asked the judges when he put down Washngton's letters. "No! I have not done the things I have been accused of! I have been slandered and abused! I am being attacked because the city of Philadelphia suffered under British rule and did not understand the discipline needed in the aftermath of the British retreat. I was a successful businessman before the rebellion began. I gave up my business to fight. Am I not allowed to carry on my life with a modicum of normalcy? Am I not expected to make investments like the rest of you? Not one of you has given up your business interests. Am I to be punished for General Howe's excesses in Philadelphia simply because I moved into the quarters he vacated?"

Arnold lowered his voice. "I ask only that you judge my actions as you judge your own."

There was more mumbling and more murmuring until the judge's voice droned. "Our verdict will be handed down on or before January 28, 1780. We ask you to return to Philadelphia and return here at that time, or sooner if notified, to hear that verdict."

"I shall," Benedict answered, his voice hoarse from his long morning of testimony.

Peggy again was at his side. She wiped her face and together they left. "It's most humiliating," she said softly. "I don't know how you can bear it."

Their carriage passed lone farmhouses, rock-strewn, snow-covered fields, small villages, and mills by riversides. "I couldn't if you were not at my side," he replied, patting her knee. Then he sank back against the plush red cushions. "I can't let these people win," he mumbled in a hushed tone. "They can't be allowed to win."

Tom lifted Madelaine down from the carriage and set her on the walk before the front door. She wore a stunning gown of rose brocade that set off her olive skin. Her dark hair was fashioned high on her head, part of it falling down on her neck. "You are as exquisite a partner as a man could wish," he said, unable to disguise the admiration in his eyes.

She lifted her skirts and he opened the door. "Would you like me to fix some tea?" she offered. "My head is light from so much wine."

The house was dark and they walked quietly down the hallway to the kitchen where, using his pipe tinder box, Tom lit a candle.

"I can't say the parties in Montreal rival the ones in Philadelphia, but the lady I escort is a rival for any woman."

Madelaine put the tea kettle on the potbellied stove. The fire still burned and the house, though everyone had gone to bed, was warm because in each of the stone hearths a fire still burned.

"You have a golden tongue," she teased. "You know, it is Frenchmen who are supposed to be great flatterers."

"I do not intend to be outdone."

"You won't be," she said mischievously. Tom looked at her for a wordless minute. This was the third occasion he had escorted her to, and they saw each other every day. Their relationship was quickly growing closer. But he had not even kissed her yet; he was trying to do as she bid him. He was trying to go slowly.

"Your perfume is intoxicating," he said in a low voice. But he knew it was not her perfume. He reached out toward her and pulled her into his arms. At first her lips were cool to his touch, then they moved beneath his, returning warmth and passion. It was a long kiss, a kiss that spoke what neither of them was yet ready to admit.

"You are bold tonight." Madelaine smiled as she withdrew from his embrace.

"And you are tempting."

Madelaine set out the cups on the table and put the tea in the pot. Then she poured the boiling water in to let the tea brew. She sat down on the wooden bench and leaned on the table. "This is a strange courtship," she said, smiling. "It is strange because we come home to the same house."

"And are seldom, if ever, alone." Tom joined her at the table.

"That may be just as well," Madelaine joked.

"Quite right. If we were alone, I would try to seduce you every hour of every day." His eyes stared longingly into hers.

Madelaine blushed and looked down. "I am too old to play the coquette. I'm not sure I would rebuff your seduction."

Tom took her hand across the table and looked at her seriously. "Not till we are married. I think too much of you, I care too deeply even after so short a time. But I would be the first to admit that having had the taste of love, having been married before, I am anxious."

Madelaine let out her breath. "I too," she admitted honestly. "When I said we did not have to hurry, it was an ill-considered request. I didn't realize I could feel so strongly after so short a time," she confessed.

He smiled and thought how much he admired her honesty. She was not playing a game with him as other women might have—indeed, as they had in the past.

"It is not a good idea to let a man know how you feel," Madelaine said, almost guessing his thoughts.

His eyes caressed her lovingly. "Trust me," he asked. "I love you and if you love me, it only makes things as perfect as they should be."

"I love you," Madelaine admitted. "I'm not sure it's wise, I know it's not prudent, I think I regret loving a soldier . . . but I do."

He squeezed her hand and lifted it to his lips, kissing her passionately. "Then tell me you'll marry me," he pressed.

195

"Tell me we can get on with our lives, make love, have children, live together in a house of our own. Tell me I don't have to wait forever to claim a future with you."

Madelaine sighed. "I feel so intensely," she confessed, "but it has been a short time."

He squeezed her hand. "In minutes, hours . . . it seemed like years. Madelaine, I love you, I love you a great deal. That won't change with time."

"It's almost Christmas," she said with a smile. "After the holidays? In the new year?"

Tom devoured her with his eyes and kissed both her hands. "In the new year, a new life. It's right, Madelaine. I know it's right."

CHAPTER XII

December 25, 1779

Will looked out across the deep blue waters of Havana's perfect harbor. It was, as always described, the model of a bottleneck harbor. Halfway between shore and open sea, a large Spanish ship floated easily on the calm swells. It was his ship in a sense, and tomorrow morning it would set sail with him and some of the six hundred men he had helped recruit.

Will walked through the loose white sand and sat down on the edge of a crumbling, ancient seawall. He examined the loose stone and turned a piece of it in his fingers, wondering what mason originally had put it in place. This, he thought pensively, is one of the oldest outposts of civilization in the New World. He glanced behind him. Up the hill in the distance he could see the spires of the Cathedral San Francisco. It had been rebuilt in 1716, but it stood on the site of the original cathedral, which had been built in the early 1500s.

Havana was quite a fine city and, had he not been so anxious to return to New Orleans, he would have enjoyed getting to know it better.

Havana had been a surprise to Will. More of a surprise than he had bargained for. He had known some of its history before he arrived, but he had not known that it was the third-largest city in the hemisphere. With its inhabitants numbering more than fifty thousand, it dwarfed New Orleans. By comparison, the streets of Havana seemed overburdened by converging humanity at all hours of the day and night. And if New Orleans retained its French qualities in spite of Spanish rule, Havana was Spanish to the core. It was a city that did not seem to sleep; a city alive with music at all hours; a city with a bustling market filled night and day with the aromas of fish, fruit, and tobacco. It was quite another world from his childhood world of isolation on the banks of the Mississippi.

The main language of Havana was, quite naturally, Spanish. The Spanish had controlled Cuba for over two hundred years, save for a short period of eleven months during the Seven Years' War, when it had been captured by the British. But that was a joke in the history of Havana. The people all said it was the other way around. The British landed and only claimed to capture Havana; but within days it was they who were captive. Captive to a commerce so active they never understood it; captive to the music, the women, and a way of life so utterly un-British that it was totally corrupting. At the end of the Seven Years' War, Havana reverted to Spain in exchange for West Florida.

But eleven months was quite long enough. Among the golden-skinned, dark-haired beauties of Havana, the British had clearly enjoyed their stay. Eleven months had been long enough to sire a generation of children, and one saw them everywhere. Even if their mothers were coal black, the children were lighter of skin and looked like coffee. If the mothers were light-skinned and Creole, the babies often were blond and blue-eyed, with skin of golden hue. Yes, Will thought the British had changed the complexion of the island, giving it new hues. Of course, the Castilian Spanish had done their share of breeding as well. As they were in New Orleans, the people of the island were varied. They ranged from black to snow white with all possibilities in between. And as in New Orleans, ladies of the evening were in plentiful supply. They had no problem earning a good living. Spanish, French, Portuguese, and Dutch ships often were in port here.

Abstractedly, Will kicked the sand with his foot. He was frustrated and angered that the Spanish commander, Diego José Navarro, had vacillated so. He refused to give Will and Estevan Miró more ships for the attack on Mobile. Men he was willing to part with, but he mumbled constantly about ships. "Oh, we must keep our fleet intact," he went on. "For defense purposes, you understand."

Will and Estevan had argued long and hard on behalf of

Bernardo Gálvez. "It would be best for your defense if Mobile were in Spanish hands."

But the commander was a nervous man, a man set in his ways, and a man committed to defense pure and simple. He refused to admit that Mobile posed any threat to him, or that having it in Spanish hands would make Havana less vulnerable. "You'll have four fine ships to transport your new troops," he told them. "More than that I simply cannot spare."

Will felt that he was returning to Gálvez with his hands only half full. He had the needed men, but he had failed to get the additional naval power. Naval power could mean a great deal, he reflected.

So, Will thought, I will bring back only what we've been able to secure and a few memories of Havana. They were, of course, memories worth having.

Diego Navarro could be accused of military shortsightedness, Will thought, but he could not be accused of being inhospitable. He had insisted that Will stay at the official residence, a huge, rambling, stucco villa, whitewashed to a brilliant purity and covered with a a sloping red-tile roof. It was the most magnificent house Will ever had been in. It boasted no less than three indoor courtyards complete with fountains and lush flower beds.

"For you, a Christmas present," Navarro promised. They had taken dinner at the hard-carved dark oak table in the main dining salon. It was a nine-course meal that included trays laden with fresh island fruits, spiced seafood dishes, and piles of Spanish rice accompanied by Arab flatbread and clove-spiced lamb. "A memory of Moorish rule," Navarro explained as he served the lamb and the flatbread, "they enhanced Spanish cookery."

"It was a sumptuous meal, *señor*," Will told his host after dinner. "And most welcome."

Navarro seemed gratified. "The least I can do. But you will have a gift, too; this is a celebration of sorts."

Navarro poured more Madeira, "*¡Felices Pascuas! ¡Felices Navidades!* We must have yet another toast and must arrange for your surprise."

Will was embarrassed and fumbled verbal apologies. "It's not necessary," he kept saying. But Will had forgotten how the Spanish could be. Formality was important and when one came, one brought gifts and was given gifts of welcome in return. To reject a gift was a gross insult, so Will said no more.

Navarro's gift was a total surprise and did not arrive until after he had been shown to his bed chamber, a large, airy room with a balcony that overlooked one of the small, secluded courtyards.

He had undressed and crawled into his bed when the door to his room opened and a beautiful young woman came in. The light from the candle near the bed flickered, but even in the shadows, Will could see her clearly. He sat in the bed, startled. Though, he reflected, not so startled that he didn't appreciate her appearance.

She wore a long white dress trimmed in red Spanish lace. Its skirts were layer on layer of deep ruffles and its plunging bodice revealed small but well-formed breasts.

"I have been sent to entertain you this Christmas Eve," she said, smilingly. Will blushed, but he could not deny she was a most unusual gift. Her hair was jet black and fell nearly to her slender waist. It was held back away from her delicate face with huge combs, and her eyes were great dark pools framed by long, thick lashes.

She glided rather than walked to the bed. She stood over him smiling; a dazzling, white smile. He remembered feeling self-conscious—young, inexperienced and foolish. He was sitting in the huge Spanish bed like a prim old maid with the white sheet pulled up nearly to his neck.

"Señor Navarro says you are a virgin. Are you?" Her eyes flashed and Will could see the look of genuine amusement on her face.

She smiled again and sat down on the edge of the bed. She reached out to him and her cool hand massaged his neck. "You don't have to answer," she said playfully. "It makes no difference. I am quite well trained."

Will closed his eyes for a second and let go of the sheet, allowing her to run her soft fingers through the sandy hair on his chest. A chill of response ran through him and as she drew closer, the sensation of her hands caused him to tingle. She lay her head against his bare chest and kissed him, moving slowly up his neck and breathing seductively into his ear. Will moved his rough hands over her bare shoulders; her skin was incredibly soft and her dress seemed to slide away at his touch.

She removed the sheet that covered him and shed her filmy white gown, then covered him with her naked body. Will felt he was living a dream. His hands moved over her and he watched with fascination as her small, firm nipples hardened. She did not have large breasts, but they were well shaped and seemed to harden at his touch. She, in turn, ran her hand slowly down his body till she grasped his organ, caressing it till it grew harder and more ready than Will ever had imagined it could. Then she slithered down the length of him and covered him with her full mouth, moving with such agonizing slowness that Will thought he would burst with pure physical desire. At the very moment he thought he could bear it no longer, she removed her full lips from his manhood and straddled him with the grace of a dancer. Will reached for her breasts, which moved seductively above his face as she hovered above him, moving slowly up and down, allowing him to enter and withdraw, enter and withdraw. Will remembered reaching for her undulating hips just as he burst forth, arching his back and letting out a gasp of relief and satisfaction.

She waited for a few seconds and then nestled next to him, stretching her body out full against his. She took his hand and directed it down over her smooth belly till it rested on her mound of dark, curly hair. She moved his fingers expertly to the spot where she wished them and then began to direct them in a slow movement. "Ah, *sí*," she murmured as he mastered the slow rhythm. Will propped himself up and watched her face. She had lain back, her eyes closed with an expression of pure pleasure on her face. "Not too fast," she begged. Will was transfixed. Her hips moved and her nipples hardened until they looked like dark stones set atop white mountains. Her lips parted and she looked almost as if she were in pain. But she moaned with satisfaction and Will discovered that he too was ready again. "Now," she murmured, and Will mounted her while she parted her legs to receive him. Her movements were sensual and he slipped

201

his hands beneath her buttocks to lift her to him. This time she too cried out and Will, unable to hold back longer, pulsated into her.

Even as he recalled the intimate details of the night before—indeed, those of their parting on this very morning—Will felt the color rush to his cheeks. He lifted his eyes once again to the harbor and let them rest on the ship he would soon take back to New Orleans. He had not gotten all he came to Havana to get, but he had received more than he expected. He smiled to himself. Havana always would be a precious memory, a kind of magical place. He had left New Orleans a boy with a man's responsibilities; now he was returning a man, having experienced that last mysterious rite that heralded his entry into the world of the adult male. He looked on Navarro's "gift" not as love but as a precious physical interlude "whereby I will know real love when I find it."

Will turned to go back and finish his last bit of business. Gálvez must have known, he thought as he recalled their last conversation. "The commander of Havana will look after you; he looks after everyone." Will had wondered why Gálvez, the adventurous lover with two dozen mistresses, had looked so very mischievous. "Now I know," Will said aloud.

A blanket of soft white fluffy snow covered the cobbled streets of Montreal, and curls of smoke rose from the great double chimneys of every house and building to disappear into a gray sky.

The Macleod house was filled with the aroma of freshly baked breads, cookies, puddings, and sweet cakes. In the center room, a large fir tree stood by the window. Helena, Madelaine, Tom, Mathew, and Helena's children Abigail and Michael were decorating the tree with candles, gay balls of crocheted yarn, and long strings of bright red cranberries. All of the decorating was being done under the watchful eyes of Captain Hans Humbolt, one of two officers billeted in the Macleod house. Dutch in origin, he had insisted that Christmas would not be Christmas without a fir tree and had, as a surprise, brought the tree as a gift for the family.

Hans wove magic Christmas tales for the children, stories

about translucent ice castles and venerable old toymakers, stories of Sinter Claes, the benevolent magician who caused presents to appear on Christmas Eve.

"Oh, not on Christmas Eve!" Madelaine exclaimed. "Père Noël, he does not come till Twelfth Night!" The round-faced Dutchman, a loyalist from New York, laughed heartily. "We are a jumble of customs!" he bellowed. "But all of them are good! There should be presents from Sinter Claes, my magician, on Christmas Eve, and more presents on Twelfth Night from your French auntie's good Père Noël! Can't have too many presents, eh? Or too many people to bring them!" The children giggled with delight and Hans drew them closer to tell them another story of Sinter Claes.

"He sounds like he looks just like you!" Michael said with enthusiasm. And it was true. Hans was a huge man with a fat round belly and full red face and a nose that did indeed resemble a cherry. "But it's red from too much brandy," Hans confided, "and not from the frosty cold."

"What does Père Noël look alike, Auntie Madelaine?"

"Much thinner." Madelaine made a motion with her hands. "He's very old and very wise. He has a long white beard, tall black boots, bright blue trousers, and a red coat trimmed with ermine fur."

"Is that like beaver?" Michael asked.

Madelaine laughed. "Only white and more valuable."

Janet paused in the doorway and looked proudly at her brood. Including guests and grandchildren, they were a large family. There were, she thought unhappily, only two missing: Jenna and Andrew. And of course Mat . . . Janet blinked back a tear, and forced the sad thought out of her mind. Tonight there was too much warmth, too much happiness.

Hans, who had replaced one of the British officers as a billet only recently, was a great improvement. He was not stoic and sullen, as the young, homesick British officer had been. Hans had brought with him a certain *joie de vivre*, albeit a loud and often crude way of expressing it.

Janet inhaled the wonderful smells of the house. It smelled of evergreen. The odor came not just from the fir tree, but from branches that decorated the doors and hung on the walls. Seldom did the Scots use a whole tree, but decorating with branches and with mistletoe was a custom as old as the Celtic people. And, for the remaining British officer, Ronald Cook, there was a Yule log burning in the fireplace. He had not yet arrived, being delayed by urgent duties.

Abigail stood up and stretched. "When are we having our feast?"

"Soon," Janet replied. "We'll wait a bit longer for Captain Cook."

"The menu's as varied as the company," Mathew announced cheerfully. "Black puddings and haggis for the Scots, plum pudding and rare beef for Captain Cook, a spicy fat sausage or two for Hans, and a pot of hot Quebec meat soup for everyone!"

"Everything is for everyone," Janet said and smiled.

"Not the haggis!" Hans said with distaste. "But the wine, yes! Lots of wine!"

"What magic will Sinter Claes perform tonight?" Michael asked, preferring to return to the magic world of Hans' stories to discussing food when his stomach was quite empty.

Hans closed his eyes and put his finger to his lips, pretending to fade away into a trancelike state. "I feel he will bring good news . . ." he intoned in a mystic voice. Then opening his eyes, he glanced at Madelaine and Tom.

Good news seemed as safe a prediction as any. They were sitting beneath the tree and though their fingertips didn't quite touch, Hans noted they were indeed close. In any case, they looked at one another much too lovingly not to be in love. The looks that passed between them were stolen, subtle glances, but Hans prided himself on being an observant man.

"It's time for a Yule toast!" Mathew smiled. "Wine or brandy?"

"Oh, brandy, please," Hans replied without hesitation. Janet disappeared and returned with a tray of brandy snifters, each containing several ounces of drink. As she passed one to each person, she heard a carriage in front. "Ah, let's wait a moment," she suggested. "I think Captain Cook is here."

In a moment the front door opened and Captain Cook came in. "You look like a snowman!" Michael called out happily. And he did: Ronald Cook was covered from head to toe with snow. He took off his heavy coat and removed his boots. The snow that had nestled in his eyebrows melted in the warm room, causing little drops of water to run down his nose and cheeks, which were red from the nip of the December night.

"Am I too late?" he asked breathlessly.

"Not at all," Janet replied. "We are only now about to toast the Yule." Ronald Cook took a brandy snifter and grasped its stem in his hand. "Ready," he announced. "And it's just what I need to warm me up."

Mathew raised his glass. "To an end of this rebellion, to peace, and to a better and more prosperous year!" They raised their glasses and each took a sip. Ronald put his glass down almost immediately. He reached into his coat and withdrew a leather pouch. He turned to Janet and handed it to her. "This is for you," he announced. "It was delivered just before I left. A message of some sort."

"A message?" Janet's heart took a sudden leap. Messages, she knew full well, could be good or bad. This year, it seemed, she had received far too many bad ones. She undid the pouch and withdrew the carefully folded parchment addressed to her. She unfolded the parchment quickly under the watchful eyes of her family. She quickly perused the page and her eyes settled momentarily on the signatures attached. "Good heavens!" The words escaped her lips and a smile broke across her face, revealing to a breathless group that the news was good and not bad.

"What is it?" Mathew asked. "Are we all to be kept in suspense?"

Janet's face flushed with excitement and with the brandy she had just sipped. "It's from Jenna!" Mathew clamored to his feet and came quickly to her side. "And Robert!" Janet exclaimed with surprise. "Jenna's with Robert!"

"In Louisiana Territory?" Helena asked with surprise.

Janet nodded and struggled to reread the letter word for word. Mathew peered over her shoulder. A frown covered

Janet's face. "Stephan was killed," she said softly. "But Jenna's with Robert in New Orleans. He is taking her back to his home upriver."

Mathew's look of concern also turned to a smile. "Jenna's safe," he repeated.

"Is she coming home?" Madelaine pressed.

"Not just yet," Janet explained. "Travel is difficult because of the rebellion. Robert thinks she should wait, then he will see to her return."

"Will he come too?" Abigail asked, her eyes large and round with childlike curiosity. Robert MacLean, whom neither Abigail nor Michael had ever seen, was a kind of legendary family figure. Their mental picture of him was second only to their mental picture of Sinter Claes. Robert MacLean was a hero—a giant of a man, an Indian-fighter who had mastered Indian ways and languages, an adventurer, a frontiersman. He had fought and won at Fort Henry; he had survived the Battle of the Plains of Abraham, he had rescued their grandmother from the ruins of Quebec City and brought her back to Fort Niagara. He had lived with the Indians and he had traveled past Thundergate and all the way down the Mississippi.

"Perhaps," Janet answered, biting her lip. Jenna was safe! She couldn't keep the tears from forming in her eyes now; her long, silent prayers had been answered.

Michael clapped his hand together. "Uncle Hans was right! Sinter Claes did deliver good news! He is a magician!"

Janet smiled at Hans. "I guess he is at that," she allowed, happy that her grandson had given the jolly Dutchman the honorary title of uncle.

"Am I then the messenger of the magical Sinter Claes?" Ronald Cook asked playfully.

"You're much too thin and more like Père Noël," Madelaine replied cheerfully, sipping her brandy.

Tom suddenly sprang to his feet. "Sinter Claes has yet another message, a good message, a very good message!"

Mathew looked across the room at his son. "Well, tell us," he urged.

Tom turned to Madelaine and took her hands in his,

206

lifting her gently to her feet. "There's to be a wedding," he smiled. "Madelaine has consented to become my wife."

Mathew walked across the room and grasped Tom, embracing him warmly. Janet did not try to stem the warm tears of happiness that ran down her flushed cheeks. She looked at Madelaine and said softly, "We will be united at last. This is more than adoption, it is a true unification of our families."

"I could wish for no nicer Christmas present," Mathew added. "I have been given two gifts tonight: My daughter is safe, and my son is marrying as fine a woman as there is in Montreal."

"And it's not even midnight!" Michael chimed in from his position on Hans' lap.

"Nor is this announcement a surprise," Hans winked.

Mathew paused. "I have a gift for Tom," he announced. "It is one he will be needing. I think I should give it to him now."

"Will that be all right with Sinter Claes?" Abigail asked.

"He's very understanding," Hans answered. "He has lots of helpers."

Mathew went to the sideboard, and from inside the bottom cabinet he withdrew a carefully wrapped package. "To wear at your wedding," he said, giving it to Tom.

Carefully, Tom undid the paper and with a broad smile unfolded a brand-new dress kilt in the Macleod tartan.

"Now," said Mathew with a broad grin, "you know you're a Scots!"

Jenna sat looking at the river. It was Christmas, but it seemed so totally unlike any Christmas she had ever known, she couldn't quite believe it. In any case, she thought, it was a terrible Christmas. In fact, every day had been terrible since their arrival in November. It had taken so long to get back upriver! And not one of them could have imagined the sadness and tragedy that greeted them. But the memory was vivid and Jenna was sure she would never forget it.

Robert had walked ahead of Jenna and James, his long legs bounding up the grassy knoll to the cabin. He had called out once, half expecting to see Angelique open the door. He had begun running, but as he reached the top of the knoll and the door was flung open, it was not Angelique who greeted him. Jenna soon learned that the disheveled woman in the doorway was called the conjure lady.

"Where's Angelique?" Robert called out. But the woman did not answer him. She stood stock still and stared at him. Her hair seemed more tangled than ever, her face was an ashen mask. "Where's Angelique?" Robert demanded, aware that he had grown shaky.

The conjure lady lifted dark eyes to him, eyes circled with black lines. "She died," the woman answered simply. "She died of the growths and we buried her." She motioned toward the plot behind the house. It had had two small, stark, white crosses before; now there were three. Angelique lay buried next to Fou Loup and Grande Mama.

Robert stopped dead in his tracks and stared past the conjure lady toward the three crosses. "Dead," he repeated as if he did not think it could be.

Jenna reached him first. She held his elbow. He seemed overwhelmed by remorse and guilt as he reached out for the edge of the doorway to steady himself. Jenna could feel his hand shaking and she could see his legs buckle. "Oh, God!" he had mumbled under his breath, "Oh, God! What have I done? I had so much to tell her, I wanted to make peace with her. . . ." And finally he had turned to Jenna with pleading eyes: "I loved her, I really loved her. . . ."

"And she loved you," the conjure lady said with some conviction. "But she was sick for a long time. She had tumors on her body. She turned you out because she had pain, she turned you away, the disease affected her mind."

Robert looked blankly at the woman. He dug his fingers into the door and turned around. James looked stricken. His hand covered his mouth. His eyes were filled with momentary sympathy for his father.

Robert was struggling to take in the reality of her illness, Jenna thought. And it's been nearly a month, and he's still trying to understand it all.

"When did she die?" Robert finally had managed to ask.

"Near three weeks ago," the conjure lady had told him.

"Where's Maria?"

It was that question that had begun the terrible series of

events that Jenna now fought to understand. Maria was the strangest of girls; she was, as Jenna soon learned, quite possessed.

The conjure lady had pointed inside the cabin. "She's sleeping. Sleeps during the day, can't sleep at night." The conjure lady leaned over conspiratorially. "She's terrified," she whispered. "She saw the white dog; see his footprints still are there."

It was with slightly glazed eyes that Robert looked down to see the white pawprints on the porch. They were faint, hardly visible. "White dog?" he repeated the phrase and through a blur he seemed to remember something. "The Haitian ghost story you used to tell the children?"

"She says her mama's ghost is coming for her," the conjure lady added.

It was James who leaned over and wiped the pawprint, then lifted the substance on his fingers and studied it. "Bleached flour," he announced. "I'll bet that dog had been into the flour stores."

"The neighbors' dog," Robert said vaguely. "Maria!" he called out loudly. "Maria!"

In a matter of seconds, Maria had appeared in the doorway, cringing behind the conjure lady. James gasped and Jenna thought it could not be. The girl's hair was as much a tangle as the conjure lady's hair. Maria's dress was soiled and her skin was sallow. She looked as if she had not eaten in a long time; her cheeks were hollow and her dark eyes were ringed with circles; she looked deathly ill and four times the age Jenna knew her to be.

She moved forward with the stealth of an animal, glancing once over her shoulder. As she stepped into the light, Jenna could see that her pupils were abnormally large and they remained so in spite of the bright sunlight. Maria squinted. "Papa?" she asked as if she did not recognize him.

Robert pulled her into his arms and for a moment she seemed to shake against him. Then she withdrew, her huge, haunted eyes meeting his. "Mama is dead! Mama's ghost is killing me!" Her voice rose and she let out a piercing scream, covering her eyes as she did so.

Robert grasped her shoulders and shook her hard. "It is

not! Your mother was a loving and kind woman!" he said firmly. Then he turned on the conjure lady accusingly. "What have you done to her?"

"She screams in the night, all night. She's bewitched! I gave her calming root, that's all. I did a spell, but the spell didn't keep the dog away! That girl's full of the devil! She's bewitched, I tell you!"

"That's nonsense!" Robert shouted. "Maria, stop this at once!"

But Maria did not stop. Her eyes opened even wider. "I saw the white dog," she whispered. "It came to me, but we killed the chickens."

Robert closed his eyes. "I'm going mad," he uttered. "Angelique is dead, my daughter is in some sort of drugged trance. There is no ghost dog! I know the dog you saw and it is quite real. But there are no ghosts, and if there were, your mother's ghost would not hurt you."

But Maria stood there like a statue. She pressed her lips together. "She would, she would, she would!"

Jenna had stepped forward then. "No mother would hurt her own child," she remembered saying.

Maria narrowed her eyes. "Who are you?"

"She's your cousin, Jenna. Janet Macleod's daughter," Robert said.

At that moment, Jenna was glad she was there. I can help Maria, she thought. I can help her because I'm not part of this. And Maria didn't question the explanation, she simply stared at Jenna.

Robert reached down and took Maria's hand. "Let's go inside," he suggested. The conjure lady stepped aside and Robert led the way into the cabin. They all took in the center room at a glance. The bedrolls had been pulled from the bedrooms into the center room. Dishes littered the wooden table, and the stench was unbelievable. There was chicken blood smeared across the walls from one end of the room to the other. And on the table, in the center of the room, three sacrificial chickens lay decaying in the summer heat, their organs removed and spread out in patterns and their heads tied together in a bunch.

Robert turned angrily to the conjure lady, but she was

gone. "She won't be back," he mumbled. "What's this?" he questioned Maria.

"A sacrifice for the white dog."

"There is no white dog!" Jenna could see Robert's temper rising. "And there's no ghost and your mother wouldn't hurt you!" He was shaking Maria by the shoulders. "Do you understand? She wouldn't hurt you!"

But Maria's eyes had grown large as she looked into her father's face. She shook her head and continued to shake her head. Then she shrieked. "Yes she would! She would because I killed her!"

Jenna remembered clearly the chill that had run through her. Maria completed her confession and then bolted from Robert's grasp, running out of the cabin. James went after her and Robert sank onto a bench, his hands covering his face.

Jenna went to him and patted his back. There were no words to say. "I will try to help," she had told him finally.

Now, Jenna thought, it is Christmas. Robert had tried to lose himself in work and James, who always was wonderful to her, did much the same. She tried patiently with Maria and finally succeeded in getting the sullen, silent, guilt-ridden child to eat three meals a day and sleep through the nights.

Jenna stood up and looked down toward the river once again. She could see James in the distance, tugging a flatboat to shore and tying the line securely. It was filled with supplies and in a few moments he began to help unload them. It might have been her father unloading supplies on the dock near Fort Niagara. A wave of homesickness flooded her. "I hope you got my letter, Mama," Jenna said aloud. She had written it so hastily and given it to a sea captain just before they left New Orleans. "Merry Christmas, Mama and Papa," Jenna said. "I wish I were home."

CHAPTER XIII

January 26, 1780

In the carriage, Peggy's hand covered her husband's. She was almost afraid to look at his face; she could feel his intensity in his clenched fingers.

They had returned to Morristown at the request of the court and, after the long journey, they had sat in Norris' Tavern while the judges streamed in, one by one, unconcerned that they were late and seemingly uncaring about her and Benedict, who waited so patiently to hear his innocence proclaimed.

But they had not proclaimed his innocence. Six of the eight charges had been dropped, but the docking pass for the *Charming Nancy* was proclaimed illegal and improper, and so was the use of the wagons to transport the goods. For these two offenses, General Benedict Arnold was to be reprimanded.

The judge who read the verdict did so in an utter monitone, droning on and on while Peggy cried, fearful even to glance at Benedict, whose rage she could all but feel across the makeshift courtroom. The judge had no sooner finished when Arnold struggled to his feet.

"Reprimanded?" he shouted at the top of his mighty lungs. "For what? For doing what each of you would do, for doing what every officer in the Continental Army would do!" His face had grown black as a thundercloud and his voice fairly rocked the tavern with its fury.

"That is our decision and it is a mild one," the judge reiterated.

"Allow me to thank the court for its—its *consideration!*" Arnold bellowed, spitting out every syllable.

Peggy had struggled to her feet and virtually run across the room to take his arm. Her blue eyes had been filled with tears as she led him away, hurrying through the crowd of curious onlookers and pushing her way to the waiting carriage.

"We shall go home," she had said firmly, "home to Mount Pleasant."

"Even I didn't believe they would do such a thing," Benedict muttered, breaking the silence at last. "I am playing the scapegoat for Washington."

Peggy sniffed. "They're nothing but uncultured louts, rebels, little people of absolutely no consequence! Benedict, you are too fine a man, too honorable a man to worry about a reprimand from a person like George Washington! Even Mr. Adams, who is one of them, says he is incompetent."

Benedict shook his head in silent agreement. "I don't even believe in their cause," he replied. "And this is the final act of treachery. I will ask George for another command, I will ask for West Point, and when it is given to me, I will surrender it to the British." He turned to Peggy, searching her face. "That is what you want, isn't it?"

Peggy lifted her blue eyes. "I want what you want. I would follow you to the ends of the earth, I would lie for you and kill for you. If you chose to remain a rebel, I would support you. If you choose to remain loyal to the King, I support you. Whatever you decide, Ben, we are in it together. I know you could only do the right thing, the honorable thing. I know you will make the best decision."

"I have made the decision; it is only the danger to you that has troubled me."

Peggy's hand went around his neck and she pulled him down, kissing his lips and moving hers seductively. "I am in no danger," she whispered.

Benedict allowed his arms to encircle her and he bent his head, burying his face in her neck. "I adore you, I adore you." The carriage bumped along and each bump brought them into closer contact. "This cannot have been easy for you," he said, moving his finger around her tiny pink ears. "Are you all right? Is the baby all right?"

"He is getting a little ride," Peggy said, smiling up at her husband. "Oh, do be prudent. If we are going to kiss

213

and play, pull down the shades on the carriage. I shouldn't want every farmer in Pennsylvania to see us kissing."

Benedict felt his face flush, but he did pull down the shades. "Are we going to kiss and play?" he asked, smiling for the first time in over two months.

Peggy threw her arms around him and playfully bit his neck. "I am seven months with child," she murmured. "Am I still attractive? Do you still want to?"

"Want to! I'm in a constant state of frustration."

"Well, it cannot be more difficult than on a feather mattress." With those words, Peggy climbed on his lap, laughing coquettishly. She adroitly lifted her skirts and struggled out of her undergarments. Facing Benedict, her arms around his neck, she looked into his large wide brown eyes. "This is naughty," she cooed. Flustered, Benedict fumbled with the ribbons that held the top of her dress. He pulled it down and away, burying his face in her ample bosom. She undid his breeches and, lifting herself slightly, slipped him into her.

"Oh, I do love you," he said, pressing into her urgently.

The carriage hit a deep rut and they bounced slightly upward together. "Oh, I think this is more convenient than a bed!" Peggy said, laughing. "Most especially in my condition!"

"I mean, she's gone," Tolly reiterated.

But he has a smirk on his face that he can't hide, Will thought. "You may be a fine poker player, but you're keeping something from me. What is it?"

"Am I?" Tolly asked. "Now, why would I do a thing like that?"

"Because you enjoy kidding me and you're still mad because I sent you back to New Orleans. What you're really mad about is the fact that I succeeded without you."

"And went to Havana without me," Tolly added, a twinkle in his eyes.

"I'm serious," Will said earnestly. "I've been back less than three hours—it took me two just to find you—and we are mobilizing tomorrow to leave for Mobile. Now tell me: Where is Jenna?"

"Oh, do have another drink. I hate sitting in taverns and having an empty cup. Besides, if you're off to Mobile, you won't be getting much good rum."

Exasperated, Will signaled for the tavern keeper. "Two more," he ordered. The man disappeared and returned almost instantly, setting down two drinks that Will paid for.

"This had better loosen your tongue."

Tolly laughed. "Might I start at the beginning?"

"Do, but don't take long getting to the important part."

"Well, I brought your little moppet safely to New Orleans. I must say, I don't know why you care so much. She's not the most grateful woman around, you know."

"On with it, Tolly."

"Well, I ensconced her—at great expense, I might add—in La Casa Roja."

"La Casa Roja!" Will exclaimed. "You took little Jenna to a brothel!"

"I should remind you that she is the same age as you, and far from little. A trifle immature emotionally, but quite mature physically. Indeed, most women of her age are happily married and not wandering about the wilderness."

"How could you take her to a brothel?" Will's voice was rising.

"Quite simply, I know the madam. Who was willing to board her, quite a moral arrangement, really. Besides, where else is there? Inns in New Orleans, such as they are, are no place for a young single woman."

Will's face was knit in a frown. "I'll go to get her right away," he said, standing up.

"No, no. She's no longer there. I keep telling you that."

Will sank back down to the bench. "And where is she?"

"Well, you remember her story, she was looking for her uncle . . . not really her uncle, but this close friend of her family's."

"Yes, I remember. But she didn't tell me his name."

"Well, he turned up at La Casa Roja, or so Juliet tells me. And your little friend went off, upriver with him, quite happy."

"That's wonderful!" Will exclaimed.

"It may be, but you don't look as pleased as you sound."

"Well, I had hoped to see her. I thought a lot about her, I wanted to help her, I . . ." Will stumbled over his words, aware that Tolly was laughing.

"Oh, you will. When you come home after Mobile!"

"What—what do you mean?" Will was puzzled. Tolly was being unusually vague.

"Well, you didn't tell her your real name and she apparently gave you her married name."

Will frowned. "I gave her the name I was traveling under, but what difference does that make?"

Again Tolly laughed and gulped from his tankard of drink. "Because the relative she was seeking was Robert MacLean, and her name, according to Juliet, is Jenna Macleod."

Will's mouth opened in surprise. "Macleod." He repeated the name dumbly and cursed himself for not urging her to tell him her whole name in the beginning. But she had been tired and hysterical and Will himself had been anxious and distracted.

"My father was here in New Orleans?"

"He was," Tolly confirmed. "And he took the girl back upriver with him. So when you go home, I expect she will be there."

"I can't believe it," Will said, rubbing his forehead. "I really can't believe it—Jenna Macleod. I might have guessed."

"How?" Tolly laughed.

Will smiled and looked down at the table. "Because my father always talked about Janet Macleod and how beautiful she was. Jenna has that same kind of beauty."

"There are lots of beautiful women," Tolly mused. "Are you supposed to recognize all of them?"

Will shrugged, an embarrassed look on his face. "It's just that it's such a coincidence." He shook his head in disbelief. "It really is hard to believe."

"What isn't hard to believe is that we have to get up at five in the morning, my friend. I suggest we get some sleep. Mobile awaits."

In the morning Will MacLean and Tolliver Tuckerman joined Bernardo Gálvez. The men and the ships had been assembled since January 18, but the weather had kept them in port.

They were in all 754 men, including the Louisiana regiment, 14 trained artillerymen, 26 carabineers, 107 free blacks, 24 slaves, and 26 Anglo-American volunteers. The main force of men that Will and Miró had recruited in Havana remained on ships near Mobile Bay and were destined to rendezvous with Gálvez when he and his force from New Orleans arrived.

The little fleet that left New Orleans was made up of twelve vessels. There was the frigate of war *Volante*, which was in reality a remodeled sloop, the *Valenzuela*, and the brigs *Gálvez* and *Kaulican*. The other eight vessels were rebuilt fishing ships specially outfitted for attack.

"We'll sail today," Gálvez announced. *The Gálvez town*, as he called his own vessel, was neither as large nor as fast as the *Volante*, but he insisted on being aboard it. "She is like a beautiful woman," he told Will. "I know her well, and we satisfy one another."

Will surveyed the rapidly moving clouds. The sky was dark from horizon to horizon and he remembered the hurricane that had struck just as they were ready to leave for Baton Rouge.

"The weather today doesn't look any better than it did yesterday," Will commented.

"We've been waiting ten days," Gálvez reminded him. "I am not the most patient of men. It's nearing the end of January and I'm anxious to secure Mobile and move on to Pensacola."

Will nodded. "The gulf is dangerous this time of year; it could defeat us before we encounter a single Tory."

"I'm plagued by the weather," Gálvez answered, looking across the gray horizon. "Job was sent warts and sores; I am tested by the wind and the rain. If I can't defeat the gulf and its storms, I can't expect to defeat the British either."

Will smiled at Gálvez' stubbornness. He watched as Gálvez gave the order to set sail, and the little armada left New Orleans and headed into the unpredictable gulf. It could, weather permitting, take five days to reach Mobile Bay. Or, Will contemplated, it could take weeks if they were caught in a storm and had to make port. Everything,

217

Will thought, seemed to be conspiring to keep him from going home. And home, he decided, was where he ought to be.

The months since their return from New Orleans had passed with agonizing slowness for Robert MacLean. Hard work and sleep offered little escape from reality. "I don't know what I would do without you," he told Jenna. "Having you here has made it easier." *She is,* Robert thought, *like a breath of clean, fresh, northern air.*

But no matter how much Jenna eased the days, she could not solve his problems. First and foremost, there was Maria, who claimed to have killed her mother and now lived behind a wall of silence. Robert watched Maria with anguish, the kind of anguish that came from not knowing what to do for her or about her. He half believed that she had killed Angelique, but he told himself it was because Maria could not stand to see her suffering so. He also believed that Maria had in fact been attacked by Belle's brother and that the attack had caused her to tumble over the edge into insanity. When Maria had first blurted out her belief that she had killed her mother, she had ranted and raved, pouring out hatreds Robert did not know she possessed. There were a thousand and one injuries, real or imagined.

Robert's second problem was James. He learned about the role James had played in the death of Belle's brother and that, because of Maria, he could forgive. But he could not forgive James for being instrumental in carrying his revenge to the entire La Jeunesse family and in chasing them off the land. He could not forgive the fact that James had claimed that land. James, Robert concluded, was greedy.

Thus between father and son there was a deep rift. Jenna played the silent arbitrator, showing understanding and affection to both of them. This Robert found himself uneasy about. He was wary of James' attention to Jenna, so he had warned him again that honor must at all times be his byword. But what more could he do? Jenna accepted James, and Robert could not deny that she even seemed attracted to him. Perhaps, he convinced himself, Jenna could reform James.

They were eating their afternoon meal and Jenna had just dished up another helping of stew. "I'm going to start building on the land soon," James announced. "I'm going to build my own place."

"It's your land," Robert replied, his tone heavy with sarcasm, "no matter how you got it."

Jenna was unfamiliar with all that had transpired between father and son. She knew that the Spanish authorities had delivered the papers and that James and Robert had engaged in a long argument when they arrived. She had heard them shouting all the way from the jetty. Robert, she knew, considered it ill-gotten land; James believed he was entitled to it. "I and my friends only did what any white men would have done." He had looked sad and he had shaken his head. "The people hereabouts would not tolerate them on the land any longer. I was not responsible for the La Jeunesse family just picking up and leaving their land grant. Should the land simply lay fallow?"

Jenna had no answer, though she might have been suspicious had she seen the look on Maria's face. When James and Jenna had their conversations she was lurking just beyond the door.

Jenna decided that Robert might have an exaggerated sense of justice. It did seem strange that good farmland should remain fallow.

"Will you move out when the house is finished?" Jenna asked, seeking to circumvent yet another argument about the land itself.

"It's time I had a place of my own."

"And doubtless you'll purchase slaves to do your work," Robert suggested.

James looked at his father steadily. "You support the army of Virginia, you help them get arms. You're a part of this rebellion."

"Because I believe in free trade," Robert answered.

"When they win, and they will win, slavery will be upheld, and the Virginians, the settlers from the Carolinas—all of them—will bring even more slaves into this territory. It's the way of the future! Slavery is the path to economic stability."

"A man has no right to own another man," Robert said forcefully.

"The clan chieftains own the lesser members of their families; the peasants who work their land merely are tenant farmers who have to turn everything over! That's slavery, it's a form of slavery!"

Robert looked distinctly annoyed. "We gave our loyalty to the clan chieftains. It's not the same as declaring another human inferior or nonhuman. It's not the same as owning somebody!" Robert suddenly was aware of sounding like one of the Quaker abolitionists. He was just as aware that his responses were emotional and that he had not, in truth, given the entire issue much thought. He had a sense of hypocrisy because he was against his son having slaves, but he did not criticize his friends who had them. He wanted the rebellion over with and he helped the Virginians, first, to make good money and, second, because he personally had judged the Virginians the lesser of two evils.

James did not answer immediately. Finally, he only mumbled stubbornly, "Voluntary submission isn't much different than enforced submission if eating depends on submission."

Jenna looked from father to son. She was quite used to political arguments. They were, indeed, one of the main sources of entertainment in the Macleod household. But Jenna would have admitted that except for her argument about Stephan and his practice of militant Protestantism, most of the arguments in the Macleod household were more on the order of airing opinions without being laced with real irritation. Children, Jenna thought, were destined to disagree with their parents on many issues. Perhaps that was more true when the parents were born in one country and the children in a new country. Ideas that parents held dear were not always the ideas children grew up with.

"Well, you can't stop me from owning my own slaves," James uttered with finality.

Robert's eyes softened and he looked away. The law of the land was likely to remain the law of the land. "No, I can't," he answered, "but I don't have to approve of it, either."

Jenna cleared the dishes from the table and when she had

220

finished washing and drying them, she wiped her hands on her apron and hung it. "I think I'll go out for a little air," she announced. The inside of the cabin was stuffy as usual, overwarm from the necessary cooking fire.

"Don't go far," Robert cautioned.

"I won't," Jenna sang back. "No farther than the barn."

She opened the front door and walked out into the night air. A light breeze wafted off the river, but the stars were obliterated by a light cloud cover. It was a hazy night; a night when low-lying fog clung to the ground and rose up off nearby ponds and riverlets. January, Jenna thought. It was January. At home the ground would be frozen solid and covered with snow. The fire would be welcome and people would come and go in sleighs. Jenna sat down on the huge rock that marked the pathway to the cabin. There just wasn't any winter here at all, and though the seasons changed, the change seemed to Jenna to be almost imperceptible. The trees went from golden brown to green and back again. There was no golden and red fall, no barren, stark, white winter, no new, fresh green in the spring. There was nothing but the warmth of endless summer; it always was the same.

"You're thoughtful tonight," the voice behind her said.

Jenna turned and looked up into James' face. In the still darkness its outlines were rugged and strong. His deep-set eyes always seemed to hold her fast and she could not deny her growing feeling for him. But Jenna did think of James as two different people. With his father, James was arrogant and stubborn. Like I used to be, Jenna admitted to herself. But with her, James was soft and he seemed kind and concerned.

"I was thinking of home," Jenna sighed. "I was thinking how different it is here."

James sat down next to her. "This is not where you belong," he suggested. "You belong in a mansion. You should be waited on hand and foot. You should have gowns and jewels, flowers for your hair."

James' hand gently stroked her hair. And for a moment, Jenna was briefly reminded of the young man who rescued her from Baton Rouge. He had caressed her hair too; there was something about James, perhaps his hand motions . . . but certainly they did not look alike. Both were good-looking, but in different ways. James was dark and handsome, Will had been sandy-haired.

Jenna started to say something, but James leaned over and closed her mouth with a kiss. "You have wonderful lips," he praised, tracing around her mouth with a finger. "You are stunning."

Jenna, startled by his kiss, admitted to herself that she found it pleasant. Her green eyes sought his dark eyes. She hadn't objected in any way and when James touched her throat with his hand and again bent and kissed her, she found herself responding, moving her lips beneath his, yielding to the pressure of his mouth.

Reluctantly, James withdrew and cupped her chin in his hand. "I love you, Jenna. I want to marry you."

Jenna knew she must look disturbed. His declaration had not come as a total surprise, but it forced other considerations into her thoughts. The first was her great longing to go home, the second was the vague but persistent memory of the young man in Baton Rouge.

"Oh," Jenna replied. "Oh, James, I'm so confused."

His hand moved lightly from her chin to her neck. His finger traced small circles over her bare white skin and he toyed with a strand of her hair that hung loose. She shivered in response to his sensuous touch for, like Stephan, James was causing her to respond physically.

"I have been married," she reminded James, "however briefly."

James smiled and laughed. His hand slid back down the front of her throat and caressed the top of her breast. "Do you think I would find a virginal creature more desirable?" He bent and lightly kissed her neck again. "Don't you miss lovemaking?" he whispered. "Don't you need it after you have known it?"

"That's not what I meant," Jenna stammered. "I meant that I have to go home. I have to."

James did not remove his hand. He was fully aware of the effect he was having on her and equally aware of his own rising desire. He looked at her warmly and moved his fingers ever so slightly, slipping his hand partially down her dress. "I would take you home," he promised. "I would take you home for as long as you want to stay. But I would

222

want you to come back here, I would want you to help me build." He dipped his head down and kissed the top of her breasts, moving his tongue softly over her cool flesh, dipping it down into the cleavage of her all-too-modest dress.

Jenna moaned slightly and leaned against him. In her mind she envisaged him making love to her as Stephan had done. But, she realized, James was stronger than Stephan. She knew she craved strength in a man—strength and gentleness. "Would you really take me home?" I could live here, she thought, but I must see my father, I must make peace with my family.

"Of course I would," James confirmed. "I would do anything for you, anything in the world."

Jenna shivered again, then she put her arms around him. "My father would never object to you, not to Robert MacLean's son. Perhaps we are fated—do you believe in fate, James?"

He nodded and covered her entire breast with his hand, squeezing it through the material of her dress, wishing this were a secluded spot, wishing they could be completely alone.

"And you will marry me?"

Jenna nodded. "Oh, James. I will."

James might have taken more caution, and Jenna would have been distressed, had either of them seen Maria peering at them from the bushes a short distance away. James would have been especially upset if he had seen her face. It was twisted into a jealous mask of pure evil as her deep-sunken eyes settled on Jenna.

It was February 10 and Mobile Bay was far from its usual blue. It was cold and gray and the dark clouds that had persisted throughout the voyage of the little armada still gave cause for concern.

They were a ragtag fleet and the wind could give them more problems than it might have offered larger ships. Gálvez, tall and handsome, was dressed in cool white breeches and knee-high, highly polished black Spanish boots with long golden tassels. His waistcoat was a dazzling green trimmed in gold braid, and beneath that he wore a shirt made of ruffled Spanish lace. His dark eyes searched the horizon through his glass and he turned to Will without smiling.

"I can well imagine," he intoned, "that you would rather be in bed with a fine Spanish mistress in Havana than here on the deck of this vessel."

"Wouldn't you?" Will ventured.

"I would, indeed, though I prefer two women. One is seldom enough. With two, one might at least have a variety of endowments. As you may have noticed, those with fine bottoms are frequently without breasts, while those without bottoms have ample bosoms."

Will smiled. Gálvez discussed women often. Next to planning battles, women were his favorite topic of conversation.

Gálvez continued to peer through the glass. "The odds might be with us, but again, damn the weather!"

Will could only agree, and a sudden burst of wind which was distinctly cooler than the hot, muggy air confirmed his opinion. "We're in for it, we're going to hit a southwester!" He muttered the words even as large drops of rain began to fall.

"¡Cristos!" Gálvez swore. "The curse of Mobile!"

"¡Mi Capitán! ¡Mira a la playa!"

Gálvez snapped around and looked toward the beach as requested. The *Volante* had run aground on a sandbar. "¡Madre de Dios!" Gálvez muttered.

Men ran for their stations and the sails of the *Gálvez town* whipped in the heavy gale-force winds. "We too will be grounded," Gálvez said prophetically. "The wind carries us too close to the sandbars; the water is far too shallow."

Will looked about. The ships were badly scattered and some of the men he and Miró had recruited from Havana were not on the vanguard of ships. The smaller vessels were still at sea, not yet having entered the treacherous Mobile Bay.

"We cannot head back for open sea," Gálvez confided. It was a statement that did not need to be made. The winds were whipping the ships in uncontrollable circles, circles that brought them ever closer to the long, narrow sandbars that guarded the harbor and lay just beneath the surface of the water, where they could be avoided only in calm weather, when depth readings could be taken.

But the weather was anything but calm and within moments, the *Gálvez town* also was aground, her bow lifted from the safety of the water and onto a sandbar.

Will felt a helplessness he was certain his captain shared. There was no leaving the ship in such a storm and no breaking free without a miracle. Meanwhile, the wind and water pummeled the vessels that were grounded and drove yet another ship onto the sandbar. The remaining vessels, more because of divine providence than by the skilled guidance of their pilots, managed to enter the bay and drop anchor.

The hours passed and the rain-drenched vessels bobbed helplessly in the water while their slanted decks became pools and their sails were mangled by wind.

Sometime close to midnight, Mobile Bay stood almost tranquil in the eye of the storm. "It surrounds us," an old seawise sailor announced. "Only half of it has passed over." It was ominously silent. The wind dropped and, as if by some miracle—a miracle every man aboard had prayed for—a high tide coincided with the temporary calm, allowing the *Gálvez town,* wet and battered, to float free of her sandy prison.

The *Gálvez town* managed to navigate into the bay, riding the tide. She dropped anchor with the other vessels and the eye of the storm passed over, allowing its windy conclusion to whip the anchored vessels for the rest of the night and well into the next day.

By noon on February 11, the rest of the storm had passed over and lashed the land, wearing itself out.

"Like a child having a temper tantrum, these storms," Gálvez said cheerfully as he drank some hot soup. "We will have to salvage what we can, make do with what is left."

Will shivered and thought that he had never felt so wet. The water had flattened his sandy hair and ran down his cheeks, even dripping off his nose. The rain was soft now, as it always was in the aftermath of a storm. Will gulped some soup and wondered why Gálvez didn't look as wet as he did. He laughed to himself as he listened to his commander giving orders and thought, This is Baton Rouge all over again. Gálvez seemed almost inspired by the impossible. When the hurricane had struck, sinking his fleet, he had taken to the overland plan quickly. And hurricane or no, he had taken the British garrison at Baton Rouge only two days off his original schedule. Mobile will be the same, Will thought. Gálvez was not easily put off by what might be described as "fate."

It took better than five days for the men to unload the vessels and to salvage the big guns from the *Volante,* which remained stranded on a sandbar. Gálvez ordered the guns placed on Mobile Point in order to guard the entrance to the bay. "We'll move inland up the Dog River in a few days," Gálvez informed Will.

"And the other men?"

"They will arrive," Gálvez replied with confidence. "It's true that they should have arrived by now, but I know Miró. He's a cautious man and will have waited for calm seas to bring his vessels in."

Will studied the maps of Fort Charlotte, their objective. Intelligence forces estimated British strength to be under four hundred men, but it was not Fort Charlotte that worried him. The main British garrison was at Pensacola, and by this time the British would be on the move trying to reinforce Mobile.

"We'll lay siege to Fort Charlotte," Gálvez said, lighting his pipe. "Captain Elias Durnford is in command and I hear he's a real gentleman."

"Time is not on our side," Will interrupted. "A siege takes time. If reinforcements from Pensacola arrive, we could be outnumbered. Caught between those in the fort and the reinforcements."

Gálvez chuckled. "Have faith."

Another two days passed and Will was awakened from a deep sleep by a joyous cry in the makeshift camp. Miró had arrived! The Spanish now were two thousand strong.

On February 28, the entire Spanish force crossed the Dog River and set up camp less than two miles from Fort Charlotte. The big guns were fired at the fort's walls and then ordered into silence. Negotiations began.

But these, Will soon learned, were not the kind of negotiations that might have been held in the usual frontier battle. This was to be a siege on the European model; it was to be a waltz of formal politeness, a battle between two gentlemen whose roots were in another world.

"We have surrounded Fort Charlotte and by virtue of strength we hold the residents of Mobile hostage. But they will not be harmed, for we are an army of gentlemen, my dear Captain Durnford. Please accept this gift I am sending, some fresh citrus fruits from Havana, a store of tea biscuits, a tin of corn cakes, and several boxes of fine Havana cigars. And while you enjoy them, consider the cannon outside Fort Charlotte. We are a strong army that lay siege to your fort, we will allow you and your men to surrender with all the honors of war. There is no need for unpleasantries."

Will delivered the letter together with the assembled gifts. He entered the gates of Fort Charlotte under the white flag of the unarmed messenger and he was ushered into Captain Durnford's quarters with great civility.

"A rare and welcome treat," Captain Durnford said, admiring a firm, round orange. "We have been cut off from imports from the Caribbean since Spain entered the war." He took a cigar and passed one to Will. "I should be most pleased if you would join me in this delight."

Will looked at the cigar and remembered his last experience with one. He took it, hoping the effect would not be the same. Captain Durnford lit it for him, using an ornate tinder box. Captain Durnford then lit his cigar and sucked on it, closing his eyes with pleasure. "Ah, a divine treat indeed."

Will took a tentative puff, careful not to inhale too much. But to his relief, this cigar was well aged and mild; its heady taste was quite pleasant.

Captain Durnford poured some wine. "Are you to be the messenger who carries our correspondence back and forth?"

"I am, sir," Will said formally.

"Your English is excellent!" Captain Durnford praised. "Is your Spanish as well spoken?"

"I hope so, sir. Negotiations can be quite delicate."

"No, no. We wouldn't want any misunderstandings." Captain Durnford sat back in his chair and sucked once again on the aromatic cigar. " 'Caps on their heads, and halberts in their hand; And parti-coloured troops, a shining train, Draw forth to combat on the velvet plain,' " he recited. "Do you know Alexander Pope? Are you familiar with his poetry?"

Will frowned and felt a tinge of both apprehension and confusion. He searched his mind. His father did possess some books in English and among them were volumes of poetry. But he did not recall Alexander Pope. "No, sir," he answered. "I know some Shakespeare."

"Ah, the immortal bard! But you must acquaint yourself with Mr. Pope. Indeed, I should like Governor Gálvez to accept this volume with my fondest regards. He writes poetry, does he not?"

"Yes, sir," Will replied, now fully aware that his apprehension was justified. This was going to be a long siege and a graceful dance indeed. Captain Durnford was buying time, time for the reinforcements to arrive from Pensacola. The captain had withdrawn a leather volume from the bookcase behind his desk. He handed it to Will. "You also will find a case of wine, a side of mutton, and some fresh chickens waiting outside. These are my gifts to your superb governor. And please tell him I cannot yet accept his invitation to surrender."

Will stood up and bowed. "I will deliver your gifts and your message, sir. But I should mention, sir, that while Governor Gálvez is a proper gentleman, he is not a man of infinite patience."

"Ah, we have world enough and time, my boy."

Will took his leave, a volume of Pope's poetry tucked into his pack and a cartful of Captain Durnford's gifts in tow.

Back in camp, Bernardo Gálvez studied the gifts with some pleasure. "I shall have to reciprocate, of course," he said, smiling and looking at the volume of poetry. "Have Captain Durnford sent some more oranges and some more cigars. I will prepare a letter and send him some of my own verses in appreciation."

"He's trying to buy time, sir. I'm certain he's expecting reinforcements."

Gálvez smiled his mocking smile. "But he buys it with such charming gifts. Am I to be ungrateful? Never! Oh, and do mention that we will commence firing on the fort at 7:00 A.M. daily.''

Five more days passed and the correspondence continued on a daily basis, complete with the continued exchange of gifts and poetry. The cannon fire also continued for one hour daily.

On the evening of the fifth day, three houses in Mobile were found in flames, their hapless occupants having barely escaped with their lives.

Gálvez surveyed the ruins and commented, "I really shall have to rebuke Captain Durnford for this act of unwarranted inconsideration. Why do you order the houses of innocent civilians burned?" he questioned Durnford in his extraordinarily polite letter.

"In order to prevent them from being used to conceal Spanish batteries," came the quite logical reply. "And do let me thank you for the Madeira. It's my favorite Portuguese wine."

And as was to be expected, Gálvez replied. "It troubles me when people's homes are destroyed. I shall not place my batteries behind any homes if you will agree not to burn any more. And allow me to say that with the addition of fine Spanish spices, the mutton was most agreeable."

The answer came with equal charm and patience. "I accept your promise not to place batteries behind homes and I give you my word that no additional houses will be burned. I also should like to mention how much I like your young ambassador, William MacLean. He is good company and quite intelligent. I am pleased that you enjoyed the mutton and hope this bottle of fine aged Scotch also will please your palate."

The correspondence continued until March 10, when Gálvez moved the guns to the more vulnerable side of the fort and began digging trenches. Inside Fort Charlotte, Will reported, trenches also were being built. Gálvez seemed undisturbed and unflappable in spite of Will and Miró's growing concern over the possibility of reinforcements.

"I should not like to be considered a bad sport," Gálvez confided. "The British take sportsmanship so seriously." On March 12 all was in place and Gálvez gave the order to open fire. But this was not, to Will's relief, the perfunctory morning cannon fire that was intended to remind Durnford that Fort Charlotte was indeed surrounded. This was steady, destructive fire; this was battle.

By late afternoon a breach had been opened in the British fortifications and, an hour later, as the sun sank into Mobile Bay, Captain Durnford ran up the white flag of surrender.

The negotiations for the actual surrender took three more days, time lost as far as Will was concerned. But at last, on March 15, the papers were signed.

Captain Durnford was accorded the honors of war. He and his troops were allowed to march out of the fort and surrender formally.

"We meet at last," Captain Durnford said, shaking Bernardo Gálvez' hand. "It is an honor," Gálvez returned. Then, taking Durnford's hand, he quoted, " 'Submit, in this, or any other sphere, secure to be as blest as thou canst bear.' I do like your Mr. Pope," Gálvez added.

But neither Gálvez nor Durnford nor Will MacLean could quite have imagined what was, at almost the moment of final surrender, going on a mere twenty-five miles from the tumbled walls of Fort Charlotte.

A Spanish patrol, sent by Gálvez the day before, encountered a vanguard of over eleven hundred men marching from Pensacola to relieve the besieged Fort Charlotte. The commander of this force was one Brigadier General John Campbell. Dressed inappropriately for slogging through the dense marshes, in the bright red dress kilt of clan Campbell, the Scot cursed both the inclement weather and the "misery of the bog."

A six-foot one-inch Highlander of some decorum and a long military history, he looked down on the leader of the Spanish patrol with some disdain. Alfredo Albenez stood only five feet, two inches in his high-heeled boots. But Alfredo Albenez was game and, at this moment, he considered Brigadier General John Campbell to be something of an apparition. Albenez commanded only twelve men and looked Campbell up and down and decided he had absolutely nothing to lose.

"Why are you in Spanish Territory?" Albenez snapped, craning his neck to look Campbell in the eye.

Taken aback by the too-obvious question, Campbell sputtered his answer. "This is war, we've come to reinforce Mobile! You are the enemy, I demand your surrender!"

"I, sir," Albenez retorted, "am the advance party from Mobile and I have come to demand your surrender. Mobile is ours and there are more than three thousand Spanish soldiers led by Governor Bernardo Gálvez. You, sir, are pitifully outnumbered and I suggest you either honorably surrender to me, or return to Pensacola at once!"

Albenez guessed correctly. A man who stood six feet, one inch, commanding eleven hundred men, looking down on a man five foot, two inches, who was leading twelve men, did not expect to be lied to.

Campbell grunted and ran a nervous hand over his kilt. "Three thousand men?" he repeated.

Albenez nodded yes. "With heavy artillery and a huge fleet from Cuba anchored off Mobile Bay."

Campbell hesitated for only a moment. Then he turned to one of his officers. "Order a turnabout at once! We're returning to Pensacola!"

The officer, an older British regular, grimaced. "Should we not try to retake Fort Charlotte, sir?"

Campbell again grunted. "We are already short of men! A Scots—especially a Campbell—has more sense than to fight over a dead horse. Mobile is a dead horse!" With that, and much to Albenez' relief, the long column did an about-face and began its long, weary march back to Pensacola.

Albenez crossed himself and rolled his dark eyes heavenward. Three thousand men! A huge fleet from Havana! "Just a small lie," he said, crossing himself again. "Back to Mobile!" he ordered his men. Albenez shook his head as he listened to the British column as it marched on and finally out of his range. "No wonder this rebellion is such a stalemate," he mumbled. It was not a compliment to either side.

CHAPTER XIV

March 20, 1780

"There must be a hundred people here!" Janet whispered to Mathew. "And look at that young Mackenzie! Ah, that lad does love a free meal."

Alexander Mackenzie was indeed stuffing food into his mouth as quickly as it was served, and he seemed to wash down each mouthful with yet another glass of wine.

"With this collection of people, we shall be fortunate if rebellion doesn't break out in the parlor," Janet commented. It was, even by Montreal standards, an odd group. There were British officers and English-speaking loyalists. The loyalists, especially if they were born in Canada or one of the Thirteen Colonies to the south, were more British than the British officers—unless, of course, they were Scots, Irish, Dutch, or German loyalists. The Dutch grew furious if confused with the Germans, and the Germans were a house divided. "Your King is really our King," a somewhat drunk German neighbor told young Cook, who billeted at the Macleod house. "Ever since Cromwell overthrew the Stuart kings and put a German on the throne of England! That's why I'm a loyalist! Your King is a good German!"

"But the Prussians fight for Washington—he has droves of German mercenaries," Cook reminded his drinking companion.

"They're another kind of German," the man retorted quickly. "And they'll cause nothing but trouble. They're addicted to fighting."

In another corner of the room, two French *seigneurs* carried out a spirited argument between themselves. And in yet another corner, two merchants were just consummating a business arrangement.

Tom, Mathew observed, had made a total conversion. Proud and tall, and dressed in his Macleod tartan, he looked every inch the Highlander. "I told you, you looked Scots," sixteen-year-old Mackenzie said, nudging him in the ribs. "Are your knees cold? I mean, the kilt takes getting used to after so many years in breeches."

"They're a bit drafty," Tom conceded with good humor. "But I still don't know what to wear in the winter."

"A mite, little wee sock," Alexander replied with a wicked glimmer in his eyes, "long and thin, specially knitted, and lovingly fitted."

Tom laughed heartily; he enjoyed the ribald humor of his people. "But not tonight," Mackenzie was quick to add. "On a man's wedding night, I'm told there should be no restrictions!" He again nudged Tom and burst into red-faced laughter as he downed another glass of wine in two short gulps.

Tom's eyes traveled the room and fell on Madelaine, who looked breathtakingly young and full of life. Her dark hair was elaborately coiffed and her deep golden gown rustled when she walked. It was trimmed in white lace, which made her olive skin look darker. Her black eyes danced with merriment, and her laughter was infectious.

It had been a long day, one which had begun the night before for Tom. All of Mathew's Scots friends had gotten together and hosted a party for him. It had been a long night of drinking, swearing, and telling stories of the Highlands. There had been songs too, and Tom almost found himself singing one of them as he looked at Madelaine. "The sweetest hours that e'er I spend, Are spent among the lasses, O, Green Grow the Rushes . . . Oh!" I love you, he thought. And I love the family I've found.

For the women, it also had been a long night. They had finished together what embroidery remained to be done on Madelaine's trousseau and each had made her a personal gift of something handmade.

The actual wedding had taken place in the home of Governor Haldimand, who had been kind enough to offer it. "It would seem quite symbolic," he admitted. And indeed it was. Madelaine was the sister of a wealthy Quebec *seigneur,* and her husband-to-be was the son of an accepted and well-thought-of Scots family. Governor Haldimand himself was a French-speaking Swiss by birth who had secured a commission with the British Army. He had been the military governor at Trois Rivières from 1758 to 1763 and knew Mathew Macleod and his sons well. Haldimand took over his post as governor on the eve of the French declaration of war against the British. He had served well during a difficult time and was both loved and respected. "Yes, it is symbolic," he declared. "I myself am a sample of mixture and because the wedding of Madelaine Deschamps and Thomas Macleod is a mixture, it is only right that the wedding be at my home. Is it not my assignment to unite the people of this province? What could be more appropriate?"

The governor provided early-blooming flowers from his own garden for the wedding. "I pride myself on my garden," he said with a smile. Janet helped to arrange them. Everyone in Quebec knew about the governor's gardening. Indeed, it was he who formulated the plan for the "edible annex" to Fort Niagara, a quite fancy name for the farms he now was encouraging. "We will not have a winter like the last one," he declared. He had made the comment offhandedly, but it still made Janet shudder. The expected famine at Niagara had materialized because so many loyalists had come into the area so late in the year. But supplies finally had gotten through, and Andrew was safe. It was that news that added to Janet's joy on this wedding day.

In all there had been over a hundred guests and they had sat on long rows of military benches. After the ceremony, performed by an Anglican, there had been a long lunch with all of the family, and now, as the evening wore on, a reception at the Macleod house.

"It reminds me of my wedding," Janet told Mathew. He burst out laughing and hugged her. She was speaking of her marriage, albeit an arranged and loveless marriage, to James MacLean. It was at her wedding that she had met Mathew.

"We'll, I hope the bride doesn't fall in love with another man!"

Janet looked at him red-faced and somewhat sheepishly. "I'd have married you if I'd seen you first."

He squeezed her hard. "If I met you before your wedding vows, even a minute before, I'd have kidnapped you and not let you marry anyone but me."

Tom and Madelaine were together now, standing arm in arm. They looked at one another with such intensity and love that Janet squeezed Mathew's arm and nodded toward them, "I think this knot is tied very tightly."

"And so it should be. I expect grandchildren. Two are not enough."

"You want to populate all of Canada with Macleods?" Janet answered playfully.

"And Macdonalds, Mactavishes, MacLeans, and Camerons. I want my children to help mold this country into a strong nation, a nation where people like us, people who come from lands stolen from them, can build new lives."

"And what about the Indians?" Janet asked.

"That will be settled, but you know I want them to have what's theirs; it's a big land, big enough for everyone to share."

"I'm glad you have a dream, Mathew. No, I'm glad you have a worthy dream." She looked up at him lovingly. "I wouldn't want a man without a dream."

Across the room, Tom whispered into Madelaine's ear, "When can I steal you away? We've been man and wife for hours and I don't feel married at all."

"You're shameful," she whispered back. "Are you suggesting we leave our guests?"

"I'm suggesting that if I stay up one more hour, or have one more glass of wine, I won't be able to make you my wife till tomorrow night."

"We're going to Trois Rivières tomorrow," she reminded him, then added, "but I don't think I care to wait that long!"

"Easy, then; I think we can escape up the back stairs, through the kitchen. I'll stay here; you go first."

Madelaine eased her way out of the crowded room and into the kitchen. She stole past the servants who had been hired for the occasion and up the back stairs to her bed chamber on the third floor. There she quickly changed into the filmy lace nightdress Major André had sent from New York as a wedding gift.

Low-cut and clinging, it fell from her hips in flowing folds. She peered into the mirror. It hardly covered her breasts, and what lace was there could quite easily be seen through. She smoothed her hair and unpinned it, allowing it to fall loose around her shoulders.

Tom opened the door and tip-toed in, locking the door behind him. "They'll never miss us," he said, kissing her neck and sweeping his vision of loveliness into his arms.

"Oh, my God!" he exclaimed breathlessly. "You are wonderful!"

"It's this outrageous gown; it's most immodest!"

"A gown is only as beautiful as the woman who wears it." He swooped her up and carried her to the bed.

Madelaine lay with her hair spread out around her, a dark fan of curls against the pillow. Her small breasts rose and fell with the rhythm of her breathing, straining against the white lace of her nightdress as if begging to be set free.

For a time, Tom could only look at Madelaine, contemplating her beauty. Then he stood up and undressed himself and lay down beside her to kiss her neck and shoulders tenderly.

Madelaine sighed with contentment as Tom lifted her gown and caressed her thighs, finally allowing his hand to come to rest on the tight, dark curls of her mound. She moaned and clung to him as he gently massaged her to life. Her olive cheeks flushed with the fire she began to feel as he touched, stroked, explored her. Madelaine lifted her hands and undid the ribbons that held the bodice of her nightgown, pulling away the lace material.

Tom bent his head and kissed the tips of her breasts, feeling them become hard. "It has been a long while," Madelaine breathed.

Tom slid down the length of her body, kissing her as he did so. Then he began again with her feet, kissing every part of her till again his ardent lips reached the thick, dark curls beneath which lay the center of her ecstasy. There he lingered until her lovely rounded hips moved rhythmically and she clutched at him, trying to reach him. Tom moved and felt her hands close on his manhood, guiding it to its destination. As he slipped into her, she seemed to close around him and Tom groaned with pleasure as she moved beneath him. In their joining, he felt his senses both concentrated and scattered, and he marveled, not for the first time, at the sheer beauty and range of sensations involved. They were like two birds, soaring to the very heights, then gliding together, then plunging into a fall in which all feeling was concentrated. Madelaine shook beneath him and cried out just as he himself felt the final sensation of fulfillment. There was a wave of nostalgia; a feeling of thirst; the rising of some primordial instinct.

When Tom withdrew from Madelaine, he pulled her quivering body into his arms. She was so small and vulnerable that he wanted to protect her always, to keep her from harm. In his lovemaking he had been slow and gentle, despite the urgency he himself had felt. And they had joined as one, making that final pledge to one another and knowing that for each, there would be the other and no one else. "I do love you," he told her.

Madelaine's hand rested on his chest, and her fingers toyed with his hair. "You are all I could ever want," she said and sighed. "It is as if we have been waiting for one another."

Tom hugged her to him. Since his first wife's death he had possessed no other woman and he knew that Madelaine had been celibate since her husband's death. Now, he thought, the long years of loneliness and of not belonging have come to an end. "Life is perfect," Tom told her. "More perfect than I ever dreamed."

Will stared up at the altar of the little Acadian church. It was Lent, so the gold cross was draped in black and the church was bare of flowers. It was not a large church—a chapel, really, a chapel built by the Acadian refugees. His eyes filled again with tears, and he blinked them back even as he clenched his fists trying to get control of himself.

He had returned to New Orleans with Gálvez' main force and found a letter pouch waiting. It had been sent downriver by his father. The letter inside was quite long, and Will could almost make out the tearstains on it.

"You must not feel guilty," his father had told him, "She was ill and had been ill for a long time. It is something we could not have known about. Believe me, she loved you and she forgave you."

I hope you can practice what you write, Will thought. His father must be even more miserable than he. "I should have been there," Will said aloud. "God forgive me, I should have been there."

Will wiped his cheeks and crossed himself. He had been sitting in the Acadian chapel for over an hour. His mother was a Cajun; it seemed the right sort of place to come, though in his heart he felt there was no right place.

"You are troubled." The voice came out of the shadows. Will started, then realized it came from the frail old priest. "I'm mourning my mother's death," he said, choking out the words.

"It is the season of mourning," the priest replied.

Again Will wiped his face and fought back the tears.

"You should not be afraid of crying," the old man told him. "It is no shame."

"I loved her, I disobeyed her, and—and I never had the opportunity to tell her . . ."

"That you loved her?" The priest's hand moved to Will's back. The old man patted him gently.

"Oh, yes. I just didn't have the opportunity to tell her. I was away when she died. I should have told her so much."

"Mourn peacefully," the priest told him. "Part of what you feel now is pity for yourself because you were not there and because you could not explain your actions. But, my son, Heaven is a place of all understanding. She knows, she understands as perhaps she could not understand in her mortal life. Mourn, it is right to mourn. But then rejoice for her soul. Stand up and go forward. Live a life that will make her proud."

Will searched the old priest's face. It was deeply lined. But his eyes were soft and sad; he looked like a man who had cried much and whose tears had worn away his skin, leaving valleys in his face, crevices that marked the unhappy times.

"My mother was an Acadian refugee. She lost her whole family; she was sometimes lonely and she grew bitter."

238

The priest nodded knowingly. "I too am Acadian," he revealed. "We are a scattered people in a strange land, we have a sadness of the soul." His eyes flickered. "But we survive, we will leave our mark."

Will took the old man's hands in his. "Thank you," he said sincerely. "You have helped me. I have made a decision."

"You will go home?" the priest asked.

"As soon as I can," Will answered thoughtfully. "Then I must take a longer journey. I think I must search out my roots, know what my mother really lost. I think I must try to return to Acadia."

The priest nodded. "Many have," he replied. "Go in peace." He made the sign of the cross.

Robert doesn't approve, Jenna reflected. He doesn't like the idea of James and me marrying. He had not said so in so many words, but Jenna could sense his reserve. He ought to be happy, she thought.

Jenna sat on the wooden steps of the cabin and watched Robert's raft as it became a tiny speck on the water, growing ever more distant. He was crossing the river to Natchez for a few days, there to meet with messengers and arrange for the onward shipment of some supplies that had recently arrived.

"The silent battle between father and son will go on," she said aloud. Robert was wonderful to her, but when she and James had told him their plans, he had looked distressed, then expressed only the most perfunctory congratulations. It was all quite the opposite of what one might have expected. Robert's attitude was all too clear. He simply did not believe James to be good enough.

Almost as soon as they were alone, Robert had asked with concern, "Are you certain of your feeling toward him?" Jenna reassured him that she was.

I suppose it is natural, she thought. Robert was so close to her mother and father. "You are good for James," Robert had told her. "He does seem to be more responsible since you came." But Jenna found Robert's suspicion of his own son puzzling. Then, too, there was Maria. She seemed to look differently on Jenna now that she and James had announced their plans. Jenna often felt Maria staring at her, and her look was not friendly. It was as if a jealousy welled within her and she could not control it. It is because we are happy, Jenna thought. Maria cannot stand our happiness because she herself is so filled with misery and guilt.

"You're thinking of home again," James said, sitting down next to her.

"And other things," Jenna admitted without elaboration. She glanced around and relaxed when she did not see Maria. Robert being gone, Jenna realized that this was one of their rare moments alone.

James was equally cognizant of the situation and he readily pressed his advantage, bending to kiss her neck.

"Please," Jenna smiled.

"Please stop or please continue?" James asked, moving his lips downward and kissing her bare shoulder. Jenna turned and his mouth fastened on hers, forcing her lips open. It was a long, sensuous kiss. "Your lips are delicious," he breathed into her ear.

James' hand moved to clasp her breast, which he squeezed through the material of her dress. Jenna's lips parted and she breathed deeply, once again feeling the fire of desire surfacing, the fire that had been buried since Stephan's death.

"We promised your father we would wait for the priest, until we're married."

James did not answer, but instead buried his face in her cleavage, lifting one breast so that it was more exposed. "You don't want to wait, Jenna. Neither do I." His hand traveled up under her skirts and he moved it slowly, tantalizingly. He grasped her roughly and through the thin material of her undergarments caressed her. Jenna felt herself going limp in his arms, desiring his touch. Curse Stephan for awakening such desires, she thought as she gave in completely to James' intimate probings. But he moved his hand away and Jenna leaned against him, a moan of anticipation escaping her lips.

"I don't want to wait," she admitted. James said nothing; he just slipped his arm under her knees and lifted her, carrying her easily to the bed chamber of the cabin and laying her down on the bed.

Jenna closed her eyes and felt him removing her clothing, covering her with his hands, exploring her with rough, urgent caresses. When he parted her downy red-gold hair and moved his hand over her with a maddening rhythm, she thought she would scream out with her sensations of pleasure. But again he withdrew, waiting for her to calm before he resumed teasing her, driving her to the edge of frenzy. In spite of the fact that he himself was bone hard, he did not try to enter her. Rather, he watched as she reached for fulfillment, only to have him deny her.

"Oh, please," Jenna gasped, clutching at him. Again his hand returned to her, but this time his touch brought instant response and she arched her lovely back as she reached the fulfillment and release she had so urgently been seeking.

Her breath came in short gasps and Jenna could feel James watching her. She knew that he relished, even as Stephan had relished, this power he had over her.

"Ah, you do enjoy it," James finally said. She opened her eyes and looked into his. "Your expression is one of pain and passion," he noted as he ran his hand over her. Jenna's milk-white, perfectly shaped body was even finer than he had imagined it, and the red-gold hair of her mysteries was inviting.

"This time for me," he said, turning her over on her stomach and pulling her onto her knees. He moved his hand forward again to explore and caress her into passion. When she moved her rounded buttocks in response, he entered her moist depths, reaching his own fulfillment almost immediately.

Robert stood on the levee outside Natchez. In a way, it was two cities. On the top of the steep bluffs behind him there were a few homes, cabins like his own. They were larger and more spacious than the cabins to be found elsewhere, but they were not the houses of New Orleans. They have, he thought, that temporary appearance that characterized the frontier. Behind the houses on the top of the hills there were scattered farms. Below the bluffs, just a few steps from the levee, was a long, winding road that followed the river. Along it were trading posts, taverns, and even a brothel. Here frontiersmen, Creole women, and merchants plied their trade. They were a different lot from the God-fearing, pious settlers above and beyond the river.

"Damn!" he said under his breath. "Damn the river!" He had come yesterday, and the water had been high and rough. But overnight it had risen incredibly and now it was a torrent of brown, swirling water, running bank to bank. The river, more often a sinuous, peaceful snake, suddenly was an alligator, thrashing its giant tail and baring its sharp teeth.

"I've lived here for sixteen years. I should have known the signs." The river always was unpredictable in the spring. But Robert had thought to chance it, hoping to finish his business and return before the angry waters of the Mississippi rose any higher. Now as he looked at his nemesis, he realized he would likely be in Natchez for a while, as long as two or three weeks, depending on the weather far upstream. There was no denying it: The river had not yet reached flood tide. When it did, the Mississippi carried the trunks of giant trees in its swift current, and it was not unusual to see a cabin, or parts of one, rushing toward the sea. There always were some hapless settlers upstream, some eastern greenhorns who built too close to the sandy banks and did not realize what happened when the sleeping river drank the waters of the melting northern snows.

"It's worse this year than last," old Kenneth Moran, the keeper of the trading post, muttered.

Robert kicked a pebble and turned to the old man, who had been working nearby and had just come over to survey the rising water. "It certainly is worse than last year," Robert agreed, giving Moran's words more meaning than the old man had intended.

Across the river, Jenna lay next to James, who slept. Her eyes studied the dark ceiling of the cabin, settling on two great notched beams that transected the roof. James is like Stephan, Jenna thought. He can make me want him, he can make me desire him physically. But why did they seem to enjoy one another separately? Shouldn't their lovemaking be done in unison?

James had pried the most rapturous feelings from her when he was touching her. He subjected her to divine torture

242

and was himself fulfilled only after he had succeeded in reducing her to a bundle of sensations, making her desirous and wanton. It had been that way with Stephan too, and Jenna wondered if it were always so. Did her parents make love this way? Each pleasuring the other, but not truly being one. "You are a foolish romantic," Stephan had told her. Jenna wondered if James would say the same thing if she asked the question.

Still, Jenna thought, James loves me. He is good to me, and that he brought me satisfaction is unquestionable. But the manner of the satisfaction left Jenna feeling puzzled and somehow lonely. Sometimes, she thought, I just want to be held.

Jenna forced her eyes closed and concentrated on James' even breathing. She forced herself to think of tomorrow's chores. She willed herself to sleep and felt vaguely guilty that Will's face returned to her just as she was on the verge of rest.

Robert awoke at dawn from an uneasy sleep. But it was not the early-morning light that woke him, it was the alarmed cries of old Kenneth Moran and his Creole wife, Mattie.

Robert tumbled from the bed pad and pulled on his breeches, his shirt, and his boots. He ran from the cabin, following the sounds of voices in the cool spring dawn.

On the levee, old Moran, his wife, and two strangers pointed off across the murderously high river. Robert squinted, then his heart began to pound.

On the far shore, the river was spilling its banks and threatening his trading post; on the hill, where his cabin was located, flames burst forth and dark, acrid smoke curled to meet the light of the new day.

A cry of anguish escaped Robert's lips. His eyes searched in vain for human figures, but the cabin was too distant, and all that he really could see was smoke and leaping, orange flames.

He pushed through the huddle of spectators to his raft. "I have to get across the river!" he shouted. "I have to save what can be saved!" His fingers struggled with the knots that held the raft to the levee. He alternated muttering curses

243

and prayers. Let Jenna, James, and Maria be safe, he prayed.

"You can't cross that river!" Old Moran had a restraining hand on Robert's arm. "It's much too high, too unpredictable!"

Robert shook off Moran and fumbled with the last of the knots. It didn't matter! Nothing mattered but getting home! Amid shouts and shrieks from those on the levee, Robert pushed the flatboat out into the raging waters of the Mississippi.

A short time earlier, Jenna, who had been sleeping lightly, awakened to the smell of smoke. She jostled James roughly. "Wake up! Hurry!"

James opened his eyes and rubbed them sleepily, properly exhausted from his lovemaking with Jenna. Then, as he inhaled, he too smelled the smoke and jumped from their bed. He flung open the door and was greeted by a wall of flame and smoke. "The window!" he screamed back to Jenna.

Jenna struggled with the sash on the shutters and then managed to fling it open, allowing a rush of fresh air into the smoke-filled room, "Hurry!" James urged. "It's only a few feet to the ground!" Jenna grasped her clothing in one hand and crawled through the window, dropping to the hard ground below. James jumped after her, carrying only his breeches and cursing.

"Maria!" Jenna called out.

James grabbed Jenna's hand and pulled her back away from the burning house. It was a mass of flames that lapped at the sturdy logs, sizzling and smoking.

"Maria!" Jenna screamed again. She strained forward, but James held her wrist firmly. "She's either out of the house already, or she's dead from the smoke!" James pointed toward the other end of the house, where Maria's room was. It was burning rapidly and black smoke poured from the window of Maria's bedroom.

"Maria!" he called too, but she didn't answer. "Maria!" he called again, but the only answer was the distant howl of a dog.

"Come on!" James eased Jenna along, leading her away

from the house and toward the river. "There are clothes and supplies in the trading post," he was saying. James paused to tie his breeches, and Jenna had slipped into her night-dress. Barefoot and trying to avoid the sharp, jagged little stones on the rutted pathway, she followed James, her mind a mass of confusion.

They reached the trading post and the adjacent dock. Across the river they could barely make out the huddle of spectators on the levee. But the figure in the middle of the river was all too visible. Robert MacLean struggled to control his flatboat amid the whirlpools and swirls of the river. Jenna screamed out and her hand automatically flew to her mouth. Robert's long, muscular legs were wide apart in an attempt to balance himself. He used the long pole not to guide the raft, or to measure the depth of the water, but to punch at debris that threatened to capsize the flatboat in the turbulent waters.

"Oh, dear God!" Jenna whispered. She found that she could not speak after her first scream; her heart pounded and it was as if time stood still.

"Father!" James' voice bellowed out across the water. Moments passed; the distance between the flatboat and the shore did not decrease. James' eyes darted about, but there was no other boat and the distance was too great to make use of a line.

"Hold on, Father!" James again cried out.

The flatboat was near the center of the river, and suddenly the flatboat seemed caught. It was as if a giant hand reached up from under the water and turned the flatboat in a full cir-cle. Robert teetered, fell to one knee, and seemed to be grasping the boards of the boat for dear life. The pole was gone! It had been jerked out of his hands when the flatboat was swirled about.

"Don't fall!" James shouted. "Hold on, my God, hold on!"

Robert struggled to his feet. His torn breeches flapped in the vicious wind, and the flatboat careened downstream but did not draw closer to either shore.

James began running along the bank, parallel to the river, trying to keep up. Her heart pounding, Jenna ran behind him, cutting her feet on the rocks. Her lungs felt as if they were bursting. James was far ahead of her, but the flatboat was ahead of him. It was Jenna who first saw the huge old cypress careening downriver on the current. It passed Jenna and it passed James. "Watch out!" Jenna screamed, again finding her voice.

It was a futile gesture. The huge tree crashed into the back of the flatboat, upending it and flipping it in the mad rush of water. Jenna came to a halt. She heard herself scream again and again, but she was paralyzed, transfixed. she couldn't move, couldn't look away from the horrible sight in the river. The water was fast, terribly fast. But to Jenna, the scene she witnessed seemed to be happening with agonizing slowness.

Robert surfaced and struggled vainly with the current as it sucked him under. He fought desperately, trying to head for shore. He surfaced again, this time a little closer, but again he was sucked under. Tears welled in Jenna's eyes and she grasped the trunk of a nearby tree to steady herself. The wind whipped her nightgown around her, and she was aware that the ground was soggy beneath her feet. She held in her breath when Robert's bobbing head surfaced again. She saw his large arms struggling, his open hands clawing at the water, grasping with the last throes of life. Then he disappeared, as if he had been eaten by the monstrous river.

James too had halted his frantic shoreline chase. He stood absolutely motionless, his eyes fastened on the river, searching the water. Then, slowly, he turned and walked, head down, back to Jenna, who leaned against the tree, sobbing uncontrollably.

He stopped by her side and inhaled. Behind them, on the hill, the house continued to burn. In front of them, the trading post was threatened by the high, rising waters that looked as if they might top the banks at any moment, making a lake of the shore. And in the river itself, debris from some unknown place upstream continued to plummet down the waterway.

"He's dead!" Jenna shuddered and her hands dropped limply to her side. She was cold and numb and her legs seemed to be buckling under her. She was aware of pain in her feet but unconcerned with the bleeding cuts.

After a long while, James shook his head, seemingly

awakening from a bad dream. "We have to move things," he said, vaguely pointing off toward the trading post. "In case the river rises more."

Jenna stared without really seeing, then nodded abstractedly. "Yes, must do something, can't think . . ." she murmured.

"Janet!" Mathew's voice rang through the house. It was filled with excitement. "Janet!" he called out again.

She came down the stairs at the sound of his voice, an expression of anticipation on her face. Mathew was aglow and Janet knew instantly that he had some sort of surprise. It's Tom, Janet thought. Since Tom came, only good things have happened. It was as if having father and long-lost son reunited broke the spell of misery that hung over the household since Mat's death and Jenna's running away.

"The best of things has happened!" Mathew announced, grinning.

"Andrew's coming home!" Janet guessed.

Mathew shook his head. "No, but we'll be together."

"Well, what? Explain, you're teasing me."

"Word from Governor Haldimand." Mathew could hardly contain himself. His dark eyes danced with merriment and he looked immensely pleased with himself. "He has opened the Niagara. Any loyalist who desires can lay claim to farmland and will be given the necessary equipment to begin working the land. The frontier's being reopened for settlement!" Mathew swept Janet into his arms and hugged her. "He has asked us especially, because we know the area and can help the newcomers. There will be farms, Janet. And Andrew too. Janet, we're going back to Lochiel! We're going home, to our real home!"

Janet leaned against him and thought of that moment so many years ago when they had built Lochiel, only to have it taken away from them. Mathew always had said the land would be returned eventually, and now it was happening.

"The throatway of the Niagara River is the key to Canada's westward expansion; it leads to the fur lands." Mathew always had maintained that belief and now he repeated it to her. "There are going to be thousands of loyalists," he said pensively, "too many to settle in Quebec, too many to settle

247

in Nova Scotia. There will be no turning back; the Niagara must be settled, the land must be held."

"What if the rebellion fails?" Janet asked. "Won't the loyalists return to New York, Pennsylvania, and Massachusetts?"

Mathew shook his head. "There are too many. They have come too far and given up too much. They'll not go back."

Mathew paused and then spoke the words that few British ever wanted to admit or even think about. "The rebellion will succeed," Mathew said. "I think that England has lost the will to fight for British North America. The Thirteen Colonies will become independent by default; only Canada will remain."

"I really don't understand it at all," Janet answered. "I hardly think they're capable of governing themselves." She shook her head. "The men who lead the rebellion are no less members of the aristocracy than the British they rage against."

"They'll establish a Roman republic, not a monarchy limited by a constituent assembly. It will be a government ruled by the wealthy traders of Boston, Virginia, and Philadelphia."

"Yankee traders," Janet joked.

"Yankee?" Mathew smiled. "That's a new word for them. Where did you hear it?"

"From one of the soldiers," Janet replied. Then she added, "You know, it's a good thing we're leaving. I think we've both caught Montreal disease. Politics is the main occupation in this city."

"It's an easy illness to catch," Mathew said and laughed.

"We have cast our lot with the loyalists," Janet reminded him more seriously. "What will happen here?"

Mathew looked pensive. "I'm not a soothsayer, but I think we eventually will be the masters of our own house. The sea that separates us from England is too wide to alter what will be. But we will have to struggle to maintain this country—the Americans are expansionist. I have seen them, I know them. They're like a horde of insects that devour land."

Janet leaned against her husband and felt his strength and understanding. He had been right before and she felt he was

248

right now. The British had not destroyed the French of Quebec, as was originally feared. They had allowed, above the objections of the Thirteen Colonies to the south, freedom of religion in the province. The clergy and French-speaking gentry respected the British. The loyalists who were now coming wanted to remain British and, Janet thought, they would make the country stronger, giving it what it did not have before—sheer numbers. And those numbers would populate the frontier.

"This will be a different sort of country," Janet said reflectively. "We are from so many countries and so many places." She thought of the wealthy Hebrew Aaron Hart, of Hans, and in her heart she knew there would be others. "We are a land of refugees," Janet commented.

"Who better understands freedom?" Mathew answered.

Impulsively, he hugged her again. "I want to go by the end of the month. Can we be ready?"

Janet nodded and closed her eyes. She could see the wide-open fields, she could feel the spray from the falls, she could picture in her mind what Lochiel would become. "I thought it was a dream crushed."

"It's still there and it is ours."

Janet's eyes grew misty with happy tears. She had missed the rolling hills, the carpet of wild flowers that covered the earth in the spring, and the tall uncut and untrodden grasses blowing in the wind. It was so like her original Lochiel in Scotland!

"Can we get a letter to Jenna?" Janet asked.

"We can try. Perhaps Tom's friend, Major André, can help. Perhaps we can pass it through British Intelligence to the colonists who fight with George Rogers Clark, then onward down the Mississippi."

Janet smiled. "Jenna will come home soon. Oh, Mathew, it would be wonderful if she came home to Niagara!"

CHAPTER XV

June 1780

Nearly three months had passed since Robert's death. James and Jenna, in the immediate aftermath of the tragedy, had saved the trading post from the rampaging river. They had worked nonstop for the better part of two days, removing the contents of the post to high ground. Then, after the river had reached flood tide, and the waters once again had receded, they had cleaned the silt from the floors, allowed the post to dry out, and returned its contents.

At first they lived in a makeshift lean-to, fashioned out of the charred boards of the original cabin. Then James, working long hours, completed a small one-room cabin around the great stone fireplace of the original cabin.

James disappeared now and again, sometimes returning with supplies, sometimes coming home empty-handed. "I have to go away by myself," he told her by way of explanation. And Jenna accepted his need for solitude without question. James had sustained the disappearance or death of his sister, he had watched helplessly while his father drowned in the swirling torrent of the river.

He needs to be alone, Jenna believed. He needs to work out things in his mind. And so they both busied themselves trying to lose the days in manual labor. During the first two months they were both too emotionally drained for anything save the comfort of holding one another. But early in June, James and Jenna began making love again. It began, as it often does, with one comforting the other and it grew into an impassioned scene during which they were both temporarily lost in the world of sensations, using them to block out the day-to-day reality.

On the fifteenth of June James had left early, telling Jenna, "I'll be back by late afternoon."

Jenna had spent the morning in the garden and when the door swung open to let in the afternoon breeze Jenna was standing lost in thought by the cooking fire, preparing a thick soup for the evening meal.

"You don't have to live here," Maria's voice whispered.

Jenna jumped and turned around. Before her, in tattered rags, stood Maria, her eyes black and deep, her face contorted.

Jenna gasped. "Maria! You're alive! Oh, thank God, you're alive! Where have you been . . . ?"

Maria did not answer immediately. She simply stood and stared at Jenna, who thought: She must never have had the face of a child. She's always had the mask of hatred. Jenna took a small step toward Maria. "Your brother will be back soon," Jenna said kindly, trying to penetrate Maria's mood.

Maria in turn stepped forward and grasped Jenna's wrist, digging dagger-sharp nails into Jenna's skin. "I didn't come to see him."

Jenna winced and tried to jerk loose of Maria's grasp. It was then that she saw that Maria held a long, sharp hunting knife in one hand, partially concealing it in the folds of her torn dress. It was like Robbie's knife, and Jenna felt herself weakening.

Maria smiled maniacally. "I'll kill you if you scream," she whispered. "I'll kill you, I will."

Jenna, her knees weak, nodded dumbly. Maria released her wrist and walked to the wooden table. There she picked up a piece of bread and stuffed it into her mouth as if she were a starving animal. Jenna watched her, unable to take her eyes off the knife that Maria held so tightly.

"Does it feel good?" Maria asked when she had finished the bread.

"Does what feel good?"

"Does it feel good when James touches you, when he does it to you?"

Maria's eyes traveled Jenna's body from head to toe; her expression made Jenna's skin crawl. Maria must have been in the woods all these weeks! She must have been watching,

251

listening! She's a sick, mad child, Jenna thought. And reluctantly, Jenna admitted to herself: She's dangerous, too.

"I don't know what you mean," Jenna stumbled. And to herself she thought: I have to keep her talking—she's mad, like Robbie.

"I suppose you call it lovemaking," Maria hissed. "But it's not, you know. It's the same thing he does with Belle. He's doing it with Belle now."

Jenna froze and stared at Maria. She reminded herself that she was only two years older than Maria and that Maria was small for her age, seemingly shrunken by her lunacy. Jenna eased forward, wondering if she could overpower Maria.

"He's with Belle now," Maria repeated.

"I don't know what you're talking about," Jenna said, trying to sound calm. Maria is jealous, she thought. It was unnatural to desire one's own brother, but then, everything about Maria was unnatural.

"Belle's a black girl," Maria continued. "James keeps her in *placage*. She's his mistress. He says he owns her."

"*Placage?*" Jenna stumbled over the unfamiliar word. It troubled her that Maria suddenly sounded logical.

"He bought her from her daddy. And he killed her brother and claimed their land."

Jenna remembered the story about the black boy who had attacked Maria—it was allegedly the incident that made Maria lose her mind. Jenna even remembered that he had been hanged and she knew that James had indeed claimed the land. He and Robert had argued about it a great deal. But who was Belle? Belle never had been mentioned.

"The boy was killed because he attacked you," Jenna explained, trying to reason with Maria.

"He didn't attack me," Maria answered quickly. "And James knew he didn't. He just had him killed so I wouldn't tell about Belle."

Her voice sounds almost normal, Jenna thought.

"James won't give up Belle," Maria added. "We're going to take the gold Papa left and build a fine house. We're going buy ourselves slaves."

"There is no Belle!" Jenna protested. "James wouldn't do such a thing. You're lying! You're hateful and jealous and you're lying."

Maria shook her head resolutely. "He's with Belle now. I follow him. He goes there all the time. He makes love to her."

"James loves me! We're going to be married!"

"He's at Belle's," Maria countered with maddening confidence.

"I just don't believe you," Jenna answered. "James wouldn't."

"Belle doesn't like it, the way you do. Sometimes he hits her or ties her up. Belle hates him, but he owns her."

The color had drained from Jenna's face. Maria looked so set, so certain, so confident. But she's insane, Jenna reminded herself. Still, her mind raced. Would James do such a thing? Was it possible? No, no, she told herself. Maria was mad, she was lying. "I don't believe you," Jenna said finally.

"I'll take you there," Maria offered. "We'll take the horses and I'll take you there. Belle will tell you herself." Maria narrowed her eyes, making slits of them. "James and I are alike," she said slowly. "We are one. Mama and Papa are dead. Will is away and we have all the gold. Everything is ours."

"I'm not going," Jenna protested. "You're making up all this to frighten me and to make me hate James."

Maria waved the knife. "I do want to go," she announced. "Move."

Jenna stook a few steps. She had no doubt that Maria would not hesitate to use the knife. To try to take it away from her would invite violence.

Maria motioned her to the door and Jenna went, knowing the girl was right behind her. Maria prodded Jenna toward the trough were the horses were tied. "Get on," she ordered. "And don't try to run away. I have a pistol in the saddlebag."

Jenna felt a helpless, sinking sensation. Surely Maria would kill her when they got away from the house. The girl was demonic.

But as they rode farther and farther and nothing happened, Jenna relaxed a bit. She did not dare glance behind her at Maria, but Jenna was fully convinced of the girl's madness. The tragedy of Angelique's death and Maria's confession came back to Jenna with a new kind of clarity. Could Maria have been telling the truth? Did she, in fact, kill her mother? It was a dreadful thought, but had Maria set the fire in an attempt to kill Jenna and her own brother? Had she known her father would see the flames and try to cross the river? Angelique's death, the fire, Robert's drowning . . . had all these events been carefully orchestrated by Maria? Jenna shuddered at the implications of her revelation; if her suspicions were correct, the magnitude of Maria's crimes was far greater than anyone knew.

Jenna hardly noticed the woods they passed through, nor the fields they crossed. The sun was hot on Jenna's back, her mind was full of questions and fears; they all intermingled with terrible memories and now with the suspicion that there even might be a glimmer of truth in Maria's accusations about James.

After a time, they approached a ramshackle cabin, "Here!" Maria called out with a note of triumph. "Here is the house James built for Belle!"

"James' horse isn't here," Jenna said with relief.

"Perhaps he finished with her and is on his way home," Maria replied, seemingly untroubled.

At Maria's bidding and because she held the pistol now, Jenna dismounted and went to the door of the cabin. Maria stood behind.

Jenna knocked gently, half expecting no answer.

But there was an answer. The door opened and Jenna beheld a truly beautiful black woman. She was dressed in a ragged white gauze dress that revealed her voluptuous body.

Jenna let out her breath slowly and in that instant she knew that Maria had told her the truth. And though Jenna still fought the reality, she felt it with the sinking agony of one deeply betrayed.

"Are you Belle?"

The girl nodded yes. "May I talk to you?" Jenna asked hesitantly.

Jenna could feel Maria's eyes on her from behind. Belle opened the door wider and ushered Jenna in, but not warmly and not politely. "Who are you?" she questioned. "Why are you here with *that* girl?"

Jenna bit her lower lip. "I'm Jenna Macleod," she answered.

Belle muttered, "A fine white lady come to visit?"

"Are you James' mistress?" Jenna blurted out. "Was he here today?"

Belle broke into sarcastic laughter. "Mistress? What a grand name for a black slave whore!" She stopped laughing and looked at Jenna. "I suppose you're the one he says he's going to marry?"

Jenna's eyes were wide. "He told you?"

Belle's face had grown serious. "He told me, and he told me he'd be keeping me here." In an automatic gesture, she pulled the material of her dress down and swirled around, revealing angry, red crisscross marks on her back. "That's what your fine white man does to women!" She turned back to face Jenna, her dark eyes filled with hate.

Jenna had gone white as a sheet and she began to shake, wanting to close her eyes against the sight of Belle, wanting to run as far from James MacLean as she possibly could.

"Why don't you run away?" Jenna stammered. "Why do you stay?"

Belle fairly sneered. "To what? I have no clothes, no money. I'm black. He even brings me the food I eat. Where should I run? My people are gone! Do I run to another white man, another man to rape me?" Her voice had reached a crescendo of emotion.

Jenna's heart pounded and her head throbbed. She stood motionless, her hand over her eyes. What was she to do? Where could she turn?

"And now that girl stays here too," Belle said in a low voice. "She's possessed of the devil; she's a she-devil, that one."

Jenna shook her head in disbelief. "James knows she's alive?" It had not dawned on her; it seemed nothing had dawned on her. She had been deceived, lied to, betrayed by a man she thought she loved.

"Of course he knows!" Belle snapped.

"Of course I do!" James' voice boomed. Jenna turned and saw him framed in the doorway.

"How could you deceive me so?" It was half a question

255

to him, half a question to herself. Her voice expressed pain, shock, and anger all at once. But she was frightened too. No wonder Robert had questioned her so! No wonder he didn't trust his own son!

James took one long stride and seized her wrist, pulling her roughly toward the open door. "We'll go home now," he said firmly. "This is none of your affair."

Jenna stiffened, suddenly resisting. She shook her arm loose. "Don't touch me! Don't ever touch me again! I'll never marry you—never!"

She didn't even see him lift his arm, but she felt the stinging slap across her face and the hot flash that followed as blood rushed to her cheek. "Shut up and come home!" he commanded. He pulled her roughly from the cabin and dragged her to his horse, lifting her into the saddle and mounting behind her. Maria was gone and so was the other horse. Janet struggled, but James held her fast by force of superior physical strength. When they reached home after what seemed to Jenna like an endless ride, he pulled her down from the saddle and shook her. "Marry me or not," he threatened, "but you'll stay here!"

Jenna broke free as they entered the house. "Don't touch me! Don't ever touch me! I hate you . . . you and that child, you're unnatural!" Her eyes were full of tears and defiance. She knew as she looked at him that she always would cringe at his touch, that he no longer had any power over her. "I'll not stay!" Jenna screamed. "I'll not!" But the vow was hollow. Jenna's energies were completely drained, and deep down a terror filled her as she looked into his dark, brooding eyes. How could she ever have found him handsome and kind?

James took a step toward her and pulled her to him. "Don't try to resist me!" he threatened. Jenna stood stiffly. "I hate you!" His fingers folded over the top of her dress and he pulled it down, ripping the material. Jenna kicked and screamed, but he forced her downward, pressing her to the bed pad they had so peacefully and lovingly shared for so many weeks.

Jenna clawed at him and shrieked. She struggled, trying to free herself. But he was too large and too strong for her.

He lifted her skirts and pressed the full weight of his body against her.

His rough hand roamed over her. Jenna felt nothing save fear, loathing, and exhaustion. He seemed to be squeezing the breath out of her and as he parted her legs, she let out a long, horrible scream of protest. Jenna barely heard the musket shot, but James tumbled off her, half naked and panting. Blood ran down his arm.

"Up!" Tolly Tuckerman commanded. "Get up and pull up your pants, man! If you are a man!"

Jenna's hands flew to cover herself. She pulled up her torn dress. Behind Tolly stood Will, his face etched with pain and bewilderment.

Will shook his head as if to rouse himself from the nightmare. "Where's Father?" he demanded of James.

Jenna blinked. This Will was James' brother? But he had given her another name.

James looked stunned. He held his wounded arm and stared blankly into Tolly's musket. "Where's Father?" Will demanded.

"Dead!" James said. "Drowned in the river at flood tide."

Will's hand reached for the edge of the table. "Where's Maria?" He asked in a lower voice.

Jenna could hold her silence no longer. "She killed your mother! And burned down the house. She's mad, completely mad!" Tears were running down Jenna's face and she began to tremble, unable to control herself.

Tolly shook his head. He was not a man to register shock, for there wasn't much in the world he had not seen, but this did shock him.

Will looked deathly ill. He was sick and he fought nausea. He had heard only fragments of what he knew was a much longer story, but he had heard enough. He turned on his brother. "I ought to kill you," he said softly and steadily. "Or let Tolly do it." James stared at Will. Jenna crawled off the bed pad. She pulled herself to her feet on rubbery legs. She grasped Will's arm to steady herself and whispered hoarsely, "He's your brother. Don't kill him. It would be wrong, no matter what."

Will looked at her. She was bruised from her struggle with James, and her eyes were puffy from crying, much like the night he had first met her. "You're defending him?"

Jenna shook her head. "I hate him, but brother shouldn't turn against brother. Will, it would be wrong to kill him."

Will turned his gaze back to James, who cringed in the corner. "He didn't kill anyone," Jenna stressed. "And Maria's mad, not responsible."

"I won't kill him," Will finally said. "I don't have to. One day his greed will kill him. It'll kill both of them."

Will shook his head. Then he leaned over and took the gun from Tolly. "Tie him up," he instructed. "Tie him up and lock him down in the trading post."

Madelaine and Tom took a rare moment away from the chores to walk in the woods near their recently completed cabin. There were three cabins in all and three land grants from the governor: one for Helena and her husband, John Fraser; one for Tom and Madelaine; and another for Janet and Mathew. The three land grants encompassed all of what once had been Janet and Mathew's original farm.

"What do you think of my Niagara?" Madelaine asked. Tom Macleod inhaled the fresh-smelling sweet grass. The land was lush and open, gently rolling hills covered with virgin forest. "It's not Philadelphia." He squeezed her arm and added, "Thank goodness!"

"The Americans will want it," Madelaine said pensively.

"Then we'll defend it," Tom answered. "I've never owned land before." He kicked the rich soil with his foot and, thrusting his hands in his pockets, he turned to look out on the newly planted fields. "I like the feeling."

They had come at the end of April, and with the help of the small community each couple had put up a one-room cabin to serve until more permanent structures could be built. They had planted too, and now the rains of June watered the neatly plowed fields.

"We'll have a good harvest," Tom said as he admired the work he had so recently completed.

"Summer's a busy, busy time," Madelaine told him. "There's much to be done in preparation for winter."

Tom turned and looked at her lovingly. "It's new to me and I love it. There's something really exciting about seeing the results of your own work, about living in a house you've built. When we have our first harvest I'll know that we did it ourselves."

"It had better be a big harvest," Madelaine said, a mischievous smile crossing her face. "And it's good you like to build like your father. Soon we'll need more room."

Tom's face lit up with anticipation. "What?" he said, almost disbelieving the implication of her words.

"I said, we'll need lots of food and more room," Madelaine teased. Then she stepped closer and put her arms around him. "I'm with child," she whispered in his ear.

Tom automatically folded his arms around her and he flushed with the joy of her news, hugging her tightly. "I'm going to be a father," he blurted out. Then, picking her up, he twirled her around and let out a laugh. "It's wonderful! I can't believe it!"

"Oh, you'll believe it," Madelaine said and laughed, her dark eyes dancing with joy. "You'll know it when you're awakened in the middle of the night."

"I'll look forward to it," he said, taking her hand. "I can't wait to tell the world!"

"Janet and Matthew will be glad," Madelaine concluded. "We'll tell them tonight."

They walked back to their cabin in silence. The sun was dropping on the horizon, and Tom held Madelaine's hand protectively.

His eyes searched the ground as he walked and, curiously, he stopped and bent over to pick up a flat, charred board that lay partially covered with loose earth.

"What's that?" Madelaine asked.

Tom shrugged and turned it over, brushing the dirt from it.

"Oh, my!" Madelaine exclaimed. "I can't believe it!"

The letters carved into the wood read: LOCHIEL: OCTOBER 1757, FOUNDED BY JANET CAMERON MACLEOD AND MATHEW MACLEOD. Tears flooded Madelaine's eyes. "Oh, Tom. I remember when Mathew put that up!" She turned to her husband. "Nothing is ever really destroyed."

Tom took her in his arms again and strangely, he felt as

flooded with emotion as she. He had lost and found his real father, he had lost one wife and found a second wife whom he loved more dearly than life itself. He was going to be a father and he had his own land. "It's never destroyed," he told her, feeling his own eyes mist. "Just postponed."

Jenna told Will all she knew about the recent events in his family. "This would not have happened if I hadn't gone off to fight," Will said, looking into the fire. He had not yet fully accepted his father's death nor his sister's madness. And James had turned out to be more greedy and more of a liar than even Will would have suspected. They had been at odds for years, they never had cared about the same things, but Will would not have believed the things that James had done.

"You've had two terrible experiences," he told Jenna. "I regret one of them was at the hands of my brother."

Jenna looked at her folded hands. "He did not always force himself on me," she confessed. "Not until today. I thought I loved him. I thought he was kind like you, that he loved me." Her voice took on a faraway sound. "I always make mistakes," Jenna said in a voice barely audible. "First Stephan, then James. Neither of them was what I thought. . . ." She felt the tears coming into her eyes again. "And terrible things happen wherever I go! People get killed!"

Will turned and looked into her weary face. He looked somehow older himself. "You loved James?"

"I thought I did. I didn't know what he was like. I deceived myself. And I'm a curse!"

"That's foolish," Will answered. "I wish I had gotten here sooner." He swore at himself for taking so long. He had been delayed in New Orleans, then he had waited for Tolly to join him. The weather had been horrendous, the trip difficult. Including the delays, it had taken him three months. "I should have left when I first found out Mother had died. But I delayed, I wrote to Father, I wanted to come home sooner. . . ."

"You're blaming yourself," Jenna said. "That's not right."

"It will take me time to understand it all," Will replied.

They slipped back into mutual silence. I have a lot to think about too, Jenna thought.

She jumped automatically when Tolly swung open the door. He smiled at her. "You can stop being so nervous," he said. Then turning to Will, he said, "I tied him up, left food and water, and dressed his wound. I expect the bastard will live."

"She's still out there," Jenna said, referring to Maria.

"She'll stay away," Will said slowly. "Her horse isn't here, so she's probably still at Belle's. She won't come around while there're strange horses out there."

"You had better try to get some sleep," Tolly advised Jenna. "And you too," he said to Will.

Jenna opened her eyes when the sun began to pour through the east window of the cabin. She shook her head to clear it, feeling she had slept the sleep of the dead. Tolly had started a small fire and was making tea. Will was nowhere about.

Jenna struggled to her feet and shook out her dress. "I was more tired than I thought," she admitted.

"I'll have tea ready in a minute or two," Tolly announced. "And there's water from the well. Why don't you get cleaned up."

"I need to," Jenna replied. "Where's Will?"

"A boat came downstream this morning. Will went down to take off the supplies."

"I had hoped things would look better this morning," Jenna said. "Yesterday was like a nightmare."

"And are they better?"

Jenna shook her head. "No, it will take me a long time. I've made bad choices. I have to consider them."

Tolly smiled. "Could be you're growing up. An admission of bad judgment certainly is a start."

"I'm trying," Jenna answered. Thoughtfully, she wondered if her mother had done as badly when she was young. Jenna remembered her mother telling her, "I made two mistakes, both of which I regret." I've made two as well, Jenna thought. But I won't make another.

Will came through the doorway. "You're up," he commented. Jenna nodded and took the tea Tolly handed her.

"Is James still down there?"

"He's still there. I can't think what to do with him or about him. I can't keep him under lock and key forever."

Jenna gulped down some tea. "You'll have to let him go," she said quietly.

Will withdrew a letter pouch. "It's for you," he said, handing it to Jenna. "It came on the flatboat."

Jenna took it and quickly opened it. "It's from Mother," she told them. "They got my first letter." She read quickly, then turned the page. "They're leaving for Niagara." Jenna's eyes traveled the second page of the letter. She learned about Tom and Madelaine. She read about Mat's death and again tears flooded her eyes. She put the letter on the table.

"My brother's been killed," she said in a small voice. "Oh, I must find a way to go home. I need to go home."

Will lifted the letter and read it. He looked at Jenna and knew she felt the way he had felt in New Orleans. He had known then that he had to come home, but now that he was here, there was nothing to come home to. James and Maria in their mutual evil had erased it all. He did not wish to remain here and fight them, nor did he wish to harm them.

Will reached across the table and took Jenna's hand. "I'm going to take you home," he said at length.

Jenna blinked back her tears. "Are you sure you want to?"

"I have nothing here," Will concluded. "Are you going to come, Tolly, my good man?"

"Not this time," came Tolly's quick reply. "I'm going back to New Orleans to join Gálvez. Pensacola awaits."

"Pack," Will instructed Jenna. "We'll leave in the morning. The sooner I leave here the better."

"Belle," Jenna said, thinking of the woman she had met only yesterday. "We can't leave her. James will hurt her."

Will, who had heard the whole sordid story, agreed. "As far as St. Louis," he said. "She'll be safe there. She'll be far enough away from James MacLean and in a territory where Negroes could live free."

"How long will it take?" Jenna asked.

"Depends on the weather, depends on a lot of things.

As you know, traveling upriver is much slower than down. It's June now; we ought to make it before winter sets in.''

"It gets cold sooner farther north," Jenna warned.

"Then we'll see," Will answered.

They left on horseback the following morning. "Faster than water," Will told her. "And safer this time of year when the current runs so strong."

Will's last words to Tolly were: "Leave him under lock and key. Go to Natchez and tell someone to have him turned loose after we're well under way."

"He won't follow?" Jenna asked uneasily.

"And leave his land and money?" Will shook his head. "He and Maria have hidden it all. He won't give up his greed. He thinks he's going to own a hundred slaves and be a rich man."

Belle, whom Tolly had brought from her cabin, spit on the ground. "Slaves," she mumbled. "I hate riding horseback!"

They began their journey side by side, but soon the trails grew narrower and they rode single file, Will in front, Jenna in the middle, Belle behind. They rode silently, stopping only to water the horses. Jenna thought she would die of fatigue.

Her legs and arms ached from the exertion. It had been too long since she rode, Jenna thought. But she did not really mind the physical pain. It took her mind off the memories of the past year.

A few miles south of West Point on the opposite shore of the rambling Hudson River was a large white frame house with a pillared porch that faced a large lawn and flower beds.

Before the war, the house had belonged to Colonel Beverly Robinson, but Colonel Robinson was a loyalist and the house had been abandoned.

General Benedict Arnold arrived at the Robinson house on August 5 and decided to make it his headquarters now that he had been given command of West Point.

Colonel Richard Varick was coming to act as Arnold's secretary and Arnold congratulated himself on the selection.

Varick was a quiet young man; a man who was more of a reader than a doer; a person who would be unlikely to notice anything since he would always have his nose in a book.

The sooner I turn over West Point to Clinton, the better, Arnold had decided. And, he mused, the act would bring him fame and fortune and the gratitude of his King. He might even be knighted, he decided. Then Peggy would be Lady Arnold.

"I do believe," Arnold told young Varick when he arrived, "that the first order of business ought to be a complete survey of West Point. I should like you to make lists of the three thousand troops under my command and mark their classifications, indicating whether they are gunners, sharpshooters, foragers, or simple infantrymen." Rubbing his chin thoughtfully, he also informed him, "I would like a survey of the ammunition and a total count of both horses and mules."

And when he is finished, Arnold decided, I will have him mark the maps with all of West Point's fortifications, including all the smaller forts hidden in the foothills.

Then there was the matter of the chain across the Hudson River. General Howe did not believe it was strong enough to hold back a large ship. Some of the logs in the boom had sunk; some of the iron links were known to be twisted.

After three weeks, Varick had completed his lists and done, as requested, a report on the condition of the Hudson chain. Arnold took them all, and by night copied them for transmission to General Clinton. On the bottom of the chain report, he wrote, "A single large ship could snap the chain."

Arnold placed all the information in a pouch and then, returning to the library where Varick worked, he told the young man to make out a pass to Mrs. Mary McCarthy. "She wants to take her children and go to New York City," he explained. "And I have some letters she can carry."

Varick frowned. "She's the wife of a British prisoner of war, sir."

Arnold shrugged. "There's nothing of importance in the pouch, only some instructions about some stock I own."

The pass was made out without further discussion. Varick, only mildly troubled, continued his research.

On September 14 Peggy arrived from Mount Pleasant with her new child. Arnold met his wife on the Hudson, going downriver on his barge, which he had decorated with flowers, banners, and flags for the occasion.

"I've missed you terribly," he breathed into her ear. She pressed herself to him. "And I you," she returned. "Mount Pleasant was not pleasant without you."

Arnold beamed at his infant son. "Tonight, because it is such a long journey, we'll stay with Joshua Hett Smith." Peggy smiled enigmatically at the name. "The gentleman you've written me about?"

"One and the same," Benedict told her.

"How is our friend Mr. Anderson?" Peggy asked, beaming.

"*Anderson*" was Major André's code name. "Coming to visit soon," Benedict told her. "When we are properly prepared to welcome him."

Between them passed secretive looks, but no one truly noticed since a man, especially a man married to Peggy and separated from her for some weeks, was entitled to some secret meanings.

That night at the Smiths' it was agreed. Mr. Smith, who was a loyalist, would meet Major André. He would bring him from the *Vulture*, which was anchored in the Hudson, upstream from the American cavalry posts.

"I have arranged it all," Benedict confided to Peggy as they lay in bed that night. "I sent orders to Colonel Elisha Sheldon at Salem and to Major Ben Tallmadge at North Castle that I was expecting Mr. Anderson, a mercantile gentleman. He will be escorted through American lines."

"And you will meet him here," Peggy pressed, speaking of the Smith house. "Yes," Arnold replied. "A personal meeting is necessary for the final arrangements."

"And then we will go to England," Peggy sighed, cuddling closer. "First England," Arnold corrected. "Then Canada, where we will be given five thousand acres of prime land."

Peggy stroked his cheek affectionately. "Soon," she promised. "Soon it will be over."

CHAPTER XVI

September 15, 1780

The trip to St. Louis was slow and arduous. When they arrived, Will made inquiries and they took Belle to a priest who knew of a few free black families with whom she could seek shelter.

"Will you be all right?" Jenna asked as they parted. Throughout the entire journey Belle had kept her silence, seemingly weaving her own plans, content to remain inside herself. She did her share of the work, often building the fire, or helping catch fish for the evening meal. The wilderness forced a closeness on them, but Belle remained reserved in spite of their physical proximity. She volunteered her work, but not her thoughts. Now, at the moment of their parting, Belle looked at Jenna and Will steadily. "I'll be all right," she replied. "I expect you think I ought to be grateful." Belle's mouth was set in a hard line and she drew herself up, tall and straight, proud in the way she was before she met James MacLean and was humiliated by him. "You're not setting me free," Belle announced. "You don't have that power. I *am* free. It's not a favor. I never was a slave."

"You didn't want to leave?" Jenna asked in amazement.

"I wanted to leave," Belle retorted, "but not with you."

Jenna opened her mouth to reply, but Will tugged on her arm. "We wish you well," he said almost formally. But Belle had already turned her back and was looking away; she was as unconcerned with their leaving as she had been with their coming.

"She's bitter," Will said when they were alone. "What else should she feel? Love between black and white is hard to come by; there's too much between. It's the curse of slavery,'' Will commented. ''Some people expect slaves to be happy if they are well treated, but no man ought to be a slave in the first place, and treatment doesn't change a slave's attitude. It's something the men of the colonies haven't thought about.'' He paused and added, ''Yet.''

''If you don't believe in slavery, why were you fighting with the Americans?''

''I wasn't,'' Will explained. ''I was fighting with the Spanish. The English don't disavow slavery, the French don't disavow slavery, the Spanish don't disavow it, and neither do the Americans. It's not an issue yet, except for some abolitionists who believe slavery is against the will of God.''

''And you believe that?'' Jenna probed.

Will shook his head in the affirmative. ''My mother was Acadian, my father Scots. Neither of them believed in slavery. My mother read the Bible every night and she read me passages against slavery. There's no army now that fights against it; if there were, I'd be in it. But first you fight for independence, then you fight against slavery.''

''Canada is loyalist,'' Jenna reminded him.

Will shrugged. ''It doesn't matter anymore. I see the rebellion differently now. James and Maria want wealth, land, and slaves. Their greed divided and ruined my family. The Virginians and the settlers from the Carolinas want the same thing. The colonies are divided. I don't think you can build a nation on division any more than you can build a family on division.''

''You don't want wealth and land?''

Will smiled. ''Of course I do. But I don't want it at the expense of someone else's broken back.''

''Will you stay in Canada?'' It had been a question much on Jenna's mind. Will was taking her home because he felt he should. He had left the river because he had not wanted to fight his brother.

Will kicked a pebble in the dust. ''I might,'' he answered. ''It depends on the opportunities.''

''There's rich land in the Niagara,'' Jenna told him.

''There's more than land to be considered,'' Will replied. Jenna looked up as they turned the corner of the dusty street. They had left the chapel and Belle behind. But down the street they now turned onto, Jenna saw the tavern where she and Stephan had stayed. She stopped short and froze. Mr. O'Hara had been responsible for Stephan's murder. Mr. O'Hara had returned to St. Louis, having escaped Robbie Ryan's murderous attack.

"What's the matter?" Will asked, seeing the expression of fear on Jenna's face.

"There," she pointed toward the tavern. "That's the place owned by Mr. O'Hara—I told you. That's the place where the nightmare began."

"He might not still be here," Will suggested.

But Jenna shook her head. "I'm afraid; I don't want to stay here." She turned pleading green eyes to him. "I can't," she murmured. "I can't go back there."

"There's a small settlement a few miles from here, where the Missouri joins the Mississippi River. We can go there and find shelter. It's where we have to trade the horses for a canoe in any case."

Jenna nodded. "I'd like that better, even if Mr. O'Hara is gone. I can't go back to that place, Will."

Will didn't argue. Instead, they walked onward. They retrieved their horses at the livery stable and continued their journey a few miles upriver. Where the two great rivers met, they crossed the water with their horses by barge, landing just before nightfall in a small farming community with a trading post.

Will arranged for them to stay with the owner of the trading post that night. "We'll have a good meal," he told her cheerfully, "and you'll have a bed to sleep in. A little rest before we head up the Illinois."

Jenna watched Will as he unloaded their packs. Will is the man Stephan and James were not, she said to herself. He is kind, strong, and honorable. In all the weeks they had been together, he had made no move toward her, treating her as he might treat a sister.

Jenna forced herself to hold back her tears as she watched Will move about. Abstractedly, she touched her stomach. She was ashamed and afraid. She had missed her blood and Jenna knew she was pregnant with James' child. I love Will, she admitted to herself. But it's too late.

Major André and General Benedict Arnold met at the home of Mr. Smith on the night of September 22. No sooner had Arnold turned over all the documents than gunfire erupted in the distance.

"Cannon fire!" Smith had exclaimed breathlessly. "They're firing on the *Vulture;* she laid anchor, but now she's dropping downstream!"

André gathered up the documents while Arnold, looking distressed, tried to assess the information. "You should have come in disguise," he said nervously. But André had not come in disguise. He had come in full dress uniform. "I'm not a spy," he said, straightening himself up.

"No, but you're behind enemy lines."

Smith, a round bumpkin of a man, looked for all the world like a nervous old woman. He fidgeted with his fingers and searched the room with his eyes as if he half expected an American soldier with a gun to pop up from behind the tapestry.

"You'll have to go by road—I can escort you," Smith offered. "There's no getting back to the *Vulture* now."

André frowned. "That may not be dangerous for General Arnold, or for you, but it's a bit of a hazard for me! More so since I'm carrying documents I should not have."

"Mr. Smith has passes," Arnold said calmly. "I did plan for this contingency."

André cocked an eyebrow. "And the documents?"

"Put them in your stockings," Arnold suggested. "And Mr. Smith will lend you some more, uh, appropriate clothes."

André eyed Smith and actually laughed. "I suspect they would be a bit large."

"Never mind your breeches," Smith said with a bit of irritation. He considered himself portly and not fat. "I'll give you a beaver hat and I do have a smaller-size purple coat trimmed in gold lace. You need only discard the jacket of your uniform."

"Is it a smart-looking jacket?" André asked. "Actually, I don't wear purple all that well."

"This is no time for humor," Smith snapped.

André shrugged. "I suppose a man in my position cannot

be too choosy about style.'' He turned and looked at Arnold a trifle more seriously. ''Go home to Peggy,'' he said. ''But be on your guard.''

General Arnold pulled himself up. ''I hardly think that I will come under any suspicion.''

''All the rebels are a suspicious lot,'' André concluded without even a hint of his usual sarcastic wit. ''That, my dear fellow, is what makes them so tiresome. They always check under their beds for loyalists, but seldom do they look in them.''

''Are you insulting my wife?'' Arnold said accusingly.

''I would never insult Peggy. My God, man, you really are defensive tonight.''

Arnold's face flushed. ''What do you expect? We could be on the verge of being discovered. I have reason to be nervous.''

''I suggest we leave immediately,'' Smith urged. André nodded his agreement and the three of them left the drawing room of the Smith house, Arnold to go home to Peggy, André and Smith to cross back into British-held territory.

At nine o'clock Smith and Major André were halted by a rebel militiaman who demanded to see their passes.

''Joshua Hett Smith and John Anderson, are you both merchants?'' he questioned.

''Bound for White Plains. What route do you suggest?''

The militiaman studied the passes again. ''Take the route through White Castle,'' he suggested at length. ''But not tonight. There's a farm up the road. Stay there for the night.''

''You are kind,'' Smith said. André tipped his beaver hat and they traveled on. ''You aren't going to take his advice, are you?'' André inquired of Smith.

''Yes. It's a warning. If we don't heed it, he might report us.''

They stayed the night, and the next morning, Smith and André left together. But Smith rode only six miles. ''This is where we part,'' he announced. ''You will continue on.''

André paused and looked at Smith. ''There are cowboys hereabouts. They're ruffians who attack travelers. I don't fancy going on alone.'' ''Cowboys'' was the term applied to the young lads of Westchester County who had Tory sympathies but who, at times, bedeviled travelers, threatening them and occasionally robbing them.

"You need not worry," Smith informed him. "Just express your political sympathies. If you're a loyalist, they won't bother you."

André looked skeptically at Smith, but he waved him off and continued on alone. André rode through the village of Chappaqua but as he crossed the Tarrytown bridge, farther on, three large, unkempt boys halted him. They had muskets, and one of them pointed at him. "Off that horse!" he commanded.

"The better part of valor is discretion," André quipped as he dismounted. He lifted a well-manicured hand and touched the barrel of the lad's musket. "That's in my face," he commented somewhat regally. "Do remove it."

The youth scowled but lowered the musket. They all look a bit slow, André thought. "Sirs," he addressed them, trying not to laugh, "I am of your politics."

The tallest was chewing tobacco and he spit on the ground. "What does that mean?"

"Well, you are *cowboys*, are you not?"

"Skinners," another replied. André frowned; the term was unknown to him. "I don't understand," he stumbled.

"Patriots," the tobacco chewer hissed. He leaned over and chucked André under the chin. "I suspect we've got ourselves a pretty British foppet."

André fumbled for his pass and withdrew it together with his fine gold watch. He handed the pass to the youth. "I trust you can read."

The young man snatched it. But the puzzled look on his face told André that he indeed could not read.

"The watch has a Tory crest," one of them sneered. André froze. They crumpled the pass and discarded it, but the tobacco chewer retrieved it. "Might come in handy later."

"Let's search him," the one with the musket suggested.

The one who had chucked him under the chin leaned forward threateningly. "I'll bet you'll love being stripped?"

André blinked and looked into the unshaven face. It's over, he admitted to himself. He smiled back at the threatening youth. "I suppose it doesn't have to be entirely unpleasant," he said dryly.

General Benedict Arnold received word of André's arrest on Monday, September 25. He read the letter and bounded up the stairs.

"You're ashen!" Peggy exclaimed. She wore a filmy white nightdress that fell off her shoulder; her blond hair was a halo of ringlets.

Benedict drew her into his arms. "I've been discovered," he said breathlessly. "I must leave at once."

"General Arnold, sir! Colonel Hamilton is here to see you, sir. And General Washington is on his way!" Major Franks' voice boomed from the hallway.

"You must go by the back stairs," Peggy urged. "Go to the *Vulture*."

"But you—I can't leave you."

Peggy kissed his cheek and then his lips. "I will join you," she promised, squeezing his arm. "I know what to do. Go now, I implore you."

Arnold kissed her one more time, then leaned over the cradle and kissed his infant son. "Soon," he said with warm eyes. "I can't stand being without you."

Peggy blinked back tears. "We'll go to Canada together," she promised. "Go, hurry, my dear."

Benedict picked up his things and opened the door. As quickly and as quietly as possible, he slipped down the back stairs, through the kitchen, and out to the stables. There he mounted his saddled horse and headed for the Hudson. It was raining lightly. When he reached the dock, he found his barge and oarsmen. "Take me to Teller's Point," he ordered. "And hurry!"

When they were in sight of the *Vulture*, Arnold waved a white flag of truce so the ship's guns would not fire on him.

Once aboard the *Vulture*, he ordered his oarsmen arrested.

"Where is John Anderson?" Captain Sutherland asked, referring to Major André.

"Held as a spy in Salem," Arnold confessed breathlessly. Arnold leaned against the rail and said a silent prayer for Peggy.

Back at the house, Peggy sent word that her husband had left for the fort so that Colonel Hamilton and General Washington would go there. At West Point, they found that General Arnold, far from making the fort stronger, had neglected it shamefully. They also learned that Arnold had been seen heading down the Hudson toward Teller's Point. And by midday, more information had been received. Major André had confessed, but had not named Arnold. Nonetheless, the information and the papers clearly revealed Arnold as the only possible culprit.

"This is treason," Washington mumbled. "I should pursue him," Hamilton suggested.

Washington shook his head. "It may only have been his raft seen heading for Teller's Point. Benedict Arnold is an officer and a gentleman. He should be given the benefit of every doubt."

"But the evidence . . ." Hamilton protested.

Washington stood up. "I make the decisions," he said hotly. "I wish to speak with Mrs. Arnold."

At Washington's suggestion, they returned to the Arnold house. "I should like to meet with Mrs. Arnold," General Washington requested. Colonel Alexander Hamilton stood by; General Lafayette, who had joined them at the fort, also stood by, more interested in meeting the legendary Peggy Shippen Arnold than in confirming the worst fears of General George Washington.

"She's terribly ill," the maid stammered. "She's taken to her bed, quite hysterical."

Washington frowned. "I shall go to her," he announced. General Washington bounded up the stairs with a curious Colonel Hamilton and a smiling, gallant Lafayette behind him. Washington knocked lightly on the door. "Madame Arnold. Please, my dear, do let me speak with you. It is most urgent. It's General Washington, Peggy. It's George."

They were greeted with a hysterical shriek. "I shan't let you kill my baby! I shan't, I shan't! Oh, George, I could never believe you so cruel! My God! My world is ending, it's ending! Heaven take me!"

Washington's face flushed a deep red. "My God," he mumbled, turning the handle and opening the door. Before them, cringing near the cradle of her child, was a wild-eyed Peggy Arnold. Her filmy see-through nightdress had dropped off one shoulder, revealing the curve of her breast. Her full mouth was partly open. Peggy's blond curls fell on bare white shoulders, tears flowed freely down her cheeks from wide blue eyes.

"No one cares about me! I'm innocent but disgraced! And you want to kill my baby as retribution! Savages! Savages!"

"I would never do such a thing," Washington stuttered. "Nor would I harm you, dear Peggy!"

"Certainly not," Hamilton blustered. Lafayette said nothing. He only eyed the incredibly beautiful Peggy Shippen Arnold, noting that her nightdress left little, if anything, to the imagination, and wishing the situation were somewhat different.

"Don't let them harm my baby, George! Please!" Peggy ran across the room and threw herself into Washington's arms. Her arms encircled his neck and she breathed into his ear, pressing herself against him. "Please, George. Please."

Lafayette could not suppress himself. A lecherous smile crept across his lips. "I should be begged too," he mumbled under his breath.

Hamilton shot him a dark look. "We would never do such a thing," he said. "You and your child are perfectly safe."

Peggy drew back, but the tears still flowed freely. "You will help me?" she said in a tiny little-girl voice.

Washington, beet red but not unmoved by her embrace, stuttered, "Of course I will help you. I'll do anything to help you."

Peggy blinked and then fainted dead away.

The court-martial that convicted Major André of spying was held swiftly on September 29. He was moved to Tappan, there to be hanged on October 2.

He went to the gallows in full dress uniform, accompanied by a Calvinist minister. He climbed to the platform gallantly and stood at attention as the noose was placed around his neck.

"Do you have any confessions to make?" the upset minister inquired.

André smiled. "My dear man, if I start making confessions, this hanging shall never take place."

The minister cleared his throat. "You're being irreverent," he said coldly.

"Ah, rebuked on the gallows," André said with a sigh.

The minister ignored him. "Do you have any last words?"

André lifted his well-plucked eyebrow and leaned forward to whisper in the minister's ear. "America's a very tiresome place," André intoned. "Very tiresome indeed." Then he added, almost as an afterthought, "God save the King."

It was midmorning on October 5. Jenna and Will had been paddling for some hours. They were close to shore and Will's thoughts were far away as he contemplated the changing scenery. The countryside was all rolling hills, but the bluffs that overlooked the river still were quite high in some places. They were, he knew, not more than twenty-five miles downstream from the settlement of Peoria. It was one of the earliest settlements along the Illinois. The name came from one of the five tribes of the Illinois Confederacy of Indian Nations. It was the former site of the French Fort Crèvecoeur, established by La Salle in 1680. The fort had been deserted and plundered; its ruins still stood on the bluffs above the river. But the land around Lake Peoria was rich, and long after the fort had been abandoned, there were French settlers as well as Americans there. It now was a farming community, a small settlement that his father had passed through years before.

"Oh," Jenna moaned.

Will, in the stern of the canoe, leaned forward. "What is it?" he asked. She looked deathly pale.

"I'm sick," Jenna said, letting her paddle go slack. "Could we beach the canoe for a time?"

Will nodded his reply and they headed for the near shore.

When they were close enough, Will jumped from the canoe and pulled it in. Then he lifted Jenna and carried her beyond the pebbly shore to the grass. She looked at him with wide green eyes, then covering her mouth with her hand, stood up and bolted for the brush, where she vomited uncontrollably.

When at last the spasm ended, she returned to a distressed-looking Will. "We'll set up camp," he suggested. "You're too ill to go on."

Jenna agreed. "Yes," she murmured. Her fingers dug into the soil beneath the grass. Winter was coming! It was fall already. They were not yet even on the Great Lakes! She felt a sudden fear that by camping they were wasting precious time. Her womb was full and her stomach was churning constantly. It was the canoe. She felt nauseated each time they got onto the water, and she knew that it was the pregnancy, because she had never gotten sick before in a canoe; she had practically grown up in a canoe. Now she couldn't bear it, and it was the only way home!

Will returned with a tinful of cool water. "Drink a little," he urged. "Just a sip or two."

Jenna took a small sip. Will bent down and put his arm around her shoulders protectively. "Are you very sick? Is it something you ate?"

"I don't know," Jenna lied. She did know. She knew she already felt better because she was sitting still and not moving. It was nothing she ate; it was motion sickness because she was pregnant. Helena had it; she couldn't even ride in a carriage for the third, fourth, and fifth months of her pregnancies. Her mother had talked about it too. "A family female curse," Janet had told her. "When we Macleod women get pregnant, we have to stay put."

Will erected the lean-to and then unpacked a blanket from the pack. He brought the blanket to her, covering her legs and tucking it up around her waist. "I'll build a fire," he suggested. Jenna shook her head. "I'm not cold," she assured him. In fact, the sun was quite bright and warm, and though it was October, it was cold only at night.

"Your color is coming back," Will said with relief. He looked at her as she stared into the grass. She's as lovely as ever, he thought. And, as always, he longed to kiss her, touch her, and hold her. But Jenna had been through too much. She was friendly to him and warm, but she seemed to keep a distance too. It was no use, Will decided. She had suffered too much at the hands of James and Maria; she had passed through a terrible journey on her way to womanhood and it had scarred her. She had no faith in her own judgment, and though he hoped that time and going home would heal her, he vowed never to trouble her or try to make love to her until they were home.

He sat down beside her on the grass. He put his arm around her to comfort her as he often did, but suddenly Jenna shook him off and, for no reason Will understood, burst into tears.

"What's the matter?" he begged to know. He put his arms around her again. This time she leaned against him and sobbed violently. "Is it something I've done?" The feel of her in his arms caused a shiver to run through him. Oh, how he wanted her. He took her shoulders and looked into her tear-stained face. "Please, trust me. Tell me what the matter is. . . ."

Jenna's eyes sought his almost pleadingly. "My shame," she sobbed. "Mine and mine alone."

Will's heart ached for her. "Tell me," he prodded. "Please tell me."

"I'm with child," Jenna confessed, covering her face with her hands. "James' child."

Will looked at her, then pried her hands from her face. "Why didn't you tell me sooner?" he questioned.

Jenna shivered. "Before," she sobbed, "before I knew about Belle . . . I thought he loved me, we were going to get married, I told you all that. . . . I thought . . ." Her voice trailed off and she turned away from him. "I can't go on, Will. I can't travel anymore. Winter is coming. I wouldn't blame you if you left me. . . ."

Will was silent for a few moments. "We're about twenty-five miles from Peoria," he said thoughtfully. "I can get work there. We'll have to stay the winter, wait for the child to be born. Then I'll take you home, Jenna."

She turned her tear-stained face to him; her eyes were full of sadness. "I'm sorry," she said softly. But Will had begun gathering firewood. He turned away from her so she would not see the pain on his face. Time, he told himself. In time she will heal.

"They're safe," Tom Macleod said, putting down the dispatches. "Arnold escaped and Peggy is well."

Mathew shook his head, "It's a pity," he admitted. "The plan for him to surrender West Point might have shortened the war."

"He plans to come to Canada," Tom said thoughtfully. "He's a real loyalist hero."

"He'll be welcomed here, but if the Americans ever catch him, they'll hang him. One nation's hero is another nation's traitor."

Tom agreed. "He did what he thought was right. But I suppose I'm happier to know that Peggy and the Shippens are quite safe."

"I owe them a debt," Mathew replied, "for helping to bring up my son."

"They were good to me," Tom said thoughtfully. "It's really terrible about Major André. He was a bit of a dandy, but a very well-liked dandy, a really fine man."

It was nearly Christmas and they were both in the barn working. There were three cows now, some pigs, and some chickens. They had worked all summer; the harvest had been excellent.

"There'll be chicken for Christmas dinner," Mathew announced, pointing off toward a large, fat bird. "And perhaps a wild pheasant, if I improve my aim."

"And all of us together," Tom added. "But poor Madelaine will have difficulty getting close enough to the table." She was nearing her time; a tiny woman whose pregnant belly was full and rounded, she appeared somehow off-balance.

Mathew's eyes suddenly became misty. The memory of Tom's birth swept across his thoughts; Tom had been born in January 1747. Tom's son would be due shortly after Christmas. He remembered listening to Ann's birthing screams; he remembered shoveling snow to take his thoughts off the birth; with sadness, he remembered Ann's death and his own parting from his infant son.

"What's the matter?" Tom asked.

"I was just remembering your birth," Mathew replied. "I'm getting sentimental in my old age."

"I shan't know what to do," Tom replied. "I want to be there when the baby comes, but I don't know if I can."

Mathew put his arm around his son. "I know what to do," he said confidently. "We'll go out and shovel snow together. That's what I did when you were born."

Tom hugged his father affectionately. "Then that's what we'll do."

Will found work on the farm of James Huggins and his wife, Sara. Jenna was to help around the house till her time came, and Will was to do the chores and help plant in the spring. The days were long and hard. They were filled with the work of survival and they passed quickly. Christmas came and went, so did New Year's and the short month of February. Jenna stayed with one of the Huggins children; Will slept in the parlor downstairs. It was a warm, loving household, and Mrs. Huggins promised to birth Jenna's baby. "I know all about it," she said with confidence. "I've got six of my own and I've birthed twelve others."

The momentous day was March 20, 1781. Jenna gave birth to a seven-pound son. "You can go talk to her now," Mrs. Huggins informed Will. "But she's tired, so don't talk for too long." Will nodded and tiptoed into the room where Jenna lay on the bed, her eyes closed.

"Are you asleep?" he whispered.

Jenna opened her eyes and looked up at him. "Did you see him?" she asked.

"He's a beautiful baby—I think he looks like you; his hair is reddish."

Jenna blinked back tears. "I thought I wouldn't like him because he was James'," she confessed. "But when I saw him, Will . . . when I held him, I loved him. He's wonderful."

Will put his hand over hers and pressed it hard. It's a first step, he thought. She loves and wants the baby and that's the best thing. "What shall we call him?"

Jenna frowned. "I haven't thought of a name yet. What do you think?"

Will thought of all the biblical names he knew and finally said, "Let's call him Joshua—Josh for short."

279

"Joshua," Jenna repeated the name. "I like that."

Will squeezed her hand again. "And in the spring when the planting is done, we'll bundle him up papoose-style and take him home."

Jenna tried to smile. "Thank you, Will," she said, fighting back her emotions.

He bent over and kissed her on the cheek. "You'll be a good mother," he told her.

Jenna wanted with all her heart to throw her arms around him, but she did not. "I'll try," she promised.

Jenna was up within a week and while she had to feed little Josh often, she managed to make herself useful around the house, delighting Mrs. Huggins by teaching the three oldest children how to read.

Spring came to the Peoria settlement before it came to Canada, and Mr. Huggins and Will planted in May. By June Will, Jenna and Joshua were able to be on their way, winding up the Illinois River, portaging to the Fox River, and then finally reaching Lake Michigan.

It was nearly July when they crossed the portage trail.

"It's breathtaking," Will said as he looked for the first time at the thundering falls. "I know now why they call it Thundergate."

"It's my home," Jenna replied. "We're only twenty miles from the farm now."

Will had set down the canoe and sat down on the grass, tired from the climb and from carrying the canoe. "Let's rest for a while," he suggested, "over there." He gestured toward a small clearing beyond the trees that lined the high bluffs of the river. It was late afternoon and the July sky was a piercing blue; the mist rose from the falls in the distance.

Jenna readily agreed. She slipped Josh off her back. The child slept peacefully. "It's really warm," Will said, wiping his brow. He took a blanket out of the pack and spread it out. "My lady," he said, smiling, "please be seated."

Jenna sat down and folded her skirts about her. Her eyes studied her son's sleeping face. She moved a little, to be under the shade of the tree, and moved the sleeping Josh as well.

"You look tired," Will commented.

"Apprehensive," Jenna replied. "I don't know quite how—or what to tell my family."

Will looked sympathetically at Jenna. She was afraid to tell her parents about the child, but she wanted to go home badly nonetheless.

"I was such a fool," Jenna admitted.

Will sat down beside her. He gently put his arm around her shoulders. Jenna loosened her bonnet and took it off, allowing the breeze to blow her hair. Will ran his hand through her hair, as he had on the night he had first met her. He's trying to comfort me, Jenna thought.

"Don't be afraid," Will told her.

Jenna could feel his hand and she wanted to throw herself into his arms but could not. She turned her face to look at him. "Will you stay?" she asked again.

"I may go on to Acadia," he answered. "I want to visit my mother's land, to know what she lost. I may go west; I really don't know." He looked into her eyes, thinking: If only you cared about me I would stay, but I have nothing to stay for without you and Josh.

"Go west . . ." Jenna said the words as if she hardly understood them, but as she said them, tears flooded her eyes. "I'll miss you so," she said softly.

Will looked into her eyes, then he drew her into his arms and held her tenderly against his shoulder. "I love you, Jenna," he whispered into her ear.

She withdrew and looked into his face. "How can you? I'm not good enough for you . . . it's a mistake."

"Good enough?" Will questioned. "Do you think I've never had another woman?" He pulled her back against him. "I love you and I want to marry you. I love Josh and I want us to raise him together as if he were ours."

"You don't want to go west?" Jenna said wide-eyed.

"Only if I have you with me . . . I know you've been hurt, I know you don't love me, I know you're afraid. But I want to look after you."

"Don't love you!" Jenna exclaimed. Her arms flew around his neck. "I've loved you all along! All these months, I just didn't think you could forgive me for . . . for . . ." She dissolved again into sobs.

Will cupped her chin in his hand and leaned over her tear-stained face, kissing her lips for the first time. It began tenderly and grew into a long, passionate kiss that Jenna returned fully.

Will lowered his head and kissed her shoulders and her neck. "We're going to be married," he told her. Jenna's eyes were closed as his lips touched hers. She felt as if she were standing on the very edge of the great falls, fearing yet desiring him. She felt caught in the torrent of waters, tumbling downward. But somehow Jenna knew it was right. There were other men, but this was *the* man. This was the man both gentle and strong. "I love you," she whispered again.

"And I you," Will pledged. Then he stood up, lifting her to her feet. "Come, Jenna," he said. "Let's go home."